# THE
# ROAD
# RENOUNCED

A NOVEL

## KAYE D. SCHMITZ

THE ROAD RENOUNCED BY KAYE D. SCHMITZ
Kensington Studios Press is a division of Kensington Media
St. Augustine, FL 32092

ISBN: 979-8-218-05183-9
Copyright © 2022 by Kaye D. Schmitz
Cover design by Hannah Linder of *Hannah Linder Designs*
Interior Formatting by Catherine Posey of *Hannah Linder Designs*

Available in print from your local bookstore, online,
or from www.kayedschmitzauthor.com

For more information on this book and the author, visit:
www.kayedschmitzauthor.com

Library of Congress Cataloging-in-Publication Data
Schmitz, Kaye D.
The Road Renounced / Kaye D. Schmitz 1st ed.

Printed in the United States of America

# OTHER BOOKS
# BY KAYE D. SCHMITZ

*THE CONSORT CONSPIRACY*

*ON DEADLY GROUNDS*

*THE ROAD REMEMBERED*

*To the memory of my maternal grandmother, Maude Irene Brewer Gibbons, a wonderful, energetic little woman whom I loved dearly. Fortunately, this story is fiction and while the real Maude's life may not have been perfect, she did NOT suffer the kind of life my fictional Maude did.*

*And, as always, to my darling husband, Michael, my best friend, my first reader, my sounding board, the one who encourages me when I throw up my hands and declare my words "garbage," and my co-collaborator through the giggles of life.*

# Letter to
# my Readers

Dear Friends,

Welcome to another historical tale about the Ryan family.

For my readers of *The Road Remembered,* you will see that the first chapter of this story is different from the one included there.

The reason is simple. As stories fill out, they often take a new twist on the way the author intended to write them. Sometimes the author makes changes to build the suspense and other times, the characters dig in their heels and refuse to allow the story to unfold as originally planned. The change to the first chapter from the one included in the last book is a combination of these two reasons. Through the years, I have learned to trust the voices in my head and go with their guidance.

I also need to explain, for you very careful readers, that my main character, "Maude" appeared as "Maud" in the last book. That's because the character is based on my grandmother and I had seen her name on my mother's birth certificate spelled without an "e." But additional research revealed the spelling half the time with an "e" and half without.

So I visited my grandmother's grave and her tombstone showed her first name ending with an "e." That's why I changed the spelling.

Thank you so much for continuing to read the words I write. I sincerely hope you enjoy this story.

Kaye D. Schmitz

# THE
# ROAD
# RENOUNCED

Kensington
STUDIOS PRESS

# PROLOGUE

Marthe
Liege, Belgium
August 4, 1914

The neighborhood market on the outskirts of Liege swelled with shoppers, eager to claim their share of the scarce goods that arrived only an hour earlier. Marthe Peeters, elated to find butter again after months without it, counted out seven francs to the clerk and waited for her change. But her focus shifted to the flickering shadows on the wall above the counter that darkened, then dimmed, then shot to the ceiling.

Around her, the other customers grew restless, their voices rising along with the commotion from outside. Hair rose on the back of her neck and she snatched up the butter and left, her change forgotten.

The market's door slammed behind her as she scrambled up the hill for a better view of the shadows' origin. As she watched, the strange glow in the evening sky twisted into vicious tongues of flame that licked the night and shot sparkling embers heavenward like a new crop of stars. Even at that distance, smoke stung her eyes and clawed at her throat, soot mixing with the bile that filled her mouth.

Her heart clenched, then filled with dread.

It was *her* house that burned, *her* family's screams that reached her above the fire's roar.

Marthe dropped her treasured bundle and raced down the hill, tucking the gold locket that held her parents' pictures into her blouse as she ran. Nothing mattered except saving her family from the inferno that had, until that moment, been their home.

The scent of burning flesh assaulted her and she followed its source to the front yard where her mother had dragged her sister. Flames sprouted from the younger girl's sweater and Marthe smothered them with her light jacket while her mother tackled the smoldering braids with her bare hands.

Beside them, Marthe's father struggled under the weight of his writing desk, dragging it down the front steps by its broken legs and then placing it safely in the grass where it tilted to one side. Marthe placed her sister next to the desk and flew up the steps to emerge with a load of blankets and pillows.

With her face blackened from smoke and her lungs wheezing from lack of air, she turned to get another load. Her father stopped her.

"Enough, Marthe. That's all we can do." His shoulders drooped and his face wore defeat.

"Papa," Marthe rasped. "How did this happen?"

Before her father could answer, Marthe saw others surrounding them, standing clear of the fire's light and partially hidden in the dim of the early evening. Soldiers. *Feldgrau* uniforms greeted her, regardless of the direction she faced. The greenish-grey jackets fed her fears.

The soldiers held her brother's arms behind him. Again, the hair on Marthe's neck rose and she turned to her father, her eyes wide, her chest bursting with questions.

"The Germans have invaded Belgium," he said. "They think your brother is a sharpshooter. A sniper. They have arrested—"

An agonized scream broke through her father's soft words.

"She's dead!" Marthe's mother sat in the grass, cradling Marthe's sister in her arms and rocking her back and forth. "She's dead! The fire killed her." Marthe's mother rose, her face contorted in anguish, and flew at the nearest soldier—an officer by his insignia—then beat his chest with her fists. "*You* did this. *You* killed her. My baby is dead!"

The soldier drew his pistol and aimed it at the woman's head.

"No!" Marthe pulled her mother away while her father knelt in front of the officer.

"No, please, sir." Her father's voice broke. "Can't you see she is sick with grief? She didn't know what she said. Please, sir, have mercy for a mother's loss."

The officer's expression never changed but his eyes left her mother and turned to her father. Time slowed and Marthe's breath stopped but she held onto her mother's sagging form, the two of them frozen to the ground where they stood.

Without a word, the officer pointed his weapon at her father's head and the crack of a gunshot cut through the night. In a haze of horror, Marthe watched her father tilt sideways, then crumple to the earth. She pulled her mother closer but a second gunshot exploded and jerked Marthe backward, tearing her mother from her arms and tumbling her lifeless form to Marthe's feet. The bullet that traveled through her mother's body lodged in Marthe's upper arm, along with blinding pain.

At the third shot, her brother collapsed.

The officer spun toward her, his Luger trained on her forehead. He cocked his gun, slashing her remaining life to seconds. She clamped her eyes shut and clutched her locket tightly in her fist, then waited, steeling herself for the momentary pain from the bullet. And the final oblivion of death.

But only the roar of the fire, along with her terror-induced whimpers, reached her ears. She cracked one eye open to see a soldier whisper to her family's executioner. The officer's arm lowered and he studied her face, then motioned with his gun.

Blood trickled from Marthe's arm and she opened her mouth to scream. Before any sound emerged, rough hands bound her arms while another clamped over her lips, sickening her with the aromas of strong cheese and gunpowder. She worked her jaws and sank her teeth into her captor's meaty hand, gratified when he cried out.

Until his fist slammed into her face.

The night spun but the soldiers holding her arms refused to let her fall. The cold steel of a gun muzzle ground into her temple and the soldiers dragged her from her home, forcing her to leave her family where they fell, huddling together in death as she had often seen them in life.

The column reached the rise of the hill and Marthe staggered along with them, determined not to pass out. At the hill's crest, she slid on the butter from her earlier purchase, ground into the dirt by the soldiers' boots. Her prior elation at finding the rare item, along with her zest for life, had evaporated.

Forever, she feared.

One foot in front of the other, she stumbled along, chillingly numb. The pain she expected her heart to feel from the loss of her family hadn't caught up to the horror her brain had witnessed. She had *no* pain, in fact, from her family's death or the bullet wound in her arm.

But her heart raged with hate. Waves and waves of it.

And an overpowering resolve for revenge.

# CHAPTER ONE

SUZANNE
2015

The dad-shaped hole in my heart ached with the pain of his loss.

My father, Sam Ryan, whom I had adored my whole life, was dead.

I still found it hard to believe. A mere two weeks ago I had accompanied him on a bucket list trip where he and his Army buddies from seventy years earlier reprised their trek across Europe—the one they made originally during World War II.

For me, it was the trip of a lifetime.

For him, the *last* trip of his lifetime. He died less than a week after our return.

As his only child, the thankless task of cleaning out the house where he'd lived for almost fifty years fell to me. Some elements would be simple, like packing up his clothes and donating them to the Veterans of Foreign Wars, his favorite charity. Most of his furniture could go there as well.

No, I dreaded the hard stuff, like going through all his papers. Not his will, of course. We'd already been through that. I mean his boxes and boxes of mementos. And books. And picture albums.

I only dreaded it because I know myself. I anticipated having to stop and look at every single picture in every single album. And, like Dad, I would have trouble throwing away such priceless treasures.

I'd already done the high-level arranging after his death ... a service in Lock Haven, Pennsylvania, where we'd lived since the early sixties, and then his final trip to the Ryan family farm, where after a service with his remaining siblings, he would spend eternity. Right next to my mother, his life companion for seventy years, who'd already rested there for eight months.

My son, Steve, had spent most of the day bringing boxes down from Dad's attic and I faced them, scattered across the floor of his den. His Zen Zone, I had called it.

Dad always got a kick out of that.

I figured the only way I could approach the boxes in front of me was methodically. That's the way I did everything.

I eased into Dad's chair and sat a minute, surrounded by his essence, as intense as if he had reached out to give me a warm hug. I felt them both there, Mom and Dad, standing behind me, arm in arm, and smiling. Believing he was with Mom again eased my pain at losing him.

My mother's memory box, the one she called "Betty's Beautiful Box," still rested beside his chair and I picked it up and put it on my lap. Dad found this decorated tin in a small bakery in Zwickau, Germany, and brought it home to Mother when he returned from World War II. At the time, it contained Lebkuchen, spicy German confections, made from a recipe the baker's family had used for more than one hundred years even then. Fewer than two weeks ago, he introduced me to the baker's daughter, Gerda Zeigler, when we were in Zwickau for his reunion. My mind still reels from what we learned that night.

A coincidence that affected my entire life.

Profoundly.

During the war, I learned, Gerda had saved almost twelve hundred Jewish children and babies from extinction in German concentration camps even though she was married to a Nazi officer who bought into the pure Aryan party line. But she couldn't stand the thought of Jewish people being killed simply because of their religion. So behind her husband's back, she worked with the resistance to save Jewish people, mostly Jewish babies.

Dad and his Army buddies met her in 1945 when they liberated the concentration camp at Buchenwald where she'd been locked in her bedroom at nine months pregnant. And in heavy labor. They delivered her baby, a girl she named Etta.

But until Dad and I attended a small gathering at Gerda's home the last night of our trip, neither she nor my dad had any idea I had been one of the babies she saved.

At Gerda's apartment, I saw the glass jars she had used to record the names of all the children and one of them had a single name in it. Even after seventy years. The name was that of a baby girl who had been whisked away the final night of escapes at Buchenwald, along with twenty-nine other children. Incredibly, Dad and his squad stopped the group in the middle of the Thuringian Forest and Dad even held me that night. He told me if he hadn't been in the middle of a worldwide war, he would have tried to find a way to take me home with him. But since he couldn't, he handed me back and everyone continued their journeys—Dad and his company to liberate Buchenwald and the thirty children and their caretakers to someplace safe.

But the night we were with her, Gerda told us the story of how the baby girl Dad held was taken to the United States in the arms of an American officer who intended to adopt her. But he was tragically killed in a car accident before he even made it home. The baby girl survived, but the officer's wife was so distraught she had a nervous breakdown and sent the baby to an orphanage in Philadelphia. When Dad asked the name of the orphanage, and Gerda told him Saint Katherine's, that's when the two of them pieced it all together.

And that's where Mother and Dad found me.

I leaned back into Dad's chair and smiled, still thrilled at Dad's and my shared connection with that small, wonderful German woman.

After reminiscing for a few more minutes, I pulled one of Dad's boxes toward me and began my task. I had to laugh. Contrary to my dad's disciplined life, the box contained a hodge-podge of stuff in all different categories and from many different decades. I found drawings I had done in elementary school that Mother had meticulously labeled with the date, my age, and what class I was in at the time. Then, without rhyme or reason, right under that I found articles and recipes from *The Ladies' Home Journal* from twenty years ago.

Obviously, Dad never went through Mother's things after she died.

I pulled items out and, as a first step, sorted them into piles that made sense to me. After the first box, I did the same with the second and then the third, figuring some of the piles could be thrown away completely and the rest arranged by year.

The fourth box changed everything.

I reached the bottom and found an old photo album, weird because I knew where he kept the others. And that place wasn't in this box.

Carefully, I pulled the album out. The faded black cover peeled, with little bits of the padded cardboard breaking off with every movement. I positioned it carefully on my lap and turned to the beginning. Black-and-white photos of babies matted on heavy black paper sported captions written in white ink.

I did a double take when I saw the first date. 1898. More than one hundred years earlier.

I knew it was Dad's family because Mom's relatives were all gone when they married and, as far as I knew, she had no family keepsakes.

The name under the first page of photos was "Henry." I had no idea who that was so I kept turning pages until I found a baby with the caption, "Maude."

Dad's mom. My grandmother. Whom I had never met.

After I found that, and based on subsequent pictures, I figured out that Henry had been Maude's brother.

Later pages bore pictures of teenagers with baseball gear, labeled "Henry and Buzz." I knew that name as well. Buzz was Dad's dad … my grandfather. I studied his picture and marveled at how much he looked like my dad when they were both young. But according to Dad, they didn't have much of a relationship, unfortunately, so I knew very little about him.

I turned each page, careful not to cause any more damage, while I enjoyed the pictures of my grandmother in all stages of her growing up years. Sadly, she died in 1944, the same year my dad entered the service.

I found pictures of her wedding to my grandfather and several after the birth of each child, showing the older ones with their younger siblings as they were born. I loved the pictures of Dad as a baby and then as a toddler and I was surprised to see several pictures of my grandfather with him, given the unpleasant way Dad always referred to him.

I went through every page quickly and when I turned the last page, I found a bulge in the paper bound to the back cover. It disintegrated under my fingers when I tried to smooth it and a large chunk peeled off, revealing a corner of red. I picked at the edges and uncovered a slender book bound in red fabric.

The pages inside, so thin they were almost translucent, revealed spidery writing in ink faded to pale purple. With gentle fingers, I turned to the first page and read aloud, "Diary of Maude Irene Brewer." The word "Ryan" appeared under that first line in darker ink, obviously added after she married.

I couldn't believe it.

I had always wished I'd had a chance to meet my grandmother. And here it was. A way to get to know her through her own words.

I adjusted my glasses, turned to the first page, and read.

*April 17, 1915*

*Dear Diary,*

*Today is my birthday.*

*But I guess you know that since you were my present. Anyway, I'm ten now. I told Mom at breakfast that I'm a teenager, but she said not until my age ends in the word 'teen.' Still, I like having two numbers in my age instead of just one.*

*Mom's making my favorite cake for my birthday dinner, chocolate with cream cheese frosting, and Helen and Ethel are coming for a sleep-over. We'll celebrate my birthday, of course, but we'll also work on an end-of-*

*year Social Studies project assigned by our teacher, Miss Delsie. She wants us to put together a timeline, she called it, of the events so far in the war in Europe. She says it's already been going on for almost a year but I don't think it affects us much here. So the whole thing seems like a waste of time to me, but she says we need to know what's going on in case America ever decides to join. Can you imagine? Why would our country do such a stupid thing? But we have to complete the project, whether we want to or not. We'll spend some time in the library and find what we need in old newspapers.*

*My brother, Henry, will be staying with his friend, Buzz Ryan, even though Mom's not crazy about his parents. But Dad told her it would be okay. The boys are out in the front yard now, playing ball.*

*Seems like that's all they ever do.*

*I'll tell you more later.*

*Your new friend, Maude Irene Brewer*

———— ❦ ————

## Prospect Park, PA
## April 17, 1915

HENRY BREWER SQUATTED BEHIND THE WOODEN TOMATO basket cover that served as home plate and positioned his mitt squarely over it. His father, Frank, crouched behind him, eyes focused on the strike zone.

"Hit me here, Buzz," Henry called. "Straight down the old pipe." He beat his fist into the middle of his glove. "Into the sweet spot."

Sixty and one-half feet away on the little rise that served as the pitcher's mound, William "Buzz" Ryan, his right side to Henry, raised his hands over his head and moved his fingers into position for his fastball. In seconds, he visualized every step of his delivery, then took a deep breath. He wound up and released. The ball flew out of his left hand and whipped over the plate.

"Stee-rike!" Frank called, moving his arm out to the right the way he'd seen the professionals do. "Good job, son. I'll bet you're as fast as the pros—Rube Waddell, even. I wish we had some way to find out."

"Coach says the same thing, Mr. B. He said it would be helpful to know for whenever big-league recruiters come around."

"You think he was serious, Buzz?" Henry said.

"I hope so," Buzz said. "That would be my ticket outta here," he added quietly.

Henry threw the ball back to Buzz and squatted again. "Let's try your knuckleball, Buzz. Remember the signal for that one ... I'll point my finger down and kind of wiggle it."

Buzz nodded, then turned sideways again. As was his routine, he visualized what he planned to do, then wound up and threw.

"Ball!" Frank said. "But really close. Try again."

Henry returned the ball and Buzz repeated his routine. But this time when he delivered the pitch, Frank yelled, "Strike! That was perfect."

The screen door slammed and Maude backed out onto the porch balancing a tray of filled glasses. "Break time," she yelled. "Mom made iced tea. Come and get it."

"Thanks, Maudie," Frank said. "Come on and rest a minute, boys."

They followed him to the porch steps and hurled themselves down, accepting the tea from Maude's tray. Henry yanked on her black hair.

"Happy birthday, Bug." She grinned at him, the blank spots from her missing canine teeth visible.

"Oh yeah," Buzz mumbled. "Happy birthday."

Maude ducked her head, picked up her own glass of tea and returned to the kitchen, letting the screen door bang behind her.

Buzz watched her go and then turned to her brother. "Why do you call her 'Bug'?"

Henry laughed. "Because ever since she started losing teeth, her smile reminds me of the cartoon bugs in some of the comic books I've read."

Buzz smiled, then stood. "Come on. Let's work on my knuckleball some more so I can use it in our game next week."

"You really think there'll be any scouts there?" Henry asked.

"Yeah, that's why I want my pitches to be sharp."

"Not many teams have left-handers," Frank said. "You could be a real contender, Buzz."

"I sure hope so. I'd give a lot to get away from here."

Frank and Henry remained silent. Everybody in town knew about the volatility of Buzz's home life with his parents, drunk and jobless most of the time. Buzz's job at the local feed mill often provided the family's sole means of support.

"Okay, Buzz," Henry said when he was in position. "I'm ready for you."

---

THE BOYS WORKED LATE INTO THE AFTERNOON.

"I think you got it, Buzz," Frank said. "That knuckleball dropped in just perfect."

"Thanks, Mr. B. You sure helped a lot."

Frank's wife, Florence, met the boys on the porch with a plate of chocolate cupcakes. "Please give these to your mother with my compliments, Buzz," she said. "I had extra batter when I baked Maude's cake and thought they might be a nice touch for your dessert tonight."

"Thanks, Mrs. B.," Buzz said without looking her in the eye. "I'm sure my mom will appreciate it."

The boys mounted their bikes and Buzz balanced the plate of cupcakes in his basket. They pedaled off down the long dirt lane and passed the Model T Roadster on its way to the house. A cloud of dust swirled around it when it stopped in front of the porch and Maude's friends, Helen and Ethel, hopped out, small suitcases and gaily wrapped presents filling their arms. Maude flew down the steps and hugged both girls, waved to Helen's father, then raced back up the steps to hold the screen door as the girls entered, all of them chattering at once.

"Would you like to come in, Tom?" Frank asked. "Florence made a fresh pitcher of tea."

"No thanks, Frank. I told the wife I'd get right back home. Good luck with all these girls tonight. I hope they don't drive you crazy."

———— ⋯⋯ ————

"GREAT JOB KEEPING MOM'S CUPCAKES FROM SPILLING, Buzz."

The boys turned their bicycles into the short lane leading to Buzz's house. Henry saw, not for the first time, the trash littering the yard, the grass uncut and bushes overgrown.

"Sorry for how it looks," Buzz mumbled. "Dad told me he would mow this week, but I guess he got busy. I'll take care of it tomorrow."

"It's no—"

Henry's words died as a bottle flew through the screen door, narrowly missing Buzz's head. A whiskey bottle. Screams reached them from inside the house.

"You filthy bitch! Put tha' knife down." A male voice. Words slurred.

"Not 'til you get the hell outta my house." Female voice, shrill.

"You can't tell me what to do, bitch. Goddam it. I'll show you!"

The boys froze while thumps and crashes reached them from inside. Buzz let his bike fall to the ground, cupcakes scattering everywhere, and raced to the door.

"Buzz wait ..." Henry yelled. "They might—"

Again Henry's words were lost in the scream that reached them.

"You damn fool! Put down that gun." Followed by another scream. Female.

"When you put down your goddam knife." A male scream. "You stupid bitch! You stabbed me!" A gunshot cracked through the air.

"Stop!" Buzz charged through the screen door. "Stop it now!"

Buzz found his mother crouched behind the overturned kitchen table. Chaos in the form of broken dishes with half-eaten food surrounded her while white sauce covered her face and matted in her hair. The entire kitchen resembled a disaster area with upended and broken chairs everywhere. Papers floated to the floor then rested on empty whiskey bottles. Garbage reeked on every surface.

Buzz grabbed his father's arm and tried to pull the gun from him. But the man was maniacal and pushed his son roughly. Buzz lost his footing and fell to the floor. "Mom," he screamed. "Get out of here. Run outside."

She rose but stumbled against the counter in her drunkenness and pitched over the table, landing at her husband's feet.

"Dad, stop!" But Buzz's words fell unheeded and he watched in horror as the bullet left his father's gun and lodged in his mother's left eye. He rose slowly, eyes locked with his father's. Each searched the other's soul and Buzz wondered which of them had only seconds to live.

Henry pushed through the door. "Mr. Ryan, please!"

The man raised his arm and Buzz closed his eyes.

"No!" Henry screamed.

But the gun fired anyway.

Buzz's father crashed to the floor, his blood splattering a red starburst in stark contrast to the dingy white wall behind him.

Henry threw up, his vomit mingling with the pool of blood that oozed down the slanting floor toward his feet.

Silence reigned in the tiny kitchen.

Until a tortured scream tore from Buzz's throat.

Before Henry could move, the sheriff burst in the door and raced past him to see if Buzz was okay.

"Come on, son," the sheriff said. "Let's get you boys outside."

On the small porch, Buzz gulped in air and Henry stood, unable to control his trembling. Buster, the sheriff's deputy, stood with Buzz's neighbors who loitered in the yard, shaking their heads. "Yer neighbors come to git me," the sheriff told Buzz. "Said it sounded real bad in there." He patted Buzz's back. "I see they was right."

The boys slumped to the steps and the sheriff eased his bulk down to join them. "I can see exactly what happened here," he continued. "So you don't have to come to the station tonight. You have a place you can stay, Buzz?"

"He can stay with me," Henry said. "And my family."

"Yer Frank Brewer's boy, ain't you?"

"Yessir. Mom and Dad will welcome him."

"I tell you what," the sheriff said. "I'll leave Buster here to contact the coroner and do what needs to be done to secure the crime scene. Let's load up yer bikes in my vehicle and I'll take you to the Brewer farm. You boys can come to the station tomorrow and give me yer statements. For the record."

The neighbors parted and formed a path to the police wagon. A couple of them even helped put the boys' bikes in, then patted Buzz on the back as he walked past.

———◦◦———

LAUGHTER FROM THE BREWER KITCHEN REACHED THEM when the sheriff knocked on the door.

"Sheriff," Florence and the girls heard Frank say. "Come in."

"I'd rather you come out," the sheriff said.

Frank joined them on the porch and the sheriff told Frank what had happened. "You boys have anything you want to add?"

"It was awful, Dad," Henry said. "Just awful."

Frank hugged Buzz and then Henry. "Oh God, boys. I'm so sorry you had to see all that. Listen, go on up to Henry's room and I'll be up in a minute with some food." The boys went straight up to Henry's bedroom without seeing the girls.

Frank turned back to the sheriff. "What'll happen to Buzz now?"

"He don't have no kin that I know of," the sheriff said. "He'll go into foster care till he's eighteen, I suspect."

Frank shook hands with the sheriff. "Thanks for bringing the boys home, Sheriff. Listen, Buzz can stay with us as long as he likes."

After the sheriff left, Frank stood at the kitchen door and motioned to Florence. He told her what had happened and asked if she would put together a couple of plates of food. "And why don't you go ahead and give the girls their ice cream and cake? I'll stay upstairs with the boys and see how I can help."

Minutes later, Florence handed plates of food to Frank, then returned to the kitchen and told the girls the boys had misunderstood Buzz's parents' plans and needed to stay at the Brewer farm instead of the Ryan house.

Then Florence lit the candles on Maude's cake, ten bright specks in the darkened kitchen, and the three of them sang to her as she blew them out. Laughter filled the room as each girl dove into a large piece of cake with ice cream scooped on top.

Florence purposely chose to keep the terrible news from the girls. For one thing, she didn't believe she should be the one to deliver that kind of news to someone else's child. And for the other, she wanted Maude's birthday to remain as happy as possible.

But when she forked her own cake into her mouth, it didn't taste as good as she had anticipated and chunks of it stuck in her throat.

————⟡————

IN THEIR BEDROOM LATER, FRANK AND FLORENCE TALKED about Buzz's parents.

"Oh, those poor boys," Florence said. "How did they seem, Frank? Will they be able to get over this?"

"I hope so, Mother." He hugged her close.

"And what about Buzz? Where will he go? Does he have any relatives?"

Frank cleared his throat. "No, no relatives at all. But I had an idea I need to talk to you about. The sheriff said he will probably go into the foster system until he turns eighteen. Well, Mother, you know that's only a few months from now. So I told the sheriff he could stay here as long as he wants to. At least until he's eighteen and finishes school. He's such a good boy and with his pitching arm ... well, you just never know where he could go. He could be recruited by—"

Florence put her hand on her husband's arm. "It's okay, Frank. You convinced me. Of course it makes sense for him to stay with us. I just …"

"What, Flo? You just what?"

"I just worry about what kind of long-term effect witnessing such a terrible tragedy might have on Buzz's life."

"I would guess it won't be much worse than what he lived through every day." Frank pulled her close and put his chin on top of her head. "We need to let him see that the way he was raised isn't normal. Let's show him what a loving family actually looks like."

# CHAPTER TWO

MARTHE
Belgium
April 21, 1915

The first few weeks after her family's violent deaths, Marthe stumbled along with her captors, dazed and endlessly angry. Her heart ached from the loss of her loved ones, but each new step through her hometown of Liege expanded the sadness to include her way of life, her very existence. Street after street, homes and businesses she knew lay in rubble, with remnants of former lives visible through broken furniture and blackened walls.

"Looks like the work of Big Bertha," one soldier said.

"I heard about that one," another remarked. "Howitzer, right? How big did they say it was?"

"Almost half a meter, four hundred twenty millimeters, I was told," the *Hauptmann*, Fritz Reiner, answered. "With a range of more than seven kilometers." The officer laughed, a short guttural sound. Marthe looked at him with contempt. Her loathing for him had only grown deeper since the day he murdered her family. "They were supposed to aim for the fort here but it looks like the shells got away from them," he went on. "Wiped out most of the town. Less work for us, eh, boys?"

The soldiers broke out in raucous laughter and punched each other's shoulders as if all the devastation and destruction had been nothing more than a game to them. Not one of them uttered words of sorrow for the loss of lives. Civilian lives that had nothing to do with their war.

Steady tears stained Marthe's cheeks day after day and month after month as she endured her forced march through the countryside of Belgium and heard the same kind of heartless chatter from the German soldiers who had viciously snatched her life from her. To make it worse, she was expected to nurse their wounds and keep them healthy when, in reality, she would gladly have seen them all dead. Since she didn't know how to arrange that, she simply clenched her teeth and did what was necessary to stay alive.

Her locket with her parents' pictures was her only comfort. But not nearly comfort enough. Despite her tears, walls formed around her heart and she constantly struggled with the question of why she lived when her whole family—and many of the townspeople she knew—had died.

She learned the answer several weeks later when she tended the wounds of a young soldier from the group.

"Thank you, *Fräulein*," he said.

She remained silent.

"I know this must be hard for you," he added. "Losing your family that way and then having to help us when we're wounded."

She studied his face and found it different from the other soldiers who joked about death.

"I recognize you," she told him. "It was you who spoke to the *Hauptmann* when his gun threatened to blow my head off. Right after he killed my whole family."

"*Ja*," the soldier said. He cleared his throat and refused to look at her. "I am sorry that happened." At least he had the decency, Marthe thought, to look ashamed. "But your brother," he continued, "begged for your life to be spared. He told me you were a nurse and I thought the captain would want to know that, since nursing skills are always in short supply. Your brother also said you speak several languages. I figured that could come in handy with prisoners."

"Thank you." Marthe cleaned the bullet hole in his arm, then applied antiseptic and a bandage. Quiet air hung between them before Marthe spoke again. "Although, to tell the truth," she continued, "I would have cursed you at first. The loss of my family devastated me.

And my desire to live died along with them." She finished tying the bandage and frowned. "But now that I've found I can make a difference for wounded soldiers—even Germans—I'm no longer sorry I was left alive." She saw that he had raised his eyes to look at her and she returned his gaze. "So at this point, I will say 'thank you' and mean it."

She knew she told the truth. While her heart maintained its hate for Germans in general, her training wouldn't allow her to let a soldier die in the field if she could help him. Already, a number of the soldiers who watched her family die and her home burn had been wounded, and she swallowed her distaste and upheld her medical vows to try and keep them alive. Her track record was excellent and the officer in charge—the one who sent the bullets into her parents' heads—ensured she was treated well. At least as well as could be expected under the conditions.

In early spring, the unit that had kidnapped Marthe marched into the town of Roulers, a mere thirty or so kilometers from France. The devastation there appalled her. More than half the buildings lay empty, their remaining few walls reaching out, baring their blackened interiors in mourning for the lost souls who had lived there.

Fritz Reiner, the *Hauptmann* who allowed Marthe to live, kept part of his unit in Roulers and gave orders for the rest to be sent to the villages of Langemark and Gravenstafel the following morning. He invited Marthe to accompany him and his officers to the local Taverne where they dined and found lodging for the night. At first Marthe resisted, her hatred for the *Hauptmann* overruling everything else. But in the end, she couldn't resist the thought of engaging in a few simple things—eating a warm, well-prepared dinner and sleeping in a regular bed rather than a thin blanket on the ground. So she accepted.

For the first time since her family was killed, she didn't hate the world and everyone in it. She even had time to look around and appreciate that, while war changed everything somewhat, a few folks, like the other diners present at the Taverne, still had their families around them and lived a semblance of their normal lives. That didn't change her desire for revenge, but it did allow her to hope that someday, when the war was over, she might be able to return to a normal life as well.

At dinner, the Taverne's owner, Herr Harti Breit, learned of Marthe's nursing skills and suggested to *Hauptmann* Reiner that Marthe be allowed to stay in the city and work with a group of nuns who had set up a field hospital in one of the larger houses spared from bombs. To Marthe's great surprise, Reiner agreed. She managed to control her excitement during the meal, but once in her room, she actually danced around, thrilled at the prospect of freedom from marching with the Germans.

THE FOLLOWING MORNING, MARTHE WOKE TO A LIGHT knock on her door.

"*Ja?*" she said. "Who is it?"

"Herr Breit. I will escort you to the nuns." He hesitated then added, "I brought you a change of clothes."

She threw off her coverlet and opened the door.

"Thank you," she said. A smile lit her face for the first time in months and she held out the clothes to inspect them. They were worn and patched but smelled of detergent and she relished the thought of removing her rags and replacing them with the kindness from this stranger.

He reached behind him and brought out shoes, then held them out to her, shyly. "I noticed when I saw you last night that only string held your shoes together."

"True," she said. "And newspapers lining the soles kept my feet from hitting dirt. I can't thank you enough. If you could please give me a few minutes, I would like to wash before putting on these beautiful things."

"Of course. I will have breakfast waiting for you when you come downstairs."

He nodded and she closed the door, then hurried to the washstand, her first luxury since before her family died. She found a small cake of soap and a comb and did the best she could with her thick auburn hair, matted from her months of marching with the soldiers. When finished, not only did she feel better, but the last thing she saw in her reflection was a brighter blue in her eyes.

She descended the stairs to find an empty dining room with only one place set. Alone, she looked around and noticed that modern electric fixtures adorned the walls rather than kerosene lamps, which was different from the upstairs rooms, still lit with oil lamps and candles. She had seen that before where she lived in Liege, especially in public buildings and inns—electricity downstairs but not upstairs. She shrugged and decided wiring in upper floors must be too expensive.

Herr Breit put biscuits and weak coffee in front of her. They both tasted like heaven.

Her eyes filled with tears.

"Oh my," Herr Breit said. "What is it? Have I done something wrong?"

"No," she said. Her voice choked. "Not at all." Herr Breit stood still, waiting for her to continue. "I'm just ... it's been ..." She breathed deeply. "I'm not used to such kindness," she said. "At least not since my family died." She clutched the locket at her throat and her eyes sought his. "I had forgotten goodness even existed in the world. And I so appreciate everything you've done for me. I hope I don't let you down. Or the nuns."

When she finished her breakfast, Herr Breit met her at the door and steered her toward a side street where most of the houses still stood. At the third one in, a white two-story with an arched door and a wide semi-circular driveway, they walked up the path and Marthe picked her way carefully to avoid mortar holes where bricks were missing or skewed sideways. Some of the path's bricks even littered the street. Shrubs on both sides of the entrance steps lay dead or dying, most infested with pests.

They reached the door and Herr Breit announced their presence by lifting the heavy knocker, then letting it fall. The large door opened before she could take in more of her surroundings.

Herr Breit bowed to the stately woman in the long black habit. "Sister Margarete," he said.

"Herr Breit," she answered. "Welcome." She moved aside and they entered.

"Sister," he said again, "I am pleased to introduce you to *Fräulein* Marthe Peeters, a trained nurse from Liege. She traveled here with a German army unit, but the *Hauptmann* has agreed to have her work with you if you can use her services."

The nun turned to Marthe and grasped both of her hands. "Oh my dear," she said. "You must have been sent from God Himself because I've been praying for someone with nurse's training. We certainly do the best we can here, but without formal training, I worry that we often fall short. Welcome, welcome."

Marthe smiled and squeezed the hands that held hers.

"You will be such an asset. Can you get started right away?"

"Of course," Marthe answered. She turned and bowed to Herr Breit. "Thank you," she said, "for your immense kindness."

He left and the nun took her elbow to steer her down the corridor. "You must be brave, Marthe. The cases we get here are probably worse than what you are used to."

"Possibly, sister, but I have traveled with a German Army unit for the past several months—" She wanted to add, "after they killed my whole family," but decided that would be a story for another day. "I tended their wounds from battles before we could get them to a field hospital," she finished.

Sister Margarete led her into a large room and the odor of gangrene assaulted her nostrils. Marthe took a quick breath and stepped back before she could stop herself.

"One never gets accustomed to the odor of rotting flesh," the nun said. "But its impact lessens after a while." The sister patted her arm.

They toured the first floor where wounded men occupied every available space—beds, cots, sofas, and makeshift cushions. They lay before Marthe in all conditions, without legs, without arms, and without eyes. Many of them writhed in agony. The two women stopped behind a man in a white coat who bent over a screaming soldier. A quick glance told Marthe that gangrene had claimed his leg all the way to his knee.

"I've brought help, *Oberarzt*," Sister Margarete told the doctor. "This is Marthe Peeters, a nurse from Liege. Marthe, please meet Dr. Oswald Fleischer, the *Oberarzt*, the senior doctor."

Without turning, the doctor, his voice brusque, said, "Good. Meet me in the surgery immediately, both of you. This leg has to come off."

"No," the patient screamed. "Don't take my leg."

"I'm sorry, son," the *Oberarzt* said. "But my job is to keep you alive. That's the only way I know to do it."

And he was gone. A new round of screaming followed him from the room.

Bile rose in Marthe's throat. She had often wondered whether she would still have chosen nursing if amputation had been her first field of study. She was fairly certain the answer would have been a resounding "no."

"Follow me," Sister Margarete said.

They entered a large room with bright spotlights. Already there awaiting the surgeon were two other nuns, blood-stained white aprons covering most of the expanse of their black robes. Sister Margarete handed Marthe an apron and showed her the sink where she would scrub. "Our morphine supply is low," Sister Margarete said, "and our ether hasn't arrived yet, so we will have to hold him down." The sister placed her hand on Marthe's arm. "Be prepared for his screaming. At least until he passes out from the pain."

Two orderlies wheeled the patient into the room and one of the nuns injected atropine into his leg above the knee. Another handed him a glass of whiskey. "Drink this down, soldier."

Sister Margarete prepared the tray of scalpels but covered the bone saw with a surgical cloth to remove it from the soldier's sight and keep him as calm as possible. For as long as possible. The atropine and whiskey helped, but he continued to whimper like a small child.

The doctor took his place beside the patient and made the first incision but the soldier flailed so violently the scalpel flew from his hand, barely missing Marthe's shoulder.

"Hold this man down! We have a job to do here."

Marthe threw herself across the patient's chest while Sister Margarete and one of the other nuns held his legs, still trembling under their strong hands. Agonized screams tore from the soldier's throat and his head rocked back and forth. From her prone position, Marthe watched the doctor scoop out the infection then cut away the skin and muscle all the way down to the bone. When the doctor reached for the saw, she lessened her pressure on the man's chest because he had fainted. Marthe sent up a silent prayer of gratitude for what little peace that provided him during the worst of the operation. Even for her, trained in amputations, the incessant grinding of the surgical saw set her teeth on edge. It dragged on for what felt like forever, swelling to a high-pitched whine as it chewed through the thickest part of the bone.

When it was over, Marthe stayed and cauterized the wound then stitched the skin flaps together. The soldier was still out, but Sister Margarete confirmed that his heart rate was normal.

"We'll save the morphine for when he wakes," Sister Margarete said, adding quietly, "and the pain returns."

"Nurse." The command came out gruff and impatient. "Accompany me on rounds."

Sister Margarete nodded to her and Marthe left with the doctor. Together they visited every patient in the building, changed dressings, and explained why they couldn't give morphine for the pain. Marthe promised to return the next day to write letters to the soldiers' loved ones.

"You probably won't have time for that," the doctor said. "If you want to sleep, that is."

She understood. Almost twenty hours had passed since her arrival.

Sister Margarete found her taking the temperature of one of the final patients. "I'm here to relieve you," she said. "You should grab a short rest while you can. The doctor will return in three hours and it will be more of the same."

Marthe was shown to a room in the attic where she collapsed on the nearest cot, thankful to be off her feet. Her last thought was to remember to ask Sister Margarete about getting different shoes with better support for her tired legs.

Only forty restful minutes had passed when a shell exploded nearby and pieces of the ceiling fell on her. She awoke and went downstairs to see how she could help.

The date was April 21, 1915. Marthe didn't know it at the time, but the following day would see a critical change—a chilling change—in the weapons of war. And the results of that change would increase her job tenfold.

# CHAPTER THREE

MARTHE
April 23, 1915
Roulers Field Hospital

Rumors flew through the halls of the hospital and ambulances crammed with wounded soldiers began arriving before daylight. Marthe had never before seen such wreckage on a human body.

The first group to arrive brought shock after shock as she recognized soldiers from the unit that killed her family and kidnapped her. Yes, she decided, she still hated them. But the sight of their devastated torsos jarred her. Little by little from their pain-induced mumblings, the battle details emerged.

Just before noon of the previous day, she learned, the German unit she had spent months loathing, clashed with two battalions of Canadian soldiers in Kitcheners' Wood, only a few kilometers from Ypres and fewer than ten kilometers from where she stood.

In an area known as Flanders Field.

She held the hand of the young soldier who had saved her life by telling the *Hauptmann* she was a nurse.

"We holed up in a big oak plantation," the young soldier told her, his breath labored.

"Shh," Marthe said. "Don't speak. Save your strength."

He tried to fill his lungs, then cried out in pain. Marthe pressed a bandage to the wound near his heart.

"Were you stabbed?" she asked.

With difficulty, the young soldier nodded. "*Hauptmann* ordered us to advance on the Canadians." Blood gushed from every wound Marthe touched and he winced. "But no reconnaissance had come through ... we didn't know how many we faced." He panted in shallow bursts. "Our ammunition ran out and we charged with the only thing we had left ... our bayonets."

"And they did the same, right? That's what this hole is, a bayonet wound?"

Again, the soldier nodded. "You're right. The Canadians responded with everything they had too," he said. "Over and over they came at us." More shallow breaths. "And in no time at all, they cleared us from both the plantation and the woods. I never saw so much blood."

Marthe cleaned the young man's face. "I'm so sorry this happened to you," she said. "I will never forget you for saving my life. Try to rest now and let me help you."

He closed his eyes but before Marthe could reach for more bandages, a wan smile found his lips. Later, she could never figure out how to describe it, but she would have sworn that a peaceful light enveloped his whole body.

Then his breathing ceased. And his heart stopped.

She closed his eyes with her fingers and whispered to ears that no longer heard her. "Rest now, soldier. Your war is over."

She hated to leave the young man alone, but knew he no longer needed her help. The next soldier brought to her was the *Hauptmann* himself, the one who had actually pulled the trigger to end her family's lives. His midsection spilled out in a mass of intestines drenched in mud. She poured water over the mass to remove the dirt and determine the source of the bleeding. But he died before she had a chance to locate it.

Despite her hatred of all Germans and the one in front of her in particular, his death failed to produce the satisfaction she expected. Instead, anger filled her heart. Anger for all of the senseless killing. For her family, for the soldiers in front of her, and for all the thousands of others caught up in forces over which they had no part in initiating and no hope of ending.

For the next two hours, more than seventy-five percent of the

Germans on whom she had vowed revenge showed up in the glut of wounded soldiers, broken and dying, the extent of their wounds so severe she had no time to feel anything but sorrow for their fate. Almost none of them could be saved.

The room serving as a morgue filled to capacity.

Marthe and the nuns worked through the morning, and when they couldn't save any more lives, they disinfected the morgue and called for the bodies to be removed. To make room for the new wave of soldiers expected that afternoon.

"I don't know what we would have done without you, my daughter," Sister Margarete said. "One of the sisters made soup. Please … take a break and get some nourishment."

Marthe nodded weakly and found the soup pot in the large kitchen. She swallowed her last bite when the bell sounded at the front door and an ambulance driver shouted, "Wounded."

Marthe rose and rushed to join the sisters on their way to the new flood of soldiers. As badly broken as the first group had been, Marthe was shocked at the type of wounds she saw with this second group. The first ambulances brought German soldiers struggling to breathe, their eyes red and swollen and complaining that their throats burned. But the ones after that included French, Canadian, Moroccan, and Algerian troops—all suffering the same symptoms as the Germans but to a much greater degree.

Marthe stood beside the doctor, who shook his head in disgust. "We can do very little for these men," he told her. "They're suffering from gas poisoning so their damage is internal, their lungs blistered." He turned toward Marthe. "Ask the sisters if they still have oxygen. That will help. But these men will need bed rest. Months of it. And we can't spare the space."

"Maybe there will be room at the Taverne," Marthe said. "I can ask Herr Breit."

Slowly they progressed from one screaming soldier to the next and Marthe's frustration built. She had never seen anything like the sickness produced by the gas and couldn't understand where it had come from or the best way to deal with it. Her anger mounted once more at the horrendous way man had discovered to kill his fellow man.

Marthe bent to tend to a German soldier and learned he had been in charge of releasing the gas from the cylinders in the trenches.

"If I'd known what it would be like when it was released," he said, his eyes still red-rimmed and swollen shut, "I would've pretended to be sick that day. I mean, I was at the front, releasing the gas, but I had no idea what would happen. Nobody ever told us that." He dabbed a wet cloth to his eyes. "We knew the cylinders were there—they'd been buried the week before. But at five o'clock yesterday afternoon, we uncovered them and lit the fuses. A thick yellow cloud poured out and moved slowly toward the opposite trench." He dabbed his eyes again. "It actually looked like a yellow wall and we could see the French troops rise from their trench and break through the cloud of gas." Tears trickled from his blind eyes. "And then we shot them." His tears turned to sobs and Marthe waited until he could talk again. "I was ashamed." Another ragged breath followed. "They were helpless. And we took advantage. The gas blinded them and it was so thick they couldn't even see each other, so they didn't know which way to turn." Marthe knew she needed to calm him, but she was helpless to interrupt his story. "Most of them suffocated," he continued, "unable to breathe once the gas settled in their bodies." He hung his head and spoke quietly, his voice tortured. "Their faces turned purple and their tongues hung from their mouths. Black. Grotesque. They didn't even know we were close." Sobs overtook him again. "We shot and never missed. Every bullet tore into a body."

"But how did it get on you?" Marthe asked. "If you released it, weren't you behind it?"

"The wind shifted at one point ... just for a moment ... but enough to give those of us in front a good dose of it. We were given pads soaked with some solution—sodium-something-sulfate, they told me. But a crazed French soldier knocked into me and I dropped mine. Once a full dose of the chlorine gas reached my lungs, I understood why they all screamed. It's horrible. Just horrible." His tears flowed unchecked.

Marthe did what she could to make the soldiers feel better, then told Sister Margarete that she needed a break to talk with Herr Breit, the Taverne owner, to see if some of the gassed soldiers could recuperate there.

On her way out, she heard her name called. She turned and walked toward the sound.

"*Ja?* Who called my name?"

"I did." The voice was weak. "Over here."

Marthe edged between the cots toward a raised hand, careful not to jostle the wounded men. She reached the cot and bent down. The horizon blue of the soldier's uniform indicated he was French. "*Qui êtes-vous?*" she asked. "Who are you?"

"*Es ist dein Nachbar,*" he answered in German. "Your neighbor. From Liege. Emery Dengler. I went to school with your brother."

Pain clenched her heart and her words faltered. "Emery … what are you doing here?"

"I thought it would be obvious," he wheezed. "I needed—"

"No … I don't mean that. Of course you need medical attention, I can see that. But it's your eyes, right? How did you know I was here if you couldn't see?"

"I heard your voice and thought I recognized your accent. Then my buddy over here described you and I knew I had to be right. I remember you."

Marthe hesitated. "What I really meant when I asked you what you're doing here is, why are you wearing a French uniform?"

"I attended university in Paris. I was there when war broke out and … it just seemed … the right thing. No family left … friends were French. So I joined with them."

"I'm really glad to see you. But I'm sorry you're hurt. Is it the gas I've heard so much about or were you shot?"

"Both … well, stabbed," he said. His voice reached her in ragged gasps. "They released that yellow-green cloud … I couldn't see … tried to get out of it. To clear my senses. But it was blinding … affected my eyes … couldn't tell which way I was going. I ran into a

German soldier. Bayonet fixed ... caught me in the side." His head sank back, exhausted after telling her his story.

"Well, I'll make certain to look out for you while you're here. Although ..." She hesitated, knowing he would probably be transported to a German prisoner of war camp.

"Yeah, I know." He grinned. "I'm probably not here for very long. But I'm glad I got to talk to you. Is your family doing okay?"

The full pain of their deaths shot into her heart, cutting off her breath. Her head dropped and she used all her strength to keep from crying, then answered quietly, "No. They were killed and our home burned."

His hand found hers. "Oh my goodness. If I had known ... would never have brought them up. So sorry."

She shook her head and squeezed his hand. "Thank you. I must go for now, but I will find you again when I return and we can talk more. It's really nice to see a familiar face again, Emery."

He stayed on her mind while she walked the few blocks to the Taverne. Sure, he was wounded. And he would certainly go to a German prison camp as soon as he was well enough. But she couldn't shake the feeling that he had done things right. He had gone to Paris and removed himself from the path of the Germans. So he wasn't forced to fight for them. He had made his own choice. And when the war was over he would do so again.

Would she ever, Marthe wondered, be brave enough to make the hard choice? To make her own path?

# CHAPTER
## FOUR

Happiness filled my heart to be reading my grandmother's words.

I was certain Dad had never seen this since it was still embedded in the back of the album until just a few minutes ago. But, oh, how he would have loved it.

I pulled the old photo album onto my lap and turned back to its beginning. I hoped the pictures might match some of the diary entries. After the photos of my grandmother with her older brother and several pictures with their parents—obvious from the captions—I found a page with a picture of two skinny teenage boys in old-fashioned baseball uniforms. The caption read "Henry and Buzz, State Championship 1915." My great-uncle and my grandfather.

The next page had pictures of the boys again with a young dark-haired girl standing between them. My grandmother. She was so adorable and I figured out from the dates under the picture that she was around ten years old. What I wouldn't give to have known her.

Her diary lay open beside the album and the next date in it caught my eye as being the same as the date on the picture. April 30, 1915.

There were so many things I needed to do, but I couldn't resist Maude's diary. I adjusted my glasses and continued to read.

*April 30, 1915*

*Dear Diary,*

*Your friend, Maude, here.*

*The boys played ball again today. What a surprise, huh? Except this time they played for the Pennsylvania State Championship. Henry said the coach was worried about Buzz ... that he wouldn't come out of his slump after his parents died. But Henry and Dad have been working with him and coach told him big league scouts will be here today. So he's been prac-ticing a lot. Mostly his special pitches. They all look the same to me, but Dad thinks he's really good. And Henry is a good hitter—gets on base almost every time and Dad says that if Henry can get on base, then he's probably gonna score. So, who knows? Some big league guy might want to take a look at both of them. I hope so. I would love to have Mom and Dad all to myself without those smelly boys around all the time.*

*Mom's calling me. More later.*

*Your still new friend, Maude*

---

## April 30, 1915

HENRY BREWER SQUATTED BEHIND HOME PLATE AND positioned his mitt to receive Buzz Ryan's fastball. His ten-year-old sister, Maude, huddled next to her father on the bleachers behind Henry and silently wished she had listened to her mother and worn her coat rather than the thick sweater she pulled tight around her.

She studied the look in Buzz's eyes. Total focus. She almost laughed. She couldn't see Henry's face but figured it held the same concentration, the same set of the jaw.

A movement beside her caught her attention and she turned

slightly. A tall man, his straw boater hat stuffed firmly on his head, stopped and casually draped an arm on the end of the row where Maude and her father sat. Her father nodded.

"That your son?" the tall man asked.

"The catcher," Maude's father said. "The pitcher is his best friend. And kind of my adopted son."

"I hear they make a pretty good team," the tall man said.

"That they do," Maude's father replied. "And let me tell you, they practice in the front yard all the time. I work with them when I can. Buzz, the pitcher, is really fast. Got his nickname because his fastball buzzed right past so many batters. Wish we knew how fast he throws, but we can only guess. These boys have played the same positions for the past four years, but they've been friends since they were born." Maude's father paused and, when the tall stranger didn't respond, he turned. "You new around here?"

"I'm from Philadelphia," the tall man said. "I actually came here to watch this pitcher. And the catcher." He faced Maude's father. "The name's Cornelius Magillicuddy. But everybody calls me 'Mack.'" He extended his hand. "Connie Mack. Manager of the Philadelphia Athletics."

Maude's father, his eyes wide, said, "I didn't recognize you, Mr. Mack. Frank Brewer, as I said, father to the catcher, Henry, and adoptive father to the pitcher, Buzz." Maude's father shook hands with the tall man. "The boys told me about you," Frank continued. "We all went to Harrington's General Store in town to listen to your final game in last year's series. Tough break, that double play in the seventh inning. We thought you would easily send the Braves packing."

"Yeah ... so did I," Connie Mack said. "But that's why I'm here. Looking for new blood. Don't want to keep losing. Lost games mean lost fans. And financial backing. We have to shake things up." He took a deep breath, removed his hat and wiped his forehead. "Plus, some of my boys are leaving to join the new Federal League. Others will be volunteering for that war overseas. Don't understand that one myself, why anyone would purposely involve themselves in a fight that doesn't concern them and probably never will. But it doesn't much matter what I think. Anyway, I heard these boys are a talented team. I also heard that Ryan's fastball has been compared to Rube Waddell's at his prime. He was a southpaw, too, you know."

"Yes, I do know," Frank said. "Really sorry about his death last year. I'm sure you miss him."

"Yeah, he was a great pitcher, but we had to let him go several years ago ... too hard to control."

Frank snickered. "I heard about his shenanigans." He searched Mack's eyes. "Did he really wrestle an alligator?"

Mack nodded, his jaw clenched. "Yes, he did, the fool. Our first season of Spring Training in Jacksonville, Florida. And later during that same camp, he held up the start of games so he could play marbles with kids outside the gate." Mack's smile didn't reach his whole face. "Many's the time we couldn't find him because he took off to go fishing when he wasn't scheduled to pitch." Mack snickered. "He was quite the character ... helluva pitcher ... but wasted so much of his talent on his drinking."

The men returned their attention to the game and watched as Buzz retired three batters with nine pitches.

"Now that's what I like to see," Mack said. "Boy's got what it takes. What's his personal life like? Is he self-disciplined ... self-motivated?"

"He's all that for sure," Frank said. "And ... he had a real sorry home life. Parents fought all the time, took whatever money he brought home and spent it on booze." Frank shook his head. "You'd think that would have ruined him ... he even watched his father shoot himself. But he's such a good boy, once his parents were gone, he came to live with us. I really think he'll do fine. Just fine."

"That all sounds good except that his parents drank. I refuse to work with anyone else who drinks after trying to keep Waddell on the payroll. How did his parents' deaths affect him? Have you known him to take a drink? I just couldn't take that kind of chance again."

"No sir. Not at all. His parents' drinking is what scared him away from it."

"That's good to hear. Both your boys certainly show the physical ability for the game. If my scouts and I can determine that they have the intelligence ... and the courage ... to do what it takes not only to play, but also to win, then our scouts will want to talk with them about their futures."

"I can assure you, Mr. Mack, my boys have both. Why don't you and your scouts come by the house for dinner tonight? My wife, Florence, is cooking a chicken casserole and we would love to host you. We'll invite the boys' coach, too, if you'd like."

"Thank you, Mr. Brewer. I accept your hospitality."

The men watched the remainder of the game and cheered when the boys' team won. Not only the game, but also the state pennant, the boys' last game of their high school careers.

*Wow.* Maude smiled. *I might get my wish, after all, and these boys will go to Philadelphia. No more teasing. Oh wow, that would be great.*

# CHAPTER FIVE

MARTHE
Field Hospital
April 30, 1915

Marthe's days in the hospital morphed from day to night, light to dark, sleeping hours to waking hours until the one was indistinguishable from the other. Every day the hospital lacked something—surgeons, nurses, medicine, bandages. Food remained scarce, partly because the Germans commandeered seventy-five percent of every commodity that crossed their paths but also because the hospital staff was considered civilian, so had to eke out its food allotment from the remaining twenty-five percent not gobbled up by the Germans. Medicines appeared more often, Marthe was told, so the German soldiers in the hospital could be healed and returned to the front lines.

Herr Breit's Taverne fared a little better than the hospital since his inn housed so many German officers. His dining room received a full allotment every month for his German "guests," even though they were neither invited nor paid residents. Regardless, the arrangement resulted in better food for the inn than the folks in the rest of the town received.

The townspeople suffered greatly under the control of the Town-Kommandant and his contingent of military *gendarmerie* who carried out their duties as if they were plain-clothes agents who had the run of the town.

Because, in fact, they *did* have the run of the town.

All citizens were required to leave their doors unlocked during the day so these agents could walk in unannounced and look around anytime they desired in their constant search for spies, snipers, even food hoarders. Their suspicions became aroused at the slightest thing. A child with a piece of fruit, for example, might signify a family guilty of an illegal food supply or a visiting relative might only be visiting in order to spy.

Finding spies was the agents' major hot button and everyone —*everyone*—fell under suspicion. Marthe had even seen it at the hospital when the *gendarmerie* questioned the nuns as if on trial at an inquisition. The German agents' overbearing behavior had earned them the nickname "Berlin Vampires" behind the closed doors of the town's residents.

Marthe had witnessed their actions firsthand the night her family died, but each time she saw it again, it surprised her. She found it hard to believe that one group of people could view themselves as superior and then act so cruelly against those they deemed unworthy. So she chose to maintain her distance and go about her tasks, keeping her head down and her nose clean.

In spite of her desire to work in the shadows, however, she had purposely come to Herr Breit to ask if some of the gassed soldiers in the hospital could be accommodated at the Taverne to convalesce. And make room for the newly wounded in the hospital.

She didn't hold out much hope, but thought she had to try.

"*Fräulein*," Herr Breit greeted her warmly, taking both her hands in his. "It is good to see you. Are you getting on with the sisters?"

"*Ja*," she answered. "They work hard and there is never enough of anything they need, but they do their jobs without complaint. I enjoy my time with them."

"*Gut*. Tell me," he added, "were the wounds from the last few days as bad as the rumors?"

"*Ja*," she said again. "The German soldiers have come to us with wounds unlike any other battle. But the French and Algiers soldiers brought to us as prisoners of war have been far worse. From exposure to poison gas. Almost all of them are temporarily blinded with their lungs burned and blistered, according to the *Oberarzt*. That's actually why I am here. The doctor says there is little we can do for them, that they need time and bed rest for their lungs to heal." She closed her eyes as the memory of the soldiers gasping for air filled her brain. "Herr Breit, we don't have enough beds to allow soldiers to occupy them for weeks or perhaps months. We have too many wounded coming in each day. I know it's a lot to ask, but do you have any room for some of the gassed soldiers here?"

Herr Breit's eyes held a look she didn't recognize. *Was it eagerness? Anticipation?* But it was gone as quickly as it appeared and the only expression remaining struck Marthe as guarded.

"*Fräulein*, we are overly full, as you well know. I could possibly make room in the attic ..." His voice trailed off and he appeared to be thinking, visualizing. Marthe remained still. "Yes," he said finally. "I think we could arrange it. We could set up as many cots as would fit in the space—I will approach the Town-Kommandant about getting them—but I'm concerned about how we would care for the men. All our hands are busy with preparing food and taking care of the rooms of our ... uh ... guests."

Marthe understood that housing German officers was not his first choice, but he obliged them because the Germans demanded it.

"I thought about that," Marthe said. "When I was a teenager in Liege, I waited tables at the inn there before I went to nurses' training, so I could help out when I finish my shift at the hospital. If you will allow it, I could take their food to them and care for their wounds and gas burns at night. I'm sure the sisters will endorse this plan since we will free up needed beds at the hospital. May I tell them it's okay?"

He remained silent for a few minutes. Emotions Marthe found hard to interpret chased across his face. Fear was plainly there and she also recognized fatigue and resignation, but occasionally caught a glimpse of something else. Something that resembled enthusiasm. She certainly didn't understand that one. "Well, Herr Breit?"

"*Ja*," he said. "Let me get enough cots first and then we will work on who can be moved. I will speak with you again tomorrow."

"*Danke,*" she said. She pumped his hand up and down, unable to understand why his agreement caused her to feel excitement. But feel it she did.

"This will only work, *Fräulein,*" he added, "if the sisters really are able to spare you the time to be here and care for the men we house. If they can't agree to that, we will have to find another solution."

"I understand, Herr Breit. I'm certain I can convince them."

"And once you're here," Herr Breit added, "I will want to talk with you about ..." His words ended abruptly and he pulled himself up as if someone had hit him in the stomach. Marthe saw that soldiers had entered the dining room, where she and Herr Breit sat, but she had no idea why their sudden presence would have affected what he intended to say.

"*Ja,* Herr Breit? Talk with me about what?"

"Nothing," he said. "I don't even remember what I was going to say."

He lied. Marthe knew it but ignored it. She couldn't imagine what had interrupted his thought but had no time to worry about it then. She had work to do.

She shook his hand once again and rose to leave. Herr Breit escorted her to the door, stopping to introduce her to Town-Kommandant Gerlach Stroebel on her way out.

"Herr Stroebel," Herr Breit said. "I am pleased to introduce you to Marthe Peeters, a nurse working with the sisters in our field hospital. She is responsible for healing your troops so they can return to the battlefield."

The man took her fingers in his, refusing to rise, and regarding her with an insolent, and, Marthe thought, suggestive look. "*Fräulein,*" he said. "How good to meet you. I hope we will be able to see more of you around here. You greatly improve the scenery of this dreadful place."

Marthe managed a small smile and removed her fingers as quickly as possible without being rude. All the hate she had ever felt for the Germans bubbled back up to her brain and she swallowed several times to remove the taste of bile from her throat. She left through the

Taverne's door and gulped deep breaths of fresh air, suddenly understanding what it must feel like to be enveloped in poison.

# CHAPTER SIX

MARTHE
Field Hospital
June 15, 1915

In the weeks after Marthe arranged for gassed soldiers' and prisoners' relocation to the Taverne's attic, both her confidence in her nursing skills and her disquiet from her constant proximity to German officers increased exponentially. No longer able to simply get through her day by going about her tasks and remaining anonymous, she resigned herself to her more visible role and endeavored to use it to her advantage.

Her higher profile had happened gradually and stemmed from her role in caring for the soldiers recuperating in the attic. On the evening of a particularly rowdy celebration by the German officers, she was in the kitchen preparing trays of food for her charges when one of the Germans burst in and demanded her attention.

"*Fräulein*," he bellowed, "more *bier*. Now!"

Marthe recognized that the officer was drunk and that Herr Breit and his staff worked in the dining room as quickly as they could to accommodate the huge influx of additional diners.

"Of course," she answered. She left her tray unfinished, picked up one of the full pitchers and followed him back to the dining room. "Who needs *bier*?" she asked, raising the pitcher. Every stein at the noisiest table in the middle of the room shot into the air and one by one, she filled them, dodging sweaty hands that reached for her backside and attempted to maneuver under her skirt, then returned to the kitchen for another full pitcher and finished the job. Herr Breit sent her an appreciative glance.

While there were downsides to endlessly dodging unwelcome German advances as she traveled to and from her patients at the Taverne, she recognized that her position was more comfortable than that of most of the remaining families in town. And certainly safer than her days traveling with the German infantry. Her food rations were better, for one thing. Herr Breit saw to it that she received not only the better quality food from the seventy-five percent controlled by the Germans, but also larger portions of it. The nuns at the field hospital benefitted from her bounty, as did her patients.

Herr Breit found her in the kitchen where she spoke with the chef.

"*Danke*, Marthe," he said. "That could have turned ugly really fast."

"Let me help you, Herr Breit," she said to him. "My patients upstairs can wait a few minutes so your tables can be served."

He loaded the meals prepared for the boisterous table on a large tray, then carried it out while she served the dishes to the diners. That helped keep them quiet, but she returned to the kitchen right away for more beer and filled all the steins again and again. She stayed to help Herr Breit and his staff deliver food and drink to other tables in the dining room and finally finished the tray for the wounded men in the attic. She headed up the stairs, balancing her tray when one of the Germans shouted to her.

"*Fräulein*," he hollered. "Halt. What do you have there?"

"It is the rations for the wounded soldiers housed in the attic," she answered.

"Who authorized that? Bring it over here and let me inspect it." The room went silent and Marthe stood perfectly still, looking to Herr Breit for help.

He approached the drunken officer. "We have permission from Town-Kommandant Stroebel," he said. "German soldiers are housed here because the local field hospital ran out of room. And *Fräulein* Peeters comes here from the hospital to care for them."

"The bar maid?"

Marthe straightened her shoulders and said, "I am a trained nurse and have worked in the hospital for months. We moved these soldiers here to make room for the more severely wounded. I poured your *bier* as a favor to Herr Breit because the dining room was so busy."

"Prove it," the officer sneered. "Let me see your papers."

A tall man appeared behind the officer. "What's the problem, Hirsch? Why are you keeping this young woman from her duties?"

Marthe almost laughed at the expression on the belligerent man's face when he turned his head and locked eyes with the Town-Kommandant. "Pardon me, sir." The man's cheeks all the way past his ears matched the crimson napkin he held. "Always on the lookout for spies, sir. And food hoarders. I thought her behavior odd."

"Well, now you know she is here under my protection. If you've finished your dinner, you may leave."

"Yes sir."

Even from her distance, Marthe saw the man's hands shake and the beads of sweat that coated his forehead. She still hated the Germans, but at least the Town-Kommandant had made it clear to his staff that she was off limits to them and their harassment. She hid her smile of satisfaction as she climbed the stairs with the tray of food for the attic's wounded.

At the top of the stairs the first patient she encountered was Emery Dengler, the French soldier who had been a friend of her brother before the war. He hadn't completely regained his sight, but he always spoke to her as soon as she arrived.

"Marthe," he said. "Welcome."

"How do you do that, Emery? I know you can't see yet."

"I recognize your footsteps. Your gait has an unmistakable pattern." She saw his grin in the low light. "Plus," he added, "I can smell the bacon. And"—he took a deep breath—"Herr Breit's home-made bread."

"Right on both counts. How are you feeling?"

"Good. Well, okay … no worse, anyhow," he amended.

Emery's puncture wound had mostly healed, but she knew his

lungs hadn't recovered. The doctor said only one of his lungs had collapsed as a result of the gas but she still worried that catching a cold that led to pneumonia could kill him. She was determined that wouldn't happen on her watch.

"I'll come back after I make my rounds, Emery. If you have any new letters, I'll read them to you."

She distributed food to the thirty patients in her care, then made her rounds as they ate. She checked the progress of wounds, applied new bandages, emptied chamber pots, and changed sheets when needed. In addition, knowing that many of the wounded had come from the trenches where rats and lice were prevalent, she patrolled the attic to prevent those pests from thriving there. She removed every crumb of uneaten food and she was vigilant about wiping down everything she saw with disinfectant-soaked cloths. Daily she inspected for lice and, if found, immediately covered the man's hair with petroleum jelly to keep the lice from getting any air. Helping the men to heal was hard enough without fighting disease and pests at the same time.

She finished her chores and wound through the cots, speaking to several of the men she had come to know.

"Hey, Nurse Marthe," the young man from Antwerp called.

"*Ja*, Leo?"

"Did you hear about the pilot who got into a dog fight?"

Marthe heard snickers from some of the closest cots. "No, Leo, what about him?"

"Aw, he's all right. He was able to *shake* his *tail*."

The men all laughed and Marthe rewarded the young man with a big smile. Moving the men to this location had been good for all of them. She really believed the atmosphere aided their healing and the small group stuffed into such close quarters generated an easy camaraderie. Even among the soldiers from opposite sides of the war. *But why not?* Most of the men around her were simply foot soldiers who had no quarrel with anyone from another country.

"Marthe, is that you?" Emery said to her when she returned to sit beside him. "You must have approached me on tiptoes. I couldn't hear your footsteps."

"Probably because the cots are so close there isn't room to walk naturally."

"I suppose that's it. Is Roland beside me?"

When he was still at the hospital, Emery had introduced her to Roland Baxter, a farm boy from England. He, too, had been caught in the gas attack.

"I'm here, Emery," Roland answered. One of Roland's eyes was clear. "It's nice to see you, Nurse Marthe. Hey Emery, since Nurse Marthe is here, you want to play chess?"

"Sure."

Marthe had helped the men play chess several times, so she reached under the cot and drew out the board. "Black or white, Emery?" she asked.

"White."

She set the pieces up and watched Emery's concentration as he visualized the squares and decided on his first move. He knew not only the names of the chess pieces but also their location on the board. She didn't know how he kept it all straight in his head, but she simply moved the pieces where he told her. The men appeared to be evenly matched in skill and shared the wins and losses. She had never been a chess player before but after having helped the two of them play, she believed she could almost hold her own.

"Pawn to d-four," Emery told her. She had learned the numbering and lettering on the board so she knew to move the fourth pawn from the left two spaces forward to the fourth row.

"Good move," Roland said. "So how are things at the hospital, Nurse Marthe? Did you get a lot of wounded today? Pawn to f-five." Even though Roland moved his own chess piece, he called his action out so Emery would know his moves.

"We always get a lot of wounded, Roland. Emery, what is your move?"

"Bishop to g-five," he said. Marthe frowned. That was a strategy she hadn't seen before.

"Are you sure?" she asked. Emery nodded and Marthe made the move.

"Black pawn to h-six," Roland said quickly. "Any new rumors reached your ears, Nurse Marthe? I heard the Germans were planning an offensive."

"I don't know anything about that," Marthe said. "And even if I did, I wouldn't talk about it here," she added. "Emery, what do you want me to do?"

"Retreat the bishop to h-four."

"Black pawn to g-five." Roland turned back to Marthe. "I'm just trying to find out if any members of my original unit are close by. Maybe they could come see me."

"You've been captured, Roland," Emery said. "Do you want them captured too? White pawn to e-four." Marthe made the move.

"Ha!" Roland said. "I've got you now. I've captured your bishop with my pawn."

"No, I've got *you*. Nurse Marthe, move my queen to f-five. Check-mate, Roland."

"Well, I'll be damned."

"Maybe you should focus more on your game next time," Marthe said to Roland, "instead of asking questions you know I can't answer." She gave him a half smile. "I have to go now. I'll see you both again tomorrow."

Roland stared at her. "You really should learn what's happening with the different battles, Nurse Marthe," he said. "For your own sake. For everybody's sake."

Marthe didn't answer but picked up the tray and retreated down the stairs. At the bottom, Herr Breit waited for her.

"I'm sorry about what happened here tonight," he said. His eyes held a quizzical expression. "Did I hear Roland asking you questions about the battles?"

She blushed. "Yes. I was afraid everyone would hear. I wouldn't talk to him about anything even if I knew."

"I know. But ... let's try to find time for us to talk tomorrow. Could you do that?"

"I guess," she answered. "But I certainly won't have any more information tomorrow than I do now. What is it you want to talk about?"

"Serving your country." He bowed and retreated into the kitchen.

Marthe stared after him. His words sent fear to her stomach. But she had no idea why.

# CHAPTER
# SEVEN

**SUZANNE**
2015

I knew this would happen.

I can't resist photo albums. And at this point, even though I'd been at Dad's house for a couple of hours, I was so hooked on my grandmother's diary I knew there was no chance I'd get much cleaning or sorting done for the rest of the day.

So I gave myself permission to settle in and enjoy.

The photo album lay open and an entire page held pictures of the two boys in sport coats and ties standing beside suitcases. The caption, in white ink, proclaimed, "They're off!" The date was July 5, 1915. Carefully, I turned to the next fragile page of Maude's diary.

*July 10, 1915*

*Dear Diary,*

*It's me, Maude.*

*Well, it's been a great week around here. The 4th of July celebration was bigger than normal this year. And really fun. Except for all those boring speeches by the town's leaders who kept talking about 'The War in Europe.' I don't know why they have to bring it up all the time. It certainly won't affect us here in Prospect Park. I think they just like to hear themselves talk and make people think they're doing more than they're really doing.*

*The boys' baseball team rode on a float since they're the state champions. You couldn't hear the band play for all the cheers the crowd gave them. Henry and Buzz even got special awards because they were chosen to go to Philadelphia to practice with the Philadelphia Athletics. Henry says it's a minor league team with the same name as the major league team. But that's fine with them. They're just happy to be going there.*

*They boarded the bus this afternoon. Mom's worried about them. It's the first time either one of them has been away from home. I say, "Good riddance," but she says she's afraid they'll become sinful. Whatever that means.*

*I'm meeting Helen and Ethel tomorrow. We're going swimming and then to the county fair. I'll tell you all about it when I get home.*

*Your friend, Maude*

---

## July 10, 1915

THE WHOLE TOWN TURNED OUT TO WISH HENRY AND BUZZ good luck as they boarded the bus to Philadelphia. Their journey to become professional baseball players thrilled the townspeople, most of whom had never traveled outside the city limits. But then, neither had the boys. While the firemen's band played a rousing sendoff, the men of the town shook hands with Henry and Buzz and the women smothered them with hugs. By the time they actually boarded, their faces blushed bright red down to their necks.

"I've never seen those boys so excited," Maude's father said on the way home. "It sure was nice of Mr. Mack to arrange everything." He put his hand over his wife's as they sat together on the front seat of the farm wagon. "They'll be okay, Mother," he told her. "You don't need to worry. They're good boys."

"I know they are," she said, wiping her eyes. "And it's not them

I'm worried about. It's those loose women in big cities I've read about. What if ..."

Frank threw his head back and laughed. "I've had 'The Talk' with both of them, Flo," he said. "They'll be fine. I promise."

In the back of the wagon, Maude heard them, but had no idea what they referred to. The next day, when Maude joined Ethel and Helen, she reported the conversation.

"What do you think your mother meant by 'loose women'?" Ethel asked.

"I dunno," Maude answered. "Do you think their arms flap funny or their legs buckle when they try to walk?" She pantomimed her description by waving her arms and pumping her knees up and down. "Maybe they look like this." The girls laughed.

"Well, both boys certainly are cute," Helen said.

"Ewww ..." Maude held her nose and pretended to vomit. "I don't know how you can say that. They always smelled like sweat and their room was filthy."

"Well, of course you would think that," Ethel said. "You lived with them. But Helen's right. They could have had any girl in school as girl-friends."

"I don't think they did, though." Maude led the way down the stairs and onto the front porch. "All they ever thought about was base-ball. I guess that's why Mr. Mack wanted them. Dad said he'd take me to a game later this summer."

"Lucky you," Helen said. "I bet they'll both look great in the A's uniform."

"Will you stop?" Maude pushed Helen playfully. "They are just smelly boys and I'm glad they're gone."

The girls continued their playful banter down the long lane and during their walk to the fairgrounds in town. Maude bought her ticket and said, "Will you girls help me remember I promised Dad I'd bring him some caramel popcorn? Ferris wheel first?"

They took off into the crowd and lost themselves in the joy of the moment.

The subject of Maude's brother and Buzz ended.

# CHAPTER EIGHT

MARTHE
Field Hospital
August 1915

**M**arthe's days began and ended in the dark.

She had moved into the Taverne when her wounded soldiers took up residence in the attic. Every day she rose before dawn in her small alcove above the Taverne's kitchen with its tiny window. She ate a quick breakfast of oatmeal, then prepared her tray for the soldiers. Several of the men had regained their mobility so she sometimes left the full tray so one of the ambulatory men could distribute the food to the others. She wished the people in charge of the wretched war could see the way both German soldiers and their prisoners co-existed peacefully in their attic room. She considered it nothing less than remarkable.

Having cared for her charges, she was often one of the first to begin rounds at the hospital. Only Sister Margarete began rounds earlier.

"How are our men in the attic today?" Sister Margarete asked.

"Getting better all the time," she answered. "And they seem to be in good spirits. One of them even told me a joke recently." She checked the pulse of a new arrival. "Have you heard any rumors of what we can expect today?"

"No, my daughter. But whatever it is, God will help us to be prepared."

No sooner had Sister Margarete spoken than the first ambulance arrived. Most of the soldiers within wore German uniforms, but two were French and one appeared to be from Algiers.

Either Marthe or Sister Margarete assumed the duty of performing triage on the arriving wounded and on this day, Marthe began with the first soldier in front of her. Quickly, she scanned the injuries and decided one of the French soldiers needed the most immediate attention. His shredded jacket barely covered his torso and his hair color was impossible to determine through the blood and mud.

"Get this man to surgery immediately," she told the orderlies. "Is the *Oberarzt* ready?" she asked Sister Margarete. At Sister Margarete's discreet shake of her head, she sighed. She and the sister would have to perform the surgery. It wouldn't be the first time they had to step in because the *Oberarzt* was occupied elsewhere, but assuming his position always unsettled her. "Did we get the ether in, sister? That will help."

Sister Margarete nodded and the two of them quickly sent the other wounded men to various parts of the hospital with instructions to the orderlies and the other nuns, then retreated to scrub up for the French soldier. They rolled up their sleeves to beyond their elbows and used corrosive soap to thoroughly wash every part of the skin that showed. Then Marthe slipped her hands into the rubber gloves Sister Margarete held for her, the signal that Marthe should take the lead.

The Frenchman lay on the table between them, the naked light bulb low over his body. Marthe cut the remains of the tattered uniform from around his abdomen and chest to reveal a six-inch piece of shrapnel protruding from his belly, just below his navel. Blood had already coagulated around it, dark red and thick. Marthe nodded to Sister Margarete, who placed a thin gauze mask slightly above the soldier's face and added a few drops of chloroform.

"*Veux-tu-compter?*" Marthe said. "Will you count?"

"*Oui. Un ... deux ... trois ... quatre ...*" The soldier's voice trailed off and Sister Margarete removed that mask and replaced it with a slightly thicker one. Into this gauze she dropped ether. They waited three minutes.

"Okay," Sister Margarete said. "We're ready."

After bathing the area around the shrapnel with an iodine solution, Marthe picked up a small scalpel.

And took a deep breath.

"You are fine, my daughter," Sister Margarete told her. "He is safe in your hands."

Marthe scraped the dried blood around the shrapnel, then tugged gently to see if she could simply pull it out. It refused to budge. She made a small incision at the base of it, enough to see that the end of it curled around the large intestine. With minute cuts, she removed the tissue around it until the shrapnel moved in her fingers. Gently, she twisted it down until the curved end released. She poured more of her iodine solution into the wound and found no bubbles coming from the intestine.

"We got lucky," she said. "The intestine wasn't punctured." But the fat and muscle around it had shredded and barely covered the stomach. She cleaned and disinfected the entire area, careful to stitch any tears that seeped blood, then sewed the wounds shut. Other deep cuts appeared on the soldier's chest and arms along with a gash in his thigh.

"What on earth caused this kind of cut?" Marthe asked.

"Something called barbed wire," Sister Margarete answered.

"I never heard of it." Marthe frowned.

"Apparently the German Army uses it extensively as a final barricade in front of their trenches. I saw it once, still attached to one of the wounded. It looks like ordinary wire but every couple of inches or so, another piece of wire, with sharp points on it, is twisted around the original strand. It catches on clothes and skin and doesn't let go."

"How horrible."

"I agree. I understand the battle that brought all of these soldiers to us happened in the dark last night. This poor fellow probably didn't even know the wire was there and got so caught up in it he couldn't escape when his Army retreated. He also has multiple cuts on his head."

"Keep an eye on him, sister. This surgery will take longer than I originally thought. He may need more ether."

Methodically, Marthe cleaned and inspected each wound, made the necessary repair, then stitched it up. Sister Margarete bandaged the wounds as Marthe finished stitching and they moved on to the next area. While they worked, one of the other nuns cleaned the man's head and then shaved his hair to expose the wounds there.

By the time the surgery ended, the doctor had arrived and he handled the rest of the necessary surgeries for the morning. Marthe assisted him and then accompanied him on his rounds.

"Good work on the Frenchman," the *Oberarzt* told her. "Your stitches are excellent." He looked into her eyes. "When this foolishness is over, you should think about going to medical school. I could help you."

"*Danke*, Herr *Oberarzt*," she said. "But I can't think about that right now."

Marthe worked through the remainder of the day and the last patient she saw was another French soldier. She inspected his wounds, inquired about his comfort level, and stood to leave when he called her back.

"*Mademoiselle*," he said.

"*Oui?*"

"*Comment est* Hugh?"

"Hugh?"

"He is the one you took to surgery first. With the shrapnel in his stomach."

"Oh," she said. "Are you two friends?"

"*Oui*," he answered. "He had a very tough time of it … sent on reconnaissance two nights ago but never returned. We thought he had been captured until we heard screams that first night. His cry sounded as if he were in excruciating pain … as if he were in his death agony. The sound stopped after several minutes and we thought it was over. But it started up again an hour later. And continued through the night." The soldier closed his eyes and shuddered. "The next morning, the sarge sent me to find out what happened to him and I found him, hanging from the wire in front of the German's trench, his whole body and even his head caught in millions of barbs." Tears oozed down his cheeks. "The soldier with me rushed over to try and get him down and the Germans shot him on the spot. They left Hugh hanging there as a decoy."

"How *did* you get him down, then?"

"Our *capitaine* ordered a party of us to rescue him. More than half were shot and the rest of us captured. Will he be all right, nurse? What he endured should never be experienced by anyone. Please tell me he will be okay."

"I'm so sorry, soldier, but it's too soon to tell. We did all we could. Now we simply have to wait and see. Maybe tomorrow you can visit him."

"*Merci.* I would like that."

Marthe checked a few more soldiers on her way out and sometime before six o'clock returned to the Taverne for a quick bite and to see to her wounded men in the attic.

Herr Breit greeted her when she entered the kitchen. A tall blond woman stood with him.

"Marthe," he said, taking one of her hands. "I want you to meet Lovisa, from Brussels."

Marthe shook hands with Lovisa and felt the woman's strength radiate up her entire arm.

"Herr Breit told me of the fine work you have done here, Marthe," Lovisa said. "He also told me he thinks you would be perfect for the kind of work I do as well."

"And that is?" Marthe said. Warning bells sounded in her head and the hand that held Lovisa's began to shake.

"I am serving my country. If you will listen, I will tell you how."

# CHAPTER
# NINE

I took a break from reading, surprised to learn my grandfather had the opportunity to practice with a professional baseball team.

Steve called to check on me and I told him the truth—that I had found my grandmother's diary and couldn't resist reading it. And that I was a little embarrassed to get so distracted. But when he laughed and told me that as a retired grown-up, I could make my own decisions, I laughed too. And then went back to Maude's diary.

*August 3, 1915*

*Dear Diary,*

*Tomorrow's the big day! Coach Mack will send a car to Prospect Park so Mom and Dad and I can go to Philadelphia to watch an Athletics' game. We heard from Henry that he and Buzz were called up from the minor league bench and might play in tomorrow's game against the Detroit Tigers. Coach Mack, he said, is disgusted with his regular pitchers, so he might pitch Buzz. And if he does, Henry will catch.*

*I'm so excited! It will be nice to see the boys again, sure, but mostly, it will be my first ride in a car! And my first time in the city. Mom spent the day making sandwiches and cookies to take with us and enough extra cookies to leave with the boys. Henry says they get good meals in their boarding house, but I'm sure he'll be excited to get Mom's cookies. She made all his favorites.*

*Okay, I'm going to try and sleep now so I can stay awake during our trip tomorrow. I don't want to miss a thing. Good night.*

*Your friend, Maude*

—◦◦◦—

## August 4, 1915

MAUDE AND HER PARENTS TOOK THE WAGON INTO TOWN SO they could meet the car Coach Mack sent to pick them up.

"Okay, ladies," Frank said. "We're on our way to watch our boys playing in their first American League baseball game."

"Do you really think it's a good idea to leave the farm, Frank?" Florence asked him. "We're behind with the crops, you know."

"I know, Mother. But Mr. Mack gave us the tickets to the game for free, so we won't have to spend money for them. Besides," he said, putting his arm around her shoulders, "when the boys left town, I started tucking away a few coins from the produce money so we could splurge like this. Don't you worry about it, Flo. We'll be just fine."

They parked their wagon at the livery depot when Frank heard Florence's intake of breath. "Oh no, Frank. Do you see that?" She pointed to the door of the military recruiting office down the street from the livery. The sign on its door read, "See Europe with the Army."

"Has that always been there or is it new for this horrid war overseas?"

"Always been there, Flo," Frank said. He patted her arm. "You don't need to worry today."

Maude stopped short. "Dad, look." She pointed to a shiny car with a small man in a dark uniform standing in front of it. He held a sign with the words "Brewer Family" printed on it.

Frank approached him and said, "We're the Brewer family. Is this Mr. Mack's car?"

"Yes sir," the man answered. "He sent me to pick you up and escort you to the ballpark."

"Thank you. We're delighted," Frank said. He turned to Florence and whispered, "We're being treated like royalty."

They followed the man to a sage green open-air Cadillac Touring Car.

"Oh boy," Maude said. "You can tell that Mr. Mack doesn't live on a dirt road. I've never seen anything so clean." She ran her hand along the smooth exterior all the way to the back door.

"Allow me, miss," the man said as he held the door open for her.

"Oh, Frank," Florence whispered, "I don't think I'm dressed well enough to ride here. I'm just a simple country woman." But the look on her face belied her words. Maude couldn't remember ever seeing her mother's smile so wide.

"Today, Mrs. Brewer," Frank told her, "you are the mother of two professional baseball players and deserve to be treated like a queen." He squeezed her arm. "Relax and enjoy it."

In the back seat, Maude ran her hands over the tufted upholstery of the interior and settled back, wishing the ride would last forever so she could remain nestled in all that luxury. It was as far removed from their farm wagon as was possible and she could hardly wait to tell the girls. And to write about it in her diary.

A flurry of activity exploded in the ballpark and the energy it generated electrified the air. The trio walking in the middle of all that excitement stared in amazement. One of Mr. Mack's representatives met them at the entrance gate and escorted them to his private box while Maude's head spun at all the new sights and sounds. They climbed several levels of stairs and wound through countless corridors until their escort stopped in front of an ornate door and knocked. Mr. Mack himself opened the door to welcome them.

"The Brewers! Welcome. Come on in and get settled." He shook hands with Frank and waved Florence and Maude over to the comfortable chairs near the large window. "I know this is kind of removed from the field," he said. "So if you'd like to get closer, I'll go down with you. You can sit right behind the dugout if you'd rather."

"That is right nice of you, Mr. Mack," Frank said. "I think we'll start out here and if Buzz or Henry gets to play, maybe we can move down then." He shook Mr. Mack's hand one more time. "This is all so generous of you. We can't thank you enough."

The Brewer family settled in, Frank with a beer in his hand and Maude with a rare Coca-Cola. Spending the money to have soft drinks in the house didn't sit well with Florence, nor did she know what long-term effects the drink might have on Maude's insides. But this was a special occasion, so Maude caressed the green glass bottle and tipped it to her lips, savoring the icy coldness all the way down her throat.

"Hot dog, miss?" Maude jumped. The white-coated waiter held out a plate with the biggest, juiciest hot dog Maude's eyes had ever beheld. "We have all the condiments here at the table," the waiter said. "Ketchup, mustard, relish. We even have onions and sauerkraut if you prefer that."

Maude cocked her head in her mother's direction. At her nod, Maude said, "Sure. Thanks."

The family filled their plates from the smorgasbord prepared for them. Maude's hot dog sported so many different items, the bun refused to close. Then she filled the remainder of her plate with chips and cookies. "They're not as good as yours, Mom," she whispered. But she ate them all.

Maude's parents followed her lead and before long, they all settled at the large open-air window balancing full plates on their laps. The announcer's voice crackled over the loudspeaker to announce the teams' line-ups. They strained their ears, but neither Henry's nor Buzz's name crossed the announcer's lips.

The Tigers batted first. Athletics' pitcher Weldon Wyckoff stared the batter down, shaking his head time after time at the catcher's suggestions for pitches. Finally, with a nod, he wound up and threw the ball right across the plate. The batter, Ossie Vitt, Maude saw from the program, never moved the bat from his shoulder. The second pitch split the plate, too, and this time Vitt knocked it to the infield where third baseman Wally Schang secured the out.

Maude's attention wandered during the next batter who popped up for an easy out, but when Ty Cobb stood over the plate, she returned to her seat. Cobb's batting average was the highest on the Tigers' team, so even she could tell that Wyckoff threw him a couple of trash pitches. But he finally got hold of one and sent it right over the head of Amos Strunk, the center fielder. It dropped in front of the fence, but Cobb rounded first on his way to second before Strunk fielded the ball and threw it to the shortstop, Whitey Witt. To the delight of the Athletics' fans, Witt ran to second and tagged Cobb out. The Tigers took the field.

The Athletics' batters didn't fare any better that inning. A pop-up to first by third baseman Schang for the first out, base on balls for center fielder Strunk followed by a bunt from left fielder Rube Oldring, who beat out the Tigers' first baseman and stood safely on the bag. The Brewer family, like the rest of the Athletics' half of the stadium, cheered like crazy with two men on. But the next two batters popped up to the pitcher and ended the inning.

With no hits on either side for the next few innings, Maude grew bored and engaged in people-watching in the stands below. A small boy stood next to a man Maude presumed to be his father. The little guy hopped up and down almost the entire time. While she watched, the man showed the child how to crack peanuts, then occasionally put the boy on his lap and pointed to various parts of the field. The little boy's head nodded vigorously at each sight. But his little face exploded in smiles when the man bought him a box of Cracker Jack and pulled out the prize.

"Buy me some peanuts and Cracker Jack," Maude sang softly to herself.

*He's so cute. I'll bet this is also his first game. Just like me.*

She wandered to the food table and found boxes of Cracker Jack, then handed them out.

With so little happening on the field, the game dragged on for

Maude until the sixth inning when the Tigers were at bat. Again, Wyckoff threw a couple of trash pitches to Ty Cobb.

Frank laughed. "You can tell the pitcher's scared of Cobb's bat," he said. "Course I don't blame him. But with Crawford batting right behind him, giving Cobb a base on balls might backfire on Wyckoff. Even with two outs and nobody on," Frank added.

Florence pretended to be interested, although Maude knew baseball held very little appeal for her. Unless her son was on the field, of course. But Maude perked up and paid attention. Just as Frank predicted, Cobb sauntered to first base when the umpire called the fourth ball and right fielder Sam Crawford strode to the plate. His practice swings whipped his arms all the way around his body and Maude thought he might corkscrew himself into the earth. Again, Wyckoff shook his head forcefully at the catcher's suggestions then finally wound up and let one fly.

Right over home plate.

Crawford swung with his whole being and the crack of the bat reached the box where Maude sat. The ball flew over the center fielder's head and before it even hit the back fence, Cobb rounded third on his way home and crossed the plate just before the catcher's mitt connected with the ball. When the umpire's arms flew out to his sides to signal "safe," the Tigers' fans erupted. Roars filled half the stadium while boos echoed in the other half.

"I knew it," Frank shouted. "See Maudie? Didn't I tell you that would happen? I just hope we can hold 'em to one run. Maybe we can make that up."

The next batter grounded out to the shortstop, leaving Crawford on third and the inning at an end.

The A's came up to bat with the weak end of their line-up. One-two-three, the batters came up and sat back down. A knock sounded on the door and one of the Athletics' assistant coaches stuck his head in. "Mr. Brewer," he said in an urgent tone. "Coach Mack sent me to get you. Your boy will be pitching in the next inning. Will you accompany me to the field?"

The whole family jumped up and followed the man back through the maze of corridors to a small door. He opened it, pushed the metal grillwork to one side, then entered the small space. "This is Mr. Mack's private elevator."

Frank strode into the car as if he'd been doing it all his life and Maude followed him, although her stomach tickled and gurgled. They both looked out the elevator door and saw the terror on Florence's face.

"Frank," she said. "I don't think I can do this. I mean, how do we know it's safe?"

"Come on, Mother," Frank said. He walked back to where Florence stood trembling. "It will be fine. I promise." He took her hand and gently guided her into the car.

At the first movement, Florence let out a little scream, but calmed when Frank circled her waist with his arm. Blessedly short, the grinding of gears and hesitant shudders vanished when the doors slid open. They exited directly at field level and hurried to seats reserved for them right above the Athletics' dugout.

Henry stood outside the dugout and waved to his family while Buzz walked to the pitcher's mound, one of the assistant coaches at his side. Buzz threw several warm-up pitches to catcher Ray Haley who then joined Buzz and the coach on the mound. They formed a cluster, their heads nearly touching, and Buzz nodded several times. After a few more minutes, Haley returned to home plate and assumed his position. The first Tigers' batter, left fielder Bobby Veach, approached the plate.

Maude almost laughed out loud. Even from that distance, she could tell that Buzz's eyes took on the same steely focus she had seen time and again when he practiced in her front yard. His right side toward the batter, Buzz raised his arms in the air and closed his eyes. Maude held her breath. Then Buzz swiveled and let the ball fly.

"Stee-rike!" the umpire yelled, his right arm snapping out to make it official.

Maude and Frank stood and cheered, along with more than half the stadium. Maude glanced at her mother to see tears streaming down her face. "Oh no," she said, covering her mother's hand with her own.

"Mom, what's wrong?" Frank whipped his head toward his wife at his daughter's words.

"I can't stop thinking," she said, "how sad it is that Buzz's parents weren't interested enough in their son's skills to see this wonderful event." Frank put his arm around his wife and kissed her cheek.

"You're right, Mother," he said. "But thank goodness he has us."

Buzz retired the next two batters in short order and the inning was over. He trotted to the dugout as the whole team turned out to slap him on the back. Coach Mack caught Frank's eye and nodded.

The A's couldn't get it together to score a run, but in the eighth inning, Buzz didn't allow the Tigers to score another one either. The crowd roared as the top of the A's line-up led the batting at the bottom of the eighth, but the first two batters popped up to the infield. The third batter, left fielder Oldring, finally got a hit with clean-up batter, Schang, third baseman, coming up next. Deafening cheers echoed throughout the stadium as he positioned himself over home plate and took a couple of practice swings. His bat caught one pitch and foul tipped it but the crowd noise thundered. He sent the next pitch down the third base line and made it safely to first while Oldring advanced to second. Nap Lajoie, the A's second baseman, stepped up to the plate.

Maude thought she could hear the collective breath-holding throughout the stands.

Lajoie hit the first pitch hard out to left field and Bobby Veach caught it for the out. A groan escaped the throats of thousands of Athletics' fans as once again, the inning ended with no runs scored. The Tigers still led, one to nothing.

Buzz returned to the pitcher's mound at the top of the last inning.

"Florence." Frank took her arm and shook it. "Look! It's Henry." Sure enough, Maude saw her brother, in full catcher's regalia, saunter to the pitcher's mound to say a few words to Buzz.

"Oh, what I wouldn't give to hear what they're saying," Frank said. His grin stretched across his whole face. Henry left the mound and trotted back to home plate and Maude was certain he caught his mother's eye with a triumphant grin. Again, tears streamed down Florence's face.

Buzz faced the top of the Tigers' line-up with Bush, Cobb, and Crawford in the mix. Even Maude felt her heart beat faster. But Buzz remained true to his routine and retired first Bush and then Cobb. Clean-up batter Crawford left the deck and loomed over the plate. Henry gave a couple of signals, but Buzz shook his head until Henry pointed down and wiggled his finger. Buzz nodded and turned so his right side faced the batter while he prepared to deliver his knuckleball. He swiveled and let it fly but it fell flat and the umpire called it a ball.

Henry went back to the pitcher's mound and got right in Buzz's face. The boys talked for a few seconds, then Henry returned to home and squatted behind the plate, his mitt positioned squarely over it. Buzz wound up and went through his routine, but this time when he let the ball go, it dropped in perfectly. With his third pitch, his fastball flew over the plate and Crawford connected with it, sending a grounder hurtling toward the pitcher's mound. Buzz scooped it up and lobbed it to first for the final out.

The bottom of the ninth presented one last opportunity for the A's to score.

Frank and Maude, along with thousands of fans in the stadium, cheered as Henry, the first batter, hit a drive to right field that flew just inside the base line and he landed safely on first.

"That's my boy," Frank hollered to all those around him. "Once he gets on base, he almost always scores. Way to go, Henry!"

Next up was Whitey Witt, the shortstop, who popped up to center. Then Buzz swung his bat at the plate and laid down a sacrifice bunt to advance Henry to second. With the top of the A's lineup coming up to bat.

Maude felt the collective sense of hope that radiated from the screaming fans, that even with two outs, third baseman Schang would get a hit to move Henry around the bases and tie up the game. He hit the ball long to center field and Cobb watched it coming, backing up the whole time. He put his glove in the air, jumped ... and caught the ball just before it went over the fence. To end the inning. And the game.

The Brewer family shared the disappointment of the Athletics' fans, of course, but they crowded the end of the dugout and Florence and Frank hugged both boys so hard Maude thought they would suffocate them.

"Nice work, boys," Mr. Mack said to them, one hand on each of the boys' shoulders. "Get cleaned up and I'll treat you and your family to dinner."

Maude's heart swelled with happiness.

The boys had done exactly what they always wanted to do.

They made it.

To the big time.

# CHAPTER TEN

MARTHE
Field Hospital
August 1915

"What exactly do you mean by 'serving your country?'" Marthe asked. "What country *is* your country, anyway?"

"Same as yours, Marthe," Lovisa answered. "I seek knowledge and pass it on."

"You're talking about spying," Marthe said softly. "Why don't you say it straight out?"

"Yes. That's what I'm talking about. Spying."

"Germany shoots spies." Her voice caught and all the pain of her family being killed in front of her eyes filled her brain and squeezed her heart. "And snipers," she added. Her words emerged as a whisper.

Herr Breit put his hand on her arm. "Marthe, you would be a great asset if you joined us. You don't have to, of course, but you're in a perfect position for it. Not only could you learn things at the hospital from German soldiers, but you could also obtain information from right here. One of your soldiers in the attic, Roland, is a member of our group."

"Of course," Marthe said. "I should have known, the way he questioned me."

"But even better than that," Herr Breit continued, "is what you could do here, with German officers. I watched you last night when you helped out from the kitchen. You have a very natural way about you and I believe officers would open up to you."

"Are you saying you want me to prostitute myself?" Her voice held an indignant edge.

"No, no, of course not."

"But you could be nice to them, Marthe," Lovisa added. "You could listen. Men's tongues tend to get loose when they've consumed enough *bier*."

Marthe hung her head. "Look, I guess I should thank you for asking me. But I lost my whole family. They were accused of something they didn't do. And shot on the spot. The Germans only allowed me to live for my nursing skills. Why would I knowingly put myself in that kind of danger again?"

Lovisa stiffened and stood straight. "For your country," she said. "For your family. So their deaths wouldn't be in vain. Do you really want the people who stole your loved ones from you to be in charge of your country? Forever?"

Again, Marthe's chin reached her chest. "I don't … I don't know."

Herr Breit increased the pressure on her arm. Reassuringly. "You don't have to decide now, Marthe. Just promise us you will think about it."

She stood motionless, then finally nodded. "I will think about it," she whispered. "But right now, I must see to my men."

She left them standing there and fixed the tray for the wounded soldiers in the attic. She resolved to steer clear of Roland until she had time to think.

At the top of the stairs, however, Roland waited for her, his one good eye huge with concern. "Nurse Marthe," he said. "Hurry. Emery is having a seizure."

Marthe handed him the tray and rushed to Emery's side. His body shook and his eyes appeared vacant, unfocused. Saliva slid from his lips. "How long has he been this way?"

"Off and on all day," Roland said. "But this last one is by far the worst."

Marthe touched his forehead. "He's burning up," she said. "Has he vomited today?"

"Yes," Roland answered. "A little this morning, but a lot more this afternoon. I got rid of it so it wouldn't make the rest of the men sick."

"I was so afraid of this," Marthe said. "But I really thought he had gotten past it." She placed her fingers against his carotid artery and counted, difficult to track because of his spasms.

"What do you mean?" Roland asked.

"The gas in his lungs," Marthe said, "actually made them shrink and killed red blood cells. Which means less oxygen is available to travel to the rest of his body." She moved her fingers again until she felt a solid pulse but it registered weak and erratic. "I will see if Herr Breit has any oxygen. Roland, will you hand the food out to the rest of the men?"

She flew down the stairs and found Herr Breit in the kitchen.

"Sorry, Marthe. I haven't had oxygen for weeks."

She returned to the attic.

"Roland," she said, "I'm going to run to ..." The expression on Roland's face cut off her words. "What is it?"

"I think he's gone."

Marthe ran to the cot and knelt beside Emery. The shaking had stopped. She placed her fingers on his neck again and felt in several spots. But she found nothing. No pulse. She leaned her head against his chest to listen to his heart. No sound. "No!" she said. She beat his chest with one of her fists, then leaned his head back, held his nose and blew into his mouth. Three long breaths. She massaged his chest in hopes of starting his heart again, then beat it with her fist once more. Roland watched as she repeated the process five more times. When she put her head against his chest to listen after the last time, Roland touched her shoulder.

"He's gone, Marthe."

"No," she said again, her tears wetting the front of Emery's shirt. "Please ... please ..."

She sat back on her heels and let her head fall to her hands. Her sobs shook her body and robbed her of breath. She had lost patients before, but she thought of Emery as a tie to her brother ... the last bit of connection to her family. And now she had lost him too. How much more could she stand?

Roland stood by and waited until she had calmed, then put his hand on her shoulder again.

"I'm so sorry," he said.

Marthe became aware that the other soldiers in the attic hovered close and those who could walk also patted her on the shoulder. They offered her condolences as if Emery had been a true family member.

"We will miss him too," Roland told her. "What can I do to help?"

She pulled herself up from the floor and stood ... her body still shaking.

"I will go to the hospital and find someone to remove him," she said. "He told me he had no family, so other than his commanding officer, I guess there's no one to tell." The thought brought more tears. "No one to miss him." She wiped her eyes, then looked up at Roland.

"Except us," he said.

For the next hour, Marthe busied herself with taking care of the dead the same way she had busied herself taking care of the living. Emery's body was removed from the attic and Marthe stripped the sheets from his cot and put them with the trash to be burned. She removed the empty dinner tray and made the rounds with the remaining soldiers, all of whom treated her with extra tenderness. She would later worry that some of the men may have been in worse pain than they were willing to let on so she wouldn't have to spend time taking care of them. But, she reasoned, she would give them more time when she returned.

The grandfather clock in the Taverne's entrance lobby chimed the first peal of midnight when she pushed through the door to the kitchen for a cold cup of soup. Over and over she forced her spoon to her lips and then made herself swallow. She couldn't even taste what she ate and almost gagged a time or two. But she knew she had to have some sort of sustenance or she would be too weak to carry out her duties for the rest of the wounded who depended on her. When she finished the last spoonful, she sat, staring into space.

"Marthe?" Herr Breit approached her quietly.

She raised her head.

He sat and took one of her hands. "My dear, I am so sorry about your soldier."

She nodded, then took a deep breath.

"Herr Breit?" She straightened in her chair and looked him in the eye. In a soft, but firm voice, she said, "I will do it, Herr Breit. Whatever you need from me. Lovisa was right. We can no longer allow the Germans to take control of our lives. We must defeat them."

He closed his eyes and breathed a long sigh. "I am so glad you made that decision. You will be a wonderful addition to our family."

"Family," she said and shook her head. "That's why I decided to agree. I considered Emery the last tie to my family. And now I have nothing left. What does it matter what happens to me?" She lifted her head. "So yes. I am ready."

# CHAPTER ELEVEN

SUZANNE
2015

I was shocked.

Nobody ever told me my grandfather actually became a professional baseball player. In fact, I had never learned much about him at all. From the few things Dad did tell me, I knew my grandfather left the family when my dad's youngest brother, Freddie, was born. Of course, Dad made it sound like he and his older brother, Walter, chased him away … told him to leave and never come back when he showed up on the porch drunk the night of Freddie's birth.

So finding out he had been responsible enough to hold a professional job surprised me. And my grandmother appeared to have been so much younger, I had trouble figuring out how they could have gotten together.

Eager to answer my own questions, I picked up the diary again and, after a few short entries about spending time with her friends, Helen and Ethel, my grandmother picked back up with a longer entry in early September 1915.

*September 6, 1915*

*Dear Diary,*

*It's me, Maude. But of course it is … who else would it be?*

*I know you haven't heard from me in a while, but it's been a busy*

*summer. I helped Mom in the vegetable garden a lot—too much if you ask*
*me. I really don't mind the planting—that's kind of fun to set out the*
*tiny little green shoots in nice, neat rows. But then, they have to be weed-*
*ed!! I hate doing that. Especially the peas with their vines spilling all*
*over between the rows. The vines have to be moved first and then the*
*weeds pulled. And Mom wouldn't let me use the hoe because she worried*
*I'd dig up the little plants. But sometimes I did anyway when she went in*
*to start supper.*

I burst out laughing. In my youth, Mom and Dad had a large
garden behind the house. Behind this house, actually. I gazed out the
window and saw the patch of grass Dad had dug up that Mom used
for raising corn and peas, and a bunch of other healthy vegetables she
tried to grow. Looking back, I find it really sad that kids, myself
included when I was one, don't appreciate growing their own food
when they're in the middle of it. I remembered feeling exactly the
same way my grandmother felt about weeding and I wondered if Dad
had felt that, too, when he had to help in my grandmother's garden? If
so, he never told me. Anyway, that passage struck me as funny.

I turned back to the page in front of me.

*But what's even worse is that then we have to pick the darn things—I'm*
*talking like every day for goodness' sake—and THEN we have to shell*
*them and can them. Oh my goodness, what a process! The only thing I*
*like about it is having Mom's tender little peas in the winter. That part's*
*great, but while I'm in the middle of it, I sure don't like it.*

*And she plants rows and rows of everything! And I have to go through*
*the same thing with every vegetable. It takes for darn ever and doesn't*
*leave a lot of time free.*

*Plus, I got in a fight with Helen because she wouldn't quit talking about*
*Buzz and how good looking he is. She made it sound almost dirty. But*
*Ethel and I are still friends. I'll see Helen tomorrow at school. We're in*
*fifth grade now, so that's good.*

*I guess you're wondering how the boys are doing in Philadelphia. They came home this past weekend and will come back once the season is over and be here until they leave for Florida and Spring Training. Even though Buzz pitched for a few games, their team's still not very good so they wound up at the bottom of the American League. Coach Mack gave them tickets to a couple of the World Series games since the Phillies are in it and some games will be in Philadelphia. I think Henry even got a ticket for Dad. He'll like that although I can't imagine what's different from the game we saw there. But he seems excited.*

*It was good to have the boys here. Dad made a new picnic table and we used it today for our Labor Day lunch. Mom made them store their baseball stuff cause she almost tripped over some of it and Henry said they put it in the old trunk that's been in the barn forever. They both helped Mom make ice cream and it tasted delicious.*

*Then we all went in town for the fireworks. We saw my teacher, Miss Delsie, and she and Dad talked about the war overseas. Mom and I get fed up with hearing about it, but fortunately somebody else called to Miss Delsie and she left us.*

*The fireworks were fabulous!*

*I love fireworks. And ice cream. So it was a really good day.*

*Well, I'm going to go try on my new clothes now and decide what I'll wear tomorrow. I'll let you know how my first day goes.*

*Your friend, Maude*

## September 6, 1915

"Here, Buzz," Henry's mother said, "have another piece of fried chicken. I imagine you boys get sick of hot dogs, huh?"

The family sat at the picnic table Frank had just made that week in honor of the boys coming home from Philadelphia.

"We can't really afford hot dogs, Mom," Henry said. "Except when we can get them for free at the ballpark. Mrs. Bailey at the boarding house cooks every night, of course, but that's included in what we pay her so it's not often anything special. Plus, we very seldom get home from practice in time to eat when it's hot. So the dinner we get is normally mushy leftovers. I don't mean to complain, though."

"Don't listen to him," Buzz said. "Mrs. Bailey's meals are just fine. And he *is* complaining, not because of the food so much as that we work long hours and still don't get to play very often. I understand, though. I wish we could play more, too, but Coach Mack says we have to earn our spots on the team with hard work and sweat." He shoved the last bit of chicken into his mouth and reached for a new piece from the platter Henry's mother offered. "Hey, I'm just happy to be there." He looked at Henry and grinned. "And except for the few months I lived here," he added, "the food's way better than anything I ever got at ... well, you know ... where I lived before."

Buzz's parents and what happened to them was seldom mentioned. He seemed to have made a marvelous adjustment to his new life, so they all figured the less said about it the better.

Henry grinned at him and turned to Maude. "So, Bug, you all ready for school tomorrow? Fifth grade, huh? You're getting up there. Coming into the hard arithmetic. It's just as well I'm not here to help you. Buzz always got good grades in math, though."

"That's right," Buzz said. "Probably my favorite subject. Never liked reading much. And hated writing."

"Maude's a great writer," Frank, said. "And speller too. And my goodness, Maudie, how many books did you read this summer, twenty-some?"

Maude nodded and spooned more baked beans onto her plate.

"School will be fine. I'll be able to handle the arithmetic. I'm pretty good at it myself."

"Well, I know you boys will have a couple of months off before Spring Training starts. Do you have plans? Or jobs, maybe?" Frank asked them.

"I'm going to talk to Mr. Muir at the feed mill," Buzz said, "and see if I can get my old job back for a couple of months. Or something, even if it's not the same thing I used to do."

"Yeah," Henry added. "I thought about getting in touch with either Mr. Harrington at the department store or Mr. Carruthers at the funeral home. You got any ideas, Pop?"

"I wondered if your coach could use help with the new team at school."

"Great idea," Henry said. "I'll contact him too."

"So boys," Florence said, "I hope you'll have a chance to put away all your equipment before we go into town. I almost tripped over one of your bats on the front porch this morning."

"Sure, Mom," Henry said. "Sorry about that. We'll take care of it as soon as we finish eating. But I sure would like to have some of your ice cream first."

"That seems fair," Florence said. "Especially since you boys both helped with turning the crank on the ice cream maker."

When they finished eating, Maude helped Florence clear the picnic table and carry the leftovers to the kitchen. Henry and Buzz gathered their equipment—bats, balls, mitts, and Henry's chest protector and knee pads—and carried it all to the barn.

"Do you have a spot in mind for these, Henry?"

"Why don't we put them in here?" Henry asked. He opened the top of a large wooden steamer trunk bound with metal strips around its side and bottom. Cobwebs coated it and spiders skittered away. "I'd forgotten about this. But it's the perfect place. We won't have to worry about the humidity getting to it."

Buzz studied the trunk and ran his hands over its wooden handles and metal hinges. "Where'd this come from? It looks pretty old but it's in great shape. Wait a minute, what's this?"

He pulled a tattered envelope from a pocket on the side, down close to the bottom. Its corners appeared to have been carved off in rounded patterns and tiny silverfish fell off as Buzz shook it. "Looks like these guys had a feast," he said, flinging the last insect to the floor. The front of the envelope still bore the name "Samuel Brewer" in faded old-fashioned script. Buzz handed the envelope to Henry. "Who was Samuel Brewer?"

"I'm not sure. Some relative of Dad's, I guess." He opened the envelope and took out a folded sheet sporting holes in its middle. "Looks like a letter. Oh my gosh, look at this, Buzz. The date is from fifty years ago—1865. Early June. Right after the Civil War." He read the note out loud.

*My dear cousin,*

*I still cringe at the thought of how easily you could have killed me when we came face to face in our last battle at Palmito Ranch in Texas, especially since I had just sent a bayonet through the stomach of your friend, John Williams. I find it ironic that the officers leading us in that charge already knew the war had ended but still engaged in that battle. What a senseless waste. If you hadn't suggested we escape into the woods, we could have been among the hundreds of dead littering that ground.*

*My mother, Lorena, sister to your father, Nathaniel, thanks you also. She asked me to have you give her best to the rest of your family there and extend the invitation for you to come and see us in Virginia when you can as we will look in on you if we ever make it to Pennsylvania.*

*I hope this letter finds you and your family in peace.*

*Sincerely,*

*Your cousin, Michael Brewer*

"Wow," Henry said. "I always knew this trunk was here but never even opened it before."

"I wonder what happened to all the stuff that must have been in it?" Buzz asked.

"Who knows?" Henry said as he stashed their gear. "Let's go ask Dad."

# CHAPTER TWELVE

MARTHE
Field Hospital
October 1915

M arthe continued to grieve for Emery despite having taken Herr Breit up on his "offer." Often, the excitement-laced fear for her new assignment was the only thing that gave her the ability to put one foot in front of the other, day after day.

For the first week after making her decision she received no instructions and began to wonder if she had imagined the whole thing out of grief for Emery. But she left the Taverne one especially chilly morning around dawn and was hailed by a man sweeping the street.

"Good morning, *Fräulein.*" He tipped his hat, its brim ragged and moth-eaten. "A fine morning, is it not?"

She nodded and kept walking but he approached her and matched her pace.

"*Fräulein,*" he said again. "I wish to give you this." He held out a small box, slightly open to reveal wooden matchsticks. "I understand some of your wounded soldiers would like a smoke but have no matches. Please accept this as my contribution to making the men more comfortable."

Marthe frowned at him but before she could speak, he thrust the matchbox in her hand and disappeared into the misty darkness of a side street, his broom with him. She stood as if fixed to the street and tried to figure out what had just happened. But she finally shrugged, stuffed the matchbox in her pocket, and continued on her way.

At the hospital, she entered the small kitchen and poured herself a cup of ersatz coffee, made primarily, she was told, from ground acorns. It lacked the full-bodied flavor she had grown to love from richly brewed beans but it tasted better than nothing on these chilly days. Sister Margarete had nodded to her as she entered the hospital, so she knew she had a couple of minutes before facing the day.

She eased into one of the mismatched chairs—the one with all four legs intact and stable—and took a long sip. No one stirred in the hallway, so she removed the matchbox from her pocket and looked at it in the light. The cover bore the regular colors and logo of the current popular brand with nothing special to distinguish it from any other box of matches.

*I guess I'm losing my mind and thinking everything I come in contact with now must be a signal for something I'm supposed to be doing.*

She picked up her cup with one hand and sipped. With her other hand she idly opened and closed the matchbox cover with her thumb and forefinger.

Open. Close.

Open. Close.

Open ... stuck.

She looked down. The cover wouldn't close. She plopped her cup on the table and pulled the cover out farther. A tiny piece of paper, intricately folded, fell from the cover onto the matches. Carefully, she removed it and looked around. She was alone.

She closed the matchbox cover and slid the paper into her pocket, then went to find Sister Margarete.

"Are things busy yet?" she asked.

"No, child. The men are quiet and we've had no new ambulances yet. There aren't even any surgeries scheduled this morning. Why? Do you need to go somewhere?"

Marthe smiled. "Only to the bathroom. I just wanted to make certain you were okay before I left you alone."

Sister Margarete smiled back. "Then go. You might as well take advantage of a lull while we have one."

Marthe entered the small bathroom and locked the door. Without undressing, she sat on the commode and carefully unfolded the paper from her pocket.

It read:

*Take the main road to Westrozebeke and come to the third farm on the left. Tap twice and ask for Lisette. She is expecting to see you at ten o'clock tonight.*

Marthe's heart beat wildly. The message in the matchbox had been for her.

*Or had it? Could it be from the Berlin Vampires?*

*Or is Lisette actually Lovisa?*

She hadn't done anything to make the Berlin Vampires suspect her, but then that mattered not at all. They suspected everyone.

She memorized the words and flushed the paper down the toilet, making certain it completely disappeared. It could be a trap. But she would find a way, she believed, to make certain the message was real. She just didn't know how.

A flushable toilet was still a novelty to her. While she had loved her home in Liege, her father had not gotten around to installing a toilet in their house before the Germans burned it. Neither did many of her neighbors have indoor bathrooms. Her mother had insisted on running water in the kitchen first with an indoor toilet to follow.

But it never happened.

The war happened instead.

As always, remembering her family and her home brought pain to her heart. Her hand sought out her locket, and the feel of it renewed her resolve for revenge on the Germans. But spying was not a job for the faint of heart.

She flushed one final time and left the bathroom to find Sister Margarete. Together, they performed the duties to keep the hospital running smoothly during the day and she accompanied the doctor on his rounds when he arrived. She treated her time as any other day rather than as the day she believed would change her life forever.

When her shift ended, she returned to the Taverne and prepared the evening's meal for her soldiers in the attic. Herr Breit hustled in and out a number of times.

"Full house tonight, *Fräulein*," he said during one of his brief visits to the kitchen.

She nodded. "Will your friend Lovisa be joining us this evening?" She said the words casually as if she couldn't have cared less. Just making conversation.

Herr Breit straightened and whipped his head toward her. His eyes burned bright. "No, *Fräulein*," he said softly. "I will not see her tonight. But who knows? Perhaps *you* will, yes?"

"I don't know. Perhaps." She continued to add items to her tray.

"I told the help here earlier that if anyone needed to leave the premises tonight, they should exit through the kitchen door rather than go through the dining room. With so many officers here tonight, the path might be crowded." He stared at her for another few seconds before nodding and returning to the dining room with a full pitcher of *bier*.

Marthe took his statement as her answer about the legitimacy of the message rather than a trap from the Berlin Vampires. Her heart contracted with nerves, then relaxed slightly. But it thumped against her chest with every step toward her wounded men in the attic. Her distraction at her looming assignment caused her to stumble on the top step, but Roland swiftly caught her elbow and steadied the tray.

"Will you allow me to help, Nurse Marthe? I know you must still be mourning Emery and may need to leave us earlier than you usually do."

She looked up at the intensity in his eyes and released her heavy tray to his hands.

"*Danke.* Yes, thank you."

The men in her care appeared to need less of her time but she diligently made her rounds, changing bandages, emptying chamber pots, and assessing overall health. Several of her men neared release and while she knew they should be back on the front, she hated to be the one to send them. Roland, especially, could easily move on. But when he did, it would be to a prisoner of war camp.

He appeared at her elbow. "The hour is late," he said. "I can get this tray back to Herr Breit." He hesitated. "In case you have anywhere you need to go."

Again, her heart beat wildly, its thump so insistent, she worried it might be seen actually moving the fabric of her dress. She glanced down to make certain, then almost laughed out loud at the ridiculousness of her thoughts.

"Thank you," she said once more to Roland. "I do think I will turn in early tonight."

Quietly, she descended the stairs and stole silently to the little alcove where she slept. She added thick stockings under her skirt, donned a sweater, and carried a cloak and her boots to the door. No one loitered in the hallway but she heard the German officers in the dining room, their voices already raised in their drunken revelry. She ducked into the hallway, then hugged the wall until she reached the dimly lit kitchen. Dinner had been cleared and the counters gleamed spotless. Close to the door sat a shot glass full of schnapps on a small piece of paper containing one word: *Marthe*. She drank it in one swallow and savored its burn all the way down her throat. Then she stepped into the chilly night air and walked the back alleys until she reached the road to Westrozebeke.

# CHAPTER THIRTEEN

MARTHE
Field Hospital
October 1915

The moon hid behind black clouds, a welcome camouflage for her journey.

Marthe left the main roads and stole through the dark woods, sticking to well-worn foot paths so she wouldn't get caught up in briars and underbrush. If she were stopped by German soldiers, her story was ready. She would tell them she was visiting a sick woman at one of the farmhouses in her capacity as a nurse and that she chose the forest path because she thought it would be a shortcut.

Though not yet winter, frost had set in and frozen the ground so the walking was easy. From time to time, soldiers with lanterns traveled the main road but she remained far enough away and kept to the shadows so she wouldn't be noticed. She walked well out of her way but eventually came out on the Westrozebeke road a short distance from her target farm. Each step that took her closer sent her heartbeat into double time and she breathed deeply to keep herself from turning around to run. Her mind screamed at her to rethink what she was about to do, but her feet carried her closer to her destination regardless.

She approached the back door of the farmhouse just as the moon broke through its thick cover. *Of course that would happen now.* She retreated back into the small grove at the edge of the yard and checked her watch. Ten o'clock exactly. When her heartbeat slowed and she ensured she had a clear route, she approached the back door to the farmhouse once again. She raised her hand and tapped twice.

*This is it, Marthe. This is your moment in time from which there is no return. Once this door opens you are committed.*

The door creaked open a crack and a muffled male voice said, "What do you want?"

She opened her mouth, but no words came. The door edged closed.

"Wait," she called softly. "I have come to see Lisette."

After a brief hesitation, grunts and shuffling of feet reached her ears. Then the door opened wide enough for her to squeeze through. She entered a dark hallway, damp and smelling of mold. A hand reached her wrist and half pulled, half shoved her up a stairwell then along a narrow passageway before rapping on a door and propelling her into a heavily curtained room with a warm fire. A woman stood before the dancing flames and Marthe experienced a momentary flashback of her house in flames the night her family died. She took a deep, gasping breath but calmed when the woman turned and she recognized Lovisa.

"Henri," Lovisa said. "Keep watch. Let me know immediately if you hear any threatening sound." Then she turned to Marthe. "I am so happy to see you." She took Marthe's hands. "You will be a great asset to our organization. And to your country."

Marthe's dry throat rendered her unable to speak. The enormity of what she had done settled in her brain and regrets filled her heart.

Still holding her hands, Lovisa said, "Marthe, from this day forward, by your own will, you have become a spy in service to your country to overthrow those who oppress your way of life and who took your family from you."

The words had an immediate impact on Marthe. She shuddered violently. Lovisa's speech brought back vivid memories of her parents and siblings killed before her eyes and of her own forced marches for months with the same soldiers who had caused their deaths. She had become complacent the last few months in her role at the hospital and Taverne. But with Lovisa's intense frown, she remembered her resolve for revenge. And this was her opportunity. She would avenge her family, help save her fellow countrymen, and who knew, maybe help to end this ridiculous war sooner. She pulled her shoulders back, stood straighter, and pushed any remaining misgivings from her heart forever.

"Are you with me?" Lovisa asked in a low voice.

"I am," Marthe answered, her voice strong. And firm. "What will you have me do?"

Lovisa squeezed Marthe's hands. "Good," she said. "Sit. We will go over everything."

For the next hour, Lovisa gave Marthe the information she needed to perform her duties.

"You will get instructions at any time," Lovisa said. "And you must carry them out to the letter. You are in a perfect position in the hospital, and at the Taverne, to get information from soldiers of any rank and to pass it along. Even if it seems trivial to you, do not judge, but simply report. Your code name is 'Sophia' and you will sign all your messages to British Intelligence by that name." Lovisa handed her a small slip of paper. "This is the code you will use to translate your messages. You must learn it by heart quickly and destroy this paper."

Marthe took the paper and tucked it into the top of her stockings. "Not there, Marthe," Lovisa said with a small smile. "That will be the first place the Berlin Vampires will look. Fold it over or roll it and tuck it into your hair." Lovisa showed her how to roll it and then tucked it into the braids on top of Marthe's head. "There. It will never be seen."

Marthe put a tentative hand to her head then nodded.

"You will receive instructions from the street sweeper who gave you the matches. When you have something to report, code it and take it at midnight to the *Rue de la Place* until you reach *Grand Place*. On the right there will be an alley which you will enter. Find the fifth window on the left-hand side and tap in this sequence—three taps, pause, then two more taps. The window will open by our agent there, Number Seventy-two. Place the message in the hand that appears and get out as quickly as possible. You must destroy every message you receive as soon as you have translated it and deliver it the same night you get it. Do not *ever* keep it with you at the Taverne or at the hospital overnight. Do you have any questions?"

"How will I know if the person giving me the paper is legitimate or is a Berlin Vampire?"

"Good question. Anyone who approaches you with a message, other than the street sweeper, will lift his or her lapel and show you two parallel white metal safety pins. We understand the Vampires have learned this trick, so make certain the safety pins rest at a forty-five-degree angle. If the pins are horizontal or vertical, act like you don't understand and go on your way. That is very important."

Marthe nodded, put her hand up to her hair again to make certain the tiny slip of paper still rested in her braids, and rose to go.

"This is not a game, Marthe," Lovisa said. "The Vampires know I am in the district so I will make myself scarce. And they are ever vigilant. You may have heard that they captured Edith Cavell, who helped hundreds of British soldiers trapped behind enemy lines escape the country. They arrested her in Brussels and executed her by firing squad this morning."

Lovisa touched the back of Marthe's hand again. "You must be careful. Take a different route back to Roulers and do not get caught. And a little general advice. You must keep your wits about you at all times—asleep or awake. Remember in everything you say and do that you must give the impression the last thing you would think of doing is spying. Do not worry about any spying activities that may happen around you. The less you know about the activity of others, the less the Vampires can wring out of you if you are caught. And if you do get caught, it will probably be your own fault." Lovisa's hand held firm to Marthe's. "We are all depending on you."

Marthe turned to the door, but Lovisa put a hand on her shoulder and turned her back around. "God bless you, child," she said and hugged Marthe fiercely. Tears stung Marthe's eyes. She had the distinct impression she would never see Lovisa again.

She hurried down the stairs and out the back door into the night.

Her entire journey back to the Taverne was her first exercise in caution. She covered extra kilometers to avoid any run-ins with

German soldiers or anyone who could possibly be a Berlin Vampire. At the kitchen door, she paused and listened for sounds but only the hoot of an owl on his nightly hunt reached her ears.

The clouds had disappeared and she stared at the moon, waxing full, while the crisp night air surrounded her. She took one last deep breath and blew a kiss to the heavens with a silent promise to her family. Peace settled within her and she fully embraced her new role.

# CHAPTER
# FOURTEEN

MARTHE
Field Hospital
December 1915

Decorations sparkled on every square inch of the Taverne's dining room and, Marthe decided, the scene appeared to be every bit as merry as past Christmases from years earlier. Before the Germans marched into Belgium.

She caught Herr Breit's eye when she entered the kitchen and an unspoken question formed within hers. He appeared to look sheepish.

"The Town-Kommandant ordered this," he told her, indicating the decorations. "He is entertaining his officers here tonight and wanted the place to look as festive as possible. I hope you will be able to join us. I have invited Sister Margarete and the *Oberarzt* from the hospital."

"Of course," Marthe said. "I will change as soon as I get off my shift and will be available to help if you need it."

"*Danke, Fräulein,*" he said.

Her wounded soldiers from the attic had all returned to their units or, as in the case of Roland, a German prisoner of war camp. With the attic empty, her evenings were a lot freer and she had even begun helping Herr Breit in the Taverne dining room during especially busy times.

The soldiers' removal from the attic also afforded her additional opportunities to discover information. In the months since she met Lovisa at the farmhouse, Marthe had been contacted twice and carried out her duties perfectly. But both times she heard about an ongoing need for information concerning the days of the week that ordnance trains, loaded with ammunition and headed for the front, would arrive at the Roulers depot. Escorting her wounded soldiers to the train station when they were sent to other locations provided her the perfect excuse to befriend the German military transport soldiers in the hope she could discover the information she needed. If she found out the days the train was expected, she could pass that on to Number Seventy-two. And then if all went according to plan, the depot would be bombed.

But so far she had learned nothing from the soldiers. So she set her sights on finding an official further up in the hierarchy. The night's party should be perfect for that.

⸻

MARTHE WALKED THE FEW BLOCKS TO THE HOSPITAL AND found it a flurry of activity. "Lots of wounded today, child," Sister Margarete told her. "The *Oberarzt* could use you in surgery."

She scrubbed and then assisted in an amputation, an arm this time. The men who lost limbs were the most pitiful of all those in the hospital, she thought. Of course, they were lucky to be alive, but she hated the thought of sending them home to wives or mothers with less than all their parts.

When the surgery ended, she accompanied the doctor on his rounds, then found Sister Margarete at the end of the day. "Will I see you at the Taverne tonight?" Marthe asked. The sister shook her head. "No, my child. But I understand the *Oberarzt* will be there. Try not to let him drink too much," she added with a smile. "We will need his wits about him tomorrow."

The afternoon had darkened with a cold front and snow threatened.

Marthe left the hospital and absently crossed a street, her head down to avoid ice-covered puddles left from the previous rain.

"*Fräulein.*" The voice startled her and she ran headlong into the coated chest of a large German.

"Oh my," she said. "Forgive me. I wasn't watching—"

"*Fräulein,*" he repeated. "We need to talk."

Marthe raised her eyes to meet his, but he fumbled with his coat collar to reveal two white metal safety pins. In horizontal lines. Not diagonal.

She frowned at him.

"Pardon, sir. Do you need something?" The frown remained on her face but her stomach clenched tight and her heart beat erratically. She had never been confronted by a fake "safety-pin" man before. She stepped back, her frown fixed in place. "How can I help you?"

"Excuse me," the man said and stepped back. "I must have mistaken you for someone else."

"No harm done, sir," she said smoothly. "I'm sorry I couldn't be of assistance." She bowed her head, stepped around him and continued on her path to the Taverne, focusing on using measured footsteps and ignoring her inner urge to run. The temperature had dropped in the past hour but sweat beaded her forehead by the time she reached her destination. She went straight to her room and sat on her bed for several minutes, gulping in large breaths to still her heart and regain her calm.

Her locket had found its way outside her nurse's blouse and she wrapped her hand around it. Lovingly. It helped her to remember her family.

Icy calm enveloped her once more. Confronted with a trap, she had passed. She had performed perfectly. Again.

With great care, she selected her most festive dress for the evening, a hand-me-down from one of Herr Breit's relatives, piled her hair high on her head and joined Herr Breit in the kitchen, ready to continue her performance into the evening.

# CHAPTER
## FIFTEEN

MARTHE
Field Hospital
December 1915

Lively music filled the Taverne's dining room and Herr Breit brought out tray after tray of delicious Belgian waffles drenched in rich Belgian chocolate. Even the German "guests" seemed to appreciate the Belgian bounty.

Marthe, intent on fulfilling her new role for the British Intelligence, passed through the crowd of high-ranking German officers with trays of Belgian truffles. Herr Breit kept the *bier* flowing steadily so after an hour, voices raised and laughter increased. Careful to only sip her drink, Marthe remained watchful.

"*Fräulein,*" the Town-Kommandant said. He slid his hand under her elbow and propelled her forward until they stopped in front of a squat, rotund German. "I would like you to meet Herr Schuster, Station Master at the train depot."

What luck. Herr Schuster was the exact introduction she needed.

Marthe laid her tray on a nearby table and dropped a small curtsy. "Herr Schuster," she said. She extended her hand and he bowed to kiss the back of her palm. As his head lowered, his expression turned her stomach and she steeled herself to keep from flinching.

"I have seen you at the depot," he said. He raised his eyes to hers. Again, nausea filled her and she wondered what she had gotten herself into. How could she ever pull this off?

"You are correct, Herr Schuster. I have accompanied my wounded soldiers there when they were ready to either return to the front or be moved to a larger facility." She swallowed hard and forced her face to smile, then lowered her eyes flirtatiously. "I have seen you as well."

The little man beamed.

"Unfortunately," the Town-Kommandant added, "Herr Schuster lost his wife last year and has mourned his loss of female companionship since then."

The Town-Kommandant's meaning was sickeningly clear.

"I am so sorry for your loss, Herr Schuster," Marthe murmured. The pudgy man's hand held tight to hers. She wanted, more than anything, to snatch it from his sweaty grasp but she pushed the thought away and assumed a sympathetic gaze. She raised her eyes to meet his.

For the first time, she was glad her parents were dead so they couldn't witness the charade she played.

The Station Master straightened and pulled her hand to the crook of his arm, then led Marthe away from the group. "Will you sit with me awhile, *Fräulein?* Perhaps we will get to know each other better."

She turned back to look at Herr Breit. "Well, if Herr Breit doesn't need me to help ..." The look she sent him implored him to save her.

"It is fine, Marthe." He motioned with his hand. "Go, enjoy yourself. I am certain Herr Schuster will allow you to return should we become more busy."

Herr Schuster led her to a secluded table in the corner of the dining room where the merriment swirled around them. "Allow me to get more *bier*," he said. He hailed a passing waiter who set two glasses of sparkling brew in front of them. The Station Master put his glass to his fleshy lips and drank deeply, then wiped his mouth with the back of his fat hand. "So," he said, "I understand you speak several languages."

"Yes," she said. "It has been very helpful in the hospital where we have had foreign soldiers captured." Her heart gave a little thump as she remembered Emery, his loss still weighing on her.

"I understand that," he said. "I have always been interested in learning French. Perhaps you will consider teaching me." He leaned close and the smell of bratwurst assaulted her nose.

"*Oui*," she said. At his look of confusion, she added, "That's French for 'yes.'" She smiled. "When would you like to get started?"

He pulled a slim notebook out of his coat pocket. "Let me check my schedule," he said. The look he gave her sent shivers up her spine. But she kept smiling. He lay the book open on the table in front of him and licked his finger to turn pages, leaving an oily stain on the corner of each one. She couldn't—she wouldn't—allow him to see her shudder with distaste.

"Here." He pointed to a page. Marthe leaned in and saw it was Christmas Eve. The words on the page opposite, December 23, read, "Ordnance train—arrive 3 a.m.—depart 3 p.m.; heavy caliber shells dropped at depot; lighter shells continue on up line by train."

"I will have time on Christmas Eve for our lesson," he said. "I can't leave the station, but we can meet in my office." He gave her a look that Marthe believed he intended as amorous.

*If he only knew how ridiculous that look came across on his chubby cheeks.*

"As it turns out, I am off duty at the hospital that day," Marthe said. "I had planned to assist Herr Breit in preparing the Christmas meal, but I am certain he can do without me for a couple of hours."

"*Gut*. It is a date." Again he pulled her fingers to his lips and kissed them. Her mouth ached from holding her lips in a smile her heart didn't feel.

"I will look forward to it," she said. "I do hope you will excuse me for a few moments right now, however. I must see if Herr Breit needs my help." She rose, dropped a small curtsy, and backed away toward the kitchen, sidestepping several wandering hands along the way.

In the kitchen, she gulped deep breaths. Herr Breit sent a questioning look her way as he carved a roasted turkey and she gave him a small nod.

"What goes out next?" she asked.

He pointed to the platters of roasted pork and fried rabbit, traditional German Christmas fare. "You can take those while I finish with the turkey. Tonight's meal will be served buffet style, so you can place those on the long sideboard."

Together they, along with two of the dining room's servers, placed all the platters and bowls within easy reach on the table serving as the buffet, then Herr Breit announced to the room, "Gentlemen, dinner is served." The German officers crowded the table and shoved each other good naturedly while they filled their plates to overflowing.

"Please excuse me, Herr Breit," Marthe said softly. "I would like to retire early." She climbed the stairs to her alcove and changed her clothes to a dark traveling outfit, then locked her door and sat down to write her message about the ordnance train in her secret code. She read through it several times to ensure she had done it correctly and there could be no mistake. Getting this right was too important to risk an incorrect word. When she finished, she stretched out on her bed to rest until the party downstairs ended.

———⚜———

AN OWL'S HOOT STARTLED HER AWAKE. SHE SAT UP AND LIT her bedside candle, noting that the hands on her clock pointed to one in the morning. She rose and grabbed her coat and boots, then tucked the coded message into the mass of curls on top of her head. If stopped, she would feign sleeplessness and say that a walk at night helped tire her out.

She crept down the back stairs, through the dark kitchen, pausing at the last second to snatch a small bottle of schnapps. Quietly, she opened the back door, slipped through it, then slumped to the steps and put on her boots. The backyard, illuminated by the waning gibbous moon, showed her path clearly and she had no problem finding her way to the alley and then the street. She stopped often and hugged building walls as long as possible, straining to hear sounds of someone stirring or possibly following her. When she reached the point where she needed to cross the street in full moonlight, she hesitated, then took a deep breath and walked across slowly, deliberately, as if she had not a care in the world. The last thing she must do was act like she was in a hurry or worried about being discovered.

Marthe forced her feet to slow, then worked on calming her heartbeat. She portrayed an air of nonchalance as she reached the center of the street. Only a few steps to go. The sidewalk on the opposite side beckoned and she wanted to run ... to get this trip over with as quickly as possible. But her pace remained steady.

She stepped up onto the sidewalk and again lost herself in the shadows of buildings or the large trees overhanging the street.

Three blocks to go.

Her heart rose to her throat and she remembered to breathe evenly and walk as if this were the thing she did every night.

Two more blocks.

A sound stopped her in her tracks and she stood perfectly still. Movement in the bushes beside her roared in her ears and she peered into the darkness searching for its source. Nothing showed itself.

She took another step.

Then another, holding her breath.

At her third step, the whole shrub moved and a cat shot out in front of her. A small scream escaped her throat and again she stopped and waited, hoping no one else had heard. She saw the dark opening between buildings up ahead that signaled the *Rue de la Place*, her destination.

One more street separated her from its entrance.

She stepped into the last street, smaller than the one she had already crossed and deeper in shadows. She didn't allow herself to look around before crossing, but simply stepped down and put one foot in front of the other, her breathing shallow until she reached the safety of her designated alley.

She found the house she sought, tapped on the window three times, paused, then tapped twice again. The hour was later than her other deliveries so she worried she would have to wait for the window to open. But in under a minute, the bottom pane raised and a hand came out. She retrieved the paper from her hair, thrust it into the open palm, and turned quickly.

Done. Success. Regardless of what happened at this point, the message would arrive at British Intelligence and they would arrange to bomb the station on the day the ordnance train arrived. Which meant her Station Master wouldn't be available to meet her on Christmas

Eve. She allowed herself a victorious smile but continued to walk, unhurriedly, toward the Taverne.

The backyard came into view. She headed toward it single-mindedly.

"*Fräulein.*"

Her heart thumped up against her throat and she jumped. "Who is it?" she said, her voice a breathless whisper.

A match struck and she turned toward the sound, seeing a face temporarily illuminated. She waited for him to speak, then noticed his uniform. Her heartbeat quickened.

A German. On patrol.

"Your papers?" he said.

"Certainly," she answered smoothly. She reached in her coat pocket and pulled out her orders to work at the hospital, then handed them to the soldier.

He lit another match and studied them, then looked up at her. "What brings you out so late?"

"I have had trouble sleeping," she said, "and find that a walk in the clear night air seems to help." She feigned a look of embarrassment and pulled the schnapps bottle out of her pocket. "I have also found that a couple sips of this seem to help as well." She held it out toward him. "Would you care to join me?"

He straightened up and stepped back. "Are you trying to bribe me?"

"No ... of course not," she said. "I just thought ..."

"You will accompany me to the station," he told her, his voice hard. "We don't like to have your kind in this town."

"My kind ... what are you talking about?"

"A prostitute. You will come with me." He grabbed her wrist in a tight grip and dragged her in his direction.

"Please ..." she said, pulling away. "Look at me. You read my papers. Do you think I'm dressed like a prostitute? Please ... stop and—"

"Your papers could be forged. Do not fight me. We will go to the station."

He dragged her along but she offered arguments at every step. He pulled her through the front door and pushed her roughly into the room ahead of him. She lost her balance and fell, the bottle of schnapps skittering across the floor to the feet of another German.

"What's the meaning of this?" the other man demanded.

"I'm arresting this woman for prostitution," the first soldier said. "I found her—"

"You are a complete idiot," the other soldier said. He reached a hand to help Marthe to her feet. She accepted his hand and met his eyes.

"Oh ... it's you," she said. "I remember you." And she did. From the night he tried to stop her from taking a tray to her wounded soldiers in the attic at the Taverne. "It's Officer Hirsch, is it not?"

The second soldier let go of her hand and bowed. "*Ja, Fräulein*. It is good to see you again." He turned to the other soldier. "This woman is a nurse at the hospital and under the protection of the Town-Kommandant. Why did you bring her here?"

Marthe watched the face of the younger soldier redden. "Well ... she ... was out late at night. I thought she was a—"

"Well, you were wrong," Hirsch said. "Return to your beat. At once."

"Thank you, Herr Hirsch," Marthe said. She turned toward the door, but he stopped her.

"*Fräulein*, wait."

She hesitated but didn't turn.

"You forgot this."

He held out the small bottle of schnapps toward her. She faced him, smiled, and reached for it. "But," he said, without releasing the bottle, "why *were* you out so late tonight?"

She hung her head. "We had a terrible day at the hospital. Several amputations and a number of soldiers who didn't make it." She raised her eyes after managing to coat them with moisture. "I know it's all part of what happens in a hospital. And ..." she stopped and took a deep ragged breath, "in a war. But some days it becomes so hard to take." She reached up to wipe a tear. "I simply couldn't sleep and thought some fresh air might help." She forced a small smile and pointed to the schnapps bottle. "Along with a couple of swigs of that."

He smiled with her and placed the bottle in her hand. "I have those days, too, *Fräulein*. Wait here, please. I will find someone to accompany you back to the Taverne."

She waited until he returned with another young officer. After he introduced them, Marthe offered her hand to Hirsch. "You have been most kind, Herr Hirsch." He shook the hand she offered and she continued. "Thank you for your help. I think I can sleep now."

The young officer accompanied her to the Taverne. "Because of the hour," she told him, "I will enter through the kitchen door. I am fine from here. Thank you." She bowed slightly and stood until he turned and walked back toward the station. Then she went around to the back of the house. At the steps, she paused to remove her boots but before she finished, the door swung open.

"Marthe? Oh, thank God," Herr Breit said. "I feared …"

She placed her hand on his arm and smiled at him.

"Not this time, Herr Breit. The delivery was successful."

Two days later, bombs hit the train depot, totally destroying the ordnance train being unloaded. Most of the depot personnel were killed, including Station Master Schuster.

# CHAPTER SIXTEEN

SUZANNE
2015

An old trunk? In the barn at Prospect Park?

I had been in that barn a hundred times as a kid and never noticed an old trunk. Who knows what might have happened to it? But it would be interesting to find out. My son and his wife, Emily, had a new hobby of restoring old steamer trunks and they would love the thought of having one that had been in the family for generations.

I turned the page in the album and my hair stood on end.

A picture of a trunk.

It must have been the same one Maude talked about in her diary. And there were the boys beside it, with their baseball equipment scattered around them. It looked like Maude's brother, Henry, held a chest protector … like what he would have used during a game. I was thrilled to find a picture of something Maude had talked about and made a mental note to ask my aunts and Uncle Freddie about the trunk when we got to the farm.

My stomach growled. Reading about the vegetables in my great-grandmother's garden and then about their picnic lunch must have worked on my stomach and reminded me that I hadn't eaten. So I picked up the diary and took it to Dad's kitchen. I'd had the foresight to bring a sandwich with me since I'd already cleaned everything out of his refrigerator and pantry.

My grandmother's passage about having to help in the garden

stayed with me and without warning, a memory popped into my head and brought tears to my eyes.

I must have been ten or twelve when Dad, in his words, "requested my presence" in the garden he and Mom had planted. Like my grandmother, I hated working in it. Especially weeding. But that day, Dad started to whistle and when I asked him what it was, he told me it was "Tweedle O'Twill," a song Gene Autry made famous back in the 1940s.

"Sing me the words," I said to him. And he did.

I don't remember all the words now but after the first line of "Tweedle O'Twill," whatever the heck that meant, I remember laughing out loud when he sang the second line, "Puffin' on corn silk."

"What does that even mean?" I remember asking.

Our corn had grown above my head by then and Dad pointed to the tassels at the end of each ear. "When the corn is ready to pick," he said, "these turn black. Remember?" At my nod, he continued. "Years ago kids used to wrap it up in paper and smoke it like tobacco."

"Ewww ... yuck," I said. "Did you ever do that?"

He laughed and said that yes, he and his older brother, Walter, did it a time or two. Until it made them sick. Then he laughed again.

I picked up my phone and asked Google to play me the song. By the time Gene Autry's scratchy voice died down and the nonsense lyrics ended, tears streamed down my face.

It took me a minute to figure out why but then it hit me. Regardless of how I felt about working in the garden, being there with Dad that day and finding out about something he did when he was a kid—something I'd never known before—made the work fly by. And now, remembering it all these years later reminded me—again—of what a wonderful father he had been.

And how much I missed him.

Nostalgia swept over me in waves.

When I could control myself, I finished my sandwich and picked up my grandmother's diary again. We were already into 1916.

*January 6, 1916*

*Dear Diary,*

*I know, I know, I haven't been here much lately.*

*Henry was right. Math is harder this year and it's taking me longer to get it through my head. Plus, Helen's still mad at me because I won't let her talk about Buzz. I don't know what she sees in him, anyway, but it doesn't matter now because I won't see him or Henry for a while. They left this morning to go to Jacksonville. All the way down in Florida. On the team bus.*

*The whole thing seems really exciting to me. I've seen postcards from Florida and it looks like there must be palm trees everywhere. I wish we could go see them. But Mom says they're there to do a job and wouldn't have time for us. But I said I'll bet they don't play ball when it's dark and then she sent me to clean my room. She does that sometimes when she can't think of anything to answer me back.*

*I guess they'll come home for a few days after their training on their way back to Philadelphia. When the regular season starts. Dad says it will be March or April.*

*I never thought I'd say this, and I certainly won't tell anybody else, but I kind of miss them. I mean, I love having Mom and Dad all to myself, but Henry's been nicer to me since he's been away. And even Buzz has. Not that Buzz was ever not nice, but he's talking more than he used to. I like it. He's even kind of cute when he smiles.*

*But I'll never tell Helen that.*

*Gotta study. Big test tomorrow. Fractions, including multiplying and dividing. I really don't like it. And Miss Delsie keeps using our Social Studies class to teach us about what's going on in Europe. It just sounds like a bunch of bullies trying to make everybody else do things their way. Again, I still don't see why we have to know about it because it doesn't affect us over here. But she insists.*

*More later.*

*Your friend, Maude*

*P. S. Mom read me a letter from Henry. He says it's cold there. And then he said, "Ha ha." It might not be as warm as he expected it to be, but I bet they aren't getting any snow there like we are here.*

—————

**Jacksonville, FL**
**January 7, 1916**

"Now that we're here," Buzz said to Henry, "I think I'll find an alligator to wrestle. You know"—he grinned—"like Rube Waddell. One of the guys told me about a place down the road in St. Augustine, the 'St. Augustine Alligator Farm.' Why would anybody want to farm alligators?"

"Yeah, I don't know about *farming* alligators. But I do know that Coach Mack would not be amused if you tried to *wrestle* one," Henry said. He stood and threw the ball back to Buzz. "That one was a little flat. Try it again."

Buzz turned to his side, went through his visualization routine, then let the ball fly.

"Better," Henry said. "Way better, actually. Do it again."

They continued working for the next hour before one of the trainers came up to them. "Brewer," the trainer said, "Coach Mack wants you guys to shake it up a little." Still looking at Henry, he said, "You're supposed to catch for Bullet Joe Bush. And Ryan, he wants you to pitch to Doc Carroll. On the double."

The boys jogged to their new positions and worked there for

another hour, then reassembled with the rest of the team and played a five-inning scrimmage. After that, they joined the rest of the guys in batting practice, taking their turns with pitching and catching and then working on their batting.

When their workday ended, they went back to the boarding house where the team stayed. "Want to go into town tonight?" Henry asked, "Jacksonville's a Navy town and I hear there's a club with girls who will dance with you. Nice girls. You wanna come?"

"Henry, you know I can't dance," Buzz said.

"You can do the waltz ... or at least fake it," Henry answered.

"Thanks, but you go without me. I'm tired anyway. Maybe I'll see an early movie."

"Suit yourself," Henry said.

Henry left with a couple of the other players and Buzz watched him leave. Henry had been his best friend his whole life. But Henry had always been a lot more comfortable with other people than Buzz. He'd often wished he possessed Henry's confidence. Buzz knew a lot of his issues with people stemmed from his family life and his parents' constant drinking. Regardless of how well he did at school or on the baseball team—or even with the Athletics—he always believed the first thing the townspeople thought, and often said, when they saw him was that his parents were drunks. And if they were drunks, then their son must be headed for drunkenness himself. Logically, he knew he could chalk it up to small-town talk and that he should let it roll off and not worry about it. But because of his upbringing, he always felt inferior. Not good enough to associate with the popular girls. He even had trouble talking to Henry's sister, Maude, and he knew she didn't care one whit about what his parents had done. Being part of the Athletics helped. And being in Jacksonville, or anywhere away from Prospect Park, helped. But until he became a famous starting pitcher, his background haunted him and he preferred to remain in the shadows.

He left the boarding house and walked the few blocks to the nearest movie theater. *The Crazy Clock Maker*, featuring Oliver Hardy, himself a Jacksonville native according to the sign outside, played twice per night and Buzz took in the early show. It felt good to laugh at the slapstick antics on screen and he really enjoyed himself.

He didn't, however, enjoy the newsreel before the movie about the escalating war overseas. Most of Europe, he learned, had already joined the conflict and the war seemed to be expanding in all directions. The newsreel narrator quoted President Wilson as saying he intended to send monetary help and supplies to the Allies. At the end of the segment the narrator said, "And just how long America can stay out of the war is anybody's guess."

The words chilled Buzz's heart. He had no interest in fighting anyone else's war. He still had too much of his own war to fight. He renewed his resolve to work even harder at his craft. He thoroughly believed that baseball players would be exempt from fighting overseas if it came to that because he thought Americans needed the game for entertainment. Once the movie began, however, he dismissed his fears as unfounded and thought the announcer was simply practicing *his* craft, which, Buzz thought, included stirring up trouble and trying to produce reactions in people.

Well, it wouldn't work with him, he decided. He would simply put his head down and work on becoming the best pitcher the American League had ever seen.

And maybe, he thought, he'd also work on his dancing. And being able to talk to girls.

# CHAPTER
# SEVENTEEN

SUZANNE

2015

I decided to take my grandmother's diary with me when I joined the rest of Dad's family in Prospect Park at the end of the week. Steve and Emily would drive there with me and I had already heard from Dad's sisters that everything was set for Dad's funeral in the town where he grew up.

Which made me feel better about my decision to keep reading instead of cleaning out Dad's house in Lock Haven. I figured I needed to take advantage of my opportunity to finish the diary now since I would leave it with the family.

I returned to Dad's Zen Zone and devoured the pictures on the next few pages of the photo album. I got a kick out of one where Maude, with a huge smile, held up a piece of paper, obviously a math test, with a very large, very visible "A+." She wrote in her last diary entry that she struggled with math so I was happy to see she had mastered it.

It also kind of surprised me. When Dad spoke about her, I had the impression he didn't think she'd been very smart. He certainly loved her and he never said outright that he thought her ignorant, but again, that's what his words implied. I made another note to ask his sisters about it when I saw them.

I looked at a few more pictures ... snow in the front yard, the boys in casual clothes and waving to the camera with their suitcases in hand, and other such family happenings. I left the album and picked up the diary again.

*March 14, 1916*

*Dear Diary,*

*Hey! It's Maude! Wait 'til I tell you! I got an A + on an arithmetic test! It was really hard but I'd studied for days and with Mom's help, I finally understood it. Of course, Buzz could have helped me, but he's still in Florida. Henry's last letter said he and Buzz will be home this month because their first game is in April. I'm excited for them to see my test too.*

*In Social Studies class we still talk a lot about the war in Europe but honestly, I think it's sooo boring. Miss Delsie told us there was a big battle in a place called Verdun. She says that's in France and they're still fighting there even though that battle started last month. The good part was she taught us a French song called* Frère Jacques *and told us it means "Brother John" in English. I came home all excited and started singing it to Mom and Dad and Mom sang with me! In French! I didn't know she could speak French. She might be smarter than I thought she was.*

*I heard them talking after supper last night and they're already planning the garden. Ugh! Dad's even thinking about making it bigger. I really wish they would stop with the darn garden, but they won't listen to me.*

*Mom's calling me to help her in the kitchen.*

*More later. Your friend, Maude*

---

## March 25, 1916

AFTER A FEW DAYS WITH THE FAMILY IN PROSPECT PARK, during which Henry praised Maude for her good arithmetic grade and even Buzz smiled at her, they returned to Philadelphia to prepare for the 1916 baseball season. They needed to return early, Henry said, because their first five games were road games in Boston, then New York.

Prior to going on the road, Coach Mack called all the players one by one into his office. Buzz thought it meant bad news for him and Henry after they watched many players leave with disappointed faces, but Henry asked one of the players outright.

"What happened in there?"

"I was sold," infielder Harry Davis told him. "Coach used to have a hundred-thousand-dollar infield but he's gotten rid of so many of us, his infield is down to around ten dollars." He saw the look on Buzz's face and added. "No offense, Ryan. You do a fine job. I'm sure Coach will keep you."

By Buzz's turn, he paced, worry plain on his face. "Henry," he said, his voice tight. "What if we get cut? What will we do?"

"We'll either find another team or go back to Prospect Park," Henry said with a shrug.

"No!"

The intensity in Buzz's voice startled Henry. "Calm down, man. It'll be fine."

"No it won't. Not if I have to go back there." Lines formed between Buzz's eyes and rage filled them.

"Buzz," Henry said. "I'm sorry. I know what it was like there for you ... with your ... family and the ... trouble you had. But please don't go into Coach's office with this attitude. I don't think we have anything to worry about. We don't make the kind of money Davis made. I think that's why he's gone. Coach told my dad the first time we met him that he wanted to bring in younger blood ... which implies less expensive blood. Which, by the way, is what you and I are." He put his arm around Buzz's shoulders. "Please calm down. We'll be fine. I promise."

When it was his turn, Buzz knocked softly on the coach's door.

"Come in," Coach Mack called. Buzz sucked air into his lungs and entered.

"Have a seat, son." The coach indicated the bench in front of his massive oak desk.

Buzz had seen the bench before and loved the way it was made, fashioned from bats and studded with baseballs. It was also the only piece of furniture in the coach's office other than his desk and chair. Coach Mack smiled at him.

"You happy here, Buzz?"

Buzz's stomach tightened and he leaned forward. "You have no idea how happy, Coach," he answered. "I feel like my life began when you hired me for the team." He knew that was a dramatic statement to make. But it also happened to be true. And if Coach waivered on the fence about keeping him, he wasn't above groveling.

"Good, good," Coach said. "I like hearing that."

Buzz relaxed slightly.

"I have big plans for you, Buzz," the coach told him, leaning forward in his chair. "You and Henry both."

"You mean here?" Buzz asked. "With the A's?"

Understanding filled Connie Mack's face and he smiled. "Of course here," he said. "You talked to some of the other players, didn't you? And they told you they'd been sold or traded, huh?"

Buzz nodded, unable to speak.

"Well, most of them had other offers," Coach Mack said, "good offers. And as a businessman … and a caring coach … I couldn't stand in their way of making more money. And by freeing up their higher salaries, that will allow me to give you and Henry a slight raise in pay."

Buzz started to shake. He came in expecting to be fired but instead found out he would receive a raise. He couldn't believe his good fortune. And Henry's.

"I was serious, Buzz," Coach said. He left his chair and patted Buzz on the back. Buzz stood and the two men shook hands. "I have big plans for you. And I want to do everything I can to help you become a full-time pitcher. Maybe not in this season, although I'll play you as often as I can, but in 1917 for sure. Is that good?"

Buzz couldn't suppress his smile and he pumped the coach's hand again. "Yes sir. Not only good, but great. I can't thank you enough."

"Okay," Coach said. "Good. You want to send Henry in? Of course, I think as soon as he sees your face, he won't be worried." He opened the door for Buzz and smiled at him again, then patted his shoulder one final time as he left the office.

When Henry went into the coach's office, Buzz gulped air again, his mind whirling.

*They'll never get me back in Prospect Park. Never. No more small towns with mean-spirited people who want to talk bad about you because of the way your parents are. Or ... were. I've made a leap into the big time.*

*And I'll never go back.*

*Never!*

# CHAPTER EIGHTEEN

MARTHE
Field Hospital
March 1916

Marthe walked slowly back to the Taverne from the hospital and enjoyed the patches of new green that lined the streets and burst from the trees. Spring always brought renewed growth and, Marthe decided, even this year, regardless of the war, new hope. She filled her lungs, and the air, fragrant with the aroma of new blossoms, lightened her heart.

She neared the town square and continued to walk leisurely while many around her appeared to be in a hurry. The closer she came to the Taverne, the more the activity increased and by the time she entered the dining room, her face skewed up in a frown. She found Herr Breit in the kitchen.

"Is it my imagination or is something going on?"

He put his finger to his lips but after a moment, said. "I need fresh herbs for tonight's chicken. Will you help me gather them?"

Marthe followed him to the herb garden in the backyard and stretched out her apron so he could lay his cuttings in it. With his eyes pointed toward the earth, he said quietly, "You are correct. Something is afoot. Lots of extra activity with little talk of what it may be. Have you heard anything at the hospital?"

"No. It's been a little less busy than normal, but there has been no news about anything unusual. Maybe we can find out something tonight from the Town-Kommandant."

"Maybe," he agreed. "I may need to call on your feminine expertise. I hate to ask, but …"

"Certainly. I will do what I can. Let me help serve tonight."

He nodded and they both returned to the kitchen.

"I will go change and come back in time to help set out the food," Marthe said with her hand on his arm.

Before she could leave, a tap sounded on the kitchen door. She opened it and saw the street sweeper. A small gasp escaped her throat. It wasn't normal protocol for them to be seen at the Taverne together. "Yes?" she said. "I will get Herr Breit."

"You don't need to disturb him," the street sweeper said. "But I heard he needs matches for his stove. Please give him these." With that, he tipped his worn hat brim and disappeared.

Herr Breit joined her at the table as she sat to look at the matches. He shook his head and pointed upward. She understood and quietly left the kitchen to open the matches in private.

She drew the curtains then flopped on her bed. The matchbox opened easily and the small piece of paper, folded many times, fell onto the matches within. She picked it up and smoothed it out, then held it closer to the light so she could read it.

*Significant rumor that Kaiser Wilhelm will visit Roulers. Can you find date and time?*

Marthe held the small piece of paper to the candle and watched to make certain it burned completely. Her mind spun and she mentally paged through her contacts to figure out who could, and most important, who *would* be willing to give her such information.

She dressed carefully, her wardrobe having increased slightly in size with the small salary she received from the hospital. She chose a bright blue skirt and vest, since she had been told the color brought out the blue in her eyes. She paired it with a white long-sleeved blouse and piled her auburn curls high on her head. At the hospital, she often coiled her braids to keep her hair from escaping when she made rounds with the *Oberartz*, but on her free time, she released it to curls which she pinned to her crown and sometimes let fall down across her neck. She wore no make-up but did occasionally pinch her cheeks to disguise the pallor of her skin.

She descended quickly and found Herr Breit and his few servers busy with finishing touches in the kitchen. Herr Breit instructed her on adding the trimmings to the side dishes and then left for the lobby to welcome his diners. The door to the dining room opened and closed as each server deposited deliveries on the long table and Marthe saw that the officers who entered wore newer uniforms, their boots polished so they reflected light. Herr Breit had made arrangements that weapons were to be left in the lobby, but Marthe remembered that the few guns she had seen in the streets during her walks to and from the hospital appeared to be polished as well, which was definitely different from what she had seen during the long winter.

Herr Breit entered the kitchen. "Marthe, I hope you will join me in the dining room. We have a new colonel visiting and the Town-Kommandant wishes to introduce you."

"Of course." She picked up the dish she had just finished and carried it to the table.

"Herr Colonel," the Town-Kommandant said, turning toward Marthe, "I am pleased to introduce you to one of our hospital nurses. The *Oberartz* there speaks very highly of her work. She has assisted him to return many of our soldiers back to the front to continue our glorious cause. Marthe, please meet Colonel Selig Unger, from Brussels."

Marthe dipped in a small curtsy, then extended her hand. The Colonel bent to kiss the back of it and when he straightened, Marthe looked into his hazel eyes. He stood more than a foot above her head and his fair hair waved back away from his brow. He was easily, Marthe thought, one of the best-looking men she had ever seen. Her stomach fluttered with a slight thrill.

"*Fräulein,*" he said. "I am so pleased to meet you. I have heard much about you."

Marthe dipped her head, then looked up through her lashes. She knew the look to be flirtatious, and it seemed to have the desired effect. "Herr Colonel, how nice of you to say. May I bring you a drink?"

His eyes crinkled with interest and his smile grew to fill his face. He allowed Herr Breit to seat him and the Town-Kommandant while Marthe brought them one of the Taverne's most popular *biers*.

"Please, *Fräulein*," the Colonel said, catching her wrist, "join us. I am certain Herr Breit can do without your help for a while."

She eased into the chair he indicated and made herself comfortable while the Town-Kommandant continued to fill the space with small talk.

"How long will you be gracing us with your presence, Herr Colonel?" Marthe asked. "I do hope you will be able to come to the hospital and greet the men there. I am certain hearing from someone in such a position would cheer them up."

"I will only be here for a day or two. I must return to Brussels for some important meetings."

"Well, I hope you will not be a stranger while you are here."

The Town-Kommandant excused himself to speak to other officers in the Taverne and the Colonel moved his chair closer to Marthe. "You are very lovely, *Fräulein*. Perhaps after dinner you will join me for a short walk in the evening spring air. You will not have to worry about the curfew when you are with me."

The curfew was recently imposed after Marthe had been hauled in front of Herr Hirsch at the police station. No one ever said she was responsible, but she wondered if her late night visit to the station had been part of what the Colonel had heard about her. If so, she decided, there was nothing she could do about it.

She hesitated. The Colonel could be the perfect candidate to feed her information about the Kaiser, but she also knew that by agreeing, she could be setting herself up for more than she bargained for. "Thank you, Herr Colonel," she said. "I have a very early morning tomorrow, but I may be able to join you for a short time." She smiled at him and lightly touched his hand.

They enjoyed a very pleasant dinner with alcohol flowing freely and officers from the area stopping by the table to introduce themselves to such a high-ranking official from Brussels. Marthe had arranged with Herr Breit to just top off her drinks rather than serving her full portions so she could keep her head where it needed to be.

After dessert and schnapps, the Colonel turned to her and claimed her hand with his. "Now, *Fräulein*," he said, his face only inches from hers, "will you join me for a short stroll?"

She nodded and rose when he pulled her chair back. He placed his hand on the small of her back to guide her out the front door and onto the sidewalk. The light breeze, sweet with spring jasmine, enveloped her. She turned her face up and breathed deeply, a slow smile lifting her lips. "I love spring," she said. "I love the beautiful aromas floating on the air and the many shades of green popping up all around." She turned to him. "It renews hope, don't you think?"

Without responding, he leaned down and let his lips rest softly on hers before moving on to her neck and planting soft kisses all the way to her throat. She stiffened.

"Relax, Marthe," he whispered into her hair. "I will never ask you to do anything you don't want to do." He tucked her hand into the crook of his arm and they strolled away from the Taverne. They engaged in small talk for several blocks then headed back the way they had come. They reached her door and he glanced at his watch. "I must leave you now and allow you to sleep since you have an early morning. As do I." He took her hands in his. "But I want you to think about something. I wish you to join me next week in Brussels for a few days. I will give you a pass so you can move freely around the city and"—he stooped and bent over her hand again—"I will treat you to real food as opposed to this provincial fare you get here. We will even attend the opera one night." He brought his face close to hers. "And you will have your own room." He kissed her again then spoke in a quiet voice. "For as long as you want it."

She smiled up at him. "Thank you for such a lovely invitation, Herr Colonel. I hope you will allow me a little time to think about it."

"Certainly. At your suggestion, I plan to come by the hospital tomorrow. You may give me your answer then." He opened the door for her, bowed, and was gone.

# CHAPTER
# NINETEEN

MARTHE
Field Hospital
March 1916

Marthe's day began before dawn. She had hoped to have a few moments to think about the Colonel's proposal, but her tasks called her from one thing to another with no time to focus on anything but caring for her charges. After lunch, the *Oberartz* called her to his office and she wondered why he had summoned her rather than simply finding her in the halls as he usually did.

"Ah, Marthe," the doctor greeted her, "please come in. I understand you met our distinguished guest last evening at the Taverne, yes?"

"That's right," Marthe said, dropping a small curtsy in the Colonel's direction. "It is nice to see you again, Herr Colonel."

"And you as well," he answered. "Your doctor friend here has spoken very highly of you," he added. "He petitioned me weeks ago to reward you for your service. So I am here to present you with this German Iron Cross for your devoted attention to German soldiers."

Stunned, Marthe's hand flew to her mouth while the *Oberartz* rose and kissed her on both cheeks. She shook hands with the Colonel and accepted the medal he gave her. "I ... I don't know what to say. Thank you both so much. I enjoy my work and am glad my service is appreciated."

The Colonel stood and shook hands with the *Oberartz*, then turned to Marthe. "You have certainly earned it, *Fräulein*," he said. "Will you show me out? I must catch my train back to Brussels."

They walked together through the halls and at the front door, the Colonel gently pushed her into an alcove and leaned in close. "Have you made up your mind, Marthe? Will you come to Brussels with me?"

She decided on the spot. "Yes, I will come for a few days if the doctor can do without me."

"He will release you. Trust me." He bent and kissed her hand, then straightened. "I will arrange everything. I will have your train ticket and your pass delivered to the Taverne. When you arrive in Brussels, a car will meet you and take you to the hotel. You will love it. Until then …" He kissed her hand again and left.

Marthe's heart thumped against her throat and emotions swirled around her. Excitement, certainly, since she had never been to a city the size of Brussels. And she loved the idea of attending the opera. But she also believed she could find the information about Kaiser Wilhelm the network had asked for. Her only misgiving concerned the Colonel himself. She knew what would be expected of her in such a circumstance and dared not let herself focus on it. She would get the information she needed first and then figure out the rest later.

Her train ticket and pass waited for her when she reached the Taverne and that night, she made a visit to Number Seventy-two with the information about her trip and her planned accomplishment while there. She suggested that an agent be stationed near if she needed help.

In two days' time, she boarded the train with one small suitcase. She had never seen the kind of luxury that greeted her in the compartment the Colonel had chosen and she couldn't help but think back to the night her parents were killed and her home burned, along with the months of forced marches with her captors when she wore ragged clothes and shoes held together with string. She touched her locket to remind herself of how far she had come since then.

Although she was not proud of what she was about to do with the enemy.

She steeled her mind to push such thoughts away and tried to calm her nervous stomach. When the porter offered her a glass of schnapps, she gratefully accepted and let the liquid fire burn her throat on its way to warming her insides. She tried reading so she wouldn't have to think but after two pages, she gave up and stared out the window. The Belgian landscape sped by and gradually changed from rural scenes to more populated areas.

Night had fallen by the time she arrived and, as the Colonel had promised, a car met her at the station to take her to the hotel. At the front desk, she received a note which she slid into her pocket until she reached her room. The bellboy deposited her suitcase and left her alone.

She studied her face in the mirror.

*Oh my God, Marthe. What have you done?*

She sat on the edge of the bed and fished the Colonel's note from her pocket. It read: *Welcome, my dear. I trust your trip was uneventful and that you arrived safely. I am in meetings tonight but will see you for lunch in the hotel dining room tomorrow. Sleep well.*

Relief engulfed her, and her heart sang.

She had more time.

She would make this work.

———◦❦◦———

SHE AWOKE SUDDENLY TO A MAID OPENING HER CURTAINS and bright sunbeams radiating to every corner of her room. "*Bonjour, Mademoiselle,*" the maid greeted her in a cheery voice, then continued speaking in French to let her know that her breakfast waited on the table. She also told Marthe that a hot tub awaited her in the bathroom and that the maid was available to help her dress or fix her hair. Then she curtsied and backed out of the room.

Marthe couldn't help but smile. Never in her life had she heard anything more ridiculous. Were there really women, she wondered, who couldn't dress themselves or fix their own hair? Still smiling, she rose and opened the covers on her breakfast to find eggs benedict and sausage. Then she opened the top of the coffee pot and breathed in its rich aroma deeply. More than a year had passed since real coffee crossed her lips and her senses rejoiced in its rich taste. It almost made her reason for being there seem justified.

Almost ... but not quite.

She ate as much as she could from the tray, then went to the bathroom and stepped into the tub. The water, no longer steaming, but still plenty warm, caressed her body and relaxed her remaining jitters. The aroma of heady bath salts greeted her and she settled in to soak. Never in her life had she had time to soak in a tub. Even when her family was still alive. Guilt at enjoying her surroundings wormed its way into her head, but she pushed it away, telling herself that what she had planned would be a service to the world. For the first time, she let herself envision what it would feel like to send her network the information with the date and time of the Kaiser's visit to Roulers. She smiled, satisfied. She hated the Kaiser and his damnable war and wanted it ended. And she, Marthe Peeters, was in a position to make it happen.

She stepped from the tub and toweled herself off, then toyed with the idea of calling the maid to help with her hair. Just to see what she would do with it. But she decided against it. The Colonel had invited her on the way she looked in Roulers and that's what he would see here.

She opened the wardrobe to find several new dresses. Irritation radiated through her at the audacity of the Colonel's familiarity. Until she remembered that she had agreed to his invitation to join him. At his expense. She didn't have to accept his generosity but decided since she had already made the trip, she would play the role.

She chose one of the dresses and smoothed the silky fabric over her hips. Then she added stockings and stepped into her shoes.

She squared her shoulders and adopted a carefree expression. She was ready.

After descending the grand staircase, she found her way to the restaurant, then asked to be seated at the Colonel's table. She saw him enter and when he spotted her, his smile broadened.

"Marthe," he said, bending over her hand to plant a kiss. "I am so happy to see you. I promise you will not be sorry you came."

She smiled. "Thank you for my room. It is beautiful."

"You will see a lot of beauty in the next couple of days. Much more than is your custom."

The Colonel ordered for them both, including a sparkling wine that complemented the fish and Marthe realized that she actually enjoyed herself. When the dishes had been cleared, he rose. "I hope you will visit the city this afternoon. I shall join you again in the evening and we will attend a party with my fellow officers." He bowed and was gone.

Marthe returned to her room and looked critically at the dresses within the wardrobe, trying to decide if they were lavish enough for an officer's party or the opera. They were. One less thing for her to worry about. So she decided to stroll the streets of Brussels and perhaps shop for minor accessories.

Even though she had never been to Brussels before, she knew it had always worn the nickname *"Petite Paris."* As she wandered the streets, all of which needed repair, she could see the name no longer fit, with the peeling paint on the storefronts and the filth on the sidewalks. She cut her walk short and returned to her room, disappointed not only in the city, but also that no other agent had made himself—or herself—known to her.

She stretched out on the freshly made bed and fell into a light sleep. When she woke, the bedside clock showed the hour of four. She was to meet the Colonel at six for dinner and then on to the party. Her body trembled at the thought of what the Colonel would expect from her that evening.

———⋅⟨⟩⋅———

TO MARTHE'S GREAT RELIEF, PEOPLE SURROUNDED THEM during dinner and at the officer's party. They even joined a group at the hotel after midnight for a nightcap. Officers who reported to the

Colonel supplied him with drinks all night and he never turned one down.

Marthe watched the other women, many of whom were her fellow Belgians, and wondered what kinds of harrowing tales they could tell about why they were in the presence of German soldiers. Some of them may have been legitimate sweethearts, but more likely, she figured, the stories would be closer to hers.

Around one o'clock in the morning, Marthe saw that the Colonel's head drooped to his chest and his eyes appeared to be glazed. Suddenly, hotel personnel appeared, helped lift the Colonel to his feet, and offered to accompany them to their rooms. Marthe's heart lodged in her throat until they dropped her off at her door and continued on with him to his room several doors away. She went inside and immediately turned the key in the lock, thrilled that she had a reprieve. For one more night, anyway.

---

AT BREAKFAST, A NOTE APPEARED WITH HER TRAY ... AN apology from the Colonel for not being able to accompany her to her room himself and that he hoped to see her at lunch. A single red rose rested atop the cover for her eggs. She smiled.

*I wonder what he would think if he knew his absence had been a blessed relief for me?*

Her day turned out to be almost an exact replica of the one before. Except at lunch he told her they would join a group for dinner before heading to the opera. Which suited her fine. The more time they spent with others around them, the less time she had to worry about his expectations.

She rested that afternoon, then pulled out the finest dress that hung in her wardrobe. Despite her misgivings about being with the Colonel, the excitement she felt at wearing so fine an outfit and attending an opera amid Brussel's dazzling finest couldn't be tamped down. Indeed, her excitement bubbled over when she saw the Colonel at dinner. Her smile flashed genuine and the Colonel appeared to relax. He introduced her to the other officers and their companions and after a perfect meal, they piled into a large, hired car and arrived at *Théâtre de la Monnaie* where Wagnerian music had returned after a two-year absence. Her group sat in a box and enjoyed champagne when a flurry of activity drew Marthe's attention to another box, close to her own.

To Marthe's confusion, the soldiers immediately jumped to attention and a hush fell over the crowd until they burst into spontaneous prolonged cheering. She struggled to her feet and looked to the Colonel with confusion. "It is The All Highest," he whispered.

His answer did nothing to relieve her confusion until he added, "The Kaiser."

With that, Marthe openly stared. The crowd continued to cheer but the Kaiser seemed to take scant notice of such adulation. To her unpracticed eye, he appeared quite ordinary and, she thought, his face held a look of what she would have called sadness, as if he suffered under his great responsibility. He acknowledged the crowd before being seated but never graced them with a smile.

The scene struck Marthe as funny. But of course, she dared not laugh.

There he was. The Kaiser. The one they referred to as "The All Highest."

The man whose whereabouts she had compromised herself to find out, now stood mere meters from her while she, a spy for the British Intelligence, planned his death.

The Colonel stared at her and she pulled her focus from the object of her treason to the man beside her. She still hadn't found out anything of use for her network and had now made herself miserable with her regret. She attempted to simply relax and enjoy the glitz and glamour while beautiful music reached her ears, but the longer the night wore on, the worse she felt and several times she struggled to hold back tears.

By the time they returned to the hotel she had made up her mind.

She would leave.

Tonight.

Her mind worked furiously. The Colonel handed her out of the car at the front of the hotel and pulled her close. "Shall we have a night-cap?" he whispered.

"Thank you, but I have had enough to drink, Herr Colonel. Please go without me."

He kissed her cheek and leaned in again. "Certainly," he said. His eyes held hers in a look she assumed he meant as seduction.

Confused, Marthe wondered about his willingness to have a nightcap without her rather than try to persuade her to accompany him. Then it dawned on her.

*Oh good Lord. He must have interpreted my reluctance as shyness ... that I wanted to be alone to undress.* She shook her head. *Men are such egotistical fools. Well fine. Let him think that. It will give me more time.*

She went straight to her room. Once there, she saw that his suit-cases sat in the middle of her floor. Rage shot through her at his lack of discretion. She knew, of course, she had tacitly agreed to a physical relationship when she agreed to join him, but she had wanted to believe she would be able to make the decisions rather than having them made for her. Regardless, seeing his luggage reinforced her resolve to leave. She changed into travel clothes, gathered her purse and the pass which would allow her out past curfew, then wrote a hasty note. It read:

*I am sorry, Herr Colonel, but I have changed my mind. I have made a serious mistake by coming here and am returning home immediately.*

At the door, she gave the room one final look to make certain she hadn't forgotten anything, then opened the door and stepped into the hallway.

And bumped into the Colonel's chest.

"Marthe. What is this? I thought we were—"

"No," she interrupted. "No ... I can't. I don't ..." She stopped and covered her face with her hands, her sobs pitiful in the lonely hallway.

He took her shoulders and propelled her gently into the room.

"Please," she cried. She pushed herself away from him. "I'm sorry but I changed my mind. I have to get home."

He still didn't seem to understand.

"You don't need to go tonight, *mein Schatz*. We can—"

Again, she pulled away and pushed against his chest, then babbled whatever words came to her mind. "I have to be at the hospital. The *Oberartz* thinks the Kaiser is visiting at the end of the week and he will need me to perform certain duties."

"I'm glad you told me your concerns," he said. "You needn't have worried. The Kaiser won't arrive until Saturday afternoon ... around two o'clock, I'm told, and will only stay an hour or two. So we have plenty of time tonight and you can still get back in time for the *Oberartz*."

And there it was.

The information she sought.

The information for which she'd been willing to compromise herself.

But she still had to get away from him.

"No!" She backed up and the washstand hit her back. She turned swiftly and grabbed the full pitcher of water, then used all her strength to fling its entire contents at him. He covered his face with his hands and stumbled. She stepped forward and pushed against his chest until he fell backward over his suitcases and sprawled on the floor.

Without taking time to see if he was okay, she grabbed her purse, checked to see that she still had her pass and left everything else. She hadn't brought anything important enough to delay her escape.

She flew down the corridor and the stairs to the lobby, then caught a hired car for the train station. Within forty-five minutes, she lay back in her berth on the train, her heart still beating violently. She gulped deep breaths and counted the hours until she reached her own bed.

Where she could finally rest.

*After* she sent the date and time of the Kaiser's visit to her network.

# CHAPTER
# TWENTY

**SUZANNE**
**2015**

I'd gotten into the habit of alternating a passage in Maude's diary with a few pages in the photo album, a great visual representation of Maude's words. The next few pictures were of a smiling Maude—with all of her missing teeth grown in—and a slightly older hairdo. In one picture, she held a large towel that boasted "St. Augustine, Florida." In another, her mother held what looked like a tiny potted plant—a palm tree, I think. And then more pictures of Buzz and Henry taking baseball gear out of the trunk I had seen in earlier pictures and then one of them wearing their uniforms. That one looked like it had been taken at a ballpark.

I turned back to the diary, eager to see what Maude wrote next.

*April 5, 1916*

*Dear Diary,*

*It's almost my birthday. I'll be eleven. Still not a teenager, Mom says.*

*Ethel will come spend the night and Mom agreed to let us go to a movie in town. Helen has a boyfriend now, so we won't sit with her. I don't know what's playing, but it doesn't matter. It's fun just to be there and to get popcorn and a Coca-Cola. Mom doesn't know about the Coca-Cola part. She wouldn't like that.*

*The boys came home from Florida and brought us lots of presents. They even brought a tiny palm tree to Mom. She said it would freeze if she planted it outside, so she plans to put it in a pot and keep it on the porch in the summer and bring it inside in the winter. Dad rolled his eyes at that, but I guess we'll see if she can keep it alive.*

*Henry brought me a big towel for when Ethel and I go swimming and some coconut candy. Buzz even brought me a present. A necklace that says "St. Augustine, Florida." I can't believe he thought of me. Helen would be so jealous. If I ever start talking to her again, I'll make sure to tell her. Dad got an ashtray and a little glass they called a "shot" glass. They said it came from the Alligator Farm. Buzz tried to tell us about it, but I still can't figure out why anybody would want to farm alligators. He said that's just the name and the alligators simply live there so people can see them up close. They even have a snow white one, he told us. Not sure I believe that, though. Buzz likes to tease me sometimes.*

*They stayed for a few days then emptied the trunk in the barn again and got on the bus for Philadelphia. We took them into town to see them off. Mom always turns her head so she won't see the poster on the door of the military office. It makes her nervous. And she still cries when the boys leave. Dad pats her shoulder.*

*I hope we can go see a game again this summer, but Dad hasn't made any promises. The crops didn't do well over the winter, he said, so money might be a little tight. Sometimes I get tired of money always being tight.*

*I'll write more later.*

*Your friend, Maude*

## April 10, 1916

SPRING TRAINING CERTAINLY HELPED BUT THE TEAM included a lot of new players and they hadn't yet learned to work together. Frustration mounted among them when all of the away games at the beginning of the season ended in a loss.

Buzz had pitched two of them, one against the Boston Red Sox and the most recent game against the New York Yankees. But even with his left-handed miracle pitches, the team still lost. Only by one run for each game, but they still counted as losses. Every night, Henry talked to him, calming his fears about being let go.

"Nobody else is winning, either, Buzz," he said. "And they all have a lot more experience than you do." Then he made Buzz practice breathing exercises to keep his nerves under control. It worked. For a while anyway, until something else happened that sent Buzz into another spiral.

His next game was on May 6 against the Washington Senators. Before the game, Coach Mack sat with him to talk strategy and Buzz told Henry later that his confidence soared after that talk. The coach suggested, Buzz said, that in addition to his fastball, which practically no batter could hit, he might add a few curveballs, something he focused on during Spring Training. It worked perfectly and Buzz's pitches resulted in only four hits for the Senators with a final score of four-to-one runs, in favor of the Athletics.

After the win, only the third one in the ten games of the season, the team scooped Buzz up and carried him out on their shoulders.

He accepted the many invitations of his teammates and he and Henry joined the others at a bar and grill that served alcohol. "Hey, Buzz," Rube Oldring said, a hand on his back, "you did such a great job today, I'd like to buy you a beer."

The smile left Buzz's face. "No," he said quietly. "But thanks."

"Come on," a couple of the other players said. "Hey, bartender," they continued. "Bring this man a beer. He won the game for us today."

Buzz rose. "No," he said with more force. His features were pinched and Henry could tell his emotions bordered on anger.

"He doesn't drink, fellas," Henry said. "But I'll take one." He picked up the beer and followed Buzz to his table, then dropped off the beer to one of his teammates and slumped into a chair. "They were just trying to be nice." Henry said. "To include you. And to thank you for the win."

Buzz looked up. "I know," he said. "And I'm sorry if I acted like an ass. But Henry, you're the only one in the world who truly understands. If I ever took a drink, I'd be afraid I couldn't stop. Just like my parents. And the thought of that makes me crazy." Buzz looked up and his eyes bore into Henry's. "So I never will."

# CHAPTER
# TWENTY-ONE

**SUZANNE**
**2015**

The next few pictures depicted family scenes around the farm until I found one that showed Maude and her parents dressed in slightly better clothes. Maude's dark hair was gathered into a large bow at her neck and hung down her back. Her dad sported an old-fashioned summer straw hat, perched at a jaunty angle.

I laughed and then said out loud, "It wasn't old-fashioned then, dumbass. We're still in 1916 here."

They posed stiffly in front of a shiny car, impossible to tell the color in the black-and-white photo, but the logo on its hood was clear. Cadillac. A big one. The whole family smiled.

The next few pictures showed the three of them with Buzz and Henry in their baseball uniforms. *So they obviously went to another game. Probably in Philadelphia.*

I read the first few lines of the next diary entry and confirmed that the game they attended did take place in Philadelphia.

*May 29, 1916*

*Dear Diary,*

*It's Maude.*

*Boy, do I have news for you! It's the best!*

*Mom and Dad kept me out of school the end of last week and the first couple of days this week so we can go to another baseball game in Philadelphia. And this one's against the Yankees! Can you believe it? Mr. Mack will be sending his car again to pick us up first thing in the morning. We're pretty sure Buzz will pitch and Henry will catch. As long as they keep playing well.*

*I spent the first part of the week helping to get the fields in good shape so we would have everything done for tomorrow. We put in really long days, but it was worth it.*

*And I'm so excited I can hardly sleep. But I'm gonna try.*

*I'll tell you all about it when we get back.*

*Good night,*

*Your friend, Maude*

---

**May 30, 1916**

THE BREWER FAMILY PACKED UP THEIR FARM WAGON AND drove the mules into town, leaving them for the day with the local livery depot.

Maude spotted Mr. Mack's driver without even noticing that he held the sign with their names. Truth be told, she spotted his car first and her fingers ached to again touch the soft leather seats of the Cadillac's interior. She reached it and once more ran her hand along the entire length of its sage green beauty and decided that the King of England himself couldn't possibly have traveled in greater luxury. Happiness surged through her heart for the entire hour of their trip.

When the driver turned onto Lehigh Avenue the background noise level grew. And Maude's excitement along with it. By the time they reached the end of that block and the entrance to Shibe Stadium, even Maude's mother couldn't help but smile.

"This must be what rich people experience," Florence said. "Frank, look at how folks are craning their necks to see who emerges from this beautiful car. I'm sure we're disappointments to them, but today, I don't care. Today, I feel rich."

He leaned down and kissed her cheek. "And well you should, Mrs. Brewer. Your boys could be the stars of the game."

One of Mr. Mack's representatives met them as before and escorted them to the same box they'd occupied the previous year. "Now Maude," her mother said, "please control yourself with all this rich food. We don't want you throwing up all the way home."

Her mouth full of popcorn, Maude nodded. "I'll be careful," she said. She reached for her first hot dog.

Mr. Mack, complete in his regular attire of high-collar shirt, tie and ascot scarf, topped with a boater hat, rather than a regular baseball uniform, showed up within ten minutes to welcome them.

"Mr. Mack," Frank said. He pumped the taller man's hand. "I don't know why you're showing us so much generosity, but please know we are extremely grateful. I doubt we'd be able to watch our boys play if it weren't for you."

"I'm happy to do it," he answered. "The day I first met you I told you I wanted new blood on our team and your boys have filled that bill."

"Well, they sure are happy to be playing for you," Frank said. "And of course, seeing them so happy makes us happy as well."

"Since they're so green to the game," Mr. Mack said, "I'm sure you understand that I pay them less than players who've been on the team for years, so I'm happy to shower some of that extra to bring their family here to watch them. They're good boys, Mr. Brewer, and they give me what I seek in ball players."

"I remember what you told me," Frank said. "That you 'value intelligence and integrity as much as athleticism.' And you're right, I'm sure you've gotten that from Buzz and Henry."

Connie Mack smiled at him, tipped his hat to both Florence and Maude, and left.

"They call him the 'Tall Tactician,'" Frank said to Maude, "because he strategizes his approach to the game through getting players with what he calls 'baseball smarts.' Did you know that?"

Maude nodded, reaching for her third chocolate chip cookie.

The announcer came on the loudspeaker and introduced the players. When Buzz was announced as the pitcher and Henry as the catcher, Frank and Florence cheered from the box. Maude watched the boys as the announcer said their names and she was certain they both looked up at the box and smiled at them. Again, her heart filled that they went after a dream and achieved it. She didn't know anyone else from their small town who had done that. And it gave her hope for her own future.

The first two innings came and went with no score on either side. Buzz even retired two batters with only three pitches each.

"Our boys are doing great, Mother," Frank said, giving her arm a squeeze. "Buzz is throwing mostly fastballs. Those Yankees just can't hit them."

Maude understood that Frank talked mostly to himself because Florence, like Maude, couldn't tell the difference between a fastball and anything else Buzz might have thrown. But it seemed to make him happy to talk about it, so they both presented interested expressions and let him continue.

"He still doesn't have his knuckleball perfected," Frank said. He got up and paced the box. "Come on, Buzz. Go back to your fastball." But Yankees' center fielder Fritz Maisel bunted and the A's Stuffy McInnis missed the ball at first base. "Not good, not good," Frank said.

"I'm sure it will be all right," Florence said.

"You're right, Mother."

Even though Buzz retired the rest of the batters in that inning, the Athletics failed to score and at the end of six innings, the score remained zero-to-zero. Henry went out to the mound to talk to Buzz and the first and third basemen joined them. From their distance, it was impossible to hear what was said, but Maude saw a lot of head shaking and pointing going on. Finally, Henry patted Buzz's shoulder and the players returned to their positions. Maude watched Connie Mack stand outside the dugout.

"Oh no," Frank said. "I hope he doesn't take Buzz out."

"Why didn't Coach Mack go out on the field with the players?" Maude asked.

"He's not allowed out there because he refuses to wear a uniform," Frank said. He chuckled. "I really think his players admire him for his conviction. The boys told me they all really like him."

In the seventh inning, Buzz went back to his fastball and no runs scored. The Athletics came to the plate with the top of their line-up and after three batters the bases were loaded, with left fielder Oldring up next. When his bat made contact with a fat pitch, he reached first base and Witt, the shortstop, scored. The hometown crowd jumped to its feet and Frank danced Florence around the box with the A's leading at one-to-zero.

"See?" Florence said. "I told you it was nothing to worry about."

Frank kissed her and Maude joined him at the open area of the box. But the rest of the batters that inning either struck out or popped up and the inning ended with three runners on base.

"I can't believe we wasted that chance to score more runs," Frank said, shaking his head.

Regardless, the Athletics were energized. Even Maude could tell from the way they ran out onto the field and slapped each other's backs. Buzz did his job and retired all the batters so after the top of the eighth inning, the score remained one-to-zero in favor of the Athletics.

"Look, Mother," Frank said. "It's Buzz's turn to bat."

"He's not very good, is he?" Maude asked.

"Pitchers seldom are," Frank said, studying the field.

The Yankees' Ray Keating sent a beautiful pitch right over the plate and the umpire called a strike. Buzz let the next two pitches sail past him without even lifting his bat.

"He's suckering the pitcher in," Frank said. "Come on, Buzz. Hit one of these next ones."

Another pitch sailed past Buzz's knees but again, the umpire called it a strike.

"C'mon, Ump!" Frank yelled, along with more than half the crowd.

The count was two and two when the pitcher wound up and let another one fly. At the very last second, Buzz moved his bat and laid down a perfect bunt. The ball rolled halfway between the pitcher and the catcher toward the third base line and Buzz took off like a shot for first base.

Again, the crowd rose, and the noise level along with them. When the first base umpire called Buzz safe, the cheers went on for minutes.

Henry came to the plate. Even Florence rose and joined Frank and Maude at the open box window. "Oh, Frank," she said. "He has to hit it. He has to."

They couldn't see Henry's face, but from his years of working with the boys, Frank knew it was a study in concentration, that he stared the pitcher down. Keating threw two trash pitches and almost got Henry to swing on the second. But he held firm. Keating wound up again and Henry swung. The crack of the ball hitting the bat rang through the stadium and reached the ears of his family in the box above. Even Florence jumped up and down as the ball sailed over the center field fence for a home run. Buzz scored and waited for Henry as he jogged around the field. By then, the whole team joined him and they cheered Henry on and then slapped him on the back when he crossed home plate.

The Yankees' coach joined the pitcher and catcher on the mound and when the coach put his hand on Keating's shoulder, the crowd knew he was about to be relieved by a new pitcher. As Keating left the mound to return to the dugout, the Yankees' fans stood and cheered. He had done a good job for most of the game. But everybody knew it was all about winning.

Urban Shocker pitched the rest of that inning but the Athletics failed to get any additional hits with one strike-out and two pop-ups to the infield before the inning ended.

The score was three-to-zero, in favor of the Athletics.

With only one inning left.

If the Yankees didn't score, the A's would win the game.

The A's took the field and Buzz did a couple of warm-up pitches to Henry. Yankees' first baseman, Wally Pipp, approached the plate.

"Come on, Buzz," Frank said under his breath. "Come on."

Buzz's first pitch dropped in perfectly and the umpire called a strike. Buzz wound up and delivered his second pitch, his curveball. Another strike. At his third pitch, he tried his knuckleball again. Pipp foul tipped it. Buzz wound up once more and Pipp popped it up to the shortstop. One out and Roger Peckinpaugh came up to bat. He connected with the pitch and sent it to right field, then made it all the way to second.

The Yankees' right fielder, Joe Gedeon, swaggered to home plate and stared Buzz down. After two pitches, his bat smacked the ball high, right into the glove of the Athletic's center fielder. Athletics' fans went wild.

Henry assumed his position. Coach Mack had trained him to place himself directly behind the plate—a position that was still fairly new since Mack had invented it himself when he was a catcher in his early career.

Two outs and one man on second. Next up was the center fielder. Maude watched as Buzz shook his head over and over at the pitches Henry suggested. When he finally nodded, Maisel's bat rested on his shoulder and Buzz turned his right side toward him with his hands together in the air. Buzz arranged his fingers around the ball. Most of the fans had no idea of the process Buzz went through, but Maude and Frank both knew that at that point, Buzz visualized the trajectory of the ball as it left his hand and flew over the plate. He turned and let it fly. Maisel's bat connected with the knuckleball but it popped up to the infield. Really high. Buzz watched it come down and stood under it. The ball fell securely into Buzz's mitt with Henry standing right beside him for backup.

The game was over.

The Athletics had won. One of their few winning games of the season. And the victory went to Buzz.

The three Brewers jumped up and down in the box. "Quick," Florence said. "Let's get on that infernal elevator thing and get down to the field to hug our boys."

By the time they got to the dugout, Buzz rode his teammates' shoulders. Maude had never seen his smile so huge. When his teammates allowed him to touch ground again, Frank and Florence were there to hug both him and Henry. While her parents talked to Henry, Buzz turned to Maude and squeezed her in a bear hug.

"Great job," she said.

"I did it, Maudie. I did it," he said to her.

His eyes actually teared and Maude's heart went out to him. She wondered if he thought the same thing she did ... that his parents really missed out on a great part of his life. But neither of them mentioned it. Then the rest of the team intruded and the moment evaporated.

Coach Mack put his hand on Buzz's shoulder. "Perfect job, Ryan," he said. "You'll have more opportunities this season. And for the 1917 season, you'll be one of our starting pitchers."

Maude knew those were the words Buzz had wanted to hear his entire life.

# CHAPTER
# TWENTY-TWO

MARTHE
**Battle of the Somme**
**July 1916**

I t had all been in vain.

Schedules changed and the Kaiser never made it to Roulers.

While Marthe was disappointed that her information hadn't been useful, she rejoiced that she hadn't compromised herself any further with Colonel Unger.

Spring transformed into summer and Marthe did what she could with the information she found in her midst. For weeks, rumors flew about a large German offensive planned for somewhere in France along the eighteen kilometers of trenches that stretched from the English Channel to Switzerland. But the information either wasn't clear or wasn't believable. And details shifted daily. She delivered a couple of messages but again, nothing happened and she feared she would lose her credibility with her network.

In the early days of July, an ambulance delivered a number of wounded soldiers from a battle in the Somme region of France, almost two hundred kilometers distant. The ambulance driver stood at the door of the hospital, appearing weary and haggard. Marthe overheard his conversation with Sister Margarete.

"Can you take wounded, sister?" the driver asked.

"Of course," Sister Margarete said. "That's what we're here for."

Relief filled his face. "Thank you. I've been to four hospitals so far but none of them can handle any more. You need to know, we have a lot of prisoners of war to be treated too."

"They are welcome," she answered, holding the door open wide. "We are here for all God's children. But what's happened? Why are so many hospitals full?"

"You haven't heard?" He wheeled his first patient down the hallway where he and the sister met Marthe.

"Heard what?" Marthe said. "How many soldiers do you have?"

"Close to a dozen," he answered. "Many of their injuries are several days old. I couldn't find hospitals for them."

Marthe did a quick examination of the soldier on the gurney then led the way to a large room with freshly made cots. "Bring him in here," she said. "I'll accompany you to your ambulance and look at the rest."

"You still haven't told us what's happened," Sister Margarete prompted.

"Big battle near the Somme," he said on his way out the door.

"But that's almost two hundred kilometers from here," Sister Margarete said. "Oh these poor men, waiting so long for treatment." She half ran with the driver and Marthe.

"Okay, men," the ambulance driver called, "they can take them here. Let's get them unloaded."

Marthe stood beside the driver and inspected each man unloaded from the ambulance.

"Take this one to the room with the other man," she said to the driver. "This man ... and this one ... need to go immediately to the surgery. Follow Sister Margarete." She continued issuing orders until all of the men, including two British soldiers and one from Ireland, were unloaded and settled. The other nuns worked on them, cleaning them up and giving them enough medicine to make them comfortable. Marthe joined Sister Margarete at the surgery door.

"What time is the doctor coming?" Marthe asked. "We need to get these two men prepped."

"Any time now," Sister Margarete answered.

They scrubbed, donned their operating gowns, and wheeled the first patient in.

"This man can't wait," Marthe said. "But it looks like he doesn't need any amputations, just clean-up and stitches." She removed his uniform coat, shredded beyond repair. "Whew," she added, "lots of stitches."

The two women got to work on the wounded soldier, beginning with a few drops of chloroform on a cloth over his nose. After a minute or two, he drifted off and Marthe made the decision to begin stitching without ether. Their supply ran dangerously low and they weren't expecting any more until later in the week.

"The stomach wound is the most serious," Marthe said. "Let's work on that one first and then do the head wound." They worked methodically for the next half hour until the doctor stuck his head in.

"Doctor," Marthe said, "please confirm my diagnosis." She stepped back and let him examine the patient.

"Good work, Nurse. Fine stitches. I would do the head wound next, then on to the legs and arms."

"*Danke, Oberartz*," she said. "That was my thought as well."

The doctor shook his head. "I heard that battle was so intense, I'm surprised any of these men are still alive. You're working on the Germans first, right?"

"*Ja*, Herr Doctor," Sister Margarete answered. "We understand there are some British soldiers and one from Ireland."

"They can wait. Germans first." Marthe was surprised to hear the doctor's statement. Normally, he didn't let politics decide the treatment. He must have been given orders, she thought.

Marthe finished with the soldier in front of her while Sister Margarete went to help the doctor. Then Marthe returned to the room where the rest of the soldiers waited. She spoke with the nun in charge.

"You may want to take this one next, Nurse Marthe," the sister said. "His wounds are deep and he is in a lot of pain."

"I'm sorry, sister," she said, "but I can't. He's British. I need to finish with the German soldiers first. Direct order from the *Oberartz*."

The sister's mouth formed a thin line that radiated disapproval. Marthe felt the same way, preferring to work on the men based on the severity of their wounds, but she couldn't disobey a direct order.

More ambulances arrived almost hourly with soldiers who'd been wounded two to three days earlier. As the ambulances progressed into the afternoon and evening, a greater percentage of them consisted of prisoners, primarily British, with an increasing number of French soldiers as well. Marthe could hardly imagine how great the numbers of wounded soldiers from other countries must have been for so many of them to end up in their midst such a distance from the battle.

Marthe, the doctor, and the nuns worked through the rest of the day and into the night before Marthe learned any details of the battle. Despite their injuries, the spirits of the German troops remained high while the few soldiers from other countries, who were now prisoners, wore defeat on their shoulders. The prisoners weren't treated until well after midnight and by then, many of the newest arrivals had died.

"They thought they could get the better o' us," one of the German soldiers smirked to his comrade. "What with their week-long mortars ahead o' time." They laughed together.

"Right," the other one said. "But we showed 'em, eh?" A spasm of coughing seized him.

Marthe checked their vitals as they joked back and forth. "How long did you have to wait after your injury?" Marthe asked the one who had spoken first. "And how does your arm feel now that we've set it?"

"Oh, only two days, Nurse." He lifted his arm out of the sling that enveloped it and smiled at her. "Feels good to have it still—hurt ever' time I moved it before. But that was nothing," he continued. "Schmidt, here, he was stuck out in the mud for most a' day." The man named Schmidt coughed again, this time bringing the top half of his body off the bed.

"Sounds awful," Marthe said.

"*Ja*. It was. And we was on the good side of it."

"What do you mean?"

"Them British dogs bombed our side for one solid week before they attacked us. But it didn't bother us none. Our trenches had already been dug extra deep and the barbed wire strung double and triple, even some of it in 'No Man's Land,' so we just burrowed down like bunnies and spent most of our time drinking. When we wasn't on guard duty," he finished with a laugh.

"'No Man's Land?'" The term was new to Marthe.

"That's what we call the ground between our trenches and theirs."

"So you're actually close to the opposing troops when you're shooting?"

He nodded. "Sometimes ten to twenty kilometers is between us. But in other places," he continued, "in most places, actually, now that we've strung so much more barbed wire coils, the distance between the trenches is no more than half a kilometer."

Marthe remembered how much damage barbed wire did to the bodies that got stuck in it—the ones she spent hours stitching back together—and she shuddered.

"That's still close enough to do a lot of damage to each other," Marthe said. "How's your pain level?" She spoke to the quieter soldier, the one who still coughed.

"Not bad, Nurse. I can make it. For a while, anyway."

She patted the back of his hand and moved to the next couple of soldiers.

By the time she had worked her way back to checking on the prisoners, another day had passed. They occupied their own room and as soon as she entered, moans from their battered throats assaulted her.

The nun on duty spoke to her immediately. "Nurse Marthe," she said, "these men are in pain. They need additional medicine, but the doctor—"

Marthe laid her hand on the nun's arm. "Don't worry, sister, I'll take care of it. What do you need?"

Marthe went to the supply room and returned with vials and syringes for the nun. Together, they administered pain medicines to the wounded soldiers, most trying to show bravery, some simply reduced to constant tears.

"Where does it hurt, soldier," she asked one man. She saw from his papers he was a lieutenant. "How can I help you?"

"You mean besides praying for me?" He tried to sit up and give her a smile, then winced, his body jolting back to its original position.

Sweat formed on his forehead. He closed his eyes and breathed deeply.

Marthe's hand found his pulse, then rested against his cheek. "You're very warm," she said. "Can you tell me where it hurts?" A fever could indicate infection and she worried they may not have found all the shrapnel. "May I check your bandage?"

With difficulty, he half rolled and she lifted his shirt. Blood soaked his bandage. "Sister," she said quietly, "will you bring me some gauze?" Together they cut the old bandage off and Marthe inspected the stitches. Two of them had pulled loose and blood oozed in the open space. The nun brought the emergency kit and Marthe numbed the soldier's wound with cocaine, then replaced the stitches and rebandaged him, making certain to wrap it tight enough to stop the blood from flowing but not so tight he would have difficulty breathing. He took another deep breath, then leaned back against his pillows, his eyes still closed.

"Is that better, soldier?" she asked.

He nodded. She put a hand on his shoulder. "Are you more comfortable now?" Again, he nodded. "And about praying for you … of course I will, but you'd be better off to have the sister, here, pray for you. Her channel is more direct than mine." She smiled at him. "I will come back and see you tomorrow … Lieutenant Fletcher," she said, looking at his chart. "Lowell, isn't it?" Another nod. "And you're in the British Army, is that correct?" He confirmed everything. That was good. His head bore a bandage, but Marthe could tell his brain hadn't been damaged.

"And now a prisoner for the German Army," he added, never opening his eyes.

"Let's just hope the war ends soon. If that happens," Marthe said, "they will probably just send you home." He cracked his eyes open and she smiled. He attempted to smile back. And failed.

Marthe and the sister visited every one of the captured soldiers and did their best to make them comfortable. Little by little, additional details trickled out, and Marthe met the lieutenant's aide, Monroe McCartney, who told her he overheard their captain tell the lieutenant that the British Army suffered its greatest one-day loss on the first day of the battle of the Somme, July 1, 1916.

"It were totally unexpected," the aide said, "since old man Haig had the artillery working overtime to bomb the bloody Boches right in their trenches. Ow. That smarts." Marthe finished cleaning his arm wound and tied the bandage. "He told our officers the Germans would mostly be killed afore we even got 'ere. But he hadn't figured on them arseholes burrowing theyselves deep underground like bloody moles. And he hadn't figured on all that extra bobbed wire, neither."

"Yes," Marthe said. "I heard about that from some of the German soldiers."

The aide snorted. "Bloody Boches."

"So you thought you were approaching an area cleared of German troops, when, they were actually intact and waiting for you, right?"

"That's right, miss. And them with machine guns just waiting for us to show our heads above the trenches. It were slaughter, miss. That's what it were."

"I also heard the German soldiers say your trenches were not far apart. Is that true?"

"Yes, miss. Where we was, the space between us stretched only a kilometer."

"Were you able to hit any of them from that distance?"

"Not us, miss. But the Boches' damned machine guns reached our trench easy. I was told those things could reach more than twice that distance. All the way across 'No Man's Land.' And then some. Many men didn't even make it over the top ... they was cut down like weeds."

"And a lot of them landed here," Marthe said.

"That's right, miss." He moved his arm and inspected it. "Thank you for the bandage."

She smiled at him, then continued her rounds.

She entered the hallway just as the front door opened. "Wounded." She hurried toward them and several of the nuns joined her.

"How many do you have, driver?" Marthe asked.

"Six."

"I'll come with you to see the extent of their injuries." She joined the driver at the back of the ambulance. Before he opened the door, he glanced around and looked her in the eye. "I have a message for Sophia, Nurse. Is she here?" He raised his lapel to reveal two white metal safety pins arranged diagonally.

Fear flew into Marthe's lungs. She swallowed hard to control her voice.

"I can get a message to her." Marthe said. "What is it?"

"Please tell her to beware. The Germans know there are spies here, so they've launched a huge counter-espionage measure."

Marthe's heart thumped, but her expression remained neutral. "I see," she said. "Is there anything else she needs to know?"

"No. But please make certain she gets the message right away."

# CHAPTER
# TWENTY-THREE

**MARTHE**
**September 1916**

Marthe's every step following the message from the ambulance driver brought new fears. Shadows loomed dark with menace so Marthe avoided side streets and conversations with anyone new. Her fixed expressions revealed no emotion and her eyes focused straight in front of her. The nuns, except for Sister Margarete, skittered away when they saw her coming.

"Is something on your mind, daughter?" Sister Margarete asked. "You have been very quiet this past week."

"I'm just trying to do my job, sister," she answered. "I don't mean to worry you."

Sister Margarete touched Marthe's arm. "No, child, you haven't. But I hope you know that if anything were on your mind, you could come to me. You do know that, don't you?"

"Yes, sister. I do. Thank you."

Marthe's head dipped in a quick nod and she left the room to check on the previous day's surgery patients. When she finished making the rounds of the German soldiers, she checked the men in the prisoners' room.

"Lieutenant," she said, her hand on the forehead of the British soldier she met the day before. "Are you feeling better today?" He nodded. "Good," she said. "Your fever is gone, so that's a good sign. Have you been able to eat anything?"

He tried to smile and almost made it. "Yes. What there was of it. I probably got a larger portion than my men, but it was still meager at best."

"I know," she said. "I wish I could make it better, but that part is beyond my control. If I find a way to help, I will."

Her mind spun with ideas to get a larger food allotment to the hospital. But caution had to rule her actions. Even so simple an act could be interpreted by the Berlin Vampires as treason. The last thing she wanted was to knowingly open herself up to inspection.

The remainder of her day was filled with surgeries from a new ambulance delivery, and dark surrounded her as she dragged her tired body to the Taverne. Her feet protested every step and she didn't ever remember being so tired. She cut through a different part of the city, one she knew as a shortcut, hoping to remain upright until she reached her room.

One foot down, then the other until she simply could no longer force them to move. The sidewalk beckoned and she let herself slip down, arranging her back against an unlit streetlamp swallowed in shadows only blocks from the Taverne.

She dozed off, but jolted awake as footsteps approached, accompanied by male voices. Her initial heart spike calmed when she recognized them—the Town-Kommandant and his right-hand man, Hirsch. Probably on their way to the Taverne for dinner. Their footsteps drew close and then passed beside her resting place. They had no idea, she could tell, that anyone could hear them, so their voices rang out, unguarded.

"It's the perfect place," Hirsch said.

"But we normally billet our regiments in the local houses, three or four at a time. It's safer that way."

"True," Hirsch said, "but this is an unusually large group, preparing for the big push to finally take over France. We could assemble them here and let the bulk of them stay in the abandoned factory at the edge of town. Even the people of Roulers wouldn't see how many soldiers had arrived, awaiting final orders. That would certainly cut down on the possibility of word leaking out to any of our spies."

"I see your point," the Town-Kommandant replied. "A definite advantage."

"If you agree, I will arrange it tomorrow. We can have them settled by tomorrow night."

"Yes, Hirsch. Go ahead. How many did you say we can accommodate there?"

"Between three and four hundred."

"*Gut.* Let me know when it is done."

"Yes sir."

They went on to discuss other subjects and Marthe listened until their voices drifted off, too faint to hear.

As if by magic, her fatigue disappeared but she stayed down until she determined that no other Germans had followed to join them at the Taverne.

Her plan fell quickly into place. At the Taverne, she would briefly visit with the Town-Kommandant and Hirsch to ensure they suspected nothing. If they did, their faces would reveal everything. And if, as she expected, they had no idea she had overhead their plans to house the large group of German soldiers in the old factory, she would retire to her room and encode her message for Number Seventy-two.

She stood. Her tired feet willingly carried her the rest of the way.

---

AFTER DRINKING A GLASS OF SCHNAPPS WITH THE TWO men and three of their comrades, she answered their questions about the hospital and told them about the large influx of British soldiers. She even related a benign fact or two she had gained from the lieutenant's aide. Satisfied that the highest-ranking men had no idea that their plan had been overheard, she returned to her room and lit a candle well away from the window to code her message.

She lay down to rest. Gradually, the sound of voices from the dining room below died down and she checked her bedside clock. Almost midnight. She rose in her stockinged feet, secured the coded message within the braids on top of her head and wrapped a dark shawl around her shoulders. With her shoes in her hand, she tip-toed down the back stairs that emptied into the darkened kitchen. Standing perfectly still, she listened for any sound, then hearing none, quietly slipped into the blackness of night through the back door.

At the bottom of the back steps, she stepped into her shoes, then stopped again to let her eyes totally adjust to her surroundings. She took one tentative step, then another until she reached the edge of the yard and slipped noiselessly into the street. She picked her way along a different route that bordered a park with plenty of places to hide if she were followed.

Winding first one way and then another, her path took her beyond her destination, then caused her to double back to ensure she wasn't followed. In total darkness, she turned into the final street, her target in sight. Again, she hesitated, listening for footsteps.

But this time, she heard them.

Heavy, deliberate footsteps. She had already entered the narrow street that dead-ended only twenty meters or so from where she stood. She was trapped.

Regardless, she rushed past her target window all the way to the back wall and threw herself behind some overgrown bushes, tucking her skirt tightly around her. The night swallowed her but she could see the rest of the alley clearly. She held her breath and watched.

A dark figure entered the street and seemed to stare into her hiding place. She shrank back. But the footsteps continued slowly to the window where Marthe delivered her messages and then tapped on the window in the exact sequence Marthe used.

She breathed a small sigh of relief. *Oh. Another agent.*

Even so, she figured, since they were not supposed to know each other, she would stay put until the message had been delivered and the messenger gone ... safer that way.

The window opened and a white hand appeared.

The shrouded figure lifted an arm and a red glow burst from the end of it. Along with two loud pops. Then the figure climbed into the window and Marthe heard a stifled scream and a muffled pop before the dark figure climbed back out and ran into the larger street.

Seconds passed before Marthe admitted to herself what had happened.

*Oh my God. He killed Number Seventy-two.*

*And would have killed me if I hadn't stayed hidden.*

Shuddering violently, Marthe pushed her back into the side of the building, taking deep soundless breaths and trying to calm herself. Nothing worked. She remained in place for fifteen or more minutes until her courage returned and she could make herself move. Pure adrenaline carried her back to the Taverne by a circuitous route, much of the time letting her feet carry her without help from her brain. Breaths left her in short little pants, like a dog left too long in the summer sun.

She reached the back door of the Taverne and almost cried out with relief. Her earlier exhaustion returned and she wanted nothing more than to drop down and sleep on the spot. But again, she forced herself up the few steps and through the door leading to the kitchen, then poured herself a glass of water. When she reached her small bed, she fell on it without removing her clothes and slept immediately.

⎯⎯◦⟐◦⎯⎯

SHE WOKE WITH A START BEFORE DAWN.

Pain rushed into her head as she remembered that her network contact had been killed right before her eyes. Her breath quickened and she sat up, then leaned over and vomited into her basin. When she finished, she reached into her hair to make certain her message remained and hadn't fallen out along the way. She didn't think her handwriting could be identified by her coded letters, but she didn't want to take that chance.

She sat on the side of her bed and her head fell into her hands, her breathing out of control. Pushing herself up on shaky legs, she paced and forced deep breaths down her throat. She needed to calm down. And come up with an alternate plan.

The first ray of sun peeked through the trees and she stood at her tiny window and studied the shadowy pattern. Daylight always made her feel better.

A truth popped into her head. Since Number Seventy-two was killed outright, that actually benefitted the network. It was horrible, of course, but at least the agent wasn't tortured, so other operatives' names didn't escape. *Her* name hadn't been reported. She was probably safe.

Another reality presented itself. She had to act as if she were innocent. No, she had to make everyone *believe* she was innocent.

She had no other choice.

With difficulty, she pulled herself together, washed directly from the pitcher without using the basin, dressed and fixed her hair carefully, then put her coded message back among her braids. She would go down to breakfast as if it were any other morning and leave early for the hospital. A germ of a plan took shape and, she thought, if luck were with her, she would meet the street sweeper and solicit his help.

She avoided Herr Breit's eyes, wolfed down a piece of bread, and left by the front door.

Several blocks sped by under her feet and she rounded the corner where she normally saw the street sweeper. As she expected, he was there.

But his hands strained behind his back, bound with rope by one of Hirsch's *gendarmes*. Marthe pretended to ignore them but saw everything. The policeman beat the street sweeper to his knees, hitting his head time and again.

She hid her distress and hurried along her path, masking her heartbreak, her face a blank.

She needed to figure out what to do next.

# CHAPTER
# TWENTY-FOUR

**MARTHE**
**September 1916**

Marthe arrived at the hospital at the same instant an ambulance pulled up to the door. She rushed over to see how she could help and recognized the driver as the same one who had warned her the previous day. He saw her and relief showed plainly on his face.

They both glanced around to see they were alone.

"How many wounded?" she asked.

"Four," he said. He leaned over to hand her the customary papers. "I heard about what happened last night," he whispered. "I feared it was you."

"No," she whispered back. "But I hid nearby when it happened. Another source gone this morning. I am without contacts and I have a report to send. Very important."

"Let's take the first three in. Then accompany me back out here for the fourth where we will have to climb into the ambulance to retrieve him. You can give me your message once we're hidden from view."

She nodded and they got to work.

They carried the first stretcher into the hospital and Marthe gave instructions for him.

Then they carried in the second and the third. Luckily, the men were not critically wounded, so they could wait briefly while Marthe helped the driver.

"Nurse Marthe," one of the nuns said. "I can help the driver if you want to get started on these patients."

"Thank you, but not necessary," Marthe told her. "If you will begin cleaning the wounds of the men we've just brought in, I will help the driver with the last soldier."

Marthe and the driver returned to the ambulance. The wounded man's eyes were closed and Marthe laid a hand on his chest. "Soldier," she said, "can you tell me where it hurts?" The man's head moved but he didn't answer, his breathing shallow. "I think he has passed out," she said. She positioned herself behind the man's head so he couldn't see anything if he happened to wake and plucked the tightly rolled paper from her hair. The driver removed a small capsule from inside his mouth and wedged the paper into it.

"I will take care of this," he told her. "Thank you."

Without a word, she picked up her end of the stretcher and together they carried the last wounded man into the hospital. Marthe gave instructions, rolled up her sleeves and the driver returned to his ambulance. Her message delivered, she engaged in normal duties for her day and forced her mind away from the events of the previous night.

Darkness surrounded her when she left the hospital to return to the Taverne. Worry filled her head and despair settled into her heart. She hoped the ambulance driver could deliver her message in time to take advantage of the massed troops on the edge of town. The more Germans eliminated, she thought, the greater the possibility this wretched war could end.

As soon as her thought took shape, guilt edged its way into her brain. She hated the thought of killing so many people ... people whose loved ones would then share the same devastation she had borne when her family was snatched from her. But that was her job. She had agreed to that when she became a spy.

She opened the door to the Taverne to be hailed by Hirsch, the German officer who had stopped her to inspect her tray months earlier. His smile puzzled her and she returned it warily.

"*Fräulein*," he called. "Please join me."

That was the last thing she wanted to do. Suffering from too little sleep the previous night, she had hoped to grab a snack and head straight to her room and fall into bed. She also worried that he suspected her, especially after the street sweeper had been apprehended that morning.

But she dared not refuse him. She approached his table and dipped into a small curtsy.

"*Ja,* Herr Hirsch," she said. "Can I get something for you?"

"Your company is what I seek."

Resigned, she dropped into a chair across from him at the small table. Herr Breit approached them. "Herr Hirsch," he said, "would you like something to drink?"

"*Ja.* I will have *bier.* And a glass for *Fräulein* Peeters as well."

Herr Breit disappeared into the kitchen and Marthe sat still, waiting for Herr Hirsch to speak. His eyes intense, they studied her face, revealing nothing of his thoughts. Her mind worked desperately, thinking of and then abandoning, one notion after another. The one that refused to leave her was that the street sweeper, under torture, had given him her name. She focused on keeping her face neutral and embraced her resolution from that morning to act in a manner that encouraged everyone to believe her innocence.

Her fingernails dug into her palms; her nerves were stretched taut.

"Your name came up this morning," he said after what seemed like an eternity.

And there they were. The words she had feared.

Her vision blurred and his voice receded, then registered as only fuzzy roars in her ears.

"Oh?" she squeaked out. She knew she should say more, but her mouth refused to work.

He smiled. "*Ja,*" he continued, "in my conversation with the Town-Kommandant."

Her head spun.

She feared she would pass out.

Herr Breit slid a glass in front of her and then delivered one to Herr Hirsch. "Can I get you some dinner?" he asked.

Herr Hirsch waved him away, his eyes never leaving Marthe's.

She picked up her glass and drank deeply, grateful for the moisture that coated her dry throat.

"We could use your help," Herr Hirsch said.

Those words offered no relief. What if the help he wanted was for her to turn in other spies?

"Of course," she answered smoothly. She hoped he couldn't see her heart beating through her blouse. "What is it you need?"

He leaned closer, his hands on the table. "The Town-Kommandant and I think you are the perfect person to bring us information."

"Information? About what?" Again, her heartbeat spiked in her chest.

"We know there has been an influx of British prisoners in the hospital in the past few days, brought here from the Battle of the Somme."

"*Ja*," she said. "That is correct." A glimmer of hope sparked.

"We would like for you to question them and let us know whatever information you can find out from them."

She coughed. "Herr Hirsch," she said, sitting up straight, "are you saying you want me to … *spy* for you?" Breath flooded her chest. If that proved to be true, this conversation was the exact opposite of the one she had expected.

He appeared to be embarrassed. "We don't like to call it that," he said. "Let's just say you would be serving your country."

She almost laughed. Those were the exact words the other side had used in recruiting her.

"How can I help, Herr Hirsch?" She relaxed for the first time since yesterday morning.

"We know that the British have new weapons, new tanks. And we understand that they plan to deploy them at Flers-Courcelette. We have already encountered tanks from a New Zealand Division but were able to eliminate them easily. What we need to learn," he said, leaning closer, his voice low, "is how the British tanks are different and how many they will deploy. Also whether or not they have any … er … weaknesses we could take advantage of." He stopped talking and fixed her with another intense look. "We hoped we could count on you to have a talk with one of your British patients." He leaned back. "And get that information."

She loathed the man in front of her, but right then she could have hugged him.

He wasn't there to arrest her.

He wouldn't be hauling her off to prison.

Or standing her in front of a firing squad.

She was safe. At least for now.

She knew she needed to clear any such activity with her network. But she also knew she should probably agree, if for no other reason than to throw off suspicion.

"I will certainly do what I can, Herr Hirsch, although I do not hold out much hope. At least not with the lieutenant." She stopped talking and tapped her finger on her chin, as if she were trying to think of what might work. "But I did meet his aide as well. He was much more talkative. I could try both of them."

His smile stretched across his whole face. "I knew we could count on you, *Fräulein*." He leaned forward again and put his hand over hers. "Allow me to buy you dinner."

"*Danke*, Herr Hirsch. But I would really like to get some sleep since I expect tomorrow to be an extremely busy day. And I would like to have my wits about me when I do your bidding. I do hope you will ask me again."

She rose and dropped another small curtsy. He nodded at her, a satisfied smile on his face. She backed away and then entered the kitchen. Where she leaned against the door, gulping deep breaths, her knees wobbly underneath her.

Herr Breit rushed to her side. "What is it?" he asked. "What's happened?"

She shook her head. "Not now. He might suspect. I need to take food to my room." He moved away and prepared bread with sliced ham and thick yellow cheese. "Here. We'll talk later. I'll tap on your door around midnight."

She nodded and left, waving to Herr Hirsch, still at his table, on her way up the stairs.

She entered her room, put her meal on her dresser, then fell to her bed. Relief from her meeting with Herr Hirsch flooded through her but she still suffered from the fear and fatigue she had experienced during the past two days, coupled with the death of Number Seventy-two and beating and capture of the street sweeper.

She buried her head in her pillow to drown out the sound of her sobs, then fell into a fitful sleep.

# CHAPTER
# TWENTY-FIVE

**MARTHE**
**September 1916**

The night of her conversation with Herr Hirsch, Herr Breit tapped on her door at midnight, as promised. She woke with a start at the sound, then after slipping into her shoes followed him downstairs and into the cellar where root vegetables and wine were stored. Herr Breit told her they would not be overheard there. Once she told him Herr Hirsch's proposal, he studied her face.

"What did you tell him?"

"That I didn't think the lieutenant would tell me anything but his aide might."

"*Gut.* That was the right thing to do."

"But won't I need some kind of clearance to ... spy for both sides?"

"*Ja.* But I can help with that. Just keep your ears open and if the aide will talk, you must listen. We can decide together what is best to pass along until we get the word from the network."

Still emotional from her two-day ordeal, tears trickled down her face.

"What is it, *Fräulein?*" Herr Breit asked. "Why do you cry?"

She knew she wasn't supposed to talk about anything, but she felt she had nowhere else to turn. "My contact on *The Place* was killed while I waited to deliver a message. And the next morning, my backup contact was beaten senseless and dragged away. I really believed Herr Hirsch wanted to arrest me. I feel like I have to give him what he wants to throw off suspicion."

He hung his head. "Yes, I knew about those. And I have an idea."

He put his hand on her back and patted in a fatherly way. "There is an old vegetable vendor … a woman that hangs out in the square. Have you seen her?"

"Yes," Marthe said. "I think she's called 'Canteen Ma.' Is that right?"

"Yes," he said. "The Germans allow her to come and go as she pleases because she brings fresh vegetables and appears to be daft." He chuckled. "If they only knew. She is one of the best. She will be here in the morning. I will set her up as your new contact."

She drew a deep breath. "*Danke*, Herr Breit. *Danke*."

He continued to pat her back. "Go now. You need rest. We will talk again once I have made the arrangements."

⁕

SHE WOKE TO THE SOUND OF LOW-FLYING AIRPLANES, their steady drone passing right over her head. Within seconds, the sound of a high whistle, followed swiftly by reverberating blasts from bombs rattled her small window. Instinctively, she knew the bombs fell on the German soldiers packed into the abandoned factory on the edge of town and guilt flooded her heart. Yes, she did the right thing for her network and she hoped that having fewer German soldiers to fight would hasten the end of the war. But knowing that the information she passed on caused so many deaths sat heavy on her soul.

She rose and began dressing, then hesitated. She worried what might be thought if she showed up at the hospital without being called. But then she figured she would be expected to help with injuries, so she continued getting ready to leave.

The tap on her door sounded as she stepped into her shoes.

"*Fräulein*," Herr Breit said quietly, "Sister Nan from the hospital is here asking for you. Soldiers have arrived with bombing injuries."

"I'm on my way."

Marthe squared her shoulders and left with the nun. She would do whatever she could to save victims of the bombing.

To help mend the devastation she had caused.

# CHAPTER
# TWENTY-SIX

**MARTHE**
**September 1916**

M arthe worked alongside the doctor, Sister Margarete, and the rest of the nuns to put German soldiers back together again as best they could.

More than two hundred soldiers died instantly in the bombing, she learned, and many of the men they saw missed arms or legs. Screams of pain echoed through the hospital corridors and the convalescing patients remained quiet, requiring little attention that day, given the severity of the new influx.

Night had fallen before she made the rounds for her regular patients.

The British lieutenant, the one Herr Hirsch wanted her to question, hadn't progressed as well as she had hoped. His fever still plagued him.

"He spent a restless night, Nurse," the lieutenant's aide, Monroe McCartney, told her. "And he's been talking out of his head. Is there anything you can do for him?"

"Has the doctor been to see him?"

The aide hung his head. "He came to the door half an hour ago, but I steered him away."

"Why on earth would you do that?"

The aide hesitated, his chin touching his chest. "As I said, Nurse, the lieutenant was talking out of his head ... saying things his superiors would rather the bloody Boches—begging your pardon, ma'am—shouldn't hear. It wouldn't do for the doctor to go repeating things to the German Army that was said in a fever. Especially since the Boches lost so many men today. They're going to be hell-bent on revenge."

"I'm Belgian," she said softly. "You need have no fear of me." She met his eyes. "I will do what I can for him."

The lieutenant's temperature had stabilized so she changed his bandages, bathed his face in cold water, and sat with him for a few minutes. His aide never left his side. "Is there anything else you can tell me," Marthe asked, "that might help me in his care?"

"No," the aide said. "Do you know where they will send us from here?"

"I do not." She stopped talking and studied the face of the aide. "But I may be able to influence your comfort level when you leave, if …"

"If …?" He raised his eyes to meet hers.

She didn't have the final permission to spy for both sides, but decided to see what she could learn, just in case. She looked around the room. The beds on either side of the lieutenant had emptied and with only German soldiers in recently, no other prisoners had been admitted to claim them. She had closed the door when she entered so she decided to take a chance.

She pulled out paper and a pencil. "I'm going to tell you something … I'm sorry … McCartney, isn't it? Monroe? Are you Irish?"

"Yes, miss. A bunch of us volunteered to fight with the British. I was lucky enough to be assigned to the lieutenant, here."

"Sergeant," she said. "I'm going to sit here and write as I talk to you so it looks like I'm writing a letter for you if anyone happens to see us. But I would like to ask you questions concerning anything you might be able to tell me about what the Allied Army is planning against the German Army."

He gasped sharply.

"Let me explain," she continued. She moved her hand over the paper, writing words of nonsense as she spoke. "I am occasionally able to get information to the British Intelligence Network. But I have recently been asked to relate things I have heard to the German government as well. If I can do that … give the Germans *something* …

it will help throw suspicion off me so I can continue with my intelligence work for the Allies." She stopped talking and fixed him with an intense look. "And in return, I can perhaps influence where the lieutenant—and you—will be sent as prisoners of war."

He remained silent.

"Is there anything ... some little thing ... you can share with me that I can tell them? Something that won't do harm and is not critical to the big picture? Something about your tank warfare, maybe?"

Monroe McCartney pulled himself to his full five-foot, six-inch height. "Not tonight, Nurse. I will take it up with the lieutenant. For now, please leave."

"I understand. I hope you will think about what I have said. I'll come back tomorrow."

------◦⟨⟫◦------

THE FOLLOWING MORNING MARTHE LEFT THE TAVERNE ON her way to the hospital.

"*Hallo, Fräulein.*"

The voice came from behind her and she didn't recognize it. She turned and saw the old vegetable woman, "Canteen Ma."

"I have some fine winter squash today," Canteen Ma said. She held up a large yellow gourd. Marthe edged closer and Canteen Ma's eyes told her it was safe. "Just feel the weight of this beauty."

Marthe reached for the squash and as it touched her hand, she saw a little hole just below the stem. She examined it as if looking for blemishes and saw the rolled ends of a tiny scroll in the opening. "You're right," Marthe said. "It is a beauty." Marthe handed her a few coins, stuffed the squash in her bag and continued on her journey. She reached the hospital and headed straight for the bathroom. Once inside, she locked the door then dug the paper out and unrolled it. In small, coded letters, it translated to:

*Cleared. Lieutenant will help.*

She read the message and understood that she was cleared to be a double agent and the British lieutenant would be her next contact. She had no idea how it all worked, but she knew she could trust Canteen Ma and that whatever she received from the British prisoners of war would bring no harm to the Allied Army but would satisfy Herr Hirsch enough to get him to open up to her. Satisfied, she flushed the message down the toilet.

If she really intended to become a double agent, her level of secrecy needed to triple.

She left the bathroom and found Sister Margarete.

"No new wounded overnight," Sister Margarete told her. "But the British lieutenant ... well, his aide ... asked for you."

"*Danke*," Marthe said, ignoring the look Sister Margarete gave her. "I will see him as I make my rounds. Do we have any surgeries scheduled this morning?"

"No. So far, we've had no new arrivals yet today."

Marthe began her rounds with the German soldiers while Sister Margarete tended to those in another wing. The nun's questioning look when she talked about the British aide concerned her a little, so she resolved to spend more time with Sister Margarete during the day and maybe even tell her what Herr Hirsch had asked her to do. The Germans suspected everyone of being a spy, so Marthe figured she'd better do the same.

By the time she entered the room where the British lieutenant and his aide convalesced, she found the lieutenant seated upright with a breakfast tray on his lap and his aide helping him navigate the fork to his lips. She sent them a tentative smile and received one in return.

"Morning, Miss," the aide greeted her. "The lieutenant wishes to speak with you."

She nodded but hesitated because so many other prisoners milled about the room. The lieutenant's eyes fixed on her. "Please," he said. "Pull up a chair."

"Would you like to have a letter written to your loved ones?" she asked in English. "I will be happy to accommodate."

"Yes, please," the lieutenant said. "My hand is still weak."

She sat beside him and pulled a pad of paper and a pencil out of her pocket.

"This message is for you, Nurse," the lieutenant said in a quiet voice. "The sergeant filled me in on what you asked and it has been cleared."

Marthe wrote meaningless words as the lieutenant spoke. Occasionally she lifted her head or leaned closer as if she were taking his words down as he said them.

"You may write to my sweetheart that one more engagement will come her way. In the ongoing tumult. And that four newfangled steel containers will reach her. Their problem is they sometimes get stuck in the street and can't cross. Were you able to get all of that?" His eyes met Marthe's and she nodded.

"I will get this out to your sweetheart right away."

From his words, Marthe figured out that the lieutenant told her in an upcoming battle in the Somme, the Allies would employ four tanks. She was a little unclear about the crossing the street part but decided it must mean that the tanks couldn't cross the trenches and would get stuck if they tried. Regardless, she only needed to pass the message along and let Herr Hirsch, or his superiors, figure out the meaning.

She made her rounds with the rest of the prisoners in the room, none of whom spoke English, so she was comfortable with her interaction with the lieutenant and his aide. As she checked each soldier, she studied their eyes to see if any suspicion came her way, and seeing none, she finished in the room and sought out Sister Margarete.

"Sister," she said, "will you join me for a cup of tea?"

They entered the break room and fixed their tea, waiting to speak until the room emptied.

"Sister," Marthe said, "I wanted to tell you why the British aide asked for me. I believe by telling you, I can help the German cause."

Sister Margarete sat straight, then leaned toward her.

"Herr Hirsch, of the Town-Kommandant's office, asked me if I learned any information from our Allied Forces' prisoners, so I asked the British soldiers to help. In return, I promised them I would intercede on where they would be sent as prisoners when they leave here."

Marthe placed her hand over that of the nun. "That's why the aide asked for me."

The nun closed her eyes and leaned back, as if she were relieved.

"I feared you thought badly of me," Marthe said. "And I would have hated that."

"My daughter," the nun said. "I knew there must be a good explanation. Did you have any luck?"

"Yes, I think I did," Marthe answered. "Assuming, of course, they told me the truth."

The two women exchanged a little more conversation then went on with the rest of their duties at the hospital.

⸺⸺

AT THE END OF THE DAY, MARTHE RETURNED TO THE Taverne where Herr Hirsch waited for her.

"*Fräulein*," he said. His hand indicated the empty chair at his table. "Please join me."

She sat and folded her hands in her lap. Herr Breit placed a glass of *bier* in front of her but she kept her head low until the German spoke.

"Well, Marthe? What have you decided?"

"I will help you," she said. "In fact, I already have information for you."

He leaned forward in his chair, his breath hitting her face. "*Ja?* What is it?"

With her voice low, she leaned forward also, her head mere centimeters from his. "The Allies plan to send four tanks to the next round at the Somme. That's what you wanted, right?"

He smiled. A wicked smile. "Exactly what I wanted. Did you learn anything else?"

She hesitated. "I don't know if it will help, but I understand the tanks can't make it across the trenches. Apparently they get stuck."

His smile widened and he leaned back. "Excellent, *Fräulein*, excellent. You have done well."

She remained silent for several seconds then raised her eyes to meet his. "Since I have already helped you, Herr Hirsch, I would like to do more. If I gain additional information, would you like for me to send it directly since you are so busy?"

He laughed. "But Marthe," he said, "then I would not be able to see you. Please don't deprive me of that pleasure."

She knew he meant it as a compliment, but his words made her shudder. She must take care not to put herself in a compromising position again. She knew all too well how badly that knotted her insides.

———— ⋘⋙ ————

DAILY CONVERSATIONS WITH HERR HIRSCH TOOK THEIR toll and Marthe's stomach churned in a constant state of agitation. Canteen Ma provided her with tidbits the network had okayed for her to pass along to the Germans.

But she received very little in return.

# CHAPTER
# TWENTY-SEVEN

SUZANNE
2015

I turned back to the album and saw a picture slightly different from most of the others because it obviously wasn't taken on the farm. I could place the location of almost all the pictures so far, even though the farm looked very different today from what it looked like a hundred years ago. And those that weren't at the farm were at a ballpark. But this one appeared to have been taken at an old-fashioned store.

*Oh geez ... there I go again ... forgetting that at the time, none of this was old-fashioned, probably all state-of-the-art. Although I doubt they used that phrase back then.*

The picture was of a rather large group posing in front of shelves full of products. A couple of barrels occupied the foreground and one post in the middle of the store was ringed with something that looked like fishing rods. But I couldn't tell for certain.

I laid the album aside and went into the kitchen where I knew Dad kept a magnifying glass. When I used it on the picture, I could read the words on a small sign. I laughed out loud. The sign read, "Buggy Whips ... 25¢."

That made total sense. I was reading about 1915 and 1916 and while there were some cars—Coach Mack had a Cadillac, after all—I figured that tiny little Prospect Park had very few of them among its residents. So of course the general store would still sell buggy whips.

The thing that surprised me was how many people were in the store all at one time—I didn't figure all those people would shop together—and they all seemed to be dressed as if they were going to church. I would have expected to see housedresses on the women and overalls on the men. But these women wore hats and gloves and the men had on jackets and ties.

Maude's next passage filled me in on the occasion.

*November 8, 1916*

*Dear Diary,*

*Dad looked really sad when he returned from voting yesterday. I asked Mom why she didn't vote and she said she wasn't allowed to. I was shocked. I didn't understand why she couldn't do something for our country that Dad was allowed to do, but she didn't seem to mind. I hope that changes by the time I'm an adult.*

*For our section on Social Studies, Miss Delsie said the war in Europe is spreading out across the seas and Germany is attacking unarmed ships. I'm not sure I totally understand what that means—or why they would even want to do a thing like that. But she seemed really worried about it. So did Mom when Dad told her the same thing. I think she's worried that the boys will have to go to war.*

*I think the boys are worried too. Not Henry as much as Buzz. Henry thinks it would be great to travel to Europe and see the sights but Buzz just wants to stay here and, in his words, "Become the best pitcher in the American League."*

*I think they all talk about war too much, but Dad's determined that we should understand where our country's headed. He even loaded us up in the farm wagon and took us into town tonight so we could go to the General Store and listen to the radio. President Woodrow Wilson was elected again, he said, and he wanted us to hear his acceptance speech. I wrote part of it down so I could get extra credit in tomorrow's Social Studies class.*

*President Wilson said, "We have formed for the first time in recent years… a party of the people … a government in response to the opinion of the people." He said a few more things before he added, "We're not talking about confidence in any particular man, but confidence in the destinies of America."*

*On the way home, Mom complained that there was an Army recruiter there who kept looking at Henry and Buzz. The boys stayed quiet about it, but Mom and Dad got into a fight on the way home because Dad said if the boys are called to serve, we should be proud. But Mom didn't agree with him. She doesn't want them to have to shoot anybody or get shot themselves.*

*Anyway, Mom and Dad weren't speaking when they went to bed, but Henry and Buzz and I went to the kitchen and finished off the chocolate cake from tonight's dessert. It was the first time they treated me like I had some brains. I loved it.*

*I'll keep you posted about the war. Buzz and I are still hoping it doesn't happen.*

*Your friend, Maude*

---

## November 8, 1916

"GOOD NIGHT, BUG." HENRY TOUSLED MAUDE'S HAIR WHEN she left the kitchen to go to bed. Buzz slumped at the table, staring at the floor.

"What do you think will happen, Henry?" he asked. "Do you think the country will be at war before Spring Training?"

"No way, Buzz. Things move a lot slower than that in the government. At least that's what Dad says. And you don't have to worry, anyway. The service is still a volunteer organization, so if you don't want to go, don't. I'm sure you'll still have a position with Coach Mack."

"Why are you talking as if I'm the only one worried about it? Don't you want to keep playing ball? You almost make it sound like you're thinking about going." He leaned forward in his chair, his eyes wide. "Oh my God, Henry. Are you? Are you planning to join the service?"

Silence filled the kitchen and fear entered Buzz's eyes. "Oh Henry, for heaven's sake. Please tell me you're not planning to become a soldier."

"Okay. I'm not. At least not yet. But just last week, I learned that Mollie Bennett, one of the girls I met in Jacksonville, was on the British ship *Lusitania* when the Germans sank it. I couldn't believe it. That was pure aggression. The Germans killed innocent people on a luxury liner, for goodness' sake." He beat his fist on the table. "Doesn't that make you angry? Doesn't it make you want to fight back?"

"Look, Henry. I didn't know that. And I'm sorry you lost a friend. But no, even that doesn't make me want to go overseas to shoot people. I want to be here. Well, in Philadelphia. Pitching for the Athletics."

"My God, Buzz. Look around you. See the world."

"I see everything I want to see right here in Pennsylvania. I just want to be able to do what I'm doing."

"Well, those days might be numbered. European aggression is closing in. If nothing is done, they may decide to come over here. And then we'll all be in trouble."

Silence filled the kitchen again. Buzz closed his eyes and inhaled deeply.

"Henry," he said when he continued speaking. "I admire you. I always have. And I understand how you can be concerned about fighting a war in another part of the world." Buzz's tortured face reddened and he rose. When he spoke again his voice shook. "But I don't want to fight anybody else's war. I'm still trying to get through my own. My internal war. I don't have enough energy to take on a war for others. For people I never met. Even for Mollie What's-her-name that you met in Jacksonville. Let them take care of themselves." By this time, his voice had risen and he stood over Henry with clenched fists. "I struggled every day of my life here in Prospect Park. To live down the stigma of my parents being drunks and my dad killing himself and Mom. It wasn't until I got to pitch in Philadelphia that I felt like my own person. That I counted for something. That people would look at me without thinking about my background first or judge me for something I didn't do and had no control over." He stopped talking and closed his eyes. A single tear slid down his cheek. "I want what I have now. Only more of it. I want to be admired for a talent I have, to be one of only a few people who can do what I can do." He closed his eyes and again inhaled deeply. "Don't you get it, Henry?" he asked in a quiet voice. "If I were a soldier, I'd have nothing to distinguish me. I'd be just like thousands of other nameless, faceless men, all of whom are expendable on the battlefield. I'd be nothing. And I would have lost everything I worked so hard to gain." He slumped into a chair. His fists unclenched and he dropped his head into his hands. "Can't you understand that?"

Henry stood, then pulled Buzz into a quick hug. "Yes, Buzz," he said. "I do. Let's not talk about it anymore. Let's just continue down the path we're on and see where it leads us."

# CHAPTER
# TWENTY-EIGHT

**MARTHE**

**November 1916**

Marthe persuaded Herr Hirsch to intervene on behalf of the British lieutenant and his aide when they healed enough to leave the hospital. Originally, they were scheduled to go to one of the labour camps at the Western Front where prisoners were routinely mistreated and lived in deplorable conditions, with little food and exercise. At Marthe's request, however, Herr Hirsch saw to it that they went to Stalag Luft III in Germany where the prisoner recreational program included athletic fields and volleyball courts.

She went to see them the day they left. "Good luck to you both," she told them. "We are all hopeful this dreadful war will end soon and we can all return to our regular lives."

"Thanks, miss," Sergeant McCartney said. "I've heard the Stalag they're sending us to isn't bad."

"I hope not," she said. "Again, good luck."

She would have followed them out to the ambulance that would take them away, except that the same ambulance had delivered a new batch of wounded. She found Sister Margarete and together they administered triage to the arrivals. Although the Battle of the Somme had dragged on for five months at this point, fewer wounded Germans came their way and almost no soldiers from other nations.

But the battle had cost more than one million lives in its duration —an abnormally large number of British and French soldiers within the first week. And then mostly Germans after that.

*But not enough. There are still far too many Germans with too much fight left in them.*

# CHAPTER
# TWENTY-NINE

**SUZANNE**
**2015**

I loved the way the pictures in the album seemed to follow along with many of the entries in Maude's diary. I opened it to the spot I'd left off and read about the Christmas celebration of 1916—the first year, according to Maude, that the boys had enough money to buy presents for everybody. She was especially touched, she said, that Buzz was thoughtful enough to get her a beautiful brush, comb, and mirror set. As I read, it became apparent in these later passages that Maude paid more attention to Buzz as a person, rather than as the best friend of her brother, even though she was still pretty young to be interested in boys.

Many of her descriptions had shortened, especially noticeable when she wrote about the boys at Spring Training in Florida. But her writing included more tidbits about the country heading to war in Europe.

By the end of March 1917, Buzz and Henry returned home for a few days before traveling back to Philadelphia. Maude wrote very little about their return except one passage where the family studied the 1917 schedule and the boys encouraged them to come to the game on April 19 in Philadelphia when the Athletics played the Boston Red Sox.

But the next passage, from April 7, 1917, threw a monkey wrench into all that.

*April 7, 1917*

*Dear Diary,*

*Here it is, just ten days before my twelfth birthday, and today at school Miss Delsie announced that President Wilson declared war on Germany yesterday, April 6. She said she thinks everybody expected it, but to me, it's still unbelievable.*

*Dad talked about it tonight at the dinner table and Mom sat and cried. He tried to calm her down by saying that the military was still volunteer, so our boys didn't have to fight. Dad said he would be willing to go but he thought he was too old. Boy, that really set Mom off and she yelled at him for saying something so foolish. "What would Maude and I do if you were galivanting all over Europe? Who would take care of the farm?" He got up and patted her back and told her she didn't need to worry and that with America entering the war, he was sure it would be over quickly and that the boys probably wouldn't even have to go.*

*That didn't seem to help much and Mom went to bed early. So I had to clean up the table myself and take care of the dishes. Imagine how surprised I was when Dad came in and offered to dry as I washed?*

*"I'm sorry you had to see that, Maudie," he told me. "And I wish I hadn't said anything about wanting to go fight Germans. But what they're doing over there just makes me so mad. But don't worry. I'm sure it will all be fine and end before summer."*

*Even our teacher is worried. It's really strange but every day feels cloudy, even though it's spring and the sun shines a lot. I don't know what might happen. Dad says we might not be able to go to the game on the 19$^{th}$. And Mom cries almost all the time. As for me, I don't cry, but I walk around scared.*

*I'll let you know as more things happen.*

*Your friend, Maude*

I stopped reading to wipe my eyes. I tended to forget that I read words written by my grandmother. Her diary simply read like a good story from some young girl and I found myself thinking, "Oh, the poor little thing," over and over.

And I hated the thought that not only did she have to go through the First World War, but also part of the Second. No wonder she died so young. It's as if her poor little heart just couldn't take any more. It sounded like the same thing happened to Maude's mother.

I turned the page and saw that the next entry made things even worse.

*May 20, 1917*

*Dear Diary,*

*It's a black day around our house. We found out at church today that on Friday a new law passed requiring every man between the ages of eighteen and thirty to sign up for something called the 'draft.' Dad tried to explain it to me on the way home but stopped because Mom started sobbing. He put her straight to bed. She's had such a hard time ever since war was declared that she wasn't well enough to go to the boys' game on April 19ᵗʰ, so we all stayed home. But we did find out that Buzz pitched the whole game again and the Athletics won. I'm so happy for him and the team.*

*Once Mom went to lie down, I made iced tea—Mom had already poured the boiling water over the tea strainer before we left for church so all I had to do was sweeten it. And Dad cut off pieces of the ham Mom cooked yesterday afternoon, so he and I had ham sandwiches on the porch while Mom slept.*

*He explained the new law to me and now I'm more scared than ever. He said the branches of the military are no longer volunteer and that Henry*

*and Buzz will have to go to a military recruiting office and sign their
names since they're both almost twenty. Which means they could get
called up to go fight in the war. Dad's too old, he said, so that's one relief.*

*But I can't stand the thought of the boys having to go overseas and shoot
at other people. And neither can Mom. I know Dad's worried, but he's
trying to be brave about it. He even told me he's planning to get copies of*
The Philadelphia Inquirer *delivered with our mail so we can keep up
with the news of the war. Mom won't like that, but I think Dad's right
… we should know what's going on.*

*We haven't heard from the boys yet, but Dad thinks that most of the
baseball team will have to sign up for the draft because they're all so
young. Poor Coach Mack. We don't know what will happen to his team.
Or if baseball will even continue. I guess we'll have to wait and see what
happens.*

*Wish us luck, that some way or other, our boys get to stay home.*

*More later.*

*Your worried friend, Maude*

---

**May 22, 1917**

"GREAT JOB, BUZZ," HENRY SAID AT THE END OF THE GAME
with the Cleveland Indians. "We've won almost every time you've
pitched. Coach will probably give you some kind of bonus."

Buzz smiled at him. But the smile never reached his eyes. "Henry,"
Buzz said, "did you see that poster at the entrance to the stadium?
The one that said, 'Uncle Sam wants you for the U. S. Army'?"

Henry's smile faded and his arm tightened around Buzz's shoulders. "Yeah, I did." He took a deep breath. "We have to do it, Buzz,"

he said. "When we get back to Philadelphia at the end of the month, we're going to have to go register for the draft. It's the law."

"Maybe Coach Mack can do something ... intervene somehow to keep us here."

"Maybe," Henry said, "but I doubt it. A couple of the boys told me that some guy named Pinckney has already been drafted. So they're serious about this."

Buzz hung his head. "I wish there was something I could do to escape it."

"I'm not crazy about hearing you talk like that, Buzz. We'll do what we have to do for our country."

"What has my country ever done for me?" He said it softly, almost as if he hoped Henry wouldn't hear.

But Henry did hear.

He stopped short and jerked Buzz's arm so they faced each other.

"Are you kidding me? You've been like a brother to me almost my whole life, Buzz, but right now I want to punch you in the jaw."

"What? Why?"

"Look, I know you had a rough life growing up. But here's what's been done for you. My parents took you in and gave you a stable home life when your own parents died. And Coach Mack gave you the chance to be one of fewer than twenty top pitchers in one of only sixteen baseball teams in the country. *In the country*, Buzz. Think about how few people get chances like that. And this team sends you all over that same country. How many times do you think you would have gotten to Florida or New York or any of the places we go without being on this team? And you're able to do all of that because *this country* gave you that chance. You've been damned lucky, my friend. Talented, too, of course, but damned lucky as well. I have to say, I'm really disappointed to hear that from you. I thought I knew you better than that."

Henry released Buzz's arm and walked away.

For the first time since they joined the Athletics together, that night on the bus ride to Detroit, Henry sat with someone else.

# CHAPTER THIRTY

**SUZANNE**
**2015**

I t was so weird.

With almost every new entry in Maude's diary, I forgot that everything she described happened a century ago. But even as a young girl her writing was so articulate that her diary read more like a novel than the musings of an almost-teen.

And what was even funnier, I knew what happened during World War I, but felt as if I had to continue reading to find out how it all ended. Even when my dad did talk to me about his mother, it was only the last year or so of her life. My guess is, he never knew much of anything from her growing up years. How I wished he or Mom had found this diary years ago instead of my finding it after they were both gone.

Of course that part was weird too. Why would she have hidden it? I really hoped I'd be able to understand that by the time I finished reading.

I turned back to the photo album and saw that the next few pictures showed Maude with her dad around the farm. Very few with her mother and none with the boys.

I read her next entry.

*June 5, 1917*

*Dear Diary,*

*School's over and it's already hot. Dad and I finished planting the regular crops and before long we'll face the drudgery of the constant care they're gonna need. It hasn't rained for a while so we have to carry buckets of water out to the fields to keep the tiny plants from dying. Ugh. I hate it.*

*Mom has been so unhappy, she spends most of her time in bed. She really can't help us. I try not to get mad at her. I know she's not unhappy on purpose. But sometimes it's hard when only two of us have to do the work that three of us used to do. I guess that's selfish on my part because, honestly, I didn't have to do a lot of the outside work except weeding and helping to pick and can. But with Mom in bed all the time, the inside work falls to me and a lot of the outside work too.*

*Dad's been great at helping with the cooking and the dishes. Miss Delsie has even started coming over once every week or two to bring us some-thing. Dad looked at me funny the first couple of times she came over and I finally had to tell him the truth—that I started crying at school about a month ago and Miss Delsie was so sweet to me I couldn't help but tell her about Mom and how worried we all are about the boys. The dishes she brings are always a great addition to the things either Dad or I know how to cook. So I'm not going to ask her to stop coming. I noticed he hasn't asked that either.*

*He and I did do something we think Mom will like, though. We set out strawberry plants and while we don't think we'll have much of a crop this first year, she will be thrilled that from now on we'll have fresh strawberries to go with our fresh vegetables.*

*Miss Delsie came over yesterday and she told us something that we won't tell Mom. Today is the day designated by the government that all men, nationwide, are supposed to actually sign up for the draft. We haven't talked to the boys yet, but we assume they'll do it in Philadelphia. The numbers will be drawn next month, she said, so we're hoping against hope that their numbers are high and they won't have to go. At least I'm hoping that … I'm not sure how Dad feels about it. And, as I said, we're not going to tell Mom.*

*I'm out of time now. I have to get outside. I will try to write again later this week.*

*Your friend, Maude*

———— ⋅✺⋅ ————

## June 5, 1917

THE ATHLETICS FINISHED A FOUR-GAME STREAK AT SHIBE Stadium against the New York Yankees, splitting the win-loss record. Buzz pitched the third game but the team lost that one. His next scheduled game was against the St. Louis Browns the following day, on June 6.

Buzz and Henry had hardly spoken since they exchanged harsh words at the end of May, which made Buzz's reliance on Henry's signals while he pitched really uncomfortable. And contributed to his loss. Henry's words stayed with him and he couldn't get past them.

He hated having Henry mad at him.

"Are you going with the others?" Coach Mack asked him during breakfast.

"What do you mean?" Buzz asked. "Where are they going?"

Coach Mack studied his face. "Buzz, I don't know what's happened between you and Henry, but it's not good for the team that you don't know what the other players are up to. Since today was designated as 'draft registration day,' a bunch of the guys are planning to go together to do just that. The fact that you didn't know tells me you're not making the effort to be a team player." The look in his eyes intensified. "And we can't have that here, Buzz. Regardless of how you feel about it, personally, the law is the law, and I won't have someone on my team who doesn't play by the rules. You should think about that."

The coach stood and left Buzz alone at the table.

Buzz was miserable. The last thing in the world he wanted to do was willingly put himself in the position of being drafted to fight in a war. But he couldn't argue with what Coach had said. Or what Henry had said, for that matter.

He knew the coach was right. The law was the law. It wouldn't do him any good to refuse to register and then go to prison. Besides, he thought, maybe he'd get lucky and his number would be really high and he wouldn't get called.

He could always hope.

He walked uptown to the nearest military recruiting office. Many of his teammates were already there, filling out paperwork. When Henry saw him, his face lit up and he strode over to Buzz. "I knew you'd do the right thing," he said. He pulled Buzz into a back-slapping hug and escorted him to the front of the line.

At the Athletics' game on June 6 against St. Louis, Buzz and Henry worked together again as a well-oiled team and Buzz pitched a winning game.

Eight days later, on June 14, American General John J. Pershing and his headquarters staff arrived in Paris. Twelve days after that, on June 26, the first U. S. troops joined him there.

The Great War had just become real for the millions of American men who waited to see when their draft numbers would be called.

# CHAPTER
# THIRTY-ONE

**MARTHE**
**September 1917**

By early 1917, the number of wounded to arrive in her hospital became so light, Marthe had time on most days to help Herr Breit in the Taverne.

Her work for both sides continued into the new year and by late in 1917, Herr Hirsch asserted increased demands, not only for additional and more dangerous information about the Allies, but also for her romantic affections. She tried kidding him out of it at first, telling him their relationship was strictly war business. When that didn't work, she ducked his passes and wriggled out of his potential clutches.

But in the fall, he convinced her to meet him at his home by telling her that several high-ranking Germans would be present and he wanted to honor her. She didn't care about that part but thought she could gain additional information for the Allied network. When she arrived, however, they were alone. He had even dismissed his small staff, so except for the two of them, the house was empty.

His table was set with delicious-looking food and he began the evening as a perfect gentleman. But when he pulled her chair out for her at the end of the meal, his hands slid down over her breasts and he whispered in her ear. Disgustingly explicit and sexual.

Indignant, she jumped up and ran, barely escaping through his front door before he could catch up to her. She didn't believe he would chase her down the street. And fortunately, he didn't. She ran all the way back to the Taverne and entered by the back door, her tears streaming. She had reached the end of her rope with the German.

Herr Breit appeared at her side instantly. *"Mein Fräulein,"* he said. "What has happened?"

She told him in a broken voice, slumped to the table and let her sobs flow. "I can't stand it, Herr Breit," she said. "I can no longer stomach the thought of being a double agent. And now, Herr Hirsch … seems to expect me to … to …" Her voice broke and again her face dissolved into tears.

She wanted her mother. She needed her. She needed womanly guidance. And love. And encouragement. And advice on what she should do next.

But that was impossible. The wretched Germans had seen to that.

Herr Breit patted her shoulder. "I understand, Marthe," he said. "It is a large responsibility you bear. And you've done it very well. Let me see what I can do with the network."

She nodded and continued to cry. Quietly, Herr Breit slipped from the kitchen.

---

THE FOLLOWING MORNING, MARTHE SENT WORD TO THE hospital that she was too sick to come in. For the first time in years, she stayed in bed and hid under the covers while her body shook. She had to make changes. Her shredded mental state rendered her useless to either side.

Late in the afternoon, Herr Breit tapped on her door.

*"Fräulein,"* he said. "I have brought you some food. And I have news. May I come in?"

*"Ja,"* she answered.

He entered with a tray that contained a bowl of soup and fresh baked bread. "We've had a tragedy in the city," he told her. A tiny smile tugged at his mouth and Marthe sat up, puzzled.

"What is it?" she asked. "And why is a tragedy funny to you?"

He placed the tray on her lap and avoided her eyes.

"It's not exactly funny," he said, "but more ironic …"

"Oh my goodness. Will you just tell me?"

His eyes met hers. "One of the Town-Kommandant's men discovered the body of Herr Hirsch this morning on the road out of town. Two bullet holes pierced his skull."

She gasped.

"After that, your *Oberartz* contacted me to inquire about your health and he told me that the decision had been made to close the hospital here since so few wounded arrive these days. He said if you were willing, he would put in a transfer for you to a field hospital in Laon, France, on the edge of the German occupation behind the Hindenburg Line. Would you like that?"

She sat up straight, spilling her soup. "Are you serious?" She couldn't believe her good fortune. In one conversation, she learned her nemesis had died and she had an opportunity to go to a new place, where she could start fresh. Where no one knew her. Where she could continue her work not only with wounded soldiers, but also with her network. The cloud that had hovered for the past several weeks disappeared and she could smile again.

"Of course I will miss you, *Fräulein*," Herr Breit said, "but I agree, it would be best."

Marthe moved the tray from her lap, stood and hugged him. "Oh, Herr Breit, thank you for such comforting news. And yes, I would welcome a transfer to France. How soon can I go?"

"Right away, my dear."

———— ⟡ ————

IN ONLY TWO DAYS, MARTHE SETTLED IN TO HER NEW quarters in Laon, France. She unpacked her few belongings in the staff dormitory where she thought she would live and was surprised to learn she'd been given a promotion and much more responsibility. Which meant she had her own room. With its own door so she could close everyone out.

That came in really handy since Herr Breit sent a few sticks of dynamite with her. He had brought them to her in a small duffel bag as she packed on her last night at the Taverne.

"Where on earth did you get ...?"

His enigmatic smile sent playful crinkles to his eyes. "Let's just say, some of our 'friends' in high places wanted to make certain you had every tool available to you since you will be so close to the front. You never know when your path might cross something the Allies would like to see disappear."

She pried up two of the floorboards beside her bed and stowed the dynamite there, then covered that part of the floor with an area rug. Just having it handy made her feel better.

She met the rest of the staff at her new field hospital and arranged to receive a pass that allowed her to be out at any time of the day or night in case she needed to travel to get supplies or medicines as part of her increased responsibility. She also found her new network contact.

---

THE DAY AFTER SETTLING INTO LAON, MARTHE LEARNED that Mata Hari, the famous Dutch exotic dancer whose myriad of high-ranking lovers revealed information to her that she fed to the French secret service, was executed as a German spy.

The knowledge made Marthe's blood run cold.

# CHAPTER
# THIRTY-TWO

**SUZANNE**
**2015**

Brevity governed the next few entries in Maude's diary, which consisted of mundane happenings in her class as her sixth-grade year drew to a close.

Most of her friends at the time, including Helen, had brothers who were also required to register for the draft. That fact, Maude said in one entry, allowed the two of them to reconcile somewhat.

In addition to her work on the farm and the state of her mother's unhappiness, Maude also talked in abstract terms about the boys' baseball games. Unfortunately, she wrote, during the summer's eighty-two games, the A's lost fifty-one of them. Worse, the team lost six games in a row three different times during the season, including some of the games Buzz pitched.

According to Maude, her parents had lost their lust for talking about every game and her mother slumped deeper into a depression over the thought of the boys going to war. The schedule on the farm, without Maude's mother helping, gave them little free time and with Florence so despondent, Frank didn't press to take Maude to Philadelphia.

I paused and thought about what Maude's mother must have gone through—probably a similar thing to what Maude went through herself when my dad and his older brother, Walter, were called to go to war. I remember how I felt when Steve had to fight during Desert Storm. But that war wasn't anywhere close to what the country went through in World Wars I and II. Plus, in 1917 this country hadn't seen a soldier conscription since the Civil War and even then, nobody had to cross an ocean. No, I was certain Florence's depression stemmed from real fear and that she had no similar experiences from which to draw courage.

I missed Maude's carefree passages of spending time with her friends and lazy summer days, none of which she seemed to have during the summer of 1917. Her short passages reflected her increased workload. And, unfortunately, her loss of fun.

Maude's diary passage from Labor Day in 1917 broke her pattern of short entries.

*September 3, 1917*

*Dear Diary,*

*I know you must be tired of hearing about the war. I sure am. But so far, there's been no news about the boys having to go. Dad and I keep watching the paper because that's where they print the numbers of the men who have to report for duty.*

*I didn't understand it at first, but Dad told me that once the men registered, they each got a number between one and 10,500. And then one of the government men, the Secretary of something-or-other, drew all the numbers out of a glass jar and the order they were drawn was recorded. Then as numbers are reached on the list, all the men from each local registration office with those numbers have to report for their training. You probably already knew that, but it was news to me. Buzz and Henry have high numbers, 9052 and 9053. Neither one of their numbers has been given dates to report so they're still safe. Dad has tried and tried to get that through Mom's head. But it hasn't worked. Nothing has.*

*So she can't relax and enjoy the fact that the boys haven't been called up yet. Dad keeps trying to get her out of it and I've taken over most of the cooking. But she either spends all of her time in bed or just mopes around.*

*And she seems so weak. Dad and I both hate that she's going through that, but we don't know how to help.*

*Of course the news only makes things worse. I've actually started hiding the newspaper Dad gets so she won't pick it up and read about what's going on. Unfortunately, the war is spreading. Last month China declared war on Germany and Austria and then two weeks later, Italy declared war on Turkey. Don't tell anybody but I didn't even know there was a country called "Turkey." Seems like a funny name for a country to me.*

*Every time I see Miss Delsie, she reminds me to keep following the war since we'll be continuing to study it in seventh grade. Which starts tomorrow, by the way.*

*Mom couldn't take me shopping for school clothes this summer, so Dad arranged with Ethel's mom for me to go with them. I didn't get much new stuff, but for the past month, Dad let me keep the egg money since Mom isn't able to gather them anymore. That helped a lot. And I learned how to use Mom's Singer Sewing Machine last school year when Miss Delsie gave us girls a sewing class. Figuring out the treadle was a little tricky at first but I finally got it. Anyway, that helped. I found some simple patterns and nice fabric at Harrington's General Store. I even made matching aprons for Mom and me in hopes that would make her want to come to the kitchen with me again. But that hasn't worked either.*

*Since we haven't been able to see the boys, I've been writing to them at their boarding house in Philadelphia. Buzz told me their final game is on October third and they will come home a few days after that. I can hardly wait. I believe that's the one thing that will perk Mom up.*

*I'll write again to let you know how the first day of school went.*

*Until then, I'm your friend, Maude*

September 9, 1917

Dear Diary,

I know I don't normally write again this soon, but I had to tell you this.

First week of school and wouldn't you know it? I started my period. It's a good thing Miss Delsie told us girls about it last year because Mom never breathed a word. And I didn't think there was any chance it would happen this early. But good ol' Miss Delsie had what I needed to get through the day.

Even worse, though, since Mom never left her bedroom the whole evening, I had to talk to Dad about it. He was so embarrassed. I really felt sorry for him. Of course I was embarrassed, too, but I needed help and Mom wasn't able to give it. He went in to talk to her and came out with supplies in a paper bag for me. Poor Dad.

I have to study now. I'll write more tomorrow.

Your friend, Maude

October 7, 1917

Dear Diary,

Good news and bad news.

The good news is the boys got home tonight. Since we knew they were coming, Mom got up and got dressed. She even sat with me in the kitchen and talked me through how to make chicken pot pie. I'd helped her a *bunch of times, so I kinda knew what needed to be done but making the gravy for it is always tricky and she did that part. We both wore the aprons I made for us so that made me happy. I even heard her humming at one point. When Dad heard that, he grabbed her and kissed her, then danced her around the kitchen. So the day started out great.*

*The bad news is that after dinner, Henry and Buzz and Dad went out on the porch to smoke—that's something the boys started in Philadelphia—and when I went out to take them their blueberry cobbler, they stopped talking immediately. I knew something was wrong. "What's happened?" I asked. Nobody answered me until finally Dad took my arm and pulled me into the front yard.*

*"The boys' draft numbers came up," he whispered. "Both of them. We're trying to keep your mother from finding out just yet."*

*My heart jumped up and I felt like it grabbed my throat. I couldn't swallow. Or talk. So I just nodded and went back up the steps. I started to go inside but stopped and hugged Henry so hard I thought I might knock him over. And then, it even surprised me, but I hugged Buzz just as hard.*

*Dad and I talked later and he said he and the boys decided not to tell Mom while they're here. Not even when they leave for their training. They'll be going to Fort Benning in Columbus, Georgia. Sounds fine to me. Maybe she'll be perked up now that she's seen them and we can get back closer to normal.*

*I'll let you know how it goes.*

*Your friend, Maude*

## October 15, 1917

HENRY AND BUZZ JOINED TWENTY OTHER YOUNG MEN IN the local military recruitment office in Prospect Park and raised their hands to be sworn in as soldiers in the United States Army. Then they all boarded the Army bus for the long drive to Fort Benning, Georgia, where they would undergo their basic training. They weren't certain of the exact time frame, but after they passed the basics, like learning how to march, how to shoot, and such things, they would be sent to Fort Dix in New Jersey, for training with machine guns and whatever else they might need to be ready for the fighting in Europe.

"I feel guilty for not telling Mom where we're going," Henry said. "But, gee whiz, Buzz, you saw her."

"Yeah. I can't believe how much weight she's lost."

"Right," Henry said. "And poor little Bug is having to do the housework and the cooking. I never knew worry could work on a person like that. I feel bad for Dad too." Henry grinned. "I swear, when he dropped us off at the recruiting office, he looked like he wished he could join us." He shook his head. "Poor guy."

Buzz remained silent and Henry put his hand on Buzz's arm. "Sorry, friend. I know you're worried. I wish you could look at it like I am." He grinned. "This could be the adventure of our lifetimes. I mean, yeah, we've had a pretty good adventure already. But we'll get to see Paris and probably London. And a lot of other places we'd never get by simply playing baseball." He leaned back and put his hands behind his head. "Yep. The adventure of a lifetime."

# CHAPTER
# THIRTY-THREE

**SUZANNE**
**2015**

I stopped reading and turned on the light by Dad's chair.

I felt so sorry for my poor little grandmother and really wished I could have known her to hug her. For some reason, I didn't feel like I got to know my grandfather quite as well, but every time Maude wrote about one of the ball games and then about the fact he was drafted, I still couldn't believe no one ever told me my grandfather—and my great-uncle, for that matter—had been professional baseball players or that they had fought in the First World War. I would have figured the farmhouse where my dad's youngest brother—my Uncle Freddie—still lived would have had some sort of memento or tribute to my grandfather. But I'd never even heard about his pitching career, much less that he'd fought in a global war.

And even when Dad told me about his World War II experiences, the only thing I heard about his father was how little time they spent together and that the last time Dad had seen him, my grandfather reeked of booze. I had a hard time picturing the Buzz my grandmother wrote about as the same Buzz my father told me about.

So I turned the page to keep reading.

*December 23, 1917*

*Dear Diary,*

*We couldn't get Mom to go to church today. Everybody keeps asking for her.*

*We've decorated for Christmas and even have a bigger tree than normal. But nothing has worked to get Mom out of bed. Once a week or so, Dad will get her in the bathtub and I help her wash and get dressed. Dad and I have done the little bit of Christmas shopping we were able to do at Harrington's General Store, and we did get a few things for the boys, but we won't get to send them in time for Christmas. I feel bad about that, but it just can't be helped.*

*We had to tell Mom the boys were drafted. One of their letters stuck out of my pocket when I went in to help her get dressed and it fell out. I hadn't noticed it, but by the time I went to look for it, she had found it and read it. Dad and I were in the kitchen and heard her scream. We went to see what had happened and saw her sitting on the bed with the letter crumpled in her hand. It took Dad a long time to calm her down and I finally left them alone so I could start dinner.*

*I'm getting to be a pretty good cook. I'm roasting a chicken for Christmas. As you probably guessed, the boys told us they didn't get any time off for the holidays, so we won't get to see them. They did tell us in one of their letters they'll get a few days off before they actually ship overseas … sometime in April, we think. I don't know what we'll do with Mom then. I wish I could figure out how to help her.*

*Anyway, Merry Christmas.*

*Your friend, Maude*

———————

**December 24, 1917**

"THIS IS GOING TO BE GREAT," HENRY SAID. "THEY'LL BE SO surprised."

The wagon stopped at the end of the long lane to the Brewer property and the boys jumped out right around dusk. They had endured the discomfort of the Army bus from Fort Benning all the way to Philadelphia where they hitched a ride to Prospect Park.

Within fifteen minutes, they navigated the lane and knocked on the front door.

Maude left the simmering stew and went to answer it since she knew her father was still in the bedroom with her mother. She cracked the door, not sure who would be knocking at this hour on Christmas Eve. The sight of two soldiers standing there caused her to scream with joy and she threw herself at Henry and then at Buzz.

"Oh my goodness! What are you doing here? We thought you'd be at your next camp by now. Come in, come in. I'll go get Mom and Dad."

"Hold it, Bug," Henry said. "Let me knock on their door."

But before he made it up the stairs, Frank appeared and looked over the railing. "Oh my God!" he said. "Mother, come here. You have to see this."

"No, Frank," she said. "I'm too tired."

Frank motioned Henry up the stairs and in seconds, he stood in the doorway.

"I came a long way to see you, Mom," he said. "Won't you come downstairs and visit with us?"

Florence burst into tears and threw herself into Henry's arms. She kissed his cheek, his neck and back to his cheek again. When she finally believed he was really there, she descended the stairs with him and Frank.

Alone in the living room with Buzz, Maude hugged him again. She thought her heart would burst at having the whole family together for Christmas.

"Thank you for coming. And for surprising Mom. It might be one of the few things that gets her out of the blues." She looked up at him. "Dad and I haven't known what to do for her. Here," she added, pulling away. "Let me help you take your coat off. Oh my, is it snowing? We hadn't even noticed. Oh, I'm so happy to see you."

"I've never heard you talk so much," Buzz said with a smile. "It's good to be home. Is that stew I smell?"

"Yes," she said. "I made it. And I made bread. It's almost ready to come out of the oven. Oh, I'm so happy you boys are here. What a great Christmas present."

"Speaking of that," Henry said. "Buzz, will you put our things under the tree?" He supported Florence down the last couple of steps and seated her in her favorite chair. "You'll join us at the table, right?" he asked her.

"Yes," she said. "But I'm so mad at you two." Her smile took the sting out of her words. "For joining the Army. And for not telling me."

"Well, Mrs. B.," Buzz said, leaning in for a hug, "we really didn't have a choice about the Army. Our numbers came up."

"Right," Henry said. "And Dad and Bug wanted to wait until you felt better to tell you so you wouldn't worry as much."

"I suppose I will worry until this infernal war is over and you're both back home for good. How long can you stay?"

"We have to report to Fort Dix in New Jersey on the first of January. Buzz and I have already arranged a ride there so we'll be here almost a week."

"I've added two more plates," Maude told them. "Come on, everybody. Dinner's ready."

They gathered around the table but before Maude served the stew, Frank looked at each gathered face. "I am so grateful we can all be together like this, let's join hands and thank the Lord."

On both sides of the table, hands joined and Florence gave extra squeezes to the ones that held hers. "Dear Heavenly Father," Frank's voice rose loud and clear, "we thank you for our many blessings, especially that we have both of our soldiers with us on this joyous Christmas Eve. Please protect them in their journeys and bring them home safely to us again. We thank you, Lord, for the bounty on this table and we ask that you bless it to our bodies. Amen."

"Amens" followed around the table and Maude served the stew, then handed the hot bread to Frank so he could pass it.

"This is going to be a good Christmas after all," Frank said.

"I still can't believe you're really here." Florence clutched Henry's hand, then brought it to her lips and kissed it. "Please tell me I'm not dreaming."

Henry reached over and kissed her cheek. "You're not dreaming, Mom. Why don't you relax and enjoy yourself?"

The next morning dawned bright and beautiful, a white winter wonderland on Christmas day. Henry and Buzz had added presents under the tree for everyone, and Maude was touched that Henry gave her a set of colored pencils and a pad of paper while Buzz presented her with a book, *Anne's House of Dreams,* a follow-on book to *Anne of Green Gables* by L. M. Montgomery which she had read earlier and loved. Maude didn't remember a better Christmas.

Ever.

---

THE WEEK WITH HENRY AND BUZZ SAW A MARKED improvement in Florence as she dressed every day and spent most of her time downstairs with the family. On Christmas day, after the present opening and a huge breakfast of bacon, ham, and eggs, Maude and Buzz went outside to gather basins of snow.

"Will you tell me how to make snow cream?" Maude asked her mother.

"Of course," Florence said. "I'll even help you."

Together, they added milk, sugar, and vanilla and folded it into the fresh snow.

"This is the best you've ever made," Maude said. "Maybe we can make more later."

The family filled the days with conversation and games until the day Henry and Maude went shopping at Harrington's General Store.

"Henry," Mrs. Harrington said. "Is that really you?"

"Yes, ma'am. I'm home for a few days after my basic training. Has Howard been called up yet?"

Silence greeted him for several seconds. "Yes," she said. Henry waited but she remained silent. No additional details about her son emerged.

"Okay, then," he said. "Take care, now. And please give Howard my best."

She nodded but said nothing else. Maude and Henry turned toward the door and saw their preacher, Reverend Townsend, holding it for them. The three of them left the store together and, as Maude stowed their purchases in the back of the wagon, Reverend Townsend put his hand on Henry's arm.

"She's embarrassed, son," he said.

"What do you mean? Why?"

"Because when Howard received notice that his number came up in one of the first few draws, he took off."

"Took off? Where did he go?"

The preacher shrugged. "I'm not sure he even told anybody," Reverend Townsend said. "My guess is he left for Canada. Although I suppose he could have gone to Mexico."

"Why would he do that?" Maude came up beside them.

"To keep from being sent to Europe."

"But we were told in basic training," Henry said, "that Canadian troops are already over there. So what good would it do him to go there?"

"Because Canada can't order him to fight overseas. I've heard that people who object to being called to serve escape there and aren't obligated to the Canadian government."

"Thanks for letting me know, Reverend," Henry said.

"I'm proud of you, son," the Reverend said with his hand on Henry's shoulder. "Of both you and Buzz. You're doing the right thing for your country."

"Yes sir. Thanks."

Henry and Maude climbed into the wagon to drive home.

"Bug," Henry said, "please don't talk about this when we get home."

"Because …?"

"I don't want to give Buzz any ideas." He was silent for a moment. "He really didn't want to join the Army but did because all the rest of us did. And, of course, because the law said he had to. Coach Mack told us we would have a spot on the team when we returned. If it hadn't been for that, I don't know what he might have done." He looked Maude in the eye. "So I don't want him to think it's okay to escape to another country to stay out of the fighting."

"Yeah," Maude answered. "I understand. But I'm more worried about Mom than anything else. If we told her about it, I'm afraid she would beg you both to move to Canada. Henry, I think she really believes you guys will be killed the minute you get there."

"I think you're right, Bug. But I'm sure it's not nearly as dangerous as it sounds."

"I hope *you're* right," Maude said.

Something about Henry's words sent shudders through Maude's body.

# CHAPTER
# THIRTY-FOUR

**MARTHE**
Laon, France
1918

At the end of 1917, when Marthe first arrived in Laon, her medical skills were stretched to the limit when the British launched a tank assault against the German Army. The British gained the most ground initially since the flat land to the west of Laon lent itself to the use of tanks, but a German rally sent the British back and eventually regained all the ground the British had initially captured. The cost in lives lost and wounded, however, soared.

By early 1918, rumors and gossip flew through the hallways at Marthe's field hospital. Each new batch of wounded soldiers brought additional tidbits to Marthe's ears, and sorting through them to decide what should be reported and what could be put to rest took extra time. Her work tasks increased daily as the Germans amassed greater numbers of troops in their trenches against the French and British forces. And they were stationed within mere kilometers of where she worked.

Most of her information concerned Germany's push to fortify the German front, the Hindenburg Line, that ran roughly parallel to the border of Belgium, but in spots surged westward almost one hundred kilometers into France. The withdrawal of Russian troops, sent home to combat their internal strife after the Bolshevik Revolution in March, allowed the Germans to relocate nearly fifty divisions from the Eastern Front to the Western Front and push west another seventy kilometers or so, past Montdidier, almost to the village of Cantigny, near Amiens.

The intensity of this advance proved deadly and a new wave of wounded greeted Marthe.

"Lieutenant," Marthe said to one young man who thrashed around on the stretcher, "please allow me to examine you to find out how we can help you."

"Just make it stop hurting, Nurse," he said.

"I will," she answered, "as soon as I find out what's wrong with you."

She inserted morphine into his arm and he calmed. "I have to get back to the general," the lieutenant told her. Marthe pulled away his uniform to reveal a deep gash in his side, his intestines threatening to spill out.

"We'll get you back, soldier," she said. "But first we need to mend this hole in your side."

Marthe sent him to the surgery and examined the next soldier, an aide to General Erich Ludendorff, the German forces commander. When Marthe found out his position, she asked, "So, do you need to get back to the general too? Like the last soldier told me?"

"He needs all of us," the aide said. He screamed in pain as Marthe moved his leg, revealing its shattered bones.

"I'm sorry, soldier," she said. "But you won't be going anywhere for a while." She also gave him a morphine injection. "Why the rush to get back?"

"The general believes that with the additional troops no longer needed to fight the Russians, we can make a final push to victory before the Americans come over in full force. He'll need everyone he can find to achieve that."

"Well, I'm afraid he'll be doing it without you," Marthe said.

She approached the next soldier, alert for more information to pass on. She knew the British lines were stretched thin already, so any details she could supply would certainly help.

Once triage had been performed on this new wave, she joined the doctors in the surgery, setting bones, stitching up skin flaps where limbs had been removed, cleaning and mending wounds, and anything else required of her. Earlier in the war, many of the wounds that reached her were days old, but because these soldiers came from a closer battlefield, the wounds were fresher with a greater chance of healing.

Exhausted at the end of the day, she slumped into a chair in the tiny area the nurses used when they needed a break. Her life at this hospital was very different from her hospital in Roulers. Much busier, for one thing. Missed friendships, for another. She had been able to count on her friendship with Herr Breit at the Taverne and she missed her time with Sister Margarete at the hospital.

She did have one new friend, a nurse from nearby Luxembourg named Jeannette Beaudelaire. Marthe enjoyed Jeannette's sense of humor but they had been too busy to really get to know each other.

Fewer opportunities to reach her network also became an issue at her new hospital. While Herr Breit had sent a new contact to see her when she arrived, the sheer volume of medical cases made leaving the hospital to get messages out difficult. So she also developed an in-house contact who helped on occasion.

She had to alert her British Intelligence Network about the series of German advances coming their way. And quickly, since the first offensive was planned for north of the Somme River in two days. She entered the bathroom with her toilette kit and removed a button that rested inside it. The front of the button looked like any ordinary button seen on a coat. But its flat, white back became her new means of communication. She fished a pen from her pocket and wrote her coded message in tiny letters and numbers in a spiral around the button's perimeter, detailing the upcoming series of attacks. She replaced the pen in her pocket, then added the button and a threaded needle. She left the room and found her way deep into the bowels of the hospital where meals were prepared.

"Nurse," Helmut, the night cook greeted her. "The chicory coffee is hot."

"*Danke,*" she said and poured a steaming cup. She wandered around the kitchen lifting lids and sniffing the smells. The orderly who assisted the cook received his instructions for the next day, then removed his apron and left for the night.

"Busy day?" Helmut asked.

"Very."

He continued to stir and she said quietly from her perch at the counter, "Helmut, I understand your coat needs a new button. I could fix it for you if you like."

The words were their code and he was her internal contact. If she had a message to send, she offered to sew a button onto his coat. The button she removed to add the coded one would serve as her communication vehicle in the future.

"That's kind of you, *Fräulein*," he said. "I will get it for you."

He left the stove and returned to hand her a coat with buttons that matched the one in her pocket. She knew which button to remove so she unobtrusively pulled out the stitching, placed the removed button in her pocket and retrieved the coded one. They continued to chat as she sewed the new button in place.

"There," she said, handing the coat back to him. "Good as new."

"*Danke, Fräulein*. I appreciate your help. May I fix you a sandwich?"

She shook her head. "I think I will try to sleep."

After returning to her quarters, she closed the door behind her, removed her shoes, and lay down on her bed where she fell asleep almost immediately.

# CHAPTER THIRTY-FIVE

SUZANNE
2015

The door opened and Steve walked in. "I can't believe you're still here," he said. Then he saw my grandmother's diary in my hands and the photo album by my side. "Oh. That's why. Wouldn't you be more comfortable reading this at your house?"

"Normally," I answered. "But it just feels right to be here." I grinned up at him. "Where I can still feel your grandfather."

He kissed my forehead. "I get it. I feel him too." He moved the photo album so he could see the pictures. "What's that?" He pointed to one of the pictures of Henry and Buzz standing in front of the steamer trunk."

"Interesting that you asked, 'What's that?' rather than 'Who's that?' Have you ever seen pictures of your great-grandfather before?"

"Not that I'm aware of," he answered. "Which one is he?"

"The one who looks exactly like your grandfather did when he was young."

"Oh yeah, I see it. But I really am interested in the trunk."

"I knew you would be."

"Is it still there?"

"I've never seen it there. But that doesn't mean anything. I suppose it would be in the barn if they still have it. We can ask when we go. I'm taking all of this stuff with me. Which is why I'm so intent on finishing the story." I hesitated and thought about my words. "That's funny. That's how I've been thinking of my grandmother's diary ... as a story that I need to keep reading to find the ending." I laughed. "I certainly know how it ends. Maude dies way too young in the same year your grandfather, Sam, enters the service." I put my finger in the spot where I left off. "But I'll bet I've learned things about her—and my grandfather—that even their children don't know. I'm sure Dad didn't. My guess is my grandmother herself hid her diary in the back of this photo album. I can't imagine why she felt the need to do that, but I don't think anybody else has ever seen it."

"Do you have a diary, Mom?"

"No. But reading this makes me wish I did. For my grandkids … and great grandkids … to read." Steve's son, Sammy, and his wife Amanda just had their first baby, Elizabeth—Lizzie to us—named for my mother. My first great-grandchild.

"Oh, I forgot." He handed me the bag he carried. "Emily sent this chicken salad over for you. She figured you hadn't eaten much today."

"What a sweetheart." And she was. I had been very lucky with my son's choice for his wife and we've been really good friends since we first met.

"If you're sure you're all right," he said, "I'll go back home. Call me if you need me." He smiled. "Although it doesn't look like you'll be lifting anything heavier than that diary for the rest of the evening." He kissed my forehead again and left.

I got up to get a fork, then returned to Dad's chair and picked up Maude's diary.

*April 17, 1918*

*Dear Diary,*

*Well, we had a really great week. The boys finished their Army training and had a week off before they had to ship overseas. So they were here the whole time.*

*Mom did great. She's been so much better ever since Christmas. But having to tell them good-bye when she knew they were headed for the fighting has sent her back to bed. And nothing Dad and I have done has worked to get her out of bed again. She did call to me this morning, though, when I went past her door. She even smiled at me and said, "Happy Birthday to my teenage daughter."*

*Finally! I'm thirteen today and at last Mom agrees that I'm a teenager. I've wanted to be one for so long. But now that it's here, I'm having trouble enjoying it because I'm so worried about the boys.*

*Dad assured me Mom would get up today and make my birthday cake. But I haven't seen it yet. War changes everything. What seemed important before just isn't that important anymore.*

*The boys told us they'd be going to France. But they didn't think they would get to Paris. Seems to me, if I went all that distance, I would sure try to find a way to go to Paris. They gave us an address, so I've already started a letter to each of them. I figured they'd rather get individual letters instead of having to read each other's letters. I took stationery to Mom and told her she should write. But I don't know if she will.*

*I tried to remind her of what the preacher told us last Sunday. That it's a waste of your time to worry about things before they happen. Because you can't change the future with your worrying and … more than likely, whatever you're worried about will NEVER happen anyway. So better to simply go through life expecting the best and only worry once something DOES happen. I don't think she listened, though.*

*Sorry, Dad's calling me. More later.*

*Your teenaged friend, Maude*

*P. S. Wow! Two really good things! When I went downstairs, both Dad AND Mom sat at the table waiting for me with my birthday cake and presents sitting in front of them. One of my presents was a beautiful Bible and Mom had written my name in it. I loved it that she thought of that.*

*But the best thing happened when Mom got up and hugged me and told*
*me she heard what I said and that she would try and stop worrying until*
*she really had something to worry about. Hooray!!*

---

April 17, 1918

HENRY AND BUZZ BOARDED THE USS *PASTORES* IN NEW YORK
Harbor, along with thousands of other troops from the American
Expeditionary Force, headed for St. Nazaire in France. One of five
United States Steamships to make the journey countless times within
the past year, the *Pastores* was escorted by four cruisers, thirteen
destroyers, and two fuel tankers to guard against the soldiers' ship
being sunk by German submarines.

"Look at all this firepower, Buzz. That should make you feel
protected."

But Buzz hung over the side of the ship, throwing up for the
second time in half an hour.

"Good God," Buzz said when he could speak again. "Is this what I
have to look forward to for the entire fifteen days of our trip? I don't
think I can stand it." He slumped to the deck but found that stirred
his stomach up worse, so he rose and stood close to one of the
buckets the Navy had graciously provided.

---

BY THE END OF THEIR TRIP, BUZZ THREW UP A LOT LESS
but rejoiced when the signal of "Land Ho!" sounded throughout the
ship. Actual fighting, he believed, couldn't possibly be worse than the
journey across the ocean.

Henry had made lots of friends and even learned how to play
poker with his time. But he mostly lost. Both men used part of every
day to compose letters to the family back home. They took great care
in their wording to Florence and attempted to point out as many

positives as they could. Buzz even refrained from telling her how sick he got. He saved those details for Maude's letters, knowing she would probably get a kick out of his throwing up for fifteen days straight. Before leaving America, Henry and Buzz learned they had been assigned to the 28th Regiment, a part of the newly formed U.S. First Infantry Division under the leadership of General John J. "Black Jack" Pershing himself. While small skirmishes involving soldiers from the American Expeditionary Forces, known as AEF among the troops, happened as early as late 1917, Pershing preferred to wait until his troops reached sufficient numbers to make a difference on their own, without acting as replacements for British or French divisions.

Upon arriving on French soil, Henry and Buzz, as part of the AEF, boarded trains that took them north of Paris to Amiens, outside the front line of the German surge. Right away, they went through a short battle training course from experienced French and British officers. The seasoned soldiers worried, especially the French, that the "green" Americans wouldn't be able to do their part in actual battle conditions.

But in late May, they would all learn about the grit that drove the American soldiers.

The objective for this first AEF skirmish was for the Americans to chase the Germans from the small village of Cantigny. The Germans had commandeered it months earlier because it sat on some of the highest ground in northern France, making it a perfect observation post for German artillery.

Buzz hopped into the designated trench first and reached up to help Henry.

"Good Lord, these packs are heavy," Henry said.

"Right," Buzz said beside him. "You think it's the two hundred twenty rounds of rifle ammunition, the three grenades, the two canteens of water, or the four sandbags?" He grinned. "Or," he added, reaching behind him, "maybe it's this shovel."

"And," Henry added, "don't forget, we're supposed to have two days' worth of food and water for ... how did the trainers put it ... 'to survive in our newly-won positions.' I truly appreciate it that they believe we will win our battle."

"Well, I believe it," Buzz said. "Don't you?"

"I sure do. I think it's poetic, call it fate, if you'd rather, that our unit, the 28th Regiment, was assigned this task on May 28th. We can't help but win."

They spent a restless few hours trying to find a comfortable position in the trench and finally gave up.

But every sense shot to high alert at 4:45 in the pitch black of morning when the French artillery units unleashed the first few rounds from their seventy-five-millimeter guns toward Cantigny to perfect their firing angle. An hour later, mere moments after sunrise, the French let loose a full bombardment, blasting the German defenders for more than an hour and lighting up the village so it looked like mid-day.

"Wow. What a show. Have you ever seen anything like it, Buzz?"

"Not since our July fourth fireworks last year." Even in the low light, Henry saw Buzz's smile and he laughed out loud.

"Okay, men, prepare to move!"

The time was 6:45 a.m. and the command came from the 28th Regiment Commander, Colonel Hansen Ely.

"This will be a piece of cake," Henry said. He leapt out of the trench and took his place on the lines. "I might lose you in this fog, Buzz. But let's just stay close to these tanks and do what we're told. I love having this huge tank battalion with us."

"I hear you, Henry. If we do lose each other, I'll find you when it's over." Buzz reached out his hand while they could still see each other. "Good luck, man. I love ya."

"Love you, too, brother."

"Move out!"

They advanced with their regiment and within minutes, the crack of gunfire surrounded them. The swampy, musky smell of fog mixed with the smoke from fired ammunition stung Buzz's throat. He pulled his uniform up over his nose and continued to shoot, ensuring that he kept close to the large shadow of the tank in front of him, unleashing continuous fire from its side guns. He did lose sight of Henry but knew that Henry would do what they had agreed to ... stay close to the tanks and shoot when possible.

By shortly after seven a.m., the fog lifted and Buzz could actually see the Germans. He stayed even with his line and continued to fire into their midst. After a particularly heavy barrage from the soldiers and the tanks, Buzz saw a massive number of Germans fall, run, and finally, from those who were left, throw up their arms in surrender.

"Cease fire!"

Buzz dropped to one knee in the dirt with those around him and waited for the next order.

"Take these men prisoner," Colonel Ely instructed. Buzz moved forward with his fellow soldiers to round up the surrendering German soldiers, then glanced at his watch.

It read 7:20 a.m. The whole battle had taken only thirty-five minutes.

"Well, hell," Buzz said, looking around him. "That wasn't so bad."

He scanned the soldiers closest to him. No Henry. He walked back the way they had come but didn't find him. Finally, he checked the stretchers being carried out by the medics. But still no Henry.

With no place else to look, he asked one of the medics, "Have other soldiers already been evacuated? I need to find my friend."

The medic pointed to a spot across the field. "You can try there," he said and continued on his way.

In the first large-scale battle with American soldiers in the global conflict, the Americans were victorious. As battles went, it stacked up as small, but the Americans proved they could fight and win. They proved it not only to the Germans, but also to the British and French.

Most of all, they proved it to themselves.

Yes, it was a very small battle as far as major battles in a world war go. Only one hundred American soldiers died that day.

But Buzz's best friend—the man he loved like a brother—was one of them.

Henry Brewer was dead.

# CHAPTER
# THIRTY-SIX

**SUZANNE**
**2015**

Finally, sweet little Maude could call herself a teenager. The thought made me smile.

And ... it sounded like her mother had come around. I couldn't help but think that Florence had been selfish by spending all that time worrying about her older child while leaving her younger child to fend for herself. It just didn't seem fair. So it made my heart happy to find out that her mother at least attempted to turn over a new leaf and join the family again. I hoped it would last.

A quick glance at my watch told me this should be my last entry. I really needed to get home. I wanted to finish my grandmother's diary but figured I could get to the end tomorrow.

I turned the page and found some of the lines streaked, as if they had been hit by water.

*June 5, 1918*

*Dear Diary,*

*I still can't believe it. Mom had finally decided to live her life again when the Western Union boy's bicycle showed up in the front yard. We were all out weeding the fields but as soon as she heard the bell on his bike, Mom fell down between the rows and didn't move until Dad confirmed the news and came to get her.*

*The telegram was from the War Department and it told us that Henry had been killed in his first battle. A second telegram came from Buzz, telling us he had found Henry and that it looked like he died instantly without suffering. I guess that should have made us feel better. But it didn't.*

*Mom's screams could be heard all over the farm.*

Oh dear. That's why the page was streaked. It wasn't water ... it was tears. And no wonder I never heard of Henry. I wonder if Dad's siblings even know their mother had an older brother.

And Henry's poor mother. Just when she got her worrying under control, the very thing she had feared for months actually happened. It's a wonder she didn't have a heart attack and die right there in the field. At least I didn't think she did. Guess I'd better keep reading.

*Mom's feeling guilty ... as if her controlling her worrying caused Henry to get shot. I'm feeling guilty, too, because I convinced her to let her fears go until something actually happened.*

*Well ... it did.*

*But even I understand that nothing Mom or I did—or didn't do—caused Henry's death. The war did. And just the rotten luck of who got in the way of a bullet. It's funny, I figured if either of them died, it would be Buzz because he so badly didn't want to go. I guess I thought that attitude would make him careless. But I was wrong.*

*The telegram also told us Henry was buried in France with other soldiers from that battle, so we won't get his body back. Even though we hadn't seen him much in the past couple of years, I can't believe he's gone. That we'll never get to talk to him again. We can't stop crying.*

*The weeds have gotten huge. But nobody seems to care. The preacher came to see us and convinced Dad to hold a memorial service for Henry on Sunday. For those who knew him to pay their final respects, he said. I'm not sure Mom will be able to go. She's back in bed and worse than ever. We may have lost her too. We walk around like ghosts, not able to even think straight.*

*Miss Delsie came to see us, along with all of the neighbors and some of the townspeople. They all brought food. But I can't even swallow. Dad convinced the preacher to take some of it to share with the Cottman family who lives in the woods across the road. They're really nice people and we've known them forever. Dad says they're descended from slaves. The mother, Josephine, has even come over a few times to help Mom with the spring cleaning.*

*Once the Cottmans received the food and found out about our sorrow, several of them showed up with hoes to do the weeding in the fields we left untended when we found out about Henry. It's hard to think about right this minute, but Dad says we'll be really happy about that come harvest time.*

*I'll let you know what else we find out.*

*Your sad friend, Maude*

⟶ ⟨◦⟩ ⟶

**June 8, 1918**

FINDING HENRY IN THE ROW OF DEAD SOLDIERS AFTER their first battle was the second worst moment in Buzz's young life. Watching his parents die had been the worst.

Buzz wanted to quit. He had never wanted to be part of the Army in the first place. The really bad thing was that in all of the scuttlebutt that reached the soldiers' ears, word was the ones in charge—the ones who sat on the hill watching after giving orders for soldiers to be put in harm's way ... without being in harm's way themselves—congratulated each other on only losing one hundred men. They celebrated, for God's sake. As if that were okay. As if those hundred lives meant nothing in the scheme of things.

But his best friend had died. His friend who had viewed being in the service as "the adventure of a lifetime." Some adventure. One battle and that was it. Sure, Buzz knew somebody had to be the first soldier to die in a battle. But why did it have to be Henry?

It would have made a lot more sense if it had been him.

He still couldn't figure out why it hadn't.

But Buzz had no time to mourn. He had to keep going.

———————

BY EARLY JULY, BUZZ'S REGIMENT MARCHED SOUTH. EVERY day … south. Rumors flew that they would fight in another small town, Montdidier, but when they reached it, the French already had the Germans under control there so they kept going.

Without Henry to keep his spirits up under the deplorable conditions of marching through forests and mud, Buzz pushed his thoughts away and attempted to focus on the moment at hand. But days and then weeks of that practice worked on him and before long he felt nothing.

Soldiers fell beside him but he plowed forward, shooting until he ran out of ammunition, then reloading and shooting again.

He had begun to believe himself invulnerable. And cared little whether he really was or not. Like a repetitive machine, mile after mile, one boot hit mud. And then the other.

Over and over without hesitation.

And without fear.

Without *any* emotion, in fact. Just as no sadness reached him when his comrades fell, neither did satisfaction fill him during victory.

Buzz no longer wanted to quit. Nor to have the war end. He didn't think. Or feel. He simply did as he was told. When he stopped to rest, he slept immediately. And when he woke, he performed his tasks automatically.

Like a machine.

A killing machine.

"Ryan," his sergeant said, "the captain needs a volunteer to scout forward."

"Sure," he said.

He gathered his gear, received his orders, then started out with another soldier, one from Virginia whose name he learned was Philip Randall.

"Heard you were a ballplayer," Randall said to him. Buzz ignored him.

"A pitcher, right?" Randall almost ran to keep up with him.

Buzz stopped short and faced his companion. "Look, I don't want to talk. I don't want to be friends. And I sure as hell don't want to remember what I 'used to do.' It's easier that way. Let's just get where we're supposed to go as quickly as possible, all right?"

The man stepped back as if he'd been struck. "Sure, man. Sorry."

Buzz turned his back and resumed his aggressive pace. Again, Randall hurried to keep up. But he let all conversation drop.

Their objective was to study the southern route laid out between Montdidier and the Champagne region and find any pockets of Germans that could impede the Army's progress to Château-Thierry, less than fifty kilometers northeast of Paris. Even among the rank and file, it was common knowledge that the Germans intended to take Paris. And they would have to go through Château-Thierry to accomplish that.

The Allies focused, in addition to keeping the Germans out of Paris, on retaking ground seized by the Germans in May and June and pushing them back to the Hindenburg Line. And farther east, if possible. All the way back to Germany.

Buzz and his traveling companion covered the ground past Compiègne, then followed the Aisne River toward Soissons before Buzz halted and held up his hand. Randall stopped behind him. "What is it?" he whispered.

"Germans ... small party." Buzz pointed toward the river. They crept through the trees and followed the sound ... laughter and singing ... until they had a good view, then squatted in place. About a dozen German soldiers bathed in the river, their guns plainly visible on the bank.

Buzz raised his rifle to his shoulder.

"What are you doing?" Randall hissed, panic in his voice.

"What does it look like I'm doing? I'm going to kill Germans." Buzz closed one eye and found his target in his sites, his finger moving toward the trigger.

Randall put his hand over Buzz's gun and pushed it down. "Stop. You can't just shoot them. You have to give them a chance to surrender."

Buzz glared at him. "What would we do with a dozen prisoners? That's not our mission."

"Well, it's not our mission to kill this many Germans when they haven't engaged with us, either. It's just wrong."

"My God, man," Buzz said softly, exasperation filling his voice, "this whole damned war is wrong. What's that got to do with it? We are supposed to discover pockets of German soldiers as obstacles in the Army's path. If we eliminate them, obstacle gone. Now leave me alone."

Buzz aimed again and shot. Twice. Three times. Soldiers fell. The others scrambled toward the bank through the chest-high water, shouting. Buzz kept shooting, then noticed that Randall had joined him. None of the soldiers made it to their clothes.

The last one fell, but a shot rang out beside Buzz. His head jerked around in time to see Randall pitch forward, blood oozing from a hole in his back. The crack of another shot reached his ears at the exact moment a white-hot pain seared through his upper leg. He fell backward, his gun still in his arms. From his position on the ground, he looked into the eyes of another German soldier, whose gun was trained on his head.

Without thinking, he pulled the trigger. And the German fell on top of him. Dead. The weight knocked the breath out of Buzz and he passed out.

He didn't know how long he'd been out, but when he woke, the German's weight remained on top of him. And dusk had filled the sky.

He freed his arms and pushed the German with all his remaining strength. The German rolled on top of Randall, and Buzz wriggled himself free. He managed to sit. Every movement shot through him and ended in blinding pain. He cut away his pants to expose his wound and saw that the bullet had gone all the way through his leg. In the sketchy medical unit from his training, he vaguely remembered that a bullet traveling all the way through a limb was a good thing. But he couldn't, for the life of him, remember why. So he stopped thinking about it and searched through his kit to find something to bind his wound. Nothing. He used his knife to cut his tattered pants into strips, then tied them together. He used part of them to make a tourniquet to slow his blood loss then stuffed other strips into the hole. And passed out again, this time from the pain.

When he came to, he replaced the blood-soaked strips, more gently this time, then wrapped one more strip around his upper leg to hold them in place and keep the wound covered. He scooted himself along the forest floor until he found a sturdy branch and used his last few strips to tie a shorter stick to its top, then padded it with his shirt. Sitting beside a tree, he shimmied his torso up its trunk to a standing position and used his padded stick as a crutch. From there, he emptied his pack of everything he considered to be nonessential, hoisted it to his shoulder and started limping along the path toward Soissons. He knew he needed medical attention and figured that town would be large enough to find it. Before leaving the area totally, he checked his coordinates so he could send somebody back for Randall.

Walking was certainly harder this way, but not as painful as he'd expected.

*Maybe because I no longer feel anything.*

He continued to follow the Aisne River, knowing it would take him to Soissons, and he traveled well into the night. Again, he moved like a machine. One foot down, drag the other.

Step. Drag. Breathe. Sweat.

Over and over.

Step. Drag. Breathe. Sweat.
Step. Drag. Breathe ...
Dark ...

<hr />

BUZZ OPENED HIS EYES AND STARED INTO BRIGHT GREEN ones.

# CHAPTER
# THIRTY–SEVEN

MARTHE
1918

"Who are you?"

"*Dèsolè monsieur, je ne comprends pas l'anglais. Une minute, s'il-vous-plaît.*"

Jeannette Beaudelaire left the American soldier and went to find Marthe.

"Marthe, *l'Américain est réveillé. Vas-tu lui parler?* Will you talk to the American?"

"*Oui.*"

The two women leaned over the bedside of the young American. "Did you have a question, soldier?" Marthe asked him in English.

He opened his eyes wide and shook his head as if to clear it. "Yeah. Am I in heaven?"

Marthe laughed. "No, soldier. You're very much alive. You're in a German hospital in France. Behind the Hindenburg Line."

He leaned back, his face pale.

"German ..." He raised his hand to his head then felt his leg. "I was shot ..."

"Yes you were," Marthe answered. "But you were lucky. The bullet went all the way through. And you were even luckier that it didn't hit bone or any major arteries."

"So I'll be able to walk again?"

"Yes. It will take time for you to heal but you shouldn't have any lasting damage. Do you remember anything about what happened?"

"Another soldier and I were watching Germans in the river. Then he got shot. Dead." He stopped talking and frowned. "Then I got shot."

"By a German, right? But he didn't kill you ..."

"No." He frowned again. "I ... I think I killed him." He closed his eyes. "Yes. I shot him and he fell on top of me. I had trouble moving because of my leg." After a moment's silence, he asked, "How long have I been here?"

"They brought you in two days ago." Marthe paused then said, "Do you remember how you got here?"

"No. I remember putting a bandage on my leg and making a crutch. Then I started walking."

"From what we could piece together, a patrol found you wandering in the woods in the middle of the night. They took you prisoner and brought you here. You were feverish and dehydrated but we got to your leg just before infection set in. I assisted on your surgery myself." Marthe put her hand on his forehead. "Your fever is gone, though. That's good. No infection. How do you feel?"

"My leg hurts."

"Jeannette," Marthe said. She didn't turn toward her fellow nurse. "*Allez-vous donner à ce soldat des médicaments.*" Jeannette nodded and left.

"So I'm a prisoner. Is this hospital in Soissons? That's where I was headed."

"Yes, you're a prisoner. And no, our hospital isn't in Soissons. We're a little farther away from the fighting than that. In Laon. But you will stay here until you are well." She smiled at him. "It could take some time so, who knows, maybe the war will be over by then." Her smile widened. "And you're our first American. So I'll get to practice my English." She extended her hand. "My name is Marthe and this is Jeannette." She indicated the other nurse who offered him a glass of water and a pill cup.

"Buzz," he said. "Buzz Ryan."

# CHAPTER
# THIRTY-EIGHT

**SUZANNE**
**2015**

I
t broke my heart to read how my poor little grandmother's writing changed from being an exuberant ten-year-old to a devastated thirteen-year-old. I suppose that's the difference in going through a war or not.

I mean, sure, I've lost people ... a couple of classmates killed in Vietnam. But other than that, the only war I remember in my adult lifetime that the United States fought in was Desert Storm and that one didn't last long. Plus, I didn't lose anybody in it. My son went but came back home in one piece.

Steve, Sr., however, my son's father, was my most devastating loss. A drunk driver snuffed out his life a little more than five years ago. And while I thought at first I'd never find a way to cope with his death, I was grown when it happened, not thirteen like my grandmother. And both my parents were still alive then and became my rocks of support, different from Maude's mother who had basically checked out.

Even when my parents died, I was certainly unhappy when it happened but Mom was in constant pain from her cancer and Dad died after we got home from that fabulous trip. And he died with a smile on his face. Almost as if he welcomed it. Plus, both my parents were in their late eighties and had lived very full, very happy lives, so while I felt sad to be without them, it didn't make sense to be sad for them.

But ... poor little Maude. I could only imagine how difficult her time must have been without having her mother's support and having to figure out how to do all the things her mother should have been doing.

I picked up her diary again to see if things got any better.

*August 10, 1918*

*Dear Diary,*

*We finally heard from Buzz today. Three letters showed up all at once. In the first one, he told us the few details he had about Henry's death. It wasn't much more than we already knew. He says they got separated because of the fog that first morning just as the battle began. He doesn't know how it happened. They were just focused on doing their jobs and that was it. The whole battle only took slightly more than half an hour … but long enough to get Henry killed.*

*I'm so mad! It wasn't supposed to be like this. Buzz said that same thing.*

*In the second letter, Buzz told us he got shot too. In the leg. He's worried about healing well enough to walk again. And especially in being able to keep his balance to pitch. As if that even matters any more. But I guess it matters to him.*

*And it gets worse from there. Germans captured him and took him to a German hospital as a prisoner of war.*

Okay. Wow. That's not better. It's worse. Much worse.

And … after reading all this bad stuff, I remembered I had planned to stop for the night.

Oh well, too late now.

*In his third letter, Buzz says that so far, they're treating him fine and there's a Belgian nurse named Marthe who even speaks English. He says she takes good care of him and keeps the Germans in charge from both-*

*ering him much, but he doesn't know what he might face when he's healed. He's somewhere in France, in a small town. I'm not sure he even knows the name of it.*

*Dad and I write to him regularly. I hope he still gets the letters ... I guess the Army is supposed to know where he is and forward them to him. I feel like he's my last link with Henry. And he was like a brother to me when he lived here.*

*I can't write any more now. I'm too upset. I'll come back later.*

*Your still sad friend, Maude*

---

## August 11, 1918

BUZZ'S STRENGTH IMPROVED STEADILY. AND WITH THAT improvement, along with all the attention he received from the nurses Marthe and Jeannette, he gradually let down his guard and the hard shell he had built around himself slowly began to dissolve. He still didn't notice a lot of feeling in his heart, but his need to have people leave him alone and not talk to him had lessened. Especially when two beautiful nurses hovered over him.

He really enjoyed spending time with the Belgian nurse, Marthe, who came to see him every day—sometimes only a few minutes at a time, sometimes as much as an hour. When no one else was around, she gave him details about how the battles were going. Earlier in the week she told him the Aisne-Marne offensive was over and the threat to Paris had ended. The Allies, she said, had the upper hand. It surprised him she would share such a thing with him. But then he found out why from their continuing conversation.

"You speak English beautifully," Buzz said to her one afternoon. "Where did you learn?"

"At college," she said. "Ghent University. I began with business courses and, along with them, I studied languages, so I also speak French, German, and Russian. I switched to nurses' training, also in Ghent, after my second year and had to suspend my time there when the war broke out."

"So you're Belgian?" he asked. *That may be why she tells me about Allied victories.*

"Yes."

"And yet, you are a nurse in a German hospital." He wanted to say more but didn't want to offend her since she took such good care of him.

Her head dipped and pain flickered across her face.

"I'm sorry," he said. "I didn't mean to cause you distress."

"You didn't." She scanned the room to see who might be listening. Her friend, Jeannette, sat in another corner, caring for a French soldier. Since Marthe knew Jeannette didn't speak English, she continued, "The day the Germans invaded Belgium in 1914, they killed my whole family and burned my home. Then they forced me to travel with them since I had nursing skills and could speak several languages." She pulled her gold locket out of her nurse's blouse and opened it for him. "These are my parents," she said, showing him the tiny portraits.

Buzz looked at the pictures, then reached out and covered her hand with his. For the first time since Henry died, his heart felt something. Sympathy. "I am so sorry," he said. "I know how it feels to lose your family. I watched my parents die in front of my eyes too."

"Oh no," she said. "Now I am sorry. Were they killed as a result of the war?"

He closed his eyes, remembering the horrible scene. "No." His voice barely registered. "Unfortunately, they were both drunks. Mean drunks. And I arrived home in time to see my father shoot my mother. And then himself." Again, his eyes closed. He couldn't believe he could talk about it with someone he hardly knew. "I really thought he would shoot me instead," he added. "Or, I don't know … maybe in addition." He took a deep breath. "I think that's why I no longer feel fear in battle. Everyone I loved has been killed. So what difference does it make if I die too?"

"Oh, you mustn't say that. Surely there is someone in the world who would be sorry if you were gone."

"I suppose the family I lived with in Pennsylvania would be sorry." He took another breath. "So ... are you still captive? Is that why you're here taking care of me?"

"No," she answered. "Now I am needed. With wounded coming in so fast, we are all needed. And no one else here can communicate with so many different soldiers. So I stay."

"Do you know what you will do when the war is over?"

She shook her head. "I haven't allowed myself to think that far ahead. Have you?"

"You bet," he said. "The very minute this is over and I can get out of here, I'm headed back to Philadelphia to my ball team."

"What is ball team?"

Buzz smiled. "I guess you may not have them here. I'm a professional baseball player." He put his hands together as if he were holding a bat and did a mock swing. "Baseball?" He made a noise with his tongue to mimic the sound of the ball hitting the bat. "Do you know it?"

"Oh yes," she said. "Some young men from The Netherlands came to campus and played a ... how do you say ... *exposition?*"

"You mean like an exhibition game? Where the same team splits into two and then plays each other? Just to show people how it's done?"

"Yes. Like that." She hesitated. "I found it a little slow for my taste. What position did you play?"

"Pitcher," he said. "I pitched all during school with my best friend ..." His face clouded and his eyes teared. "Sorry," he said. "My best friend, Henry, and I played together. I lost him in our very first battle." Two tears slid down his cheeks. "I miss him so much."

She put her hand on his. "I am sorry, Buzz. It is difficult to lose someone you love."

He nodded and leaned back against his pillow. "I hate this damned war," he said quietly. "I really hope the American participation will make it end quickly. I want to go home."

She studied his face then stood.

"Maybe there will be a way for you to help." He strained to hear her.

"I don't see how ... from this bed ... as a prisoner."

"You may be surprised," she said cryptically. "I'll come see you again tomorrow. We will even get you up and have you practice walking. With crutches. Until then, rest."

# CHAPTER THIRTY-NINE

MARTHE
1918

Marthe's days flew by with her hospital duties, leaving her very little time to perform any aid to the Allies.

She did, however, find time to spend with Buzz, the dark-haired American soldier. *He is so attractive. He looks like a movie star.*

Sometimes she read to him from books written in English. She wanted the practice, she told him, and occasionally asked for his help with a word that was new to her. In the evenings, they played cards and dominoes.

Even though he was a prisoner of war, Marthe protected Buzz from any bad treatment by the Germans. She had no idea what might happen when he healed completely and had to leave. But so far, the wound in his leg had a way to go before he could be released.

Week after week, the fighting raged on and new soldiers arrived. As always, Marthe performed her duties with her usual efficiency, but her time with the American soldier became precious to her.

"Good morning." She made a point of greeting him brightly every day and looked forward to the way his eyes lit up when he saw her. She had even, without realizing it at first, begun taking more care with her appearance. "I brought the crutches again," she said. "Are you ready to walk?"

"Absolutely," he answered. "I think I'm even ready to see if I can stand well enough to try and pitch. Any chance there's a ball and a mitt around here?"

Marthe laughed. "No. As far as I can tell, no one here plays ball.

No one else, that is." She helped him sit up and then stand, fitting the crutches under his arms. "Take your time."

He took a few tentative steps and then a few more once he found the rhythm of walking with crutches.

"Bravo," Marthe said. "You are doing great."

They traveled up and down the hallways and when Buzz thought they were alone he stopped to face her. "Nurse Marthe, you recently said something to me about a way I could help to get the war over with quicker. What did you mean?"

Panic filled her face. "Not here," she said. "But I have an idea. You must trust me."

———— ✦ ————

EVERY DAY, BUZZ PRACTICED WALKING WITH CRUTCHES. And every day, his strides became longer and his confidence greater. He didn't ask her his question again but waited patiently for her to talk to him about it.

In August, Marthe told him the fighting had moved farther north in France so the influx of new wounded into her hospital had waned. A couple of days later, she handed him his crutches. "Time for a walk." His eyes lit as usual. "But first you must get dressed."

"Fine," he said, throwing back his covers. "Where are we going?"

"I have a surprise." Her eyes twinkled. "Come with me."

Marthe guided him through the halls they traveled daily on his crutches, then turned toward the outside. His face held questions but he refrained from putting them into words. She led him through a door and into the grassy yard behind the hospital where several men stood around.

"What is this?" he asked.

Then a man Buzz recognized as an orderly came through another door, his arms loaded with sports equipment. He dropped it on the ground and Buzz saw bats, mitts, and baseballs, among other things.

"Seriously?" Buzz turned toward Marthe. "How did you arrange this?"

She flashed a smile. "I found out that the *Oberartz,* the head doctor here, loves baseball. So since you are a baseball player, I convinced him it may be good for morale to have our wounded soldiers play a game. I figured you could practice your pitching."

"You are incredible," Buzz said. He moved toward the equipment and chose a mitt. Soldiers from both sides, German troops and prisoners of war from the Allied countries moved in as well and picked up equipment and the *Oberartz* himself took charge and got behind home plate. Buzz selected his team from the prisoners he knew and, once they found out he was a professional pitcher, even some of the German soldiers volunteered to join him. Marthe translated whenever necessary.

Marthe stood beside Buzz to make certain he didn't fall as he attempted his first pitch with a bum leg. Propping himself up on one crutch, he turned his right side to home plate, put his hands in the air, and, Marthe saw, closed his eyes and moved his fingers over the ball. A German soldier stood ready at home plate, bat over one shoulder. Buzz turned and let the ball fly.

"Ball," the *Oberartz* shouted. Buzz grunted.

"Did that hurt?" Marthe asked.

"Nah," Buzz answered. "Except that I think that pitch might have been a strike." He grinned.

He went through his routine again and flew the ball over the plate.

"Ball," came the shout again.

He rearranged his legs slightly to get a more grounded stance. Since he had no signals worked out with the catcher, Buzz decided to test his whole repertoire to make certain he could still pull off each of his signature pitches, even though his leg wasn't completely healed. His knuckleballs had fallen a little flat, so he wound up again and released his fastball.

"*Schlagen!*" the *Oberartz* shouted. The men on the other team groaned. Buzz looked toward Marthe, a question in his eyes.

"He said 'strike,'" she said with a smile. "That's good, right?"

"That's very good." He smiled back.

Pitch by pitch, Buzz let the ball fly, sometimes pleased with the result and sometimes not. After the equivalent of five or six innings, he slumped onto his crutches and his face paled.

"I think I've done all I can do today," he told Marthe. "But I can never thank you enough for arranging this."

Marthe called to the *Oberartz* that Buzz needed to rest and the head doctor came toward him and shook Buzz's hand. He said something in German and Buzz turned to Marthe to translate.

"He said 'thank you for giving the men something to cheer about.'"

Buzz nodded and smiled, then turned back to Marthe. "I think it's time for me to lie down for a while. Will you help me?"

She put an arm around his waist while he navigated his crutches until they reached his cot. He sank onto it gratefully. He turned to her, his eyes shining. "Marthe, I never dreamed I would find someone like you. Especially as a prisoner of war. You are …"

She watched his eyes and saw that he struggled with what he wanted to say, then he finished with, "…wonderful. Just wonderful."

Her heart filled and left her with a happy glow.

They were alone in the room and a quick glance told her that of the few soldiers remaining, none of them spoke English. She pulled a chair up to the side of his cot.

"Will you let me check your wound?"

"Sure," he said. He pushed his blanket away from his legs and removed his pants. Marthe bent over him, her locket falling toward him from her blouse.

"I want to make certain it hasn't begun to bleed again." She pulled scissors from her pocket and cut away his bandage. "Good," she said. "The stitches have held. No infection. It's healing nicely. Does it hurt?" She raised her head and looked into eyes gazing at her with such tenderness, her breath caught in her throat.

"No," he whispered. "It doesn't hurt."

"I … um … have to get a new bandage. I'll be right back."

She rose and rushed from the room toward the storage closet. Her hands shook as she focused on the supplies to bind his wound again. Finally, she took a deep breath and simply stood for a moment to calm herself. Then she put her supplies in a basket and returned to Buzz's cot.

She bent over him to rewrap his leg and spoke to him in a soft voice. "It's time we talked. About how you can help the Allies win the war sooner," she added.

He sat up straighter in his bed. "Oh," he said. His face held disappointment but he said, "Certainly. Talk."

"I have a way to get information to the British Intelligence Network," she told him, her head still bent. Careful to keep her voice low, she continued. "If you happen to know anything that might help, I can pass it along."

"Unfortunately, I don't," he said. "I wish I did. But is there anything I can do to help you?"

That was exactly what she hoped he would say.

"Maybe," she answered. "I have been told there is a German ammunition depot not far from here with heavy mortar shells and lots of machine gun rounds. It is headed for a huge offensive at the edge of the Argonne Forest. The Allies would benefit if it were destroyed. But … I can't do it alone."

"Count me in," he said without hesitation. "When?"

"I will let you know. For now, rest. You will need your strength when the time comes."

Marthe finished his bandage and tied the last knot. Without any conscious thought from her, she patted his leg softly, then raised her hand to caress his face. They sat, staring into each other's eyes.

Neither of them saw Jeannette Beaudelaire hidden in the shadows and watching them from the door.

# CHAPTER FORTY

**SUZANNE**
**2015**

I knew I should have returned to my own home, but instead I curled up on Dad's couch and pulled his comforter over me to sleep for a few hours. A lot of things still needed to be done before Steve and Emily and I made the trip to Prospect Park. But, even though I couldn't explain it, I felt a powerful need to finish reading Maude's diary. As if there were something in it I needed to know before we returned. Logically, I knew it didn't make sense, but I felt it regardless.

After a nap, I awoke, propped myself up on the couch and turned the light on to continue reading. Maude wrote a lot less often but when she did, her entries were longer.

*September 20, 1918*

*Dear Diary,*

*I know. It's been a while. Sorry about that. But we're kind of struggling around here.*

*I'm back in school—8th grade this year. I did my own school shopping since Mom hardly ever gets out of bed—again. You'd think now that she's had time to get used to the idea of Henry being gone, she might begin to accept it and rejoin us.*

*But that hasn't happened yet.*

*Dad says we had a pretty good harvest. At least good enough to get us through the winter. We saved a lot of the vegetables to can, and Miss Josephine Cottman, from through the woods, came over to help me do it. That part was really great because she even made ketchup and something she called "pasta" sauce. I'd never had it before, and the only pasta we had was macaroni. Dad was skeptical at first, but decided he liked the taste. Miss Josephine said I could even add meat to it the next time—beef, pork, or chicken—and serve it over different kinds of noodles, like spaghetti or linguine. I'm eager to try that. It will really add to the number of meals I know how to cook.*

*I made a lot of my clothes for school and I had to have Dad help me pin up my skirts for hemming. He made me laugh at the beginning, but we got through it just fine.*

*In Social Studies class, as usual, we're still following the war, so Miss Delsie asks those of us with relatives fighting over there to read their letters aloud in class. So far, I'm the only one who gets letters from a prisoner of war so she always has me read mine. Every time somebody reads a letter, if there's any information in it about where they are, Miss Delsie shows us on the world map. It's kind of interesting, to see how far away they are.*

*We got three more letters from Buzz this week. In one of them he told us about his nurse, Marthe, arranging a ball game at his hospital. He sounded like he really enjoyed it. In another one, he said his leg continued to get better but that he wasn't sure where he would be taken to an actual prison when the time came. The last letter didn't have much news but he sounded happy. Mom didn't like that one. She only wants to hear about Henry and doesn't think it's right for Buzz to be happy when Henry's dead. I told her I didn't think it was fair of her to feel that way, but then she started to cry again so I stopped talking to her.*

*Time to start supper. I'll write later.*

*Your friend, Maude*

---·❦·---

## September 20, 1918

BUZZ DIDN'T GET A LOT OF NEWS ABOUT THE WAR OTHER than the few tidbits Marthe could tell him. But she also said she was being watched so she hadn't been able to spend as much time with him lately as she had at first. He hesitated to bring up their conversation about the ammunition depot but knew that sometimes Marthe left the hospital to scout areas close by where it might be located. She had been able to tell him recently that her main contact—the one she'd used since coming to Laon—had disappeared. And she didn't know what might have happened to him.

He missed his time with Marthe terribly. Other than Henry's family and Coach Mack, no one had ever been so nice to him. Or done so much for him ... like making certain he could practice his pitching. He wished he knew who watched her. He really wanted to help and he grew impatient with not being able to destroy the ammunition depot. Or to do anything at all that might help end the war.

He noticed that Jeannette, the nurse from Luxembourg, tended to his needs most of the time now. Jeannette was pretty but didn't have the same personality as Marthe. And it was obvious Jeanette threw herself at him. Mostly, the clues were subtle, letting her hand rest too long on his thigh after changing his bandage or giving him a backrub when she helped him get dressed. Which he no longer needed. He believed she knew that as well but seemed to hang around regardless.

And ... she didn't speak English. She tried to teach him a few words in French, but they only got as far as *bonjour*, the French word for "hello," and *merci*, the word for "thank you." He spent more time sleeping and writing letters than he had when he'd been able to be with Marthe.

He unfolded one of the letters he had just received from Maude.

*Hi Buzz,*

*Dad is writing, too, but I know he won't be honest with you. I think he's hoping you will be able to go back to Philadelphia and pitch but now that you've been shot, we both wonder if you will really be able to do that again.*

*We need help around here, Buzz. I'm doing all I can in the fields, but I also have school and cooking and all those other things Mom ~~won't~~ can't do anymore.*

*Of course you still want to pitch and we all hope you can. But if not, please come on home and help until we can get Mom back on her feet. Or until I get out of school and can help full-time.*

*I hope you're still healing well. Looking forward to hearing from you.*

*Your almost sister, Maude*

His stomach tightened as if he had been punched. That was the last thing he wanted. He'd never wanted to be here in this godforsaken war and he sure as hell didn't want to go back to a small farm and try to eke out a living on truck crops.

He had to be able to pitch again. He *had* to. And it looked like he could, from the pick-up game Marthe had arranged. No, pitching was absolutely his priority. As soon as he could get the hell out of here and get back to the States.

Baseball was his future.

Baseball.

And Marthe.

Since he'd had to spend so much time without her, she consumed his thoughts. His heart raced when he thought of her and he thought of her constantly.

In fact, he admitted to himself, he loved her. Totally and completely.

# CHAPTER FORTY-ONE

MARTHE
September 1918

"I will give the American his medication," Jeannette told Marthe as they began their rounds. They always spoke French when only the two of them were together. "It looks like you are really tired today. Late night? New boyfriend?"

Marthe sat at the small table in the break room with her head in her hands. It *had* been a late night. She had walked many kilometers in search of the ammunition depot the Germans hid. With her contact gone and no one coming forward as her new connection with the network, she was operating blind. She hadn't seen any "safety-pin men" for months. And to top it off, Jeannette looked at her with constant suspicion in her eyes. "No, Jeannette. No boyfriend at all."

"I thought you were sweet on the American," she said. She waited for Marthe's reaction and when none came, she continued. "He is so handsome. Don't you think?"

Without raising her head, Marthe said quietly, "Yes. He is."

"I may volunteer to go to his prison camp with him when he leaves," Jeannette said. Again, she waited for a reaction that never came. "That way, I think I can make him fall in love with me and take me to America with him when he returns after the war. What do you think of that?"

Marthe knew Jeannette baited her, tried to get a reaction from her. And she was disappointed at the thought that the woman she believed was her friend would treat her that way. It could be because of the American. Marthe had spent a lot of time with him and it was obvious

Jeannette wanted to spend more time with him. But it didn't matter what the reason was. Marthe simply knew that with Jeannette around she would always have to be on her guard. She lifted her head and said, "I think there's not a lot of chance that any of those things will happen." Marthe stood. "Now, if you'll excuse me, I think I hear ambulances arriving."

Marthe walked briskly to the front door of the hospital where, sure enough, an ambulance wagon had parked. She descended the stairs and smiled as the ambulance driver she had met in Roulers months earlier greeted her. "Nurse," he nodded and inconspicuously raised his lapels to show two diagonal white metal safety-pins. "Nice to see you again. I heard you had transferred here. I have a few wounded for you. Overflows from the battle in the Argonne Forest. Here are their papers." He handed her a sheaf of loose pages and turned toward his ambulance. Then he stopped abruptly and turned back toward her and reached into his coat pocket. "I also heard you had a scarcity of matches around here, so I brought you some." He placed the small box in her hand, tipped his hat, and returned to his vehicle.

"Thank you," she said and slipped the matchbox into her pocket.

The driver left and Marthe did her triage, sending some soldiers to wards to be cleaned up and others directly into surgery when their wounds required it. In the surgery room, everything appeared to be under control, so she slipped into the bathroom and locked the door. Seeing a former contact lifted her spirits and she opened the matchbox to retrieve the tiny message.

*Depot is located on road to Reims in burned out church. Destroy if possible.*

There it was. The information she needed. All she had to do was figure out how she would destroy it. And when. And who would help her.

She dropped the paper into the water and flushed the toilet in case someone listened outside the door. She needed to make it appear that she had gone to the bathroom for the usual reasons, rather than to read a message from her spy network. She flushed it down the toilet but before leaving the room, checked to make certain the tiny paper completely disappeared.

Her mind spun with possible plans to destroy the depot. Silently, she sent a grateful prayer of thanks to Herr Breit for insisting she bring several sticks of dynamite with her to Laon. It would work to do the job. So that would be the "how."

And she believed the "who" would also be easy.

Buzz. The good-looking American. He would be glad to help her.

The only thing left for her to figure out was the "when." And the sooner the better.

⸻ ❧ ⸻

MARTHE LEFT THE HOSPITAL AGAIN JUST BEFORE midnight and traveled the road to Reims, making certain to carry her pass that allowed her to be out at any time of the day or night. Regardless, she stuck to the edges of roads and hid herself in the trees whenever anyone passed. She didn't want to risk recognition.

Her goal was to find the depot and time her route to it from the hospital. Once she did that, she would figure out how to sneak Buzz out to accompany her.

She stayed on her path, thankful that dark clouds covered the moon during most of her journey. After another kilometer the clouds parted momentarily and she saw the skeleton of the charred church steeple outlined against the moon. She stole around to the back of the church and searched the area. She found nothing. Then she entered the bombed out building and searched every corner of it until she found the stash of ammunition, stored in the church's basement under a large canvas cover.

Satisfied, she decided to head back to the hospital when she heard voices. She knew fighting was still going on in the area, so she shrank back against the inside wall of the church and listened until they passed. Germans. Maybe half a dozen from the sound of their voices.

She gave them plenty of time, then left the church and cut through the woods to bypass the part of the road they traveled.

A little more than two hours later, she returned to the hospital without further incident. Satisfied she could reach the depot in a

reasonable time, she had also assured herself she had enough dynamite to handle the job. But she worried that Buzz might not be able to
walk that far at the pace she needed and decided to rethink the plan.
Having help would make the task so much easier, but she couldn't
afford to be slowed down.

The hour was late and the hospital quiet so she risked a quick trip
to see Buzz. She stood by his cot, studying his face.

His eyes opened and he smiled at her. "I *am* in heaven, huh?" he
asked her softly. "And you're my angel."

Her heart thumped in her chest and she smiled back. "I hadn't
seen you in a while," she whispered. "I just wanted to look at you. To
make certain you're all right."

"I'm better than all right, Marthe. Now that you're here, I'm
perfect."

"Buzz ..."

"No ... wait," he said. "Please let me talk. I've thought about you
so much. And here you are. As if it's meant to be. I ... Marthe ... I ..."
He took a deep breath and grabbed her hand. "I love you," he finished.
"I want to spend my life with you. Back in the States. In Philadelphia.
Where I'll return to pitch." He studied her face. "Don't answer now.
Just think about it."

She squeezed his hand. "We'll talk tomorrow," she said. "And ...
thank you."

# CHAPTER FORTY-TWO

MARTHE
1918

Marthe spent a fitful night, unable to sleep and obsessed with the two things on her mind, destroying the depot and Buzz's proposal. She imagined each scenario through to conclusion and when the first rays of dawn filtered into her room she had made her decision.

She had a plan.

She rose and dressed quickly, intent on setting her plan in motion.

She would visit Buzz first. To give him her answer.

But before she reached him, the *Oberartz* called out to her. "Nurse. Join me in surgery right away. We have another case of gangrene."

She knew what that meant. Amputation.

Declining was not an option so she followed the doctor to the surgery and scrubbed up.

———◦◦◦◦———

*"BONJOUR."*

Buzz opened his eyes into the bright green ones of Jeannette Beaudelaire, hovering inches above his.

*"J'ai ton médicament."*

"I'm sorry," Buzz said, "but I don't under—"

Jeannette held up the little cup with Buzz's pills.

"Oh, right ... pills. How did you say it?"

*"Médicament."*

He repeated the word and she laughed. *"Bon."* She cocked her head as if to think, then added, "Good."

"Oh," he said. "English. Very good."

"I ... study."

Buzz smiled. "Well, you did just fine. Good for you."

He sat up and swallowed his pills. Jeannette perched on the side of his cot, her face close to his.

"Buzz," she said softly.

Her pronunciation of his name emphasized the final letters and reached his ears as a soft hiss. "I learn for you."

His eyes widened. "Well, thank you," he said. "But why? I won't be here that much longer, then I guess they'll send me to a prison camp. You won't see me again."

Her face showed momentary confusion then cleared and she took his hand. "I ... love ... you." She said the words slowly but clearly enough for him to understand. Dismay filled his features. And his gasp filled the room.

"Thank you, Jeannette. *Merci,*" he said. His free hand found his forehead. He'd never been in this situation before. "But ... I love Marthe." He watched her face change. "I'm so sorry. I've asked her to marry me."

She rose abruptly. She understood.

But anger surged into her.

Then exploded.

She pulled her hand away and left in a huff.

———— ·⚜· ————

THE SURGERY WAS BRUTAL. A BRITISH SOLDIER LOST BOTH legs all the way to his pelvis. He begged the doctor not to take them, said he had a young wife and a baby and needed to be able to walk, to carry his daughter.

But the doctor cut them both off anyway.

His actions sickened Marthe. The gangrene hadn't been that bad and she had gotten really good results by using the Carrel-Dakin technique, a simple procedure that consisted of regular irrigation through rubber tubes placed in the wounded area. It had already begun to work on the British soldier. But the doctor refused to listen to her.

Her relationship with the *Oberartz* had changed. Subtly, yes, but irrevocably, she was certain. Maybe her mind simply worked overtime due to her guilt from plotting against the Germans by night and nursing their wounded by day. Or maybe she was overly tired from her reconnaissance activities of the past few nights. But she had begun to sense suspicion from every quarter, with the *Oberartz* at the top of the list. Certain lingering looks he sent her way told her he thought she spent too much time with the prisoners—trying to heal them when simply amputating a diseased limb would accomplish the same result, but quicker.

The surgery, Marthe believed, conveyed a message to her from the *Oberartz*, an overt signal that the prisoners would suffer if she failed to remember her place with the Germans. And a British soldier's life became forever altered because of her actions.

She raced to the bathroom and emptied her stomach.

"The damned Germans," she said under her breath. "The damned brutal Germans." She flushed the toilet, wiped her face, and straightened her shoulders.

She had planned to decline Buzz's proposal. Not because she didn't love him, but because she thought he would be better off without having a new wife when—or if—he returned to the States. But the actions of the *Oberartz* confirmed in her mind that she could never live among the Germans once the war ended. She had nothing to keep her in Germany. Or even, at this point, in Belgium. So she would marry Buzz and allow herself to find happiness. At last. After everything she had been through. She smiled through her tears and left the bathroom.

⸻ ⟡ ⸻

"BUZZ," MARTHE SAID SOFTLY, HER HAND ON HIS.

His eyes opened and when he saw her, he smiled. He put his other hand on hers and said, "I'm so happy to see you. I love you."

She smiled back. "I love you, Buzz. And ... I will marry you."

"Oh Marthe ... I wish I could kiss you."

"You will," she said. "I have a plan." She spoke very softly even though no one appeared to be close to them. "Let's take a walk. I brought your crutches. And a cane if you think that would be easier."

"Yes," he said. "Let me try the cane."

She helped him get up and they went outside to the garden. They walked to the edge of the property without touching.

"May I kiss you now?"

Marthe smiled. "Not yet. But here's my plan. I will come and get you tonight and sneak you out of the hospital. We will take an ambulance and destroy the ammunition depot. I will need you to help me with the wicks for the dynamite."

"Where on earth did you get ... never mind. I think I'm better off not knowing. And then what?"

"And then we will find Allied soldiers and I will help you escape. I will even stay with you. I'm certain they can use a nurse on the other side, don't you think?"

He stopped walking and gazed at her. "I definitely do think so. And we can have an officer marry us to be certain you will be allowed to come to America with me." His grin filled his whole face. "I would like nothing better than to take you in my arms right now."

"I agree. But not yet. We have to be careful about letting anyone see us." They walked for a while longer and then Marthe said, "Okay, let's go back now. I will come to you tonight around midnight. I will bring German clothes so if we are stopped it will look as if we're simply out to pick up German wounded. You should probably get some rest."

"I will try," he said, his eyes shining, "but I doubt I will. I'll be ready when you come."

They turned back toward the hospital.

Neither of them saw Jeannette appear from the hedge where she had gone to cry. Her English wasn't very good, but with the studying she had done, she understood enough words to figure out Marthe's plan.

And she vowed to stop it.

———— ⦕⦖ ————

SHORTLY BEFORE MIDNIGHT MARTHE PRIED UP THE BOARDS in her floor and pulled out the duffel bag that held the sticks of dynamite. She made certain the detonating wire nestled among them, then added a box of matches to her pocket. She replaced the floorboards and covered them with the small rug, then dressed in dark clothes and carried another set for Buzz. After a final look around to make certain she hadn't left any tell-tale signs of her plan, she closed her door and headed downstairs.

Quietly, she slipped outside and found the ambulance she planned to use. From her work with wounded in the field, she knew the drivers kept the keys in the ignition so the vehicles were ready at a moment's notice. She stashed her gear and laid the clothes for Buzz on the front seat, then stole back inside to get him.

He waited for her, dressed and ready. At her signal, he stood with his cane and followed her down the hospital steps to the ambulance.

She motioned for him to sit in the driver's seat and put the car in neutral, then pushed the ambulance through the hospital gate as she had watched the drivers do countless times. Despite its size the ambulance moved easily. They cleared the gate and she jumped in, turned on the ignition, and rolled out on the road to Reims.

Just inside the door, Jeannette hid in the shadows. As soon as the ambulance cleared the gate and rumbled to life, she strode down the hallway and awoke the *Oberartz,* who roused hospital security.

———— ⦕⦖ ————

BUZZ PLACED HIS HAND OVER MARTHE'S. "I CAN'T BELIEVE we're finally here, together."

Even in the dim light, he saw her smile. "We are. But let's get the tricky part done first."

She focused on the road. Driving to the site rather than walking meant they would reach it much sooner, so she paid close attention to her surroundings. When the charred steeple became visible, she slowed and pulled into the church grounds, then drove around to the back of the property, hiding the ambulance from view by anyone passing on the road.

"The ammunition is in the basement," she said softly. "You must be careful. It may be hard for you to navigate the stairs."

"I'll manage," he said, hoisting himself out of the vehicle.

They crept into the church and down the stairs until they reached the piles of mortar rounds and bands of machine gun ammunition. Buzz whistled softly when he saw the sheer volume of firepower.

"You tie the detonator cord to each stick of dynamite, leaving several feet at the end," Marthe instructed. "Then I will place them. After that, we will tie the cords together so they can all be detonated with a single match. Got it?"

He nodded and she handed him a small knife and the cord. Carefully he removed each stick and did as instructed. Once finished he handed the sticks to Marthe and she placed them strategically within the stacks of ammunition. When all the dynamite was placed, Marthe tied the cords together, then unrolled the main line all the way up the steps and out the church door. With matches in her hand, she pulled her locket out of her blouse and with her eyes closed, she kissed it. When she opened her eyes, she saw Buzz watching her, a small smile on his face.

"Buzz, will you get back in the ambulance? I will light this and we'll leave."

He waited in the passenger's seat and Marthe hopped in beside him after touching a lit match to the wicks.

She pulled out onto the road and drove far enough to clear the church yard. Then she stopped and turned to Buzz. "Would you still like to kiss me?"

"You bet!"

He moved across the seat and took her in his arms then covered her mouth with his.

He pulled back and looked deeply into her eyes. "I love you, future Mrs. Ryan."

She laughed. "I love you, t—"

Lights flashed through the windows and guttural shouts reached them. They broke apart.

"What the hell?" Buzz shielded his eyes.

*"Kommen sie mit erhobenen händen heraus!"*

"Oh no." The gasp that left Marthe's throat robbed her of breath momentarily. Then she turned to Buzz. "He said to get out of the car with our hands up."

"How ...?"

"I don't know for certain," Marthe answered. "But I have an idea."

They eased out of the car, their arms raised, and faced the group of German soldiers with guns pointed at their heads. Shading her eyes against the blinding headlights, Marthe recognized most of the soldiers as hospital security. Doors of the second car in line opened and the *Oberartz* stepped out of one side. Marthe's eyes narrowed as she watched the second occupant emerge from the other.

Jeannette Beaudelaire.

She came to the front of the car and smirked at Marthe.

"Are you happy now?" Marthe asked her in French. Jeannette remained silent.

"Marthe Peeters," the *Oberartz* said, "you are under arrest for treason. You will be tried and, when found guilty, you will face a firing squad. Same with the American." He gave her a disgusted look. "Sergeant, send your men to the church to see what they were doing there."

All but two of the soldiers trotted toward the church. The other two came toward Marthe and Buzz and tied their hands in front of them, then herded them toward one of the German cars.

A blast filled the night, sending fire and debris high into the sky. Round after round of mortars and machine gun bullets exploded, set off by Marthe's dynamite. Screams echoed through the night and the soldiers pushing them took off running in the direction of the church. The *Oberartz* froze and Buzz used the distraction to dive under his car, pulling Marthe with him. He rolled out the other side and prepared to run toward the woods after bending to retrieve Marthe.

Another explosion hit right in front of him and sent him flying backward to the trees. When he woke, he scrambled to his feet, swiping at the blood clotting his eyes.

The German car, ablaze from the blast, shot flames in all directions and edged toward what remained of the *Oberartz's* body, draped across the hood.

Buzz ran to get Marthe.

He found her in the road.

Face down in the dirt. She had cleared the car and appeared to have headed for the woods when a large piece of shrapnel hit her and lodged in her back.

"No!" He turned her over and saw that the shrapnel had pierced her heart, a dark stain blossoming across her chest. He rubbed her face, caked with bloodied mud, and untangled her locket, wound tight around her throat. "No, no, no, no ..." The last syllable ended in a wail. He held her to him and rocked with her, telling her over and over again how much he loved and needed her. And imploring her to wake up.

Rough hands pulled him under his arms and forced him to let go of his beloved.

"Stop," he screamed. "Leave me alone. What are you doing?"

"You're American," a voice said, sounding surprised. "What the hell are you doing out here, man?"

"What?"

"We're part of the Eightieth Division of III Corps. Lieutenant Harold Wood. Who're you?"

Ignoring the question, Buzz asked, "Did you bomb this car?"

"Yeah," the soldier answered him. "We heard the Germans stored ammunition at a church near here and we came to destroy it. Your head is bleeding."

Buzz reached up and found the wound, then dropped his arm.

"You're too late," Buzz said. Tears fell unchecked and he pointed to Marthe. "She took care of it." Raw grief spilled from his throat and his sobs filled the night.

"Who was she?" the soldier asked gently.

When Buzz could speak again, he said, "Marthe Peeters. A Belgian nurse. A spy for the Allies. And my fiancé." He broke down again.

"I'm sorry, soldier." The lieutenant waited until Buzz could speak again. "What unit were you with?"

"The Twenty-eighth. I was captured two months ago with a bullet wound in my leg. Marthe nursed me back to good health." He dropped his head and spoke softly. "We were going to destroy the depot and then try and find you. Or a unit like yours. But instead ..."

"Again, I'm sorry, soldier. It sounds like your fiancé is a hero. As are you. We'll take you with us and notify your unit that you're safe. No prisoner of war camp for you. What's your name, anyhow?"

"Ryan. Private Buzz, well ... William ... Ryan."

He accompanied the soldiers to their vehicles and as he passed Jeannette, who lay beside the car like a rag doll with arms and legs askew, he lifted her head by her hair and with his good leg, kicked her face with all his might. Then he let her head fall back to the mud.

He turned to look at Marthe. "Can you give me a minute?"

At the lieutenant's nod, he knelt and removed her locket, then gently kissed her face and held her to him one last time.

"We will bring her with us, soldier, and give her a proper burial," the lieutenant said. "Again, I am so sorry."

# CHAPTER FORTY-THREE

**SUZANNE**
**2015**

I found it curious that my grandmother appeared to like it that my grandfather had found happiness with his Belgian nurse. It didn't seem to fit since she was the one who ended up with him. None of it made sense to me, but that confusion made me more determined than ever to finish Maude's diary. I took it with me to Dad's kitchen and made myself some coffee, then sat down at his table to keep reading.

Oddly, since her entries had become farther apart, Maude's next entry was only a week and a half later.

*September 28, 1918*

*Dear Diary,*

*I'm feeling a little guilty because earlier this week Dad and I had an argument. I was so tired with schoolwork and housework and cooking and helping with the harvest that I hollered at Dad when he asked me to do something. It was nothing, what he asked me. I don't even remember it now. But it was one more thing. And I just exploded.*

*He came over to me and put his arms around me while I cried. And he apologized. Then I apologized. And I think we both held back from complaining about how Mom's being in bed all the time has driven us to this point.*

*Later on, he came to me and said that a number of people from town are planning to take the bus to Philadelphia tomorrow, Sunday, the 29th, to go to the Liberty Loan Parade. He said this will be the fourth parade to raise money with Liberty Bonds for the war effort. "We can't afford to buy any," he said, "but we can enjoy the parade. We'll ask Mom to go, but if she doesn't, I'll see if Miss Josephine will come and stay with her while you and I go."*

*I loved it. And I was so happy. It would be a chance to have fun for a day without having too many things to do at once. Yes, I do feel guilty for the way I feel, but sometimes I can't help but resent it that Mom doesn't get out of bed to help with anything. I can't even have Ethel come over to spend the night anymore. I feel like my life is over and it doesn't seem fair!!*

*I know, I know. Mom can't help the way she feels.*

*But then, I guess, neither can I.*

*Your friend, Maude*

———————

*September 29, 1918*

*Dear Diary,*

*Mom said she didn't want to go to the parade, so Dad and I went to Philadelphia with a lot of other people from town—including Miss Delsie and Ethel—and we had a wonderful time. Dad told me the parade stretched more than two miles long and that 200,000 people were there —either marching or watching. We saw a lot of sailors and soldiers who had been overseas and were back at home. I don't think I've ever seen anything more spectacular. And lot of people on the bus did buy bonds, even though Dad and I didn't.*

*So now we're back home and I'm laying my clothes out for school tomorrow. Mom made out fine without us for the day and I feel much better about things. I really had fun spending time with Ethel again.*

*Okay, I'm going to sleep now.*

*Your friend, Maude*

✦ ─ ⋘✦⋙ ─ ✦

*October 27, 1918*

*Dear Diary,*

*I haven't been able to write because we've all been sick. I can't believe how bad it's been.*

*Everybody—to a person—who traveled to Philadelphia for the parade has gotten sick. Miss Delsie said it's the Spanish Flu. She seemed to have more information than anyone else, so she told us what she knew before school was closed. She said the officials in Philadelphia knew some of the soldiers had been sick but thought they had it contained to the bases.*

*When soldiers marched in the parade, though, apparently some of them were still sick. Within three days of getting back home, both Dad and I had it. And we gave it to Mom. We started wearing masks around her, but not soon enough.*

*Miss Delsie also said they probably should have canceled the parade, but she heard they didn't because of something called the "Sedition Act," which asked people to report anyone "who spreads pessimistic stories that might encourage the enemy." Even I can tell there's a big difference between spreading stories and giving people information to keep them from getting sick.*

*With all of us sick, Miss Josephine—who always wore a mask anyway—came over to help us, because we couldn't get the doctor to come out to the farm due to all the sick folks in town. Besides, we found out there was nothing he could do for us even if he had come.*

*Mom got the sickest. I guess she was so weak already, she didn't have anything left to fight the infection. Her symptoms were much worse than ours. Her skin turned blue and Dad said her lungs filled with fluid to the point that she suffocated. It was horrible.*

*He and I had to sit there and watch her die. There was nothing we could do.*

*We had her funeral today. Almost nobody came. They're either too sick or too scared of getting sick.*

*Dad and I agreed that at least she would get to be with Henry again.*

*I have to write to Buzz to let him know. I don't know how long it will take a letter to reach him, but I guess he'll get it eventually.*

*I'm going to lie down for a while first. I'm having trouble thinking straight.*

*Your friend, Maude*

---

## October 27, 1918

FOR DAYS AFTER BUZZ CHECKED IN TO THE ALLIED hospital, he lay in his cot, despondent and depressed. Happiness had been within his grasp—in his arms, in fact—only to be viciously snatched from him. All because Jeannette had been jealous of his beloved Marthe.

Even the thought of Marthe brought tears to his eyes and pain to his heart.

A piece of shrapnel from the explosion had caught his head, so the hospital staff stitched up the wound and put him on bed rest.

The pain from his head didn't come close to touching the pain in his heart. Everything he thought about reminded him of her. Her locket rested around his neck and he caressed it constantly. One nurse asked him to remove it so she could clean the blood from it but left in tears when he screamed at her never to touch it.

He knew he needed to write to Maude and the Brewers, but at first, he simply couldn't make himself do it. Finally, after two weeks, he wrote a few lines to let them know he had escaped from the German hospital and was back with the Allies and almost ready to rejoin his unit. At the end, he included a short paragraph to let them know that Marthe had died heroically. He didn't elaborate since he knew the censors would delete it anyway.

He heard the news from the front every day and found out that the so-called "Lost Battalion" had held on through incredibly horrible conditions—having no food, medicine, or ammunition—and had finally been rescued. At great loss of life, everyone said. Buzz noticed that when people talked to him about it, they often shook their heads as if to say, "How could they have made it through that?" According to what he heard, seven hundred soldiers went into the battle and got cut off from the rest of their troops. They held their ground and finally made it out under the leadership of Lieutenant Colonel Charles Whittlesey. But only around two hundred of them were left alive at that point.

The other news that reached him the previous day was the heroic story of Corporal Alvin York, who, after being denied conscientious objector status because of his religion, had nevertheless led a charge against a German machine gun nest. Corporal York had single-handedly killed close to twenty Germans and then captured one hundred thirty-two enemy soldiers with his squad of only seventeen men.

Those stories made Buzz stop and think. Other than the first battle he was in … the one that killed Henry … he had seen little action.

Most of his time had been spent in a German hospital. With Marthe. He knew he should be grateful to have been spared time on the battle-field with all those bullets flying at him, but his heart ached so acutely, he had trouble wrapping his head around anything else.

The soldiers who rescued him had been successful in contacting his original unit and Buzz would join them in the next push of what was termed the Meuse-Argonne offensive. His leg had healed completely and his head wound caused no pain. By the time his wounded head could tolerate his helmet again, his unit had come to collect him and, after almost five months away from the front, Buzz headed back into the thick of the fighting.

# CHAPTER FORTY-FOUR

**SUZANNE**
**2015**

My heart went out to Maude for the loss of her mother. I could tell from her diary entries that she grieved, but I suspected she also felt a sense of relief that the torment in her mother's soul had ended.

I based that on my own experience with my mother. By the time she died, she had been in so much pain for so long, I was glad she had stopped suffering.

I missed her. Of course I did. But the day I realized that I missed my mother from twenty years earlier—or even ten years earlier—and not from the way she was when she died, the pain in my heart eased and I could rejoice in the time I'd been given with her before she got sick.

I sincerely hoped that dear little Maude had reached—and recognized—that point as well.

The date on the next page coincided with the end of the war.

*November 11, 1918*

*Dear Diary,*

*Dad just returned from town and gave me incredible news.*

*He said he heard it on the radio in Harrington's General Store. Germany has agreed to stop the fighting. Dad called it an "armistice." I don't know how much that will really change things because there are still shortages of a lot of goods. Dad really misses his coffee, especially. And many, many people are still very sick, but it might be the beginning of getting back to normal. Somewhat, at least.*

*Of course our lives won't ever return to normal because "normal" included having Mom and Henry with us. But maybe Buzz will come back here. Although the last we heard from him, he still plans to bring his nurse, Marthe, with him when he returns to the States. So I don't know how she will feel about living on a farm. I know he will go to Philadelphia to see if he can get his pitching job back, but I am hopeful we will get to see him and meet Marthe before he's gone for good.*

*Okay, just wanted to give you the good news. Now I have to start supper and then study. Miss Delsie writes out our assignments for a week at a time and puts the list in our mailboxes so we can keep up with our work until school reopens when everybody gets well.*

*Your friend, Maude*

---

## November 11, 1918

ONCE AGAIN BUZZ WORE FULL BATTLE GEAR AND CHARGED east with the rest of his unit. They followed along the Meuse River, crossed it and penetrated the German lines, then continued east toward Metz. That city lay barely into the German border in the area known as Lorraine—land that had long been disputed between the French and Germans.

Rumors flew through the ranks for days that an armistice was in the works and would be signed at any time. But that morning, when a fellow soldier asked the captain about the rumors, the captain said that's all it amounted to—rumors. The unit would continue, the captain told them, to fight with everything they had until General Pershing himself gave the order to stop.

On Monday morning, November 11, just before eleven o'clock, Buzz's unit secured their position at the top of a ridge outside the city of Metz. From their vantage point, they saw a pocket of Germans below.

"Ryan," the captain said. His voice was soft so it wouldn't carry to the enemy. "You're the baseball player, right?"

"Yes sir."

"Pitcher, right?"

"That's right, sir."

"We're a little short on grenades. So let's take advantage of your ability to hit the mark and pitch a grenade right into the middle of those Germans down there. Use this one. It has a bigger payload."

Buzz took the grenade from the captain and edged closer to the ridge, then stood quickly and raised his pitching arm over his head to let it fly. Just as he released the grenade, the machine gun below fired up and bullets found Buzz's wrist, breaking the bones there and in his hand. White hot pain shot up his hand and into his forearm and he screamed with the intensity of it. The soldier beside him, John Gunther, dropped down dead.

The time was 10:59 a.m.

On November 11, 1918.

Seconds later Buzz's grenade landed right in the middle of the gun nest with a huge blast that sent body parts flying. Then, all was quiet.

The following minute, at eleven in the morning, the American captain called to his men.

"Cease fire! The war's over. But be prepared to defend yourselves until we're sure someone has told the damned Krauts the war is over."

The captain looked over at Buzz, who held his bloodied arm against his chest. "Medic! Get over here."

The medic loaded Buzz into an ambulance and took him to yet another hospital.

# CHAPTER
# FORTY-FIVE

**SUZANNE**
**2015**

I filled my coffee cup, appreciating that I've never had to endure a coffee shortage the way my ancestors did. Maude's next entry was around Thanksgiving.

*November 23, 1918*

*Dear Diary,*

*Dad and I are trying to make the best of things.*

*A few businesses have opened back up in town but school and most of the other businesses are still closed. Nobody except the two of us for Thanksgiving dinner this year and it won't be much different at Christmas. Even our church has closed down.*

*The sickness is much worse in Philadelphia, Dad says. The newspaper he gets from there lists the number of deaths in the city. In mid-October, the paper listed 700 deaths, but almost 5,000 one week later. I'm glad Prospect Park hasn't seen anything that bad. Dad won't let me go into town with him and the few times he's had to go, he wears a mask. There are signs all over the place, he said, that forbid spitting. I guess somebody figured out the germs in spit make it worse. I don't see how, but then I'm not a doctor or a nurse.*

*We finally got a couple of letters from Buzz. We were saddened to hear that his girlfriend, Marthe, was killed. But at least he was rescued by the Americans so he didn't have to go to a prisoner of war camp. But then his last letter said he got shot again. In his left wrist. The same day the war ended.*

*He's really worried that his arm might not heal well enough to pitch again. He sounded upset that he was shot right as the cease-fire was called. I don't blame him. I would have been too. But he did say he would be kept in a hospital in Paris for a while to see if those doctors could make his wrist and hand better. That's really good he's not coming back here yet since so many people are dying in Philadelphia. I sure hope Mr. Mack is okay.*

*Tonight at supper Dad and I decided we would put up a Christmas tree after all. We have both always loved Christmas and we know Mom and Henry would have wanted us to still make it as festive as we can. So early in December we will go out in the woods and cut down a tree, then come back and decorate it. I think that will make us feel better. At least I hope so.*

*I know I'm not writing as often as I used to, so if I don't come back to write for a while, Merry Christmas. It's been a very hard year. I only hope next year will be better.*

*Your friend, Maude*

A picture of my grandfather began to form in my head. Not what he looked like—I knew about that because I had pictures of him right in front of me. No, I mean an idea of what must have been going on in his head. He endured so much in a short time, beginning with his father depriving him of both parents when he was only seventeen by first killing Buzz's mother and then shooting himself. The way it looked to me, every time he finally had something that made him happy—earning a spot on the Philadelphia Athletics baseball team with his best friend, Henry, or falling in love with the Belgian nurse, Marthe—something else came along to take that away from him. In this case, World War I. From what I had read so far, while the war was hard on everyone, including Maude and her father, it seemed to just be slapping the crap out of Buzz.

I remembered from history that General Pershing hadn't agreed with the armistice. He wanted to keep on fighting until he wiped the Germans out completely. So even though the peace agreement calling for a cease-fire on November 11, 1918, at 11:00 a.m. had been signed at 5:00 that morning, Pershing never bothered to tell his officers about the end time of the war, so on its final day before 11:00 a.m., eleven thousand soldiers—thirty-five hundred of them Americans—became casualties. That number was considered so unacceptable that Pershing was called before Congress to explain why he had so many losses on the final day of the war. I looked it up once to find out what happened as a result of that inquiry and I remember being incensed that not only did he receive no reprimand, but he also continued to be honored. If I had had a family member killed that morning, I remembered thinking at the time, I would have wanted his head.

As it happened, Buzz got shot at the last second when the war should have already ended. And while I didn't yet know what else might have happened to him, the picture of what had caused him to sever ties with his family certainly became clearer.

--------◦⟨⟩◦--------

## December 20, 1918

ALL AROUND HIM, CHRISTMAS FESTIVITIES INCREASED IN his hospital ward but Buzz's only concern was whether his hand and wrist would heal enough for him to pitch again.

How ironic, he thought from time to time, that the reason his hand was hit in the first place was because he was a pitcher. He believed the captain asked him to throw the grenade because he thought Buzz would do the best job of landing it where it needed to be. And, he had.

The grenade wiped out the machine gun nest but cost him the bones in his hand.

The doctors had already made great progress and he had some movement in his fingers. Most of the bones in his hand had been repaired along with some of the ones in his wrist. But the doctors couldn't operate on everything at once, so he needed time between each surgery to do rehabilitation work. Then as soon as he reached a certain point, another surgery would take place. And the process began again.

He kept to himself in the hospital. No soldiers from his unit had landed there, although he had met soldiers in another ward who were American. He also met some who were British but the men in his ward were all French. As were the nurses. One of the nurses tried to get him to teach her English, but his heart hardened against becoming friendly with any nurse who wasn't Marthe. And face it, he thought, no one else would ever be Marthe.

So he spent his time exercising his hand, reading books, and dictating letters his nurses then sent to Maude and Mr. Brewer. Maude, especially, wrote regularly and he always loved receiving news from home. Mr. Mack had even answered one of his letters and told Buzz to certainly come and see him when he returned to the States.

Of course, Buzz had neglected to tell Mr. Mack about his injury. He really wanted to believe the doctors could fix his hand to the point that he would be able to pitch just as well as ever. His obsession with returning his pitching hand to its former abilities helped somewhat to overshadow his obsession with his love—and grief—for Marthe.

Yes, his hand obsession helped ease the pain of losing Marthe. Some. But not totally.

# CHAPTER
# FORTY-SIX

**SUZANNE**
**2015**

I returned to Dad's chair in his Zen Zone, and the photo album lay open to the last page I had seen. Pictures of Maude, her father, and Buzz filled the next page but they were obviously older. The caption dates on the previous page had been 1918, but on this page right after it, the caption date was 1922.

One of the pictures showed the three of them in a city—the caption said Philadelphia.

A lot must have happened between the last diary entry I read and these pictures. I sincerely hoped Maude's diary didn't contain that wide a gap because if I couldn't learn about her from her own words, I didn't think I'd learn about her from anywhere else.

I picked up the diary and continued to read.

*August 30, 1919*

*Dear Diary,*

*I told you this might happen. That it could be a long time before I came to see you again. With everything going on in the world, confiding in you has had to wait.*

*But a lot has happened.*

*For one thing, our crop sales did really well last year because of the sick-*

*ness and so few other people having food to sell. I know some businesses in town charged a lot more for their goods because everything was still scarce. The law of supply and demand, I learned in the take-home lessons Miss Delsie sent us. But we charged our normal prices and Dad sold everything we harvested. So that's good.*

*And because we had a little extra money from the crops, Dad has hired Miss Josephine's grandsons to help in the fields. He pays them really well and Miss Josephine is pleased. We've been able to plant extra acres and expand the strawberry fields.*

*As I told you earlier, Miss Delsie called the sickness "The Spanish Flu" although she says it didn't originate in Spain but was simply reported on from Spain first. Anyway, it has died down now and very few people are still sick. We've heard that cities, including Philadelphia, have had another wave of sickness, but that wave wasn't as bad as the first one. So Dad only goes into Prospect Park a couple of times a month and I never go.*

*The last time he was there, though, he brought me several yards of different patterned fabrics so I made all my school clothes for the year. We will still have to wear masks in school, but that's okay with me. I had that stupid flu. I don't want to get it again.*

*I make a big pot of soup or stew every week and Dad and I have our meals from it until it's gone and then I make another one. I'm still able to help him in the fields—at least until school starts again and I have less time.*

*I'll be in the ninth grade—extra hard arithmetic this year. The last time Miss Delsie came over in May to bring homework assignments, she added a note that said a young woman from Prospect Park, Jane somebody-or-other, who had her teaching certificate would join her in the fall so they could teach different subjects. And teach more of us at a time. It's fine with me. Maybe I could even skip a grade and be finished sooner.*

*We hear from Buzz sometimes. He's still overseas and the doctors are still operating on his hand. His last letter made it sound like he might be back in the States before the end of the year. It would be really good to see him again. He never mentions Marthe anymore, so neither do I.*

*I'm not sure when I will get back to write again, with school starting and all, but just know I haven't forgotten you.*

*Your friend, Maude*

————— ❦ —————

March 25, 1920

*Dear Diary,*

*I'm back.*

*Just wanted to let you know we heard from Buzz and he's back in this country. In Philadelphia. I think Dad's a little disappointed that he went straight there instead of coming here first. And actually, maybe I'm disappointed too. But at least he let us know he was back.*

*He told us he went to see Mr. Mack and that Mr. Mack is going to let him come to the park and try out for the team again. He said Mr. Mack would have preferred he had gotten home in time to attend Spring Training, but if he could get Buzz back to pitch he'd be thrilled.*

*Buzz invited us to come to the stadium and watch his tryout on March 27. He said if all goes well, he could be back pitching again by the opening game against the Yankees on April 14th. Dad already has it worked out with Mr. Harrington at the General Store, to borrow one of his delivery vans for the day so we can drive to Philadelphia to see Buzz pitch. And I'm off from school since it's a Saturday.*

*I'll let you know how it goes.*

*Okay, I know you don't believe me. But I will. I'll come back to write about how he does.*

*Your friend, Maude*

⎯⎯⎯⎯ ⚬⚬⚬⚬ ⎯⎯⎯⎯

## March 27, 1920

MAUDE PACKED SANDWICHES AND MADE LEMONADE TO take with them on their trip to Philadelphia. They drove the farm wagon into town early in the morning and left the mules with the local livery depot, then picked up Mr. Harrington's delivery van at the General Store.

"I feel kind of fluttery," Maude said. "It's been so long since we've seen Buzz. And, Dad," she added softly, "I'm afraid I might cry. Because the last time we saw him, Henry was with him. I think it will be strange to actually lay eyes on one without the other."

"I know what you mean, Maudie," Frank said. "I'm feeling that way myself." He drove in silence for a few minutes, then added, "Oh my goodness, I hope the boy can still pitch." He glanced over at his daughter. "I know we would both like for him to come back to the farm and live with us, but I also know that all he has ever wanted to do was pitch. To be a professional pitcher and be away from Prospect Park and all of the terrible family memories it holds for him. Even though we gave him better memories, he can't erase the first seventeen or so years from his life, you know?"

Maude nodded and stared out the window. She didn't know what to expect when they saw Buzz. She was fairly certain he would look different, just as her father told her she did. In two-and-a-half years' time, everybody looked different, she figured. Especially given what they had all been through.

They pulled into the familiar lot at the stadium but no one came to

THE ROAD RENOUNCED | 267

meet them as had happened before. "I guess this is the difference in being the family of a celebrity pitcher and not, huh?" Frank said. He smiled at Maude, put his arm around her shoulder and led her to the field. They spotted Buzz at the dugout and when he saw them, he loped over toward them, his face wreathed in a smile.

Frank reached him first and enveloped him in a bear hug while Maude hung back. Then Buzz spotted her and surprise filled his eyes.

"Maude! My God, you're all grown up. How did that happen?" He reached her and hugged her hard. As she had feared, tears oozed from her eyes and trickled down her cheeks.

"Oh Buzz, I'm so glad to see you. I only wish ..."

His face sobered. "I know, Maude. I do too. I guess we'll always miss him."

"Is there anything else you can tell—"

"Maudie," Frank said quietly with his hand on her arm. "Let's not bring that up first thing when we finally get to see Buzz again."

She nodded.

Connie Mack saw them and came over to shake Frank's hand. "Maude," he said. "You've grown up. And become a lovely young woman." He looked at both of them. "Welcome back."

"Thank you for allowing us time to see Buzz," Frank said. "Where can we sit so we'll be out of the way?"

"Why don't you sit with us in the dugout?"

Frank's face beamed and the two Brewers took seats at the far end of the dugout, closest to home plate. Buzz waved and sauntered out to the mound.

Ed Wingo in full catcher's gear squatted behind home plate. Connie Mack himself bent behind Wingo to see Buzz's pitches.

"Okay, Buzz," Mr. Mack said, "let one fly."

Buzz looked the way he always had when he stood on the mound, except with a more chiseled jaw and a leaner body. A year in the war and then in rehab hospitals had taken a toll in fine lines around his eyes and beside his mouth. But his warm-up looked just the same. He turned his right side toward home plate, put his hands in the air and did what Maude knew to be his visualization process.

He turned and let the ball fly out of his left hand. It sailed across the plate.

"Ball," Connie Mack called.

The catcher stood and threw the ball back to Buzz.

Buzz's face wore a look of total concentration. Total focus. Again he wound up, went through his routine, and threw.

"Ball," Connie Mack called. "Why don't you try your fastball?"

"Oh dear," Maude whispered to Frank. "What if that *was* his fastball?"

Buzz nodded. Then he went through his routine, wound up, and let the ball sail from his fingers.

Connie Mack straightened up and said, "Still a ball, Buzz. Try again."

Frustration filled Buzz's face. He dropped his head, closed his eyes, and took a deep breath. Then he resumed his position on the mound, took a little longer with his routine, and finally released the ball. It flew over the plate.

"That's more like it," Connie Mack said. "Strike."

Relief hit Buzz's face before his smile.

He went through a few more pitches, more balls than strikes, and his face reflected his weariness. And disappointment.

Mr. Mack held up his hand. "Buzz," he said. "Why don't you have lunch with your family and we'll pick this back up tomorrow?"

Frank and Maude left the dugout to meet Buzz. Frank shook Mr. Mack's hand. "Thank you again for allowing us to come and see Buzz here. It's great to see you as well."

Mr. Mack nodded at the Brewers and they left the field with Buzz. Buzz's chin sank to his chest and Frank tried to cheer him up. "Come on, son. Let's have lunch. Do you have a favorite place around here?"

"No."

"Okay, then. Let's just walk until we see something we like."

They found a restaurant they could all agree on and ordered the blue plate special—meatloaf.

"This is good," Maude said. "But not as good as what Mom used to make."

"I was so sorry to hear about her death," Buzz told them.

Frank put his hand on top of Buzz's. "Just as we were sorry to hear about your nurse friend. I know she was very special to you."

"She had agreed to marry me." He stopped talking and looked up, tears filling his eyes. "Just before she was killed."

"Oh Buzz," Maude said. "You've been through so much."

He looked at her and tried a smile but fell a little short. "You have, too, Maudie. We all have. War makes a hell out of everything. But at least I still have my pitching. I'm going to make it work again. Just you wait. I'll get it back and be stronger than ever."

"I'm sure you're right, son," Frank said. "But just know you have us waiting for you if it doesn't come back."

Again, Buzz tried to smile. But his insides knotted up with the thought of spending his life working on the small farm in Prospect Park.

---

THAT AFTERNOON, BUZZ ASKED ED WINGO, THE A'S catcher, to work with him some more. Buzz tried all his different pitches and worked with Ed until dusk. "My knees can't take any more, Buzz," Ed told him. "And my guess is that your arm could use a rest. Let's pick it back up tomorrow, just as Coach Mack suggested."

"Sure," Buzz said. "Thanks, Ed."

The catcher left but Buzz continued to work on his pitches until he could no longer see where the ball actually landed.

# CHAPTER FORTY-SEVEN

**SUZANNE**
**2015**

t this point, the album date—1923—had passed the diary date, so rather than speculate, I returned to the diary to find out what had happened in between.

*June 28, 1920*

*Dear Diary,*

*Sorry it took me so long to get back to you. But see? I told you I would come back to let you know how Buzz did with trying again to pitch for the team. He let us know that Mr. Mack took him back but he has to earn his way to reach the top again. He will be a relief pitcher for the team until his arm becomes stronger and he throws more strikes than balls. But his letters sounded upbeat.*

*We aren't planning to go to Philadelphia again since he's not scheduled to start pitching anytime soon. If he is put into the lineup on a regular basis, Dad said, we can go see him then. But in the meantime, there is always too much work to do on the farm. I help out full-time now, at least until school starts again. Dad's even started paying me, so that makes it easier to go out into the fields.*

*I'll be in the tenth grade in the fall. I found out recently that if we lived in Philadelphia, I would have gone to a different school for grades seven through nine and still another one for grades ten through twelve. But here, in Prospect Park, we're still in the one-room school with Miss Delsie and her assistant, Miss Jane. I'm really glad. I wouldn't have liked getting used to that many schools.*

*Miss Delsie told me recently that with my grades, I could combine my studies and finish school in eleven years instead of twelve. She even suggested I go to secretarial school after that. I'm not sure I could leave Dad, but it's something to think about.*

*This is going to be a very busy summer so I might not be able to write much. I'll be back as soon as I can.*

*Your friend, Maude*

*P. S. Earlier this month Congress passed the Nineteenth Amendment to the U. S. Constitution. Miss Delsie told us about it. It gives women the right to vote. I'm still not old enough yet but will absolutely exercise my right to vote when I am. I remember how awful I thought it was when Mom couldn't vote, so I'm glad that's changed now. Also, as we learned about the Nineteenth Amendment, we also learned about the Eighteenth Amendment, which prohibited the sale or transportation of alcohol in this country. It doesn't really affect anyone I know, but I thought I would mention it.*

It happened just the way I feared. The diary entries stopped until 1922. Apparently, life continued to be very hard for Maude and her father during the early 1920s and must have taken precedence over Maude having time to record her daily activities.

I was so curious. Did she ever date? Did she see her long-time friends Ethel and Helen? Did she finish school? Go to secretarial school? I hoped she would fill in some of the gaps in her 1922 entries.

Only one way to find out.

I turned the page ...

*April 16, 1922*

*Dear Diary,*

*As you know, tomorrow is my seventeenth birthday. I was able to complete my high school requirements and will graduate next month.*

*As if that isn't big enough news, you'll never guess what else happened today. Dad and I had just sat down to Sunday dinner when we heard a knock on the door. It was Buzz! He just showed up at the farm. Dad and I were so surprised. Not only to see him at the farm without warning, but also to see that he had been drinking.*

*That was the most surprising of all, given the way he had vowed never to drink because of his parents. And, even though I thought it would never affect anyone I knew, the Prohibition Amendment had been passed a couple of years ago. So whatever Buzz was drinking had to have come from illegal sources.*

*He stumbled on his way into the kitchen and when he got closer, his breath still smelled like spirits. I had no experience with any kind of liquor, so I couldn't tell what it was. But the fact that he drank at all was heartbreaking.*

*Several days' stubble protruded from his chin and his hair curled around and over his collar. His eyes appeared vacant, as if he hadn't been sleeping well.*

*He told us he was cut from the baseball team two months ago because he hadn't won a game for almost two years. His arm and the fingers in his left hand just never came back as strong as he needed them to be. Mr. Mack even encouraged him to try and pitch with his right hand, but he wasn't able to make it work after months of trying. He said Mr. Mack was generous enough to give him an extra month's pay. But that had run out and he was without a place to stay.*

*Of course, Dad immediately asked him to move in with us. And he accepted. He joined us for dinner and afterward, I offered to cut his hair the way I do for Dad. While he sat there, I even gave him a shave. He looked way better after that.*

*Buzz and Dad talked about how it would work to have him living here and Dad said he wouldn't have to pay anything if he was willing to work in the fields.*

*Buzz agreed.*

*I'm glad he's back. And I know Dad is thrilled. But I worry that Buzz isn't cut out for farm work. I mean he's twenty-four and hasn't had a job other than pitching … and being a soldier. I guess that has to count for having a job. But his only job that required physical labor was when he was in high school and worked at the feed mill. And I remember he hated that. So I suppose we'll see.*

*I don't know if he drinks a lot or if he just started because he got cut from the team. Maybe now that he's here, he can be content to be back home and drinking won't be a problem. I sure hope so because having him here certainly would make Dad and me very happy.*

*Now that I'm back, I'll try to do a better job of letting you know how it's going.*

*Your friend, Maude*

———— ⋅⟨⊛⟩⋅ ————

## April 16, 1922

BUZZ AND MAUDE'S FATHER LINGERED AT THE TABLE AFTER dinner with their coffee and strawberry shortcake while Maude cleaned up the kitchen and did the dishes.

"Maude," Buzz said, "I totally forgot ... happy birthday. I'm really sorry. I didn't think to bring you a present."

"That's okay," Maude said. "Dad gave me my present this morning even though I'm not officially seventeen until tomorrow." She held out her wrist to show Buzz her new watch.

"Maude graduates next month, Buzz," Frank said, his pride evident in his voice. "She skipped a grade and did two years' work in the space of one. Miss Delsie wants her to go to secretarial school, but she hasn't made up her mind about it yet."

"I don't think you can do without my help on the farm," she said.

"Well," Frank said, "maybe now that Buzz is—"

"We don't need to decide that today," Maude interrupted him. "Let's just let Buzz get settled in."

"You're right, of course," Frank said. "Sorry, son. I didn't mean to jump the gun." He put his hand on Buzz's shoulder. "I'm glad you're back, Buzz, although I'm as sorry as I can be that your hand and arm never healed up and got as strong as you wanted." Frank reached for his hat. "I need to check the fences on the back field. Deer keep getting in to eat the young corn sprouts." He nodded and left Maude and Buzz alone in the kitchen.

"I noticed a gold chain with a locket when I cut your hair, Buzz," Maude said. "Is that new?"

Buzz reached inside his shirt and pulled it out. "It's the only thing I have left of Marthe," he said. He opened it up to show Maude the pictures inside. "These were her parents. They were killed by the Germans right in front of her eyes." His head stayed down. "Watching our parents die was one thing we had in common."

"The Germans killed her parents but she still worked for them in German hospitals?"

"Yeah ... I had the same questions," he answered. "But they kidnapped her at first since she had nursing skills and could speak so many languages. And once she was no longer captive she stayed for two reasons. One, because she was dedicated to making people well and second ..." he hesitated.

"And second?"

"She spied against the Germans. Working for the British Intelligence Network. I even helped her the night she died." He heard Maude's quick intake of breath and looked up. "We had just blown up an ammunition depot when Marthe and I were arrested for being spies. I honestly expected them to shoot us both on the spot. But the Americans were close by and blew up the German vehicles. Unfortunately, Marthe got caught in the explosion." His voice was tight. "And died instantly."

"Like Henry," Maude said.

"Yes ... like Henry."

"I'm sorry you lost her, Buzz." Maude put her hand on Buzz's shoulder and he put his hand on top of hers.

"Thank you. But since I've been back, I've seen a lot of anti-German sentiment around." He hesitated, then added, "I loved her. I wanted her to be my wife. But I see, now that I'm back, she would have had a hard time in this country."

Maude removed her hand and sat across from him at the table. "But didn't you say she was Belgian?"

"Yes, but most people here don't know the difference. And besides, she worked in a German hospital. People wouldn't have taken the time to understand that she didn't agree with the Germans and would have made it hard for her." He looked at Maude and tried a grin. It only touched his mouth and never made it to his eyes. "Especially now that I don't have a job."

"Are you serious about your willingness to stay here and help on the farm, Buzz? I know that's not what you wanted."

He drew a deep, ragged breath. "No, it isn't. But none of this is what I wanted. You know what I mean?" Maude nodded. "I never wanted to go into the service in the first place," Buzz continued. "I never wanted Henry to get killed." His mouth hardened and his voice deepened. "And I sure as hell never wanted to get shot during the very last battle of the war so that I can no longer pitch. That's just so ..."

His fist beat the surface of the table and Maude saw that something dark rested just beneath the surface of his soul. Something she had never seen in him before. It took her a minute, but she finally identified it.

Rage.

Buzz's whole being throbbed with his rage.

Her mind flew to the stories she'd heard about his father's rage. Especially the rage mixed with alcohol. She shivered involuntarily.

"So when did you start drinking?"

Buzz's chin found his chest again. "Last year. When my pitching didn't improve, I joined a couple of the fellas at our local joints—speakeasies they were called. I refused everything for a while. Then it started with just one beer. Then a second. And so on. Then I tried gin. I didn't do it all the time because it's not that easy to get." His hand found hers across the table. "I'll stop, Maude. I know it's not good for me. And your father has treated me like his own son. I won't let him down. I won't let either of you down."

"I'll help you, Buzz. We both will. Let's just see how it goes."

Buzz climbed the stairs to the room he had shared with Henry and unpacked his bag. In the very bottom of it was a small flask, filled with the moonshine he had picked up when he reached the edge of town. He stared at it, then descended the stairs and walked into the backyard to pour it out.

For a long time, he simply held it, then finally removed its top. His arm stretched out and hovered, parallel to the grass.

But after several long minutes, he moved the flask to his lips instead.

And drained it.

# CHAPTER
# FORTY-EIGHT

**SUZANNE**
**2015**

U h-oh.

Maude's last entry sounded like the beginning of the end. Buzz had already started drinking even though he had sworn he never would because of his parents. My late husband had an alcoholic parent so he always monitored his alcohol intake since he feared the addiction gene may have transferred to him but he never had an issue with it. For which we were both relieved.

I feared Buzz hadn't been so lucky.

—◦◦◦◦◦◦—

MAUDE'S DIARY ENTRIES CONTINUED TO HAVE MONTHS between them. I turned to the next one.

*August 12, 1922*

*Dear Diary,*

*Dad sent Buzz to pick me up from my secretarial classes again today. He even sent money for us to have a malt at the new lunch counter at Harrington's General Store. I can't believe how much that store has grown since the war ended. I was thinking that might be a good place for me to get a job when I finish classes at the end of the month.*

*Buzz looks a lot better these days. His eyes aren't quite as haunted and I keep his hair cut so he never looks as scruffy as he did when he first came back to the farm. I know he didn't want to do farm work, but he seems to be making the best of it and, as far as I can tell, he doesn't drink anymore. At least I don't see him drink.*

*We spend a lot of time together in the evenings on the porch swing and occasionally go into town to the movies. My favorite so far was* Beyond the Rocks *with Gloria Swanson and Rudolph Valentino. My goodness, Gloria Swanson's gowns were all beautiful. And of course, Rudolph Valentino is absolutely dreamy. I'm not sure Buzz enjoyed that one, though. I think he liked* North of the Rio Grande *best, with Jack Holt and Bebe Daniels. I really believe what we share about movies is the love of being taken out of ourselves and our lives into places we've never been. To be able, for a little while, to imagine ourselves in someone else's more exciting life than ours.*

*Regardless, when we went to the movies tonight, Buzz kissed me. A lot. And then on the way home, he pulled the wagon over and we kissed again. It's a little strange since he was almost like a brother to me. But I never felt brotherly close to him like I did with Henry. We stay away from each other once we get home. I don't want Dad finding out about the kissing. Not yet, anyway, until I know what Buzz is really thinking. As I'm writing this, I'm laughing because all I can think of is what Helen used to say about Buzz and how handsome she thought he was.*

*Well, she was right. But I'll never tell her that.*

*I have to sleep now. Early day tomorrow.*

*Your excited friend, Maude*

## August 12, 1922

MAUDE'S BEDROOM DOOR CREAKED A LITTLE WHEN BUZZ opened it. Moonlight streamed through her open window and a slight breeze billowed her curtains into the room, almost touching her bed. Quietly, Buzz sat on the bed beside her, then put his hand on her bare shoulder. She bolted upright, her eyes wide.

"What are you doing here?" she hissed. "You shouldn't be here. What if Dad—"

Buzz interrupted her protest with his lips. The kiss was long and deep.

Tentatively, he lifted the sheet that covered her and prepared to slide in beside her.

"Buzz, no."

"Maude, please."

"No, Buzz. We're not married. Or even engaged. My God, you've never even told me you love me. Shouldn't all of that happen first?"

"Is that what you need, Maude? For me to love you?"

"Well ... yeah. I mean, we certainly know each other well enough. And I've always had feelings ... well, I'm not sure what you would call it. But I've certainly always been very aware of you. Have always thought you were extremely good-looking. Even though I never admitted it—even to myself. So, I just can't ... won't—"

Buzz stood. "Okay. You're right. I'll wait." He closed his eyes and took a deep breath. "But I'm not sure how much longer I can live in the same house with you and not show up here every night. Maybe this is love. I just ... I don't know. I'm sorry. I'll see you tomorrow." He leaned down and kissed her forehead, then left her room soundlessly.

Maude couldn't sleep the rest of the night.

# CHAPTER
# FORTY-NINE

**SUZANNE**
**2015**

O kay ... the plot thickens. Finally, Maude's diary indicates that she and my grandfather are about to get together. At least they've started kissing. That's something. I turned to the next entry.

*August 26, 1922*

*Dear Diary,*

*A lot has happened in the past two weeks.*

*First, I finished my secretarial course and got my completion certificate. Dad and Buzz came to my graduation. I was also hired at Harrington's to do their bookkeeping and typing. So far, it's just mornings. Which is fine with me. They're paying me twenty-five cents per hour! Almost minimum wage. Which means I'll be making almost four dollars per week. That will help out a lot. And I'll still be able to work on the farm in the afternoons. Dad says I can take one of the mules to the store every day.*

*Second, Buzz has been coming to my room at night. At first I told him we couldn't do anything and sent him away. But when he came back, he was so insistent and his kisses were so deep. And then he told me he loved me. So on the tenth night he showed up, I let him get into bed with me. I'm not sure either of us knew what we were doing. I sure didn't. But I finally felt something push into me. It really hurt at first but then it got better. That first time, I didn't understand what the big deal was, but it really made Buzz happy. So that was good. But he told me he loved me when it was over, so I have chosen to believe him.*

*He's come to my room every night for a week. I like it better now.*

*It's getting harder to keep Dad from finding out.*

*More later.*

*Your friend, Maude*

---

*September 19, 1922*

*Dear Diary,*

*I went to see Miss Delsie today to have her remind me of what she taught us in health class about our periods. And lack of them. Then she confirmed what I had suspected.*

*I'm pregnant. The way we figure it, the baby will arrive around the end of May next year. She talked to me about a couple of things that have been known to work to get rid of the pregnancy since she knows I'm not married. But I would never think of such a thing. This baby was conceived in love and will be born in love.*

*I plan to tell Buzz tonight and we will figure out the rest together. Like telling Dad. And getting married. I'm sure that won't be a problem. Buzz loves me. And I love him.*

*I'll give you our wedding date after I talk to Buzz.*

*Your friend, Maude*

---

## September 19, 1922

"BUZZ, WILL YOU JOIN ME ON THE PORCH SWING?"

His face lit up and he followed her to the porch. Maude sat on the swing and Buzz just stood there, confusion evident in his eyes.

"You mean you really want to swing? I thought you meant ..."

Maude laughed. "Maybe later. But first, let's talk for a few minutes. It's a beautiful night out. Perfect to swing on the front porch, don't you think?"

"Sure," Buzz said. He sat beside her and their feet worked in unison to send the swing back and forth.

Now that Buzz was beside her and it was time for Maude to tell him her secret, shyness overcame her. Music from the radio she had given her father for his birthday with her discount at Harrington's reached them through the screen door. The two young people rocked in silence.

Back and forth.

Back and forth.

Buzz's feet stopped moving and the swing stilled. He turned to her.

"Okay, Maude. What is it? What do you want to talk about?"

For a moment, the words stuck in her throat. Buzz's eyes never left hers. "Maude ..."

"I'm going to have a baby," she blurted out. "At the end of May next year."

He hit his forehead with his hand. "Oh my God." His words ended in a groan.

Fear filled Maude's head, then traveled to her heart. She had convinced herself he would be pleased. She sat still before her body began to shake.

"Are you sure?" he asked. "Could there be a mistake?"

Tears filled her eyes and she dropped her head to her hands. "I thought you'd be happy." Her words were so soft he had to ask her to repeat them. She lifted her head. "I thought you would be happy." Her voice rose. "My God, Buzz, you didn't think this was a possibility?"

"Is there anything you can ... you know ... do?"

Maude jumped up from the swing. "No!" The word came out as more of a scream than she intended. She heard her father shuffle to the door from his chair.

"Something wrong?" he asked.

"No," Buzz and Maude answered together. Maude left the porch and stormed down the long lane with Buzz right behind her. In two steps, he caught up to her and took her in his arms.

"I'm sorry, Maudie," he said. "We'll get married. I'm sure we would have anyway. We'll just do it sooner."

She rested her head on his shoulder and they stood like that for a long time.

"How about Saturday?" she asked.

"For what?"

She pulled back and looked at him, disbelief in her eyes. "To get married. What did you think I would be talking about?"

He smiled at her. A smile that almost reached his eyes. But not quite. "Saturday it is," he said. "We can get the license tomorrow when I pick you up from work."

They walked back up the lane, arm in arm.

That night, when he joined her in bed, she smelled liquor on his breath.

# CHAPTER FIFTY

**SUZANNE**
**2015**

*September 23, 1922*

*Dear Diary,*

*We did it. Buzz and I got married today.*

*You should have seen how happy Dad was. He said he had always hoped we would get married but he knew better than to suggest it. He simply waited to let us figure it out for ourselves.*

*I haven't told Dad I'm pregnant yet. But I know he'll be thrilled about becoming a grandfather.*

*I bought some fabric at Harrington's—I love having a discount there— and made myself a very simple wedding dress. Buzz used Henry's suit coat and Dad lent him a tie.*

*We had a very small ceremony. The two of us and Dad and Miss Delsie as witnesses. The preacher was very accommodating and we all went to dinner in town afterward. It was wonderful. Except that Buzz took several swigs from the flask he carried. He tried to hide it but I knew. And so did Dad and Miss Delsie. He could still walk, but I wasn't thrilled at the thought of him drinking around other people like that. And then when we went to bed, he slumped down and slept right away. I undressed him to put his pajamas on him and saw that he still wore the gold locket. The one that belonged to the Belgian nurse. It stabbed my heart but I decided not to let it bother me. She was dead, after all, and he was married to me.*

*And by the way, we'll be married for a long time. It's all fine.*

*I'll write more later.*

*Your friend, Maude Irene Brewer RYAN*

———◦✦◦———

*September 28, 1922*

*Dear Diary,*

*It's me—Mrs. Ryan.*

*I never get tired of saying that. When I went back to my job on Monday after our wedding, Mr. and Mrs. Harrington gave me an envelope with ten dollars in it! That was so generous of them. They also said I could have tomorrow off since Buzz and I are going to Philadelphia to watch the A's play the Washington Senators. It will be our honeymoon.*

*Buzz got in touch with Coach Mack and he offered to take us to dinner when we come. I asked Buzz if it will be hard for him to watch a game knowing he can't play in it and he promised me he would be fine with it. We will stay in the boarding house where Buzz and Henry used to live when they both played for the team.*

*I am really enjoying being married. I wish Mom could have been here for our wedding, but I'm sure she's better off where she is.*

*I have to sleep now. We're leaving early in the morning.*

*Your newly married friend, Maude*

——— ·⋘⋙· ———

## September 29, 1922

M aude had been right.

Buzz had a very hard time sitting in the stands and watching his team play ball rather than being on the field with them and helping with the win. That was the good part. The Athletics beat the Senators both games in the double header. But it didn't make Buzz feel much better. Having a full flask with him helped but didn't totally eliminate his pain.

Buzz went down to the dugout to talk to some of the guys between games. But he knew very few of them these days. Many of the ones he had played with didn't come back after the war. A number of them had been killed—like Henry.

On their way back to the boarding house after the game, Maude saw that Buzz's mood was very dark with the rage she had recognized earlier seething just below the surface. Once there, he removed his hat and threw it across the room.

"That was horrible." He flopped on the bed.

"What? Your team won. What was horrible?"

"My team? That's funny. It's not my team anymore. And never will be again. I would have been better off to get killed outright than have to return here and watch something I can no longer be a part of."

Maude was appalled.

"My God, Buzz," she said. "Do you think Henry would have chosen death over being wounded to the point he could no longer play ball? If you had asked him that morning on the battlefield, what do you think he would have said?"

"It was different for him." Buzz spat out the words at her. "He didn't have anything to prove ... no rotten family to escape. Plus, he loved the farm and didn't mind working there. You need to know this, Maude. I *don't* love working on the farm. I hate it. Every second of it."

His eyes narrowed as he looked at her. Then he stood, clumsily. "Fine. Let's go."

Their walk back to the boarding house held the same silence as their earlier walk from it.

When they reached their room, Maude decided to broach the subject.

"Buzz, the coach and I talked about you joining the team as some sort of assistant. But he said ..."

He turned on her and towered over her. "Why would you do a thing like that?"

Her expression reflected her shock. "To help you. To make you feel better. To—"

"You stay out of it."

"But I just thought ..."

"Well stop. I have everything under control."

He didn't have anything under control. Maude knew it. And she knew he knew it. But she decided not to fight about it. She put on her nightgown and got in bed. She heard him moving around the room, bumping into first one piece of furniture and then another. Until he left.

He didn't return until almost dawn.

# CHAPTER
# FIFTY-ONE

**SUZANNE**
**2015**

I loved hearing my little grandmother sound so happy to be married from her diary entries. I worried, though, since I knew the outcome of their relationship—that my grandfather left home for long periods at a time and, according to my dad, "only came home to get her pregnant again before leaving once more." Funny, even though I knew the history, I hoped I would find something different in my grandmother's words ... something my father and his siblings didn't know that would paint my grandfather in a better light. It was a long shot, sure, but I could still hope, right?

With very few pages left to read, I turned to the next entry.

*December 15, 1922*

*Dear Diary,*

*It's almost Christmas and with my salary and the discount I get at Harrington's I've gotten really good presents for Dad and Buzz. Dad and I already have our Christmas tree picked out and we'll put it up in another week or so.*

*Things have been mostly good since Buzz and I returned from our "honeymoon" in Philadelphia. That was kind of a rough trip because I saw Buzz drinking quite a bit. I hadn't realized he drank so much but when I talked to Coach Mack about it, he knew. And he even told me that was why he hadn't asked Buzz to be a part of the team in some way other than pitching. He said he couldn't count on Buzz not to drink. So it was more serious than I thought.*

*He keeps himself under control on most days and does his part on the farm even though he told me he hates it. "Every second of it," was the way he put it. I tried to tell him that Coach said if he could prove himself sober for two or three months, he could possibly become an assistant coach or something like that. But every time I bring up his drinking we have a fight. And I really hate fighting with him. He's such a sweet man and I know he only drinks because he's had so many disappointments in his life. When he's able to keep it under control as he has done lately, I know we'll be fine.*

*We told Dad about the baby and, as I figured, he's thrilled. I did talk to Dad about Buzz's drinking and he was already aware of it. He had an idea about working with Buzz to try pitching once more, so they've been spending time outside working on it until just recently now that it's so cold and gets dark early.*

*Dad told me he and Buzz also had a heart-to-heart talk about the work and Buzz finally admitted to him he wasn't happy working on the farm. So Dad suggested he get a job in town. He said the two of us could even ride together until I had to quit when the baby is born. So in January, Buzz will go back to his old job at the feed mill, although they promised him he could move up and take on more responsibility as openings occur. That seemed to make him happy.*

*So things are good. Mostly, anyway.*

*The baby is growing and has just started kicking. That's something Buzz and I love to share together. He loves to feel my belly when the baby is active. I think he'll be a good father although I notice that some days he looks really worried. It will be fine. I'm sure of it.*

*If I don't get back to you before then, Merry Christmas. I'm looking forward to what 1923 will bring—in addition to my child.*

*Your friend, Maude*

———— ✦◦✦ ————

*June 4, 1923*

*Dear Diary,*

*I'm a mother! My baby boy, Walter, was born early this morning. The doctor just barely made it here in time. But the baby is absolutely beautiful! Perfect! All his fingers and toes right where they should be. I'm so happy.*

*Buzz has held him some, although he seems to be a little scared of him. That strikes me as really funny that a man as big as Buzz could be afraid of a person who is so tiny. My dad is as proud as a peacock and we've both talked about how happy Mom would have been to be a grandmother. But I'm sure she's happy in heaven. Just as I'm sure Henry is.*

*I left my job at the end of April and, honestly, I kind of miss it. I will have plenty to keep me busy with my new little fella, but I did like working there. And I loved the discount, which I will miss. But I bought everything I would need for the baby before I left the job, so we're fine right now.*

*And Buzz is doing okay with his job. Turns out, though, he's not much happier working at the feed mill than he was with working on the farm. I guess for somebody with his talent, it's hard to settle for something less than what you know you can do. Or could do, before the war. He still drinks too much—almost every night after work for a while. But Dad suggested they start working on his pitching again, so he's done better at* coming home in time for that until it gets dark. Maybe keeping that up will help.

I have to feed my precious boy. I'll come back to you when I can, but I know I will be really busy for a while. So just know I haven't forgotten about you.

Your busy new mother friend, Maude

———— ⋘⋙ ————

December 20, 1923

Dear Diary,

It's Walter's first Christmas and we're all excited. He's a perfect little baby. And so smart. He rolled over at three months and he's already started sitting up on his own. He laughs a lot and hardly ever cries. Sometimes he cries when he sees his father, but Miss Delsie said that a lot of babies are afraid of men. Of course, he doesn't cry when Dad holds him, but who knows what happens in that tiny little baby brain?

Buzz got a promotion at work so he has to stay later a lot of days. Some nights, he stays in town rather than come home so late. I wish he wouldn't, but he says if he wants to get ahead, he has to play their game. I'm not sure what he means by that, but I'm so busy with Walter I don't have a lot of time to miss Buzz. He told me he'll be here for Christmas, though. So that's good.

More later, Maude

———— ⋘⋙ ————

*June 5, 1924*

*Dear Diary,*

*Walter just turned one year old and he's walking.*

*Buzz missed his birthday party. He got home really late. And he'd been drinking. Only a couple, he said. I don't normally know where he gets it, but it isn't worth fighting about.*

*Anyway, Walter is the joy in my life and now that he's here, I can't remember what I did without him. I guess I was born to be a mother.*

*I help on the farm when I can. Walter actually loves being out in the fields—especially the strawberry field. I found him yesterday sitting between the rows stuffing not only strawberries, but also leaves and dirt into his mouth. Miss Delsie says a little dirt will never hurt babies, so I try not to worry.*

*Gotta run.*

*Your friend, Maude*

---

*October 3, 1924*

*Dear Diary,*

*Well, I'm pregnant again.*

*Buzz didn't take the news very well, but I reminded him I didn't get this way by myself. Dad likes the thought of another baby, so the two of us are figuring out how we'll rearrange Walter's room to move him into the bed Henry used when he was alive and then the crib will be free for the new baby. It will be fine.*

*Fortunately, I haven't been as sick this time. Which is good because Walter, that darling little devil, is getting into everything. And oh my goodness, the increase in the laundry!*

*I talked to Mrs. Harrington about coming back to work a couple of afternoons during the week. She said they would welcome me back to help with the holiday rush. Buzz's salary, what we see of it, doesn't go as far as it used to, and now with a second baby coming, we could use the extra money.*

*I also talked to Miss Josephine about having one of her daughters come over to babysit with Walter when I go back. She told me Elsie could come and would even start supper for me. The good news is, I won't have to pay her as much as I can make at the store, so it will be worth it.*

*Have to start supper. Don't know if Buzz will be here, but the rest of us have to eat.*

*More later, Maude.*

———— ⋙⋘ ————

*March 30, 1925*

*Dear Diary,*

*Mr. Muir, the owner of the feed mill, came to see me at Harrington's today and asked if Buzz was sick since he hadn't shown up at work. I guess he could tell from my surprised expression that I didn't know what he was talking about. I thought Buzz was at work because he didn't come home last night, so I figured he stayed in town to get to the mill before everybody else.*

*I took an early lunch hour and went to the boarding house in town where Buzz told me he stayed on the nights he didn't come home. Mrs. Brady said he hadn't been in for several days.*

*That was my second surprise.*

*So I went to the restaurant. I had learned by now that they run an illegal liquor joint in one of the back rooms. A "speakeasy" I heard it called. So that was the next place I looked.*

*And there he was, asleep on one of the couches, all rumpled up and smelling like stale spirits. When I shook him to wake him up, his hand shot out and he almost hit me. I backed off and screamed at him to get up and get himself straight. I still can't believe I did that, but fortunately no one was around to hear me. I hated being that kind of wife.*

*He finally got up and started walking toward the farm. I didn't know if he would make it, but figured I had to travel in the same direction in a couple of hours, so I would find him if he didn't.*

*Then I went to see Mr. Muir and told him that yes, Buzz was sick but I would see to it that he came in tomorrow. He looked at me kindly and said, "I'm sorry to have to tell you this, Maude, but if he comes to work drunk again, I will have to let him go."*

*My third surprise.*

*I had no idea he drank during the day and was showing up at work drunk.*

*I went to see Mrs. Harrington and told her I needed to take the rest of the day off for family matters. Then I started home and found Buzz lying in a ditch. I got him up and into the wagon. Dad was on the front porch when we pulled up, so he helped me get Buzz to bed. Not in our bed … in the small bed in Henry's room he used to sleep in. And*

*I told Elsie she could go home since I would be there to take care of Walter.*

*It was a horrible day and I don't know if things will ever be fine again.*

*Your heartbroken friend, Maude*

⁕

## March 28, 1925

BUZZ SAT ON THE EDGE OF THE SMALL BED AND DROPPED his head to his hands, the gold locket he always wore falling out of his open shirt. The earlier sunlight had faded and the room dimmed with dusk. His head pounded.

"You deserve to be in pain, you sorry son of a bitch," he told himself out loud.

"I couldn't agree more."

His head shot up to see Maude standing in the door, her arms crossed over her chest and resting on her swollen stomach. The sudden movement brought an onslaught of new pain to his already throbbing head.

Maude crossed the room and handed him aspirin and a glass of water.

He attempted a smile but his lips refused to cooperate. "I don't deserve you," he said.

"You're damned right about that," she agreed. It was the first time he had ever heard her use a swear word. "But what's more important," she continued, "is that I don't deserve a husband like you. I can't believe you have chosen to throw your life away like this."

"I know. You're right. But ..."

"But what, Buzz? You're disappointed with your life? That you got shot in the war? That you lost the woman you loved? That you can no longer pitch? Or that you have refused to accept those things like a man and grow up to take responsibility for your family?"

Tears streaked his cheeks. "All of that, Maude. All of it. I haven't been able to get past it. Not being able to pitch." He stood. "Don't you understand?" He moved closer to her. "I had the talent. I was in demand. I was supposed to *be* somebody. Not just another jerk who works for an hourly wage and lives with his wife's father. I was supposed to get out of this one-horse town, to give you a big house, a car, servants to help with the baby. Everything."

His eyes were glazed. Feverish. As if he were still suffering from the effects of the drink.

Maude sat on the side of the bed and pulled him down to sit beside her.

"Okay, Buzz," she said quietly. "Thank you for what you would like to have done for me. But that didn't happen. And as long as you stay drunk, there's no chance of that ever happening. So what's your plan now? What are you going to do about it?"

His head dropped back into his hands. "I don't know," he whispered. "Please help me."

She put her arm around him. "Of course I'll help you. I love you. But are you willing to help yourself? I can't do anything for you unless *you* want to change. And the first thing necessary for that is to accept that your life is different from the way you expected it to be. That it will *never* be the way you expected it to be. Or wanted it to be. Can you do that, Buzz? Is there any way you can be happy with the path your life has taken so you can stop refusing the road you're on because it looks different from the road you originally wanted to be on?"

"I don't know. I honestly don't know."

"I never told you this, because every time I brought up your drinking you simply got mad. And I finally stopped bringing it up because I was tired of fighting all the time. But the last time we saw Coach Mack he told me if you could prove that you've been sober two or three months straight, he would consider having you back with the team in some sort of assistant role. I know you would like that better than working on the farm or at the feed mill. Is there any way you would consider working toward that? If your children and I are not enough incentive for you to stop drinking, would that be?"

"I don't drink all the time, Maude. I only have a few. And I can stop any time I want."

"Fine," Maude said. "Prove it. Stop drinking and start acting like the family man you've become."

Neither of them had seen little Walter come to the door, but he looked at his parents, then teetered across the floor in a rush and landed with his little hands on his father's knees.

"Da-da!" Buzz reached down and hugged the tiny boy to him.

"I will, Maude," he said. "I'll stop drinking. I will. I'll prove it to you."

# CHAPTER FIFTY-TWO

**SUZANNE**
**2015**

Maude's last couple of entries sounded more like what I had always heard about my grandfather. My heart went out to her. To both of them actually. Fortunately, I never had to deal with alcoholics in my family. I guess technically, my dad could have inherited the addiction gene from his father, but to my knowledge, he never had an issue with drinking. Or any other addictive substance that I ever saw. And neither did my husband nor my son.

And again, to my knowledge, none of Dad's siblings struggled with any kind of addiction either. But until I started reading my grandmother's diary, I never knew how lucky we all were that the family didn't have to deal with that. Being able to have a social drink without having it lead to anything more is just something we've all taken for granted.

It also strikes me as a sign of the times that with all of the trauma my grandfather endured—watching his father kill his mother and then himself, having the dream pitching job he'd always hoped for only to have it ripped from his grasp with the First World War, losing his best friend in the first battle he faced, loving a Belgian nurse only to have her die in front of his eyes, and then having his arm shot up, only minutes before a cease-fire was called, to the point that he could never go back to pitching—he didn't have anyone to talk with about it except my grandmother and her father. But they weren't trained in how to help him. And they were both too close to it emotionally.

From my perspective, I absolutely understood how Buzz could have been so disappointed he would self-medicate rather than come to terms with his life. And just as easily, I understood that my grandmother's first reaction was anger since she, alone, had to deal with whatever messes he made as a result of that. I'm sure she tried to help him but she probably had very little bandwidth left for a wayward husband, since she was raising children and trying to keep the farm together so they had a roof over their heads.

My heart actually ached for them. And I kept thinking, "if only" even one of those things had happened differently, Buzz would have been better able to face what his life had become. What I wouldn't give for a time machine to be able to travel back and help them.

I wondered how many thousands of people have thought that over the years. I guess the good news in all of this is that at least some lessons have been learned from history. Post-Traumatic Stress Disorder is a recognized ailment, for one thing, with resources for soldiers to deal with it. And women having equal footing in business and families, for another.

While those things made me feel better for today, none of it was there in time to help Maude and Buzz. They had to muddle through on their own with very few resources. As Maude's words show.

I turned to the next entry.

*June 9, 1925*

*Dear Diary,*

*We've had another tragedy. My father has been badly hurt.*

*He had been on the porch, waiting for Buzz to come home. We had all been excited about Buzz's progress in his attempt to stop drinking. After that day Mr. Muir came to see me at Harrington's, Buzz and I had a heart-to-heart talk that night. And he promised he would prove to me he could stay sober for two to three months so he could approach Coach*

*Mack about an assistant position with the Athletics. And he was doing great. As far as I could tell, he kept his word.*

*Mr. Muir let him return to the mill and Buzz went to work every day and came home every night. Dad and Buzz even began working on Buzz's pitching again so Buzz could figure out how to teach some of his signature pitches to new pitchers on the team.*

*But yesterday, Buzz had an argument with his supervisor at work and when he left for lunch, he went straight to the speakeasy and had a drink. And then another. And another. Through the whole afternoon. When he finally went back to the mill, Mr. Muir fired him. On the spot. So Buzz left the mill and continued drinking until it was dark.*

*I was so upset, I went into false labor, so Dad waited for Buzz on the porch. When Buzz climbed the steps and Dad saw how bad he was, he hollered at him. Told Buzz he had just thrown away his last chance at the kind of life he dreamed of.*

*When I heard them, I went to the door and saw the whole thing. Buzz cleared the top step and reached the floor of the porch, then brushed past Dad. At that point, Dad was so angry with him, he reached out and spun Buzz around to face him. Then Buzz started to laugh at the depth of Dad's anger, which only made things worse. Dad actually took a swing at Buzz, but he ducked, so Dad only connected with air. Dad swung so hard, that when he missed, it threw him off balance and he fell backward down the porch steps. And hit his head on the concrete steppingstones that lined the driveway.*

*There was so much blood!*

*I rushed out and Buzz was suddenly sober, his eyes wide. "He fell," Buzz hollered. "I didn't do anything. I swear."*

*"I saw it," I told him. "Help me get him inside."*

*Buzz picked him up and put him on the living room couch. I turned his head to clean the wound. But when I saw how large it was and that it appeared to have actually cracked Dad's skull, I sent Buzz into town to get the doctor. "And for God's sake, come straight back with him. No stopping to drink along the way."*

*I did what I could to clean the gash but it wouldn't stop bleeding. And Dad's heart was still beating, but I couldn't get him to wake up. When the doctor finally got there, he stitched up Dad's wound and told me he was in a coma. That's why I couldn't get him to wake up. The doctor said the next twenty-four hours would be critical and hoped Dad's brain didn't swell. He told me he would come back tomorrow.*

*Your heartbroken friend, Maude.*

---

*June 10, 1925*

*Dear Diary,*

*My wonderful father has died.*

*Buzz is as heartbroken as I am. And he blames himself.*

*We will have Dad's funeral tomorrow. His will be the second grave in the family cemetery at the edge of the woods behind the house. We buried my mother there seven years ago. Since we didn't get Henry's body back after the war, he's buried somewhere in France.*

*I can't believe both of my parents are gone.*

*I'll write again when I've pulled myself together.*

*Your friend, Maude*

July 6, 1925

Dear Diary,

My second child was born yesterday. Another boy. I've named him Sam.

Buzz has worked the farm since my father's death. He's doing a good job, and as far as I can tell, he's remained sober. We are trying to make things work.

Buzz no longer works on his pitching or talks about joining Coach Mack to help with the team. I believe he's doing penance for my father's death, even though I know my father simply fell and the only thing Buzz had to do with it was to come home drunk.

Again.

I am trying not to blame him. But some days it's really hard. I plan to try and get my job back at Harrington's in the fall so we have some extra money. My dad had a small insurance policy but I haven't told Buzz about it. I have put it away in case I ever need it for the children and me. No use taking chances.

Sam is a sweet little boy and his older brother is crazy about him. Buzz has only held him once but he takes care of Walter so I can tend to Sam. That works. For now.

I will get pictures in the album.

Your friend, Maude

# CHAPTER
# FIFTY-THREE

SUZANNE
2015

Oh no. What a horrible thing to happen to Maude. Good Lord, she certainly has had to deal with a lot of issues herself. I'm going to finish reading because I have so few pages left. But, oh God, I am so depressed. Especially since I just read about my father's birth when in a day or so, I have to take him back to his birthplace to be buried.

"Mom?"

"Steve—hi, honey."

He stood in the doorway and looked at me. "I thought I'd find you here. But I never dreamed you'd be in the same clothes you wore yesterday and in almost exactly the same position where I last saw you. Have you eaten anything?"

"I had breakfast. I think. Why? What time is it?"

"Almost two o'clock in the afternoon. Emily sent me over with a chicken salad sandwich. She knows how much you like it."

"Bless her heart. Yes, I do." At the mention of food, my stomach gurgled and I wolfed down the first half in only a couple of bites.

"So," he said, "this story must be very absorbing. Who would have thought a diary from a hundred years ago would have kept you glued like this?"

"I've almost finished. It really is heartbreaking. But I've learned a lot about both of my grandparents. And I'm really looking forward to being able to enlighten my aunts and Uncle Freddie since all they've ever heard is the bad stuff my grandfather did to the family. I'm guessing they know nothing about the bad stuff that was done *to* him."

"Like what?"

"I'll make a deal with you," I said. "I'll tell you and Emily all about it on our way to the farm. But right now I want to finish reading."

"You think the story from the diary will turn out differently from the one in real life?"

I laughed. "No. I'm not expecting that. I'm just really anxious to read the last few entries. Maybe there's a clue as to where my grandfather went after he disappeared."

"Do you think his remaining children are really interested in that?"

"Probably not. But even though the diary is reading the way the story was told in life, that my grandfather was less than a stellar person, I can now understand how the extenuating circumstances contributed to that. And he can almost be forgiven. Almost, but not quite."

"Why not quite?"

"Because he never accepted the fact that his dreams were no longer a reality. He never grew up and moved on. So he threw away a beautiful family to nurse his disappointments."

He leaned over and kissed my forehead. "Okay. I'll let you get back to it. Call me when you've finished."

"Okay. Tell Emily thanks again for the chicken salad."

Steve left and I turned back to the photo album. Sure enough, Maude added a picture of my dad just days after he was born. And one beside it with Walter holding him. A few pictures of Walter and Dad as toddlers followed, but by then, they were with more babies. The twins—my Uncle Richard—whom I never met—and my Aunt Kathleen. Born the year after my father. Later pictures showed the last two girls, Aunt Sarah and Aunt Winnie, as toddlers, along with pictures of Dad and Walter beside the steamer trunk I had seen in earlier pictures. The caption said they were ten and twelve years old. The ironic thing was, the two of them stood beside the trunk, still filled with baseball equipment, in almost the exact same pose my grandfather and Great-Uncle Henry had been in twenty years earlier. A few pictures after that showed all of the kids engaged in a ball game with my dad pitching. It was so cute.

I made another mental note to check where that trunk was when I reached the farm. Steve and Emily would love to have it if no one else in the family was interested.

I picked up the diary again and saw that after Maude's father died, the entries were few and far between. For the next few years, the entries consisted of dates followed by a sentence or two with only little snippets about the children. And Buzz's drinking. Almost as if Maude were chronicling a timeline the way I saw some of my friends do years earlier when they weren't getting child support from their exes.

*July 16, 1926*

*Dear Diary,*

*Sam started walking today and says three words: 'mama,' 'Wally,' and 'up.' Twins cry a lot. Walter is a great brother, keeps Sam occupied while I deal with the twins.*

*Buzz drunk for three days so I needed help with the fields.*

*Your friend, Maude.*

Occasionally, she mentioned that Buzz still wore the Belgian nurse's necklace but to her, it was one more example of Buzz not being able to grow up from his disappointments.

By the end of 1926, the entries included Buzz's rages through the house where he threw things, narrowly missing Maude and the children, and by 1928, Maude chronicled that Buzz had started beating her. Normally, there would be a really small entry following one of those about how sorry he was and that he promised he wouldn't do it again. Sometimes Maude would add a sentence or two about what a hard life Buzz has had and that she knew he still had trouble dealing with it. So when he begged for forgiveness, she always gave it.

And then in another two or three months, the cycle repeated.

In looking back and forth at the timelines between the diary and the album, I was surprised to see very few pictures of my grandfather with his children. Geez, with three boys so close in age, you'd think he'd have taught them to play ball. And as I had already seen, there were later pictures of the boys—and even the girls—playing ball. But I would have expected to see the children of a professional baseball player playing baseball with their professional baseball player father.

Who knows why that didn't happen? Maybe Buzz just didn't like having his picture taken. Yeah, right ...

*December 28, 1929*

*Dear Diary,*

*Kind of a grim Christmas this year. Although Buzz actually showed up to celebrate with us and he was in pretty good shape. We'll see how long it lasts.*

*A couple of months ago, the newspapers reported what they called the "Stock Market Crash." Miss Delsie tried to explain it to me, but I still don't understand why the loss of fortunes of some wealthy men in New York would affect us here in Prospect Park. She said when their money dried up, that took money away from businesses and everything else people depended on and with less money going around, there was less work to be had and so on down the line.*

*I'd been successful in getting my job back at Harrington's a few months after Sam was born and then had to stop again when I had the twins. But I've been working this time since the twins' first Christmas and Mrs. Harrington has promoted me and given me more responsibility and raises. She told me she will keep me on as long as the store is able to stay open. It's a constant source of conflict with Buzz since he's always trying to get part of that money.*

*For months, however, I've given Miss Delsie money to put away for me. She told me she puts it in a Mason jar and submerges it in her well. When I give her the money, I make absolutely certain no one—and I mean no one—sees me or knows about it. I pass over some of the money I've earned from Harrington's and all the money from my dad's insurance policy. Buzz must never find out about it. At least now when he screams at me to give him money, I can honestly tell him I don't have any.*

*The other good thing is, our neighbor, Mr. Reynolds, has rented twelve or so acres of our farmland for the past three years and says he will continue to do so because people still need food. So as much as I can spare of that income goes to Miss Delsie too. Buzz hasn't bothered to figure out how the land continues to get farmed with him not here and me caring for all these children, so as of yet, he doesn't know about that money.*

*And of course, since Buzz hasn't been able to hold onto a job anyway, we're not missing any income from him.*

*We'll make do as best we can.*

*Sure, I get worried, but we'll be fine. As long as things don't get a lot worse.*

*I'll keep you posted.*

*Your friend, Maude*

---

*March 2, 1930*

*Dear Diary,*

*I just found out I'm pregnant again. Must have happened around Christmas when Buzz was on especially good behavior. Damn. Another mouth to feed during these hard times is not a choice I would have willingly made. Although, I guess I did do it willingly. He hasn't resorted to rape, so I only have myself to blame.*

*Don't get me wrong. I love having children. But times are tough and I will not be able to work once the baby is born, so I haven't figured out yet what I'll do. I'll try to take time soon to sit down with all the expenses and figure things out and whether I will need to give less money to Miss Delsie. I'm sure it will be fine. It has to be.*

*Your worried friend, Maude*

⸻ ⧉ ⸻

*July 5, 1930*

*Dear Diary,*

*We just had a birthday party for Sam and the twins, whose birthdays are two days before his. Sam turned five and the twins are four. Money's getting a little tighter, so they only received birthday presents I could make for practically nothing. But the kids didn't seem to mind.*

*Miss Delsie was here and Miss Josephine came with some of her grandchildren. I marveled to see my kids playing perfectly with the little colored children. It struck me then that the prejudices some of the folks in town have against the coloreds has to be learned behavior, since my children played with them as if they saw no differences at all. Miss Josephine and I shared a few smiles at that.*

*Then I saw Buzz coming up the lane and I motioned to Miss Josephine to round up her grandchildren. "We'll be going home now," she said. And I agreed it would be for the best since I didn't know what Buzz's attitude would be. I promised to send cake over for them later.*

*I sent the children upstairs to their rooms and before long, Buzz came charging through the door. Drunk. What a surprise. He came over to me and got right in my face, but I didn't back down. "Did I just see my children in the yard with a bunch of colored kids? Did I?"*

*"You did," I said quietly. "What about it?"*

*He stood six or seven inches taller than I am under normal conditions. But he was in such a rage, he actually raised himself on his toes and I watched his fists clench and unclench. He brought his nose to within an inch of mine. "I won't have it! I won't have any child of mine in the company of those … those …"*

*"Child of yours?" My voice was shrill. "The only thing you have to do with those children and the one in my belly is a random sperm. Do you ever spend any time with them? Do you even know anything about them?"*

*He drew back his fist and it was headed for my face. I was ready to duck when I heard a click. He stopped in mid-swing as his eyes lit on the barrel of my dad's shotgun. Held steady and trained on his head by Miss Delsie.*

*"If you throw that punch, young man," she said quietly, "it will be the last thing you ever do."*

*He backed down and lowered his fists. But his eyes still held fire.*

*"Buzz," Miss Delsie said. "I know you've had a tough life. You've had a lot to deal with. And some real disappointments. But you know what? When I saw you coming at your wife like that and raising your voice to her—with no provocation, I might add—you sounded just like your*

father. Is that what you wanted, Buzz? Did you hold your father in such high esteem that you wanted to grow up to be just like him?"

His face transformed into a look I had never seen before. Kind of a mix between shock and embarrassment. As if it had never occurred to him that he was anything at all like his father.

It was actually the first time I had thought about it too. And what's worse, when I thought about how I had screamed at him, even though I wasn't drunk, I knew that the two of us sounded like the two of his parents that last night before they died.

I couldn't believe we had come to that.

I faced something else with that thought. Buzz's father had actually killed his mother. In a drunken rage. Very similar to the one I had just seen from Buzz. And I was about to deliver his fifth child. Where would our children be if their father killed their mother?

Miss Delsie, still holding the shotgun on Buzz, spoke again. "You find somewhere else to stay tonight, son. I'll remain here with your family until you sober up."

Without a word, Buzz turned and left the house. Miss Delsie lowered the gun.

"Maude," she said. "We have plans to make. You cannot afford to have him come here in a drunken rage like that around your children. Especially with this gun in the house. It's just lucky I was still here. There's no way you would have had time to go into the living room to get it from the rack." She clicked the safety switch on and placed the gun back in its spot over the fireplace.

"Thank you for threatening him, Miss Delsie. I think he believed you would have actually pulled the trigger."

*"You bet your sweet patootie I would have pulled the trigger. The man was dangerous. If I hadn't been here, he could have given you a miscarriage. Or worse, beaten you to death. Honey, you owe it to those sweet children to save them from finding their mama dead."* She gave me a quick hug. *"Now I'm going to ride into town and bring the sheriff back with me. Then together, we'll figure out what you should do next."*

*And she did. When we sat down with the sheriff, he told me he couldn't arrest Buzz because Miss Delsie stopped him before he actually struck me. He also said he couldn't arrest Buzz for simply showing up drunk because we were still married, and in a court of law he could contend he was there for his marital rights as my husband. But he advised me to lock all the doors and not let Buzz in again until at least tomorrow afternoon. He also said I should take the shells out of the shotgun and hide them where only I could find them.*

*Then once the sheriff left, Miss Delsie reached into her purse and produced a derringer that fit perfectly in my palm. She passed extra ammunition over to me as well and told me she would help me devise a holster I could wear under my clothes so the children would never find it and put themselves in danger.*

*Personally, I thought it was all a little much until I remembered, once again, that Buzz's father had killed his mother in a drunken rage. Then I decided to follow everything Miss Delsie and the sheriff talked about.*

*That night, I gathered all the children with me in my bed and told them we were having a sleepover. Miss Delsie slept below us on the couch with my father's shotgun in her arms.*

*Buzz didn't show up again for a week.*

*Your friend, Maude.*

# CHAPTER
# FIFTY-FOUR

**SUZANNE**
**2015**

I was shaken to the core after reading that last entry in Maude's diary and had a lot more trouble forgiving my grandfather after that. Yes, he certainly had been dealt a bunch of bad blows, but everybody during that time had suffered bad breaks. After all, there was a World War, for God's sake, followed swiftly by a global pandemic and then a stock market crash. Of course everybody suffered.

The difference was, Buzz had wallowed in his disappointment for so long and, coupled with his addiction gene, had allowed his life to go from manageable to uncontrollable.

Maude delivered baby girl Sarah in late fall 1930 and baby girl Winnie in 1935. The new baby pictures showed up in the photo album along with older versions of their siblings.

But the entries during the last ten or so years before Buzz finally took off for good never mentioned times when Maude felt tender enough toward him to welcome a sexual interlude. I guessed I would never know. And just as well. I'm sure Maude's remaining children didn't want to think about their parents having sex. Just as no child ever wants to think about that.

But I hated the thought of a woman as strong and capable as Maude giving in to Buzz just because she was starved for adult affection. I knew it was none of my business, and I knew I couldn't view her life in terms of life today, but still. She raised seven children on her own and brought each of them up to be strong and self-reliant as well. What a great legacy.

I was down to only a couple of pages in the diary and remembered I had been looking for clues as to where Buzz could have taken off to after Freddie, the youngest, was born. And honestly, the more I thought about it, the angrier I became with him. Why should he have been allowed to run off footloose and fancy free, living a life of who knows what while his wife was left alone to raise all his children? With no support from him.

I speculated all sorts of different things—that he had returned to Europe and met another woman like Marthe and fallen in love. Or had another woman in another state and a whole second family. Although as much as he drank, I couldn't quite picture that happening.

More likely, he committed even worse sins on someone else than he almost committed on Maude and spent the bulk of his remaining life in jail. That one certainly seemed more plausible.

While there were small entries with the births of the last two girls, they hadn't had the level of detail as the entry in 1930. In these last few pages, there were only two entries of any length. The first was at the end of August 1939, almost ten years later.

*August 30, 1939*

*Dear Diary,*

*I finally got all the little ones to sleep. We had a big day today with lots of fun. We started out at Harrington's for school shopping. The store had just gotten in a lot of new fabrics, so I bought several bolts to make dresses for the girls. And, bless her heart, even though I haven't worked there for a while, that wonderful Mrs. Harrington still gave me my old discount. I suppose it should have made me feel bad—like she was offering us charity—but I chose to look at it as friends helping friends. And she has always been a good friend.*

*So with that discount and the money from Mr. Reynolds, who continues* to rent the farmland, paying for the fabric to make school clothes for so many children came a lot easier this year.

I've even taught Kathleen to sew and that makes the process go faster. One of us can be on the machine while the other does handwork. She's really good, but she worries if one of her seams doesn't turn out perfectly. I tell her the way Miss Delsie used to tell me ... "It'll never be seen on a galloping horse." The first time I said that to her she looked at me like I was crazy and said, "What does that even mean?" So I explained that one mistake on an entire project—in her case, a dress—will never be noticed by anyone. She laughed and now she says it all the time to the younger ones.

Anyway, after our shopping, I splurged to take us all to the county fair. The little kids gorged on cotton candy and caramel popcorn—my dad's favorite—and the older ones raced each other to go on all the rides. We stayed for the fireworks and they were spectacular. On our way home, Walter and Sam carried the younger girls on their shoulders and Richard and Kathleen raced each other. Ever since Richard's bout with rheumatic fever, Kathleen has been able to beat him. He hates that.

As we walked, they all talked at once about what they wanted to do at the fair next year. The boys want to enter the cows, Bonnie and Belle, in the agricultural part of the fair and Kathleen wants to be in the Farm Queen contest. She'll be fourteen then, so I guess that will be okay. I may even enter my camellias—they've been so beautiful the last few years.

We don't see a whole lot of Buzz these days but he came to find me at the fair. I know he gets odd jobs in town and he told me he was running one of the rides and helping at the fair in other ways. He said the pay was pretty good. He was very thin, but surprisingly, I didn't smell liquor on him and he had shaved. But he did need a haircut. Ironic, I thought, now that Prohibition had been repealed I would have figured he spent every minute drunk.

*Regardless, it still breaks my heart to see him the way he was tonight. I remember what a sweet, ambitious guy he used to be when he could still pitch ... before he started drinking.*

*If only we could go back ...*

*But we can't. Too much has happened. And when I do see him, I never know which Buzz I will get—the sweet, remorseful Buzz or the mean, raging drunk Buzz. It makes me so sad. I'm just glad I've been able to keep moving forward in life and that my children are doing so well.*

*I need to sleep. I told the children we could make ice cream tomorrow.*

*Your friend, Maude.*

*P.S. I want to write this because I need to tell somebody and you've always been there for me. I went to the kitchen to lock the front door, but before I could, Buzz opened it and walked in. And ... you guessed it. He'd been drinking again. I'm figuring he took the money he was paid for working at the fair and put it all into booze. I offered to make coffee for him but he had no interest in sobering up. Gee ... what a surprise ...*

*It was a horrible scene and I'm so glad none of the kids woke up. I could tell he was angry—who knows why—and he started shoving me around the kitchen. He called me terrible names and said I was keeping his children from him.*

*"Buzz," I said. "You know you can see them anytime you want. But not when you've been drinking. I can't trust you not to hurt them when you're drunk."*

*"You're so high and mighty, trying to set yourself up as better than me."*

*He came toward me again, still pushing. "I want to see them right now." He was shouting. "Right now! I'm going to go and get them."*

*He started toward the stairs but I stood in his path. I watched his face transform from merely angry to engorged with rage. It was both comical to see the level of his anger over so small an issue and horrifying at the same instant.*

*He swung his fist and caught me in the cheek.*

*Miss Delsie would have been disappointed in me because I had stopped wearing the little holster and derringer she'd given me.*

*But I couldn't leave him there with nothing between him and the children.*

*I fought back.*

*And, of course, that made him even madder. Despite the amount he drank, he was still really strong. And at that point, I didn't care what he did to me as long as he left the children alone.*

*So, when I could move, I edged back toward the kitchen. I figured if I could get to the door, I would run out and hope he followed me. I made it to the table but he dove for my knees and pulled me down. My chin bounced against the back of a chair and then the floor. I tasted blood.*

*In less than a second, he was on top of me. With one hand he turned me over and with the other pushed my skirt to my waist. My hands were free, so I beat his head but that didn't stop him. He entered me roughly and reached up to hold my hands still. I tried to scoot away from him on the floor, but his full weight was on top of me and I struggled to breathe.*

*It didn't take him long.*

*I'm embarrassed to tell you that when he was done, he simply got up and left. Without a word. But I lay on the floor and cried. From pain. From embarrassment. And, I realized, from relief. That he was gone. And hadn't bothered the children.*

*After a few moments, I picked myself up, locked the door and even bolstered it by putting a chair under the handle. I didn't really expect him to come back tonight, but I refused to take any additional chances.*

*On my way up the stairs, I had a revelation. If I had been wearing the little derringer Miss Delsie gave me, I would have killed him.*

*Or he would have grabbed it and killed me. That's how bad it was.*

*So I decided to continue the way I had been and not keep the gun with me. If he died, I thought, the world wouldn't miss much. But I would probably go to jail. Worse, if I died, that would only leave him to care for the children.*

*With that thought, I threw up everything I had consumed for the past month.*

*Maude*

# CHAPTER FIFTY-FIVE

**SUZANNE**
**2015**

O h. My. God.

He raped her. Oh my God!

But there was nothing she could have done about it. Back then, the law would have been on his side and the courts would have decided that all he did was claim his marital rights. And if she had killed him, she probably would have, as she had written, gone to prison. A plea of self-defense would never have worked since he was still legally her husband.

Regardless of my earlier thoughts about how much I wished Mom and Dad had found the diary instead of me, at this point, I was so glad I'd been the one to read it. And that last entry changed my mind about sharing it with Maude's remaining children. I would never let them know that their father raped their mother.

I suspected that was when my darling Uncle Freddie was conceived. He certainly didn't need to know that. And I was pretty sure my grandmother never told him.

The entry after the one I had just read confirmed my suspicion.

*September 30, 1939*

*Dear Diary,*

*I was afraid of this. I'm pregnant. Again. From that drunken fool.*

*I'll keep it to myself as long as I can.*

*Damn.*

*Maude*

———— ⊷⊶ ————

*December 10, 1939*

*Dear Diary,*

*Finally, the morning sickness has eased somewhat.*

*Kathleen guessed I was pregnant and she told the others. Walter and Sam are embarrassed, since they will be seventeen and fifteen, respectively, when the baby is born. The younger girls are thrilled at the thought of having a baby to play with.*

*I'm just really tired.*

*Buzz has been coming around fairly regularly for the past few months. Ever since that night. He has done a good job of showing up sober. The boys avoid him but the girls are nice to him and he usually brings them little presents. He has asked to see us on Christmas day and I agreed— only if he is sober. He promised he would be.*

*But I'm not counting on that. I've already had a talk with Walter and Sam and instructed them that they are not to leave my side while he is here. They're pretty big boys and really strong. I honestly don't believe he would try to hurt me—or them—when we are together.*

*I'll let you know how it goes.*

*Your friend, Maude*

December 25, 1939

Dear Diary,

It was okay. Buzz came after dinner and had dessert with us. He was sober and brought presents for each of the kids. They were nice to him and the oldest boys stuck by my side. But fortunately, Buzz was calm.

He's really thin. And has lost some teeth. He's not taking care of himself at all. Oh my goodness, he used to be so handsome. I hate what he's done to himself.

But I can't change it. And he doesn't want to change it. So there it is. Done.

If I don't make it back to you, Happy New Year.

Your friend, Maude

July 5, 1940

Dear Diary,

The damned fool showed up again. He's been so good about only coming when he's sober lately. But not today.

We were all outside, doing chores to get ready for the birthday party for Sam and the twins. The twins turned fourteen two days ago and Sam is fifteen today. What fine young men he and his older brother are.

I was on a ladder, washing windows. Kathleen tried to keep me from *climbing since I'm almost due, but I told her I would only do the down-stairs windows and she could do the ones upstairs. So she saw the whole thing.*

*The boys were in the garden and the younger girls were in the barn.*

*Kathleen was the only one around when he showed up.*

*I could see he was drunk from the minute he stood at the bottom of the ladder, looking up at me. God, I wish I knew what brought these spells on, but I'm not even sure he knows. Anyway, he told me to come down so he could talk to me. But I ignored him.*

*Not very smart of me.*

*He started shaking the ladder. I told him to stop, but he kept on. Harder. I finally climbed down a few steps but it was too late. His anger had already gotten the best of him and his final shove was huge. The ladder and I both tumbled to the ground and I fell on my back. Hard. With the ladder on top of me.*

*Kathleen screamed at him from one of the upstairs windows. Shock showed on his face. He thought we were alone. Kathleen went inside and I heard her feet on the stairs.*

*That damned coward took off running rather than face his daughter for what he had done to her mother. Of course it suited me fine. I was in a lot of pain.*

*And, as it turned out, labor.*

*My water broke as I lay on the ground. And there was blood too. Kathleen helped me get into bed and then she ran to get Mrs. Gibbons from the farm down the road rather than try to get Doc Garrett in time.*

*I'm still in a lot of pain.*

*Your hurting friend, Maude*

*P. S. My seventh child has been born. I hope Sam doesn't mind sharing his birthday.*

*Thank God, the baby is fine. Another boy. I've named him Frederick but we've all started calling him Freddie. He is a beautiful little creature.*

# CHAPTER FIFTY-SIX

**SUZANNE**
**2015**

I couldn't believe it.

That was it. The last entry.

I went through the rest of the pages in the album and saw a few pictures of Freddie as a baby with one or the other of his siblings holding him. The last picture was dated 1940. At Christmas.

Additional photo albums rested in other boxes, so I pulled them out, one by one, and turned to the last page to search for another diary that picked up the story after this one stopped. But I found nothing.

Almost in a frenzy, I emptied several boxes but couldn't find anything else that even remotely resembled the rest of my grandmother's life story.

I was so disappointed. I wanted to know more.

I picked up the diary again and pored through it one more time, searching for pages stuck together. Or something that would yield additional entries. But again, nothing.

In desperation, I inspected the binding.

There was my answer.

Pages had been torn out. But there was no way to know if the pages had been deleted before or after they'd had Maude's words written on them. It was possible she tore out a page or two to make notes to herself or to leave for the kids. But that was as far as I could go with it.

Pure speculation.

No facts.

And no conclusion as to Buzz's disappearance.

I remembered Dad telling me that his father had shown up on the front porch, drunk, the night Freddie was born and that he and Walter had sent him away. Now that I knew he had shown up earlier, I'm guessing Maude never told the boys about that encounter. But Dad said none of them ever saw him again after that night.

As much as I had hoped otherwise, Buzz's whereabouts would forever remain a mystery. I figured at that point I was the only one who cared about what had happened to him.

But I did.

And I hadn't been able to find out.

Sighing, I repacked the albums in their box and got them ready to accompany us to the farm. I had already decided not to share my grandmother's diary with her remaining children. There were things I had read about their father that they didn't need to know. I could simply tell them about the good parts.

Or never even mention the diary at all.

I caressed my mother's "Beautiful Box" one last time, carried the box with the photo albums to my car and washed the dishes I'd left in Dad's sink. Even though I hadn't accomplished what I had come over to do—to go through Dad's things and clean out his house—I knew that could wait. There wasn't any hurry.

When I was satisfied I had left his house in good shape, I turned off the lights, locked the door, and went back to my house to pack for our trip to the farm.

———— ·❦· ————

WE DROVE UP THE LONG LANE UNDER ITS CANOPY OF trees. Uncle Freddie had black-topped the lane years earlier, so no dust cloud accompanied us as we reached the huge, manicured lawn surrounding the Ryan family farmhouse. The picture it presented always took my breath away with its well-kept grounds and profusion of colorful flowers set against the white latticework that surrounded the porch.

My heart soared to be back among so many people I loved, then clenched as I remembered why.

The funeral. For my father, Sam Ryan.

The huge wrap-around porch wore a new coat of white paint since my last visit and bulged with more than half the family. Members from four generations sprawled across every available space and overflowed from the porch swing.

My dad's youngest brother, Freddie—my grandmother's last child whose birth I had just read about in her own words—still lived in the house with his wife, Sally, and their youngest children. My dad's sisters, Winnie and Sarah, had both built houses on the fifteen-acre family property after Mr. Reynolds and his sons stopped renting it for farmland so they were already there, along with their children and grandchildren.

Unfortunately, Dad's oldest sister, Kathleen, had succumbed to cancer a couple of years ago. Only three of my grandmother's original seven children remained.

We stashed our bags in the upstairs bedrooms and, after a brief visit, Uncle Freddie approached me. "Are you up for taking a stroll to the family cemetery to see the spot we picked out for Sam?"

My eyes filled, but I nodded.

I leaned into Uncle Freddie as he steered me to the dirt path that ran beside the small patch of woods bordering the back of the house. White blooms dotted the deep green forest magnolias and shared their palette with yellow and purple-flowered vines entwined among them. Small blue clusters of wild violets burst from the grass below and completed the breathtaking canvas.

We reached the cemetery and Uncle Freddie unlatched the gate in the wrought iron fence.

"Oh," I said. "This fence is new since last year when we buried Mother."

"Right," Uncle Freddie said. "Winnie insisted we add it when the deer ate the camellias she planted on your grandmother's grave."

Immediately, my mind went to the passage in Maude's diary after they had all been to the fair. The night my grandfather raped her. But she had written earlier that she intended to enter her camellias in the county fair.

I wondered if she ever did.

The grounds inside the small cemetery were pristine with freshly cut grass, free from leaves even though one side of the fence rested only inches from the first line of trees. The moss-free headstones formed a neat row with flowers peeping up beside them.

I knelt at my mother's grave and another bout of sadness overwhelmed me. "You know what hits me the hardest when I look at this?" I asked.

Uncle Freddie shook his head and I pointed. "This line between her birth year and death year. That's such a measly little symbol to commemorate an entire lifetime. It doesn't seem right to reduce all those wonderful years to this small a space."

His hand squeezed my shoulder, then he helped me stand and pointed to several little orange flags on metal stakes. "We saved this spot for your dad, right next to your mom. His grave will butt up to the fence so it will be the last one in this line."

I blew a kiss to my mother's grave and we left the small cemetery. A few feet along the path toward the house, we moved aside for the Carruthers Funeral Home truck and Uncle Freddie waved to the driver.

"That's Harvey Carruthers," he said. "His grandfather started the business and was the one who took care of my brothers and mother when they passed."

"I love the continuity of life here," I told him. "Makes me homesick for a simpler time."

Uncle Freddie left me in the yard so he could check on some fencing and I returned to the kitchen. My aunts bustled around the large space and as I watched them, I visualized the kitchen as it would have appeared to Maude, although I knew it had gone through a number of renovations after she died.

My aunts and I worked on preparations for dinner so the knock on the screen door startled us and interrupted our easy laughter. We looked up to see Harvey Carruthers framed in the doorway with Uncle Freddie coming up behind him.

"Hey, Harv," we heard Uncle Freddie say. "Did you find the flags I put out for my brother's grave?"

"Yes sir. And I'm awful sorry to bother you, but that's what I'm here to talk to you about."

"No problem," Uncle Freddie said. "What's up?"

The man named Harvey cleared his throat before speaking. A spark of excitement filled his eyes. "We found something, sir, and ... well, we're not sure what ..."

He wiped his brow, then spoke again, his hand on Uncle Freddie's arm. "Please, Mr. Ryan ... you should ... somebody ... needs to come and look at what we found before we can continue."

# CHAPTER
# FIFTY-SEVEN

**SUZANNE**
**2015**

Uncle Freddie left with Harvey and fifteen minutes later Steve joined us women in the kitchen.

The photo album was open to the page with a picture of my grandfather and my great-uncle Henry standing next to the old trunk.

"What a coincidence," Steve said. He pointed to the picture. "This is what I came to talk to you about. If this trunk is still here and nobody's using it, Emily and I would like to buy it. We restore old steamer trunks as a hobby."

"Oh, don't be silly," Aunt Winnie said. "If it's here you can have it. You're welcome to go look in the barn right now if you like."

Uncle Freddie came back in the kitchen and dropped into a chair. "What are you looking for in the barn?" he asked.

"That old trunk that used to be there."

I pushed the album in front of him with one of the trunk pictures showing. "This one," I said.

"Did you ever see it, Freddie?" Aunt Sarah asked. "Is it still there?"

He shot her a funny look. "This is the first I ever heard of a trunk being in the barn. But you remember it, huh?"

"Yeah," she answered. "I was six or so the last time I really remember seeing it. Why are you looking at me like that? Do you know where it is?"

"Yeah," he said. "Well, at least I guess it's the same one."

"Same one what?" Aunt Winnie asked.

"Trunk," Uncle Freddie said. "Harvey Carruthers and his crew found an old wooden trunk buried in the spot we had designated for Sam's grave. And he was really excited about what it might contain."

"That old trunk was buried in the family cemetery?" Aunt Sarah's voice rose two octaves. "What did he think was in it?"

"Gold."

"Gold? Why gold?" Aunt Winnie said. "And who on earth would have put it there?"

"Beats me," he said. "I was hoping you girls would know. But Harvey said that for years—I think his grandfather told him about it— there have been rumors about the Confederate treasure—mostly gold, he said—that was stolen by the Union Army and brought North. But never found. That's what he thought might be in it." He shook his head with a little laugh. "But then, I never even knew we'd had a trunk in the barn. And," he said, pointing to the album, "this picture shows it open with no gold. So we know Harvey's rumors aren't true."

"What *is* in it?" I asked.

Uncle Freddie shrugged. "No clue. We couldn't open it. We hit the lock a few times with one of Harvey's shovels, but it didn't break. I need to hook a chain to the tractor and haul it out of there so Harvey can finish with Sam's grave."

"I'll help you," Steve said.

Within minutes, we heard the roar of the tractor and I decided to join the two of them at the cemetery to watch them remove the trunk. By the time I got there, Steve had jumped into the hole and fastened the chain around the trunk's middle and Uncle Freddie put the tractor into drive. The chains lifted the trunk, little by little, and Steve guided it out of the hole and onto firm ground. Clods of damp earth clung to it along with worms and multi-legged creatures. I shivered.

None of us had any idea how long the trunk had lain buried, but its metal strips, placed every two or three inches, appeared to be intact and apparently had been responsible for preserving the integrity of the wooden parts. Remnants of what looked like leather straps were visible and overall, it appeared to be remarkably well preserved.

Steve examined the lock that held the trunk's lid closed. "Corbin

Lock Company," he said. "I have several trunks with this same lock. Corbin made the best locks for years and last century even began making decorative door hardware. This could be valuable."

"Looks like a worm farm to me," Uncle Freddie said. "But if you want it, have at it. I'll haul it back up to the barn so Harvey can finish with Sam's grave. You can determine if you really want it after you've seen it up there."

"What I don't understand," I said, "is if Aunt Sarah remembered seeing this trunk in the barn, who would have buried it back here? And why?" I had almost messed up and mentioned that Maude talked about it, but then I would have had to explain how I knew that.

"Great questions, Suze," Uncle Freddie said. "But I don't have any answers for you."

# CHAPTER
# FIFTY-EIGHT

SUZANNE
2015

The following day, I walked from the cemetery after Dad's gravesite service arm-in-arm with my dad's remaining sisters, Sarah and Winnie.

The funeral went off without a hitch. I really think Dad would have been pleased. And the weather was perfect for the gravesite part at the family cemetery. We did the full military funeral with the flag folding and the gun salute—a part of an old tradition I had learned about that signified fallen soldiers had been cared for. When "Taps" was played, we all wept.

Dad's Army buddy, Dickie, from New York, had managed to come with help from his grandson, Adam, both of whom I had met a couple of weeks earlier in Europe. Dickie said it best, I think, when he remarked that even God Himself had smiled on Dad's final send-off.

I was thrilled to welcome Dad's other Army buddies, Simon and Sarge, who had traveled from New York with Dickie. Erwin Davis wasn't able to make it from Texas but the German woman, Gerda, whom Dad had met more than seventy years earlier, surprised us all by showing up just before the service.

"Look who's here," Sarge said, bringing Gerda up to greet me. "I let her know about Sam's passing, never thinking she'd come all this way for the funeral. But here she is!"

Just seeing her and knowing the part she had played in changing my life brought tears to my eyes. She even stood at his service and told everyone about my origin and that we had only found it out two weeks earlier when we were all together in Germany. After she finished her story, there wasn't a dry eye in the house.

The rest of the afternoon passed with practically everyone from Prospect Park showing up at the farmhouse. It seemed that the whole town had some connection or other with members of the family and came to pay their last respects to my father. Meeting his Army buddies was a highlight for all of them.

———⋅❧⋅———

DUSK HAD SETTLED AROUND THE HUGE FARMHOUSE BY THE time it cleared of company and I retired to my room to pack for our trip home. No one had gotten the trunk open yet, but Steve had arranged with the rest of the family to rent a truck and return the following week to get it.

I opened my suitcase, threw a few things in, and then simply sat on the bed, my mind wandering to times spent with my dad and eventually flitting around to all the wonderful things I had learned about my grandmother. I was still disappointed I didn't know what had happened to my grandfather, but it was obvious from Dad's remaining siblings that they never gave him a second's thought.

So I was glad I hadn't brought up her diary to them. The more I thought about it, the more it felt as if I would betray Maude by telling her children anything about her most personal thoughts. Or the horrible things their father had done to her.

I hadn't realized it, but as my mind wandered, my eyes faced in the direction of the bookshelf beside my bed. Without any conscious thought on my part, they suddenly focused on the middle book on the middle shelf.

A Bible.

Little tingles shot through my spine and I knew I had to touch it.

I picked it up and it vibrated in my fingers.

I swear ... it actually vibrated.

The first page proclaimed it to be the property of Maude Irene Brewer and she had received it on her thirteenth birthday. As had happened a lot during the past few days, my mind shot back to her diary entry about receiving it.

I loved holding her Bible just as I had loved holding her diary and I felt a closeness with her even more pronounced than before. She had marked a number of passages with small pieces of paper and even though she had never come across to me as particularly religious, each passage made sense from something she had written.

The last section was marked with thin sheets of paper, folded over. In the book of Ephesians, Chapter Four. She had even underlined verses thirty-one and thirty-two:

*Let all bitterness, and wrath, and anger, and clamour, and evil speaking, be put away from you, with all malice:*

*And be ye kind one to another, tenderhearted, forgiving one another, even as God for Christ's sake hath forgiven you.*

I knew from her words she was the master of forgiveness, but I found it surprising that she had marked a verse about being forgiven herself. I couldn't imagine what she thought she had done wrong.

I put her bookmark back in the Bible and closed it, then continued packing.

Seconds later, I straightened up and my breath almost left me. I grabbed the Bible and turned again to Ephesians. To the thin sheets of paper Maude had used as a bookmark.

I removed two pages, so thin they were almost translucent with spidery writing in ink faded to pale purple. There was a date at the top of the page: July 8, 1940.

The missing pages from Maude's diary.

# CHAPTER FIFTY-NINE

**SUZANNE**
**2015**

My hands shook.

The missing pages.

I had to read them. For my own peace of mind.

I adjusted my glasses, unfolded the thin pages with trembling fingers, and began to read.

*July 8, 1940*

*Dear Diary,*

*As you know, my baby boy was born on July 5. Little Freddie. He is so beautiful and considering the turmoil surrounding his birth, appears to be a perfect little angel.*

*Although, my goodness, from what happened last night, it could have gone really, really bad. Let me take that back. It did go really, really bad. Just not for Freddie or me.*

*I couldn't write about it then because it was too fresh. Too raw. But I have to tell you now and then I will probably never write to you again.*

*Sam and Walter told me Buzz had come to the door late the night Freddie was born. He told them he wanted to see his son. But they sent him away.*

*They said he seemed to be fairly sober, but that he reeked of stale beer and vomit. That didn't surprise me at all.*

*I was glad they sent him away. I wished fervently I could have found a way to keep him from ever coming over again. But even having him arrested wouldn't have worked to take him away forever because he would have been released as soon as he was sober.*

*And while he was better sober, he still wasn't great.*

*So last night, I gave the oldest boys some money and asked them to take the rest of the children to the fair. They all deserved to be treated to cotton candy and the rides. Kathleen came to see me and said she didn't want to go—that she wanted to stay with me and help me take care of Freddie. I suppose I should have insisted she accompany them, but honestly, I was glad for the help. I had lost a lot of blood and was still very weak. She brought me soup when the kids left for the fair and then she changed Freddie's diapers. What a sweet little woman she is.*

*She had gone to the washroom to take care of my nightgowns and Freddie's clothes when I heard her coming back down the hall to the room where Freddie and I were—the back room we used as a den—since I couldn't climb the stairs.*

*I called to her. "Did you forget something, honey?"*

*Then my heart froze as I heard his voice. "It's been a long time since you called me 'honey,'" he said. He staggered into the room and fell against the doorjamb. His face was bloated with drink and his eyes glazed.*

*To my mind, he had never looked more menacing.*

*"Why are you here?" Even to me, my voice sounded small, weak.*

"I'm here to see my son," he said. "Those jerks you raised wouldn't let me see him the night he was born."

I held my tongue rather than feed his anger. He walked over to the basket where Freddie lay but I beat him to it. I thought maybe if I held the baby, Buzz could get a good look and then leave.

How stupid of me.

"I want to hold him," he said and tried to wrestle Freddie from my arms.

"No, Buzz," I said it in a calm voice, but I didn't feel calm. "I will hold him. You just look at him."

Rage filled his face and he reached out to strike me. His fist hit my jaw but he continued to try and take Freddie from me with his other hand.

I screamed and backed up. Unfortunately, against the wall. I had nowhere to go. But I heard Kathleen's footsteps. Which was both a relief and a worry.

"Stop!" she screamed at him. "Leave her alone."

She hit his back and he turned on her, swinging with everything he had, sometimes making contact, most times not. He backed her up against the other wall.

A rage flew into me such that I had never before experienced. I could put up with the bastard hitting me. But I drew the line when he hit my children. I lay Freddie on the bed and went after him, beating his back with my fists. I told Kathleen to run.

But she pulled one of my kitchen knives from behind her back and struck at him, catching him across his arm. He roared and charged at her, then knocked her to the floor and twisted the knife from her hand. She rolled *away from him but he went after her. "Buzz, stop!" I screamed. "Think about what you're doing. That's your daughter. Hit me as much as you want but leave her alone!"*

*He turned and screamed at me. Terrible, vicious things. "No two-bit farm girl is going to keep me from my children." His fist caught my chest. "I'm not even sure this baby is mine." That was too much.*

*"You bastard," I screamed. "You know damned well this baby is yours from the night you raped me."*

*Of all his rages I've witnessed through the years, this one was by far the worst. And at that point, I really believed he would kill Kathleen and me as well as the baby.*

*I'm sorry, Diary. I thought I could tell you this, but it's too painful.*

*I have to stop now. I'll tell you the rest later.*

*Maude*

———— ·⊰⊱· ————

## July 8, 1940

BUZZ, HIS FACE DISTORTED IN HIS DRUNKEN RAGE, stormed toward Maude, knife held high.

Sobbing, Kathleen pulled herself up by the doorframe and prepared to attack him again.

But Maude stood her ground. Tears streamed steadily, but the fear left her face and calm filled her. She held her hands up, palms toward him, and spoke softly. "Please, Buzz. Think about how this same situation when you were a teenager affected your entire life. I can't believe you would want to put your daughter through that." And in an even softer voice, she added, "Please ... don't be your father."

The arm holding the knife hovered in the air.

But the rage left his face and his eyes cleared somewhat. He stared at Maude for a long time, then took a deep breath. Behind him, Kathleen stood motionless.

"You're right, Maudie. My father should never have taken both of my parents away."

He raised the knife and slit deeply into his own throat.

Maude gasped. "Oh Buzz ... you damned fool!"

Sounds of death filled the room.

Blood gurgled, then spurted out of his neck and grunts mixed with choking sounds emerged from what was left of his throat. Every link of the chain that supported Marthe's gold locket clogged with blood and when that was filled, the blood continued to spray from his neck and flew to the front of Maude's nightgown and her face. Buzz collapsed to the floor.

Maude fell to her knees and bent over Buzz, his eyes huge and full of fear. She clutched at his neck, trying to stop the blood from gushing.

But he had cut too deep.

There was no way she could help him.

He died within minutes.

She closed his eyes and cradled his head in her lap, rocking him back and forth. "Oh Buzz ... why did you do this to yourself? To us? Why couldn't you have accepted what happened to you in the war and been content with your wonderful children? Even if you no longer loved me. You could still have had a great life. You fool. You damned fool."

Tears streamed down her cheeks.

But her hands had stopped cradling him and her fists beat his chest. Little squirts of blood surged from his neck with each blow.

Kathleen stilled her hands, then pulled her mother away from her lifeless father.

# CHAPTER
## SIXTY

**SUZANNE**
**2015**

Without hesitation, I unfolded the final page. I needed the rest of the story.

*July 8, 1940*

*Dear Diary,*

*Okay, I'm calm now. I can finish this.*

*Once Buzz got the knife from Kathleen, he stormed toward me, the knife high, waving, menacing. The only thing I could think of was when he watched his parents in their final fight and how hard that was on him for the rest of his life.*

*So I reminded him of that and asked him not to be his father.*

*I didn't know if those words would make any difference to him, but for some reason, they did. His eyes cleared somewhat and even though he still held the knife high he no longer moved toward me.*

*Then he told me his father never should have done what he did.*

*But before I had a chance to absorb the meaning of those words, he slashed his own throat. Deep. Blood spurted out everywhere. I couldn't believe he would do such a stupid thing. I tried to stop the surge, but it was too late. He died right away.*

*I'm embarrassed to tell you, but I beat his chest with my fists. I was so angry with him for wasting his life in the bottle. For refusing to embrace the great life he could have had with his wonderful children. And for always rejecting … renouncing … the road we could have walked together because he never grew up enough to move on from his past disappointments.*

*But it was done. It was over.*

*At least I never had to worry about his showing up at the house drunk again.*

*But I did have to decide what to do at that point.*

*I needed the children to believe that Buzz listened to Walter and Sam the night Freddie was born when they sent him away and told him never to come back. They must always believe that he heeded what the boys told him and went away for good.*

*Kathleen wanted to go to the sheriff, but I thought better of it.*

*So we buried him in the family cemetery.*

*I hated putting that burden on Kathleen, but he could have killed her and she's still shaken from it. She says she hates him.*

*I still wish things hadn't happened this way, but I won't miss him. He was never able to get out of his teenage dreams of being a professional baseball pitcher. And once his dream was realized, nothing else was ever enough for him. He was never able to content himself with being a regular guy with a family. What a pity. And what a loss.*

*So this is my last entry, Diary. You and Kathleen and I will take this secret to our graves. I just hope Buzz can find his way to heaven.*

*Your long-time friend, Maude Irene Brewer Ryan*

———————

## July 8, 1940

MAUDE LEFT BUZZ'S DEAD BODY AND HUGGED KATHLEEN.

"Oh honey," Maude said. "I'm so sorry you had to go through that." She pulled away from Kathleen and continued. "But here's what we're going to do. We'll bury him."

"But Mom," Kathleen said, "let me go get the sheriff. He killed himself. We won't get into trouble."

"We don't know that for certain," Maude responded. "Your fingerprints are on that knife and even though we both have the same story to tell, the sheriff might believe I was only trying to protect you and that you did the killing." Maude hugged her daughter again then looked her in the eye. "Kathleen," Maude said, "you need to know this. I'm not sorry he's dead. He's made my life a living hell—except for giving me all of you wonderful children—so I won't miss him. And everybody in town knows what a drunk he was, so no one there will miss him, either. I won't chance losing you because of that bastard, however remote the possibility."

"Okay," Kathleen said, "but—"

"I have an idea. We'll use that old steamer trunk in the barn. You know what I'm talking about, right? Have you seen it?"

Kathleen nodded. "But why can't we just bury him in the dirt?"

"I don't feel right about that," Maude said. "I know he can't feel anything now, but I can't stomach the thought of simply dumping him in the dirt and letting insects have their way with him. I know it won't help forever, but I'd like to protect him as long as possible." She shook her head. "I know it doesn't make a lot of sense, honey, but please just go along with me on this."

Kathleen left to find the trunk and Maude nursed Freddie in hopes that he'd sleep through what they were about to do.

Once she located the trunk, Kathleen emptied it, then put it on a piece of oilcloth and dragged it to the family cemetery. She dug a hole as close to the woods as she could get and when it was large enough, wiggled the trunk into it. The hole wasn't very deep and Kathleen had to take a little more off the corners for the trunk to fit. But she was finally satisfied. She left the trunk's top open then ran back to the house.

"Okay, Mom," she said. "The trunk is ready."

Maude had rolled Buzz up in a blanket, the knife along with him, and washed the blood from the floor.

"I think he's too heavy for us to carry. Will you get the rope from the barn?"

Kathleen came back with both the rope and the oilcloth she had used to drag the trunk.

"Let's put him on this," Kathleen said. "It's kind of slick and seems to slide better."

"Good thinking."

They put Buzz on the oilcloth and tied the rope around everything, then dragged him back to the family cemetery.

"Mom, I know you're not supposed to be lifting anything this heavy after just having a baby."

"You're right, honey. I'll rest tomorrow. Right now, let's finish this."

At the cemetery, they pushed Buzz into the trunk.

"He doesn't fit," Kathleen said. "Now what?"

Maude leaned forward and bent him over. Then slammed the lid down and locked it.

"Why don't you go back to the house, Mom? I'll fill in the hole."

Maude sat down. "I'll go later, but right now I'll rest here and keep you company."

Kathleen filled in the dirt and smoothed the top then sprinkled leaves and twigs over it.

"Kathleen," Maude said as they walked back to the house, "we have nothing to feel guilty about. Your father was an alcoholic who was dangerous when he drank. And one more thing you need to know … if he hadn't killed himself, I would have tried to find a way to kill him. It's just as I told him, beating me up is one thing, but coming after my kids is where I draw the line."

"I know that, Mom. But I always wondered why you never had him arrested."

"Because it wouldn't have helped."

"Why not?"

"The way the courts see things, when he comes to the house and comes after me, he's only demanding his rights as my husband. So I would lose out there. And even if I had him arrested when he was drunk, he'd be released again as soon as he was sober. And probably madder than ever. No, Kath, I've thought about it from every angle and it would never have worked long term."

"Well, what happened tonight sure will."

Maude squeezed her shoulder. "Honey," she said after a minute, "you know you can never tell anyone about this. Not your sisters or your brothers. Not your best friend or teacher. Not even the preacher. We have to keep this totally to ourselves."

"I know, Mom."

"And we have to forgive him."

"What? Why? With everything he—"

"His life has been much harder than it needed to be."

"Geez, Mom, so has yours."

"Yes, but I've always been stronger than he was. Watching his parents die right in front of him was horrible. Of course you've experienced part of that yourself tonight. But then he reached his dream for a while only to have it shatter when he was drafted into the war and then got his hand shot up in the very last battle. Plus, he was in love with a nurse over there—they were even engaged—but she was killed the night he escaped from the Germans. No, he had his dreams smashed in front of him time after time."

"But—"

"You're right. He still should have been able to grow up and accept the reality of his life rather than constantly refusing the gift of a wonderful family we all tried to give him. He should have been able to deal with his disappointments without booze. That was his worst mistake ... and totally his fault. That he never tried to make himself better." She stopped talking and brushed away a tear. "Or to see that being with us would also have been a great life even though it was different from the great life he had envisioned. Unfortunately, it never measured up to the one thing he thought he wanted. So he refused it."

They reached the house and changed clothes; then Kathleen joined Maude in the room she and Freddie shared on the first floor. They were there when the rest of the family came in and happily piled on Maude's bed to tell her all about their fun night at the fair.

Maude loved having her whole family by her side. Happy together.

And safe.

Forever.

# CHAPTER
# SIXTY-ONE

SUZANNE
2015

I ran to the bathroom and threw up, thankful the rest of the family had gone out for ice cream and hadn't seen my mad dash down the hall.

I sat on the bathroom floor, my head still over the toilet and wished I hadn't been so insistent on finding out what had happened to Buzz.

Served me right.

Maude didn't say it outright in the last page of her diary, but I was certain Buzz was in the trunk. And had been there for seventy-five years.

My whole body shook.

I returned to the bedroom and sat on the bed, trying to figure out what to do. As had happened earlier, my mind flitted all over the place and I couldn't pin down a single thought.

I was more convinced than ever that I would betray Maude by sharing her diary with her remaining children. And she made the decision herself to never tell them what had happened to their father. So I determined to honor her wishes and never tell them about either the diary or their dad.

My heart went out to my Aunt Kathleen who carried that secret by herself for close to seventy years after her mother died. But it's obvious she never told her siblings.

I would certainly tell Steve about its contents since the trunk was now his. I wondered what, if any, legal ramifications there would be.

But I had no idea. My guess was that since the death occurred so long ago, that it was a suicide—with Maude's diary as backup to prove it—and that the two people involved in burying him were also gone, it would be a nonissue, legally.

But that left Steve and me to figure out what we would do with his remains.

Cremation seemed obvious. But then what?

I mean, yes, he was my grandfather, but from all the things Maude had written about him, it wasn't like I would keep his urn in my house as a shrine to him.

My mind went blank and I just sat for a long time.

Then a germ of an idea sparked and before long it blossomed into a full-blown plan.

# EPILOGUE

SUZANNE
2015

Steve took the old steamer trunk from the cemetery back to Lock Haven with him the following week. I had already told him what I had learned from the missing pages of Maude's diary, so he was prepared when he finally got the trunk opened. As expected, the inside was stained almost black and contained a skeleton still wrapped in the remnants of an old blanket.

Steve had arranged for one of his friends, a town policeman, to be with him when he opened the trunk and his policeman friend corroborated what we had thought. There were no legal issues. Steve's friend said that the only crime that may have been committed was burying a body without registering the death. But since it happened in 1940 and the people who did the burying were also dead, he didn't see a problem. The policeman did, just to be on the safe side, run Buzz's legal name through both the cold case and missing persons files, and came up empty on both counts. So he said Buzz's remains were ours to do with as we wished.

And I had a plan. A good one, I thought.

We took the trunk to a crematorium and picked up Buzz's ashes the following week. The lady there handed me the urn and then gave me a large manilla envelope. I looked inside to find the rusted blade of a large kitchen knife with a remnant of rotted wood held on by a metal screw. And a gold chain with a locket dangling from it.

"This chain," the lady told me, "was caked with what appeared to be crusted blood but I cleaned it up for you. It's made of very expensive gold and seems to be really old. The name of a store is engraved on the back of it so I looked it up. It's from early in the last century in Liege, Belgium. I assumed it contained pictures of your grandparents."

I was able to pry the locket open and there were, indeed, spots for pictures inside. But if any pictures were still there, they were completely blackened with age. And who knew what else?

"Thank you," I said. "You did a wonderful job."

I tucked the locket into my purse—I'd figure out what to do with it later—and took the urn to my car. Steve and the crematorium owner hauled the trunk to Steve's truck and loaded it.

"Are you sure you'll be all right on your drive, Mom?"

"I'm sure," I told him. "It's only three and a half hours and won't take me long once I get there. I've made all the arrangements."

I tuned my radio to a station playing songs from the seventies and hit the road.

When I arrived, I located my contact.

"I really appreciate this," I told him.

"Well, it is an unusual request," he said. "But the timing worked since the field's empty."

We reached the pitcher's mound at Citizen's Bank Baseball Stadium in Philadelphia. It wasn't exactly the same since Shibe Park— renamed Connie Mack Stadium in 1953—was demolished in 1976. And that location now houses a church.

But this was the closest I could get since we were standing in the stadium used by the current Philadelphia baseball team when they're in town. Not the Athletics—they were moved first to Kansas City, Kansas, and later to Oakland, California, where they still reside. No, this was the home of the Philadelphia Phillies, who happened to be out of town that day, playing the New York Yankees.

Which is why I was allowed on the field.

The grounds keeper removed his cap as I slowly poured the ashes of William "Buzz" Ryan, Philadelphia Athletics' pitcher in 1916 and 1917, on his favorite place in the world.

Sure, it wasn't exactly the same spot where Buzz had stood, but I didn't think he would mind.

He was finally back home, on the pitcher's mound, where he'd always wanted to be.

# ACKNOWLEDGEMENTS

Many people helped me through the process of writing this book and I am so grateful to all of them. Unfortunately, because of the timing, I was not able to interview World War I veterans the way I had interviewed World War II veterans for *The Road Remembered*, so my research consisted of books, movies, and countless hours on the Internet. Google and I have become very close.

Huge thanks go to my cousin, Tammy Zeigler, and her husband, John, who spent hours on the phone with me, teaching me about the making—and refurbishing, which they do—of old steamer trunks. Tammy described the way the trunk would have to be used as a casket, how two small women would have to go about getting the trunk into the ground and then adding the body to it ... and even doubling it over, if necessary. I had that scene cemented in my head before the first word of the story was even written. Tammy and John also agreed to be among my early readers and their insight was awesome.

Thanks as well to my other early readers, in addition to my darling husband, of course. They include one of my best friends since first grade, Larry McDorman and his wife, Vivien, who corrected some of my baseball terms, ensured my German names were believable, and made other great suggestions to make certain the story rang true. Additionally, I'd like to thank my corps of early readers among my neighborhood buddies, Susan Foster, Kathy Granieri, Lorna Jones, and Candi Lennox, who have been early readers for all of my books so far (and told me they like this one the best—woohoo!!). Thank you to a new neighborhood reader, Judy Thomas, who for years has invited me to speak about my books at her book club. All of these wonderful women have offered valuable feedback, and in the process, stroked my ego. Thanks also to good friends and early readers, Scott and Jeanne O'Malley Sylvester. As with *The Road Remembered*, Scott offered me books and other information about the first global conflict and Jeanne helped me see that some of my hundred-year-old language may have been too modern. Jeanne also had me speak at her book club when her members read *The Road Remembered*.

I'd also like to thank my brothers—my older brother, Noel Dykes, well versed in the history of the global wars, and my younger brother Alan Dykes, who gave me the insight to bring World War I into Maude's world a little sooner so readers had a flavor of the experiences of normal folks from both sides of the ocean during this global conflict.

A big thank you to my sister, Dr. Patricia Walker, who painstakingly listened to story lines and offered suggestions, then proofread the finished manuscript for me.

Above and beyond thanks to Ann Tatlock, my wonderful editor for this novel. Ann made such a huge difference with my last novel, I arranged with her as soon as I knew this one would be written to edit it as well. And huge thanks to Hannah Lindner, who designed the book cover and Catherine Posey who designed the interior.

And, of course, my undying gratitude to my darling husband, Michael, who reads every word I write and gives me honest feedback —especially when he doesn't like the direction I've taken with a character or an ending. And believe me, for this one, there were many times he didn't like what I had done. But once he sent me on a different path, he even suggested the final scene for this book, which I hope people found as satisfying as I did. Michael is also a huge factor in my social media and in helping me to navigate the publishing world. Even after all of our years together, my Mikey is still my most ardent fan, my loudest cheerleader, and always, always, my best friend.

# AUTHOR'S NOTE

Much of this book is based on true events and the character of the Belgian nurse, Marthe Peeters, was inspired by a real-life World War I heroine, Marthe Cnockaert McKenna, as told in her memoir, *I Was A Spy!* In addition, the character of Maude Irene Brewer, as noted in the Dedication, shared her name with my maternal grandmother, whose life, fortunately, was different from my character's life.

Many of the events cited during World War I are based on actual events with any differences noted in the pages that follow.

If explanation for a chapter has been skipped, that simply means there was nothing that needed to be explained or verified.

## PROLOGUE

- The German Army invaded Belgium on August 4, 1914, even though Belgium had announced they would remain neutral in the growing turmoil in Europe.
- One of the homes targeted by the German Army was that of Marthe Cnockaert, from Liege, because they believed her father to be a sharpshooter; the big difference is that while Marthe's home was burned, her family was not killed and she was not kidnapped. She was, however, under German suspicion but decided on her own, later, to offer her services as a trained nurse.

## CHAPTER ONE:

- To my knowledge, my grandmother did NOT keep a diary. But, oh, how I wish she did.
- My older brother, Noel Dykes, called me "Bug" when I was young for the same reason Henry gave that nickname to Maude.
- The names of Maude's parents, Frank and Florence, were actually the names of my grandmother's closest sister and her husband, my Great-Aunt Florence and Uncle Frank.
- A Model T Roadster would have been a vehicle of the time.
- The name of "Buster" for the deputy is a nod to my children's paternal grandfather, who was, in fact, a policeman.

## CHAPTER TWO:

- The description of the massive gun, Big Bertha, as well as when it hit Liege, is accurate.
- The real Marthe's family operated a tavern and Marthe helped out in it when she could.
- The description of the amputation is accurate.
- The reason the date at the end of the chapter is significant is that the following day gas warfare was begun for the first time in history.

## CHAPTER THREE:

- The description of the battle at Kitchener's Wood, in the area known as Flanders Field, is accurate.
- The description of the release of the gas, as well as the conditions of the soldiers suffering from gas inhalation, is accurate.

CHAPTER FOUR:

- The description of Connie Mack, manager, and in 1936, owner of the Philadelphia Athletics, as well as his coaching philosophy, is accurate.
- The description of the left-handed pitcher, Rube Waddell, once a part of the Philadelphia A's, is accurate as is the description of all of his shenanigans, including wrestling an alligator. He died young from his drinking.

CHAPTER FIVE:

- Descriptions of the German's conscription of seventy-five percent of the food allotment as well as the nickname of "Berlin Vampires" is accurate.
- The description of what the Germans considered suspicious behavior is accurate.

CHAPTER SIX:

- The joke told by Leo was a common joke during the First World War.
- The chess moves are accurate to result in a win early in the game.

CHAPTER SEVEN:

- Henry and Buzz took the bus from Prospect Park to Philadelphia because train service was not in place in Prospect Park in 1915.

## CHAPTER EIGHT:

- The description of the use of barbed wire is accurate. World War I is the first war that saw extensive use of this defense medium.
- The description of the French soldier left hanging on the wire as a decoy is an actual occurrence documented by an eye-witness survivor.
- Marthe was recruited to spy against Germany with the phrase of "serving your country."

## CHAPTER NINE:

- The description of the Cadillac Touring Car is accurate for the time.
- The description of the game is for an actual game that took place on August 4, 1915, in Philadelphia between the Philadelphia A's and the Detroit Tigers. All the players' names, the score of the game, and even the order of the line-up is accurate with the exception that I inserted my fictional players, Henry and Buzz, within the mix.
- Cracker Jack was available at the game.
- Baseball had NOT begun using an organist at that time.
- Elevators had been invented but not used by many country people at that point. I was not able to determine if an elevator had actually been installed at Shibe Stadium, so my description of the elevator as Mr. Mack's personal conveyance is my invention.

## CHAPTER TEN:

- The description of Emery's death is accurate as a consequence of gas poisoning.

CHAPTER ELEVEN:

- As a child, my parents always had a huge garden and I shared Maude's dislike of having to go out and work in it. Until I was grown and away from home. Then, whenever I went to visit, I always joined my mother in her garden. And loved it.
- Samuel Brewer was actually the name of my grandmother's father.
- The last battle fought in the Civil War is reported to have happened in Palmito Ranch, Texas, after the official end of the war; the officers in charge of that battle supposedly knew the war had ended but fought anyway.
- John Williams is reported to have been the last soldier to die in the Civil War fighting.
- As noted in Acknowledgements, all descriptions and facts about steamer trunks came to me from my cousin Tammy Zeigler and her husband, John.
- The name of Lorena is a shout out to my paternal grandmother.

CHAPTER TWELVE:

- The description of using matchboxes as delivery vehicles for spy messages is accurate.
- The words on Marthe's message about where and when to go to learn about spying is word for word the way she wrote about it in her memoir, *I Was a Spy!*
- Flushable toilets were in many of the public buildings and expensive homes as early as the 1880s; the toilet in the building in my story, however, is my invention.

CHAPTER THIRTEEN:

- The instructions Marthe received to do her spy work are exactly as outlined by the real Marthe in her memoir.
- Even though watches were not common at this time, the real Marthe had received an engraved watch from her father; it was this watch which, again in her real story, led to her capture when it slipped off her wrist in the tunnel she used to bomb armaments.
- Edith Cavell, who ran a nursing school in Brussels, rescued more than 200 British soldiers trapped behind enemy lines and helped them either return to duty or escape the country. She was arrested by the Germans and shot as a spy in October 1915.

CHAPTER FOURTEEN:

- The description of Marthe being stopped by a fake "safety pin" man is as covered in her memoir.

CHAPTER FIFTEEN:

- The description of Belgian waffles drenched in Belgian chocolate is accurate and is considered a traditional Belgian Christmas treat.
- The description of Marthe meeting the Station Master at the train depot as well as the bombing of the ordnance train is accurate from Marthe's memoir.

CHAPTER SIXTEEN:

- Suzanne's description of working in the garden with her father and having him sing the Gene Autry song, "Tweedle

O'Twill," is one of my own memories with my father. I still get weepy when I think about it.

- Even as early as 1916, northern baseball teams held Spring Training in southern—mostly Florida—towns. The Philadelphia Athletics did, in fact, hold Spring Training in Jacksonville, Florida.
- The movie, *The Crazy Clockmaker,* was shown during February 1916 in Jacksonville, and Oliver Hardy is supposedly a Jacksonville native.

CHAPTER SEVENTEEN:

- The name of Maude's teacher, Miss Delsie, was actually the name of my mother's teacher in the one-room school where she was taught. My mother finished school in eleven years and was graduated valediction, by the way.
- The war talk described by Maude in her Social Studies class is accurate.
- The description of Connie Mack getting rid of more expensive players to keep less expensive ones is accurate, as is the description of his office and his bench made from baseball bats.

CHAPTER EIGHTEEN:

- The request that came to Marthe to find information about a visit from the Kaiser is accurate.
- The description of Marthe meeting a high-ranking German official who invited her to accompany him to Brussels is accurate from her memoir.

CHAPTER NINETEEN:

- The description of Marthe receiving the German Iron Cross is accurate. She received it for her dedication to caring for wounded soldiers.
- Marthe did accompany a German colonel to Brussels and she had all the experiences described in this chapter. Her thoughts came straight from her memoir about how torn she was between her actions and her words.
- The opera Marthe attended was at the *Théâtre de la Monnaie* in Brussels where Wagnerian music was played for the first time in more than two years.

CHAPTER TWENTY:

- The Alligator Farm in St. Augustine, Florida, began in 1893.
- There are white alligators still living there.

CHAPTER TWENTY-ONE:

- Connie Mack was known as "The Tall Tactician."
- The description of the game against the Yankees is accurate as far as date, venue, hits and runs, final score, and names of players, with the exception of Henry and Buzz.
- It is true that Coach Mack was not allowed on the field because he refused to wear a baseball uniform and opted instead for his customary suit, ascot, and straw boater hat.

CHAPTER TWENTY-TWO:

- Details for the Battle of the Somme are described accurately, including that the British bombarded the German trenches almost nonstop for a solid week prior to the battle, but the

Germans had gone underground and very few were killed. The British suffered their worst one-day casualty count on the first day of this battle, July 1, 1916.

- Anesthesia described is accurate for the time, as is the use of cocaine to numb wounds and relieve pain.
- The descriptions of trenches in the Battle of the Somme, as well as "No Man's Land," and how far the guns could reach across it are accurate.
- The Irish soldier named "Monroe McCartney" is in honor of the first names of the daughters of Kelly Winwood, who bought the rights in a charity raffle, to have their names appear as characters in this book.

CHAPTER TWENTY-THREE:

- The housing of soldiers in an abandoned building in town is accurate and the real Marthe was responsible for having the structure bombed and the bulk of the soldiers killed.
- The description of Marthe's contact, Number Seventy-two, being killed is accurate.

CHAPTER TWENTY-FOUR:

- Marthe's ambulance driver contact is my own invention; she didn't write about any such person in her memoir.
- Marthe was recruited to be a spy for the Germans as well. Her network approved it and she carried out the duties of a double agent for a time.

CHAPTER TWENTY-FIVE:

- The fruit vendor, "Canteen Ma," was a real person and is depicted accurately as written about in Marthe's memoir.

CHAPTER TWENTY-SIX:

- Marthe was responsible for tending the wounds of the soldiers caught in the abandoned building bombing and learned that more than two hundred of them died instantly.
- Sister Margarete's character is my own invention; her suspicion stemmed from the fact that the Germans taught *everyone* to be suspicious of everyone else.

CHAPTER TWENTY-SEVEN:

- Women did not have the right to vote in 1916.
- Very few homes had radios in 1916, so the residents of small towns often congregated at the town's General Store if something important was being broadcast.
- Woodrow Wilson was re-elected on November 7, 1916, and gave his acceptance speech the following night. The words Maude quoted from his speech are accurate.
- The Germans did sink the luxury liner, *The Lusitania*, on May 7, 1915.

CHAPTER TWENTY-EIGHT:

- The number of casualties quoted for the Battle of the Somme are accurate.
- The description of Stalag Luft III prison in Germany during World War I is accurate.

CHAPTER TWENTY-NINE:

- President Woodrow Wilson did declare war on Germany on April 6, 1917.

- The draft was reinstated for the country for the first time since the Civil War.
- *The Philadelphia Inquirer* was begun in 1829 and is still being published today.
- Soldier John Pinckney was among the first American men drafted for the war in Europe.

CHAPTER THIRTY:

- June 5, 1917, was designated as "National Registration Day" when men whose ages fell within the draft guidelines were supposed to register for the draft.
- The date for General John J. Pershing's arrival in Europe, June 14, 1917, as well as the date the first U. S. troops joined him there, June 26, are accurate.

CHAPTER THIRTY-ONE:

- The real Marthe was recruited to be a double agent and her German recruiter, a man she identified as "Otto," became increasingly demanding. He was found dead on the road out of town with two bullet holes in his head.
- Mata Hari, the famous Dutch exotic dancer and spy, was executed in October 1917.

CHAPTER THIRTY-TWO:

- The accounts of China declaring war on Germany and Austria and then Italy declaring war on Turkey are accurate.
- My grandmother taught me to sew on her Singer Sewing Machine (with a treadle) and the first thing she had me make was an apron. It was yellow with a green waistband

and ties. She helped me with the pocket which was in the shape of a pink tulip bloom.

## CHAPTER THIRTY-THREE

- *Anne's House of Dreams* by L. M. Montgomery was the follow-on book to *Anne of Green Gables* by the same author.
- Snow cream was quite a treat for my family when I grew up and served as an inexpensive way for the family to have ice cream.
- I was surprised to learn that even during World War I, men who objected to fighting but were not eligible for official exemption status escaped to Canada.

## CHAPTER THIRTY-FOUR:

- The description of the German Hindenburg Line and its perimeters is accurate.
- The Russians did pull out of the war in 1917 to deal with a revolution at home and freed up German troops for large-scale attacks before the Americans reached them in full force.
- The button Marthe used to get a coded message to her network is an accurate means of communication open to her spy network during this time.

## CHAPTER THIRTY-FIVE:

- The passage about Suzanne's son and daughter-in-law refurbishing old steamer trunks is a nod to my cousin Tammy Zeigler and her husband, John, who spent hours on the phone with me teaching me some of the nuances of the art.

- U. S. Soldiers during this time frame did travel to Europe aboard the USS *Pastores* and took fifteen days to complete the journey.
- The description of the naval escort for the *Pastores* is accurate.
- The name given to the U. S. fighting force was the "American Expeditionary Force."
- General Pershing did, in fact, want to have a fighting force of his own rather than have American troops as part of the British or French Army, although some U. S. troops did fight on a limited basis prior to Pershing assembling his entire Army.
- The description of items in the kit bag is accurate.
- The description of this first battle outside of Cantigny is accurate; only one hundred Americans were killed.
- Many fallen soldiers were buried in France, for both the First and Second World Wars.

CHAPTER THIRTY-SIX:

- The names and descriptions of towns where fighting took place in this chapter are accurate.
- The scouting mission for Buzz is my own invention but is based on research for similar missions.

CHAPTER THIRTY-NINE:

- The real Marthe did destroy a German ammo dump but within the city of Roulers rather than in the field.

CHAPTER FORTY-ONE:

- The descriptions of the ammo dump in a burned-out church on the road to Reims is my invention.

CHAPTER FORTY-TWO:

- The Carel-Dakin technique to treat gangrene was used at the time and had proven beneficial to the patient; its description is accurate.
- This is not the way the real Marthe died. She did blow up an ammunitions depot and in the process, lost her engraved watch. It was found and she was captured. At first, she was sentenced to be executed but because she had received the German Iron Cross, her sentence was commuted to life in prison. When the Allies won the war, she was released, married a man named John McKenna and became an author, writing, in addition to her memoir, a number of spy novels.

CHAPTER FORTY-THREE:

- The description of the Liberty Loan Parade, one of which was held in Philadelphia on September 29, 1918, and its devastating consequences of releasing the Spanish Flu from sick soldiers is accurate. There were four such parades and for this one, the Philadelphia officials knew the parade should have been canceled but proceeded with it anyway.
- The description of "The Lost Battalion" and the heroics of Sergeant York are accurate.
- The Meuse-Argonne Offensive was one of the last large battles of the war.

CHAPTER FORTY-FOUR:

- General Pershing did not agree with the armistice that was signed on November 11, 1918, at 5:00 a.m. So he refused to allow his officers to stop fighting, insisting instead that they continue to gain ground, since whatever ground was held by the Allies at the cease-fire would remain with them when the spoils of war were divided. That last day of fighting saw more than eleven thousand casualties, thirty-five hundred of which were Americans and General Pershing was later brought in front of Congress to explain the losses. My research did not turn up any disciplinary actions. General Pershing actually received an additional star posthumously.
- John Gunther is documented as the last soldier to die in World War I.

CHAPTER FORTY-FIVE:

- Even though Thanksgiving was not made an official national holiday until 1941, people   celebrated Thanksgiving on the fourth Thursday of November as originally laid out by President Lincoln.

CHAPTER FORTY-SIX:

- Ed Wingo was a catcher for the Philadelphia Athletics at the time.

CHAPTER FORTY-SEVEN:

- The anti-German sentiment Buzz described was real; I even heard it in the mid-1960s.

### CHAPTER FORTY-EIGHT:

- The names of the movies and the actors are accurate and were popular at the time.

### CHAPTER FIFTY-TWO:

- The mention of Maude's lack of rights in her marriage is accurate; during that time, she really didn't have any.

### CHAPTER FIFTY-FOUR:

- The saying "It'll never be seen on a galloping horse" is something I heard my grandmother say my whole life. I don't know if she invented it or if it came from somewhere else, but she's the only one I ever heard say it. When I knew I was going to write a book with her name as one of the major characters, I knew I needed to include one of my favorite memories of her.

### CHAPTER FIFTY-SIX:

- Stories have circulated for years about Confederate gold that has never been found; this rumor has been the basis for a number of interesting novels.
- Corbin Lock Company did provide locks for many steamer trunks.

### CHAPTER FIFTY-NINE:

- My cousin Tammy Zeigler described the way two small women would have used a steamer trunk as a casket before the first word of this book was even written. She described how it would make more sense to bury the trunk first and then throw the body into it. And that probably the body would have to be doubled over to fit. I think her description worked perfectly and I thank her from the bottom of my heart.

## CHAPTER SIXTY:

- Maude's assessment of either her or Kathleen's getting into trouble for Buzz's death may have been unfounded, given that everyone knew Buzz was a drunk and a mean drunk. But she had so few rights at the time, she never wanted to take that chance.

## EPILOGUE:

- The name of the ballfield where Suzanne spread Buzz's remains is accurate as well as the description of what happened to the former Shibe Park.